MRS. MORRIS AND THE WITCH

Charlene peered inside the empty shop. Five minutes till ten. Why was the place obviously closed when Morganna had said she'd be open later tonight?

She cupped her hand against the double-paned glass of the front door, the toes of her boots bumping the wooden bottom half.

Kevin joined her. "What's wrong?"

Charlene tugged on the handle, but it was locked. "I'm not sure . . . I thought that Morganna was going to be working late on the witch balls—she said she'd be open until ten and this place is dark, except for the back room."

"She works on a special machine," Kevin said, brow drawn with worry. "It gets pretty hot to melt the glass." He, too, cupped his eyes to stare into the store.

"What do you see?" Charlene asked.

"A leg." Kevin knocked loudly. "Something's wrong."

Jim used his elbow to break the glass above the lock. "Call nine-one-one," he told Kevin.

The fireman lunged forward, Charlene at his side. "This way." She led him through the shop, past the counter with the cash register. She smelled something hot.

The door was slightly open to the work space, and Charlene slowed as the knee and hem of Morganna's costume came into view.

Morganna's blond curls splayed across the floor, the red witch hat to the side. No blood anywhere that Charlene could see. But Morganna wasn't moving. Her eyes were wide open, her crimson mouth gaping wide. Charlene's stomach knotted.

The witch was dead. . . .

Books by Traci Wilton

MRS. MORRIS AND THE GHOST

MRS. MORRIS AND THE WITCH

Published by Kensington Publishing Corporation

MRS. MORRIS AND THE WITCH

Traci Wilton

KENSINGTON BOOKS
www.kensingtonbooks.com

Patrice Wilton would like to dedicate this book to her granddaughters—Caelan, Blake, Bryn, and Andrea—also a romance author, the Salem B and B mystery series is the first that the children can read!

Traci Hall would like to dedicate this book to her kids, Brighton and Destini, and to her granddaughter, Kennedi—you all inspire me to be the best I can be!

ACKNOWLEDGMENTS

We'd like to thank our agent, Evan Marshall, our editor, John Scognamiglio, the Kensington publishing team, Christopher Hawke at Community Authors, our families, for understanding deadlines, and our friends who have supported us along the way!

CHAPTER ONE

"All Hallows' Eve—Salem's most celebrated night of the year," Charlene Morris said to Jack Strathmore, seated next to her on a love seat in the privacy of her personal suite. "And my first Halloween as a bed-and-breakfast owner." She wasn't sure which was more elegant: Doctor Jack Strathmore, dressed for cocktail hour in a dark blue Armani suit, or her recently acquired historical mansion.

Less than two months ago she'd moved from Chicago to get away from the memory of her dead husband and had bought this seven-bedroom house sight unseen. It was ridiculously underpriced, and her sleazy realtor, Ernie Harvey, had neglected to mention the place came with a resident ghost.

"It's been crazy, but we did it, Jack. Opening night, right on time for Halloween. Fully booked too," she added proudly.

He unfolded his legs and stood, the action bringing a chill she'd come to associate with Jack's particular energy. "Not we, Charlene. *You* did it. Congratulations, my dear. You've made this place into a home. Well done."

Regarding him from her seat, she thought back to the first night they'd met—she'd been awakened by a howling wind and rain pelting against the windowpane. When she'd opened her eyes, she'd seen a shadowy someone watching her. Terrified, she'd tried to run away and hide, but there was no hiding from a ghost.

Her frightened brain had fought hard to be rational—she did not believe in spirits or ghosts—yet here Jack remained. Charming, extremely handsome, with thick, wavy black hair and the bluest of eyes. Jack liked to dazzle—hence the Armani suit. He'd told her once that he created his image for her, right down to the detail of the striking silver at his temples.

"Thank you, Jack. I can't wait to see what the buzz is all about for Halloween." She checked the time on her cell phone, both excited and nervous about the private ghost tour she'd booked for her houseful of guests, following happy hour she'd organized to start at four. Fifteen minutes. Charlene wiped her damp palms on a tissue—she couldn't bear for anything to go wrong.

Jack peered down at her with amusement. "You're lovely, as always. Are those silver spiders hanging from your ears?"

She reached up to touch one, missing the familiar weight of her diamond studs, a gift from her deceased husband, Jared. "Yes—this is my nod toward a costume tonight." She'd chosen black skinny jeans, a black turtleneck cashmere sweater, and a looped Halloween scarf with pumpkins and black cats. Her long dark hair was loose around her shoulders.

"It's just right," Jack said. "Perfectly you."

Hiring a tour bus to take them out to see ghosts when she had one right here might seem counterintuitive, but she didn't want to exploit the fact that her B and B was haunted. The idea of having paranormal seekers and crazed ghost hunters clamoring around didn't sit well when she wanted "Charlene's" to be the most elegant place in town, not the cheesiest.

"Our guests should be coming downstairs soon. Please behave. You know how awkward it is for me when you whisper things and I can't answer."

Neither of them knew why Charlene was the only person who could see and hear Jack, and he thought it amusing to try to trip her up.

After leaving her suite of rooms, with Jack right behind her, Charlene entered the kitchen. Minnie, her housekeeper and cook, opened the oven to release the scent of cinnamon, spice, and everything nice. "Smells great. You need any help?"

"I've got it all under control." Minnie's full face was flushed, and she mopped perspiration off her brow with a paper towel before taking a sip of water from a ceramic mug. Gray curls, quick to laugh, Minnie Johnson and her husband, Will—his dour face and lean body the complete opposite of his cheery wife's—had been her first real hires, and both priceless. "Will has the wine and champagne chilling on ice. Iced tea and lemonade in the fridge. I'll make fresh coffee."

"Perfect. We don't have a lot of time, as Kevin will be here between five and five thirty." Charlene snagged a cookie from the tray. "The kids will love the ghost-shaped cookies and the gooey witch hats." Minnie had formed chocolate cake mix and pudding into a cone, set with orange icing.

The Jensens, Ted and Katherine, had arrived from England for Halloween because their son, Peter, had studied the witch trials in school. Their precocious daughter, Hailey, was very much about dressing up in costume. Charlene adored having children in the house as she and Jared hadn't been fortunate enough to have their own. It remained her greatest regret.

"You bet they will." Minnie set her mug down with a clatter. "Is that concern on your face?"

"I don't want anything to go wrong." She and Minnie exchanged a look, but neither woman brought up the last party, which had ended in disaster. Jack's murderer had held a knife to Minnie's throat, right where they were standing.

"Everything will work out," Minnie harrumphed, her big bosom lifting and falling with her exaggerated sigh. "The guests will mingle and have some cheer before the big night you've planned for them."

Charlene hadn't done much. "I can't believe how this place goes wild for Halloween. All weekend there's been the Psychic Fair and Witch Festival. Yesterday was a parade. Tonight is the Witch Ball at the Hawthorne Hotel."

"Will and I have gone to that ball a few times," Minnie said, placing cookies on trays. "There's a prize for best costume. You should go at least once to check it out."

"Maybe next year." Charlene adjusted a loop on her Halloween scarf and peered out the kitchen window at the yard beyond. Even at dusk it was a gorgeous piece of property, with a lawn in the front and around the side leading to a screened porch and private garden in back.

The mansion had seven bedrooms on two floors—four double rooms and three single—her suite behind the kitchen on the main level, and an ornate wine cellar below.

She'd spent the past few months selecting furnishings for each room, buying from estate sales, combing through antique shops, and bargain hunting online. Now, she just had to keep her beautiful home and business filled with happy guests—to satisfy the bankers—and stay out of the poorhouse.

Minnie gave her a sly look. "Kevin was extremely nice to offer this tour tonight, being Halloween and all."

Kevin Hughes was a bartender at a popular bar in town, Brews and Broomsticks. Sandy-blond, midthirties, and a Salem native, the part-time tour guide was also single.

"I got lucky there. Kevin knows so much about the rich history of this place, really fascinating stuff that doesn't make the books."

"Well, he's a fine gentleman, and must have taken a liking to you," Minnie said with a wink.

"It's not that!" Charlene hurriedly explained, glancing around guiltily for Jack, who had a jealous streak.

"Kevin feels protective, after what happened at last week's party." He'd played the bartender role to keep her guests preoccupied as the police arrested Jack Strathmore's killer—had it been only a week ago?

She felt a chill beside her.

"I am glad he's watching out for you," Jack's husky voice whispered in her ear. "But is it more than that, Charlene?"

Since she couldn't tell him to scoot, she used her hip to get Jack to move. She gave him a reproving look, which was answered by his sardonic smile. *Handsome devil.*

Jack folded his arms. If somebody had told her a few months ago that she'd not only talk to a ghost but live with one, and anticipate their private moments alone . . . she'd have said they were three-ring-circus, stark-raving-mad kind of nuts.

She smoothed a strand of hair behind her ear, the silver spider dangling. Jack's jealousy of other men was pretty irrational considering he was dead. He'd been jealous of Detective Sam Holden, too, but with more reason. The detective was smart, witty, broad-shouldered, masculine. And alive. That was a really big plus. Who knew that would need to be a benchmark?

Charlene turned her back to Jack and spoke to Minnie. "After the tour, Kevin is giving us an hour of free time at the Witch Festival. The guests will love that."

"You should get your fortune told." Minnie took cheese balls from the refrigerator. "I had mine done while I was still in high school, and the psychic predicted I'd marry a man whose name started with *W*, and have a full life." She set the cheese platter on the counter next to the pretty tray of cookies. "Spot on."

"Wish I'd had mine done," Jack lamented. "Maybe I wouldn't have married Shauna. Or gotten myself killed. Perhaps I would be out dancing with you tonight."

Charlene offered a look of comfort. It wasn't right that he'd died so young. A strong, vibrant man, dead in his forties. Like Jared. Life was not fair.

Minnie, oblivious to the nuances in the room, asked, "So what do you think of Kevin?" Her eyes lit with mischief. "He could be the special someone you deserve."

Jack scowled, and she wanted to hug him—he didn't have to worry. Kevin, while charming and fun, was younger than her and not her type. She seemed to prefer dark-haired men.

"I'd like to know how you feel too." Jack sat at the kitchen table that Minnie had pushed to the side and stacked with goodies, and rested his chin in the palm of his hand.

Damn him for always appearing so elegant, and a teensy bit snooty, as though being deceased gave him special powers. Which of course it did. *She* couldn't slip through closed doors and walls or go flying around the widow's walk at night.

"I like Kevin very much," she told them both. "He's easy to be around, a good conversationalist, and funny. But would I ever get romantically involved? No—he makes too good of a friend."

Minnie exhaled so hard she blew a gray curl off her own forehead. "Delegated to the friend zone already?"

Jack sank backward, pleased.

Just then the front door opened, and Charlene was grateful for the reprieve. The Jensen family entered with laughter, which warmed her heart. Eleven-year-old Peter was dressed as a pilgrim—a costume he'd had made for his play at school and now got to use again. Hailey, eight, was dressed as a fairy with purple wings. Katherine wore a queen costume with a red velvet cape while Ted had taken the easy route in a black sweatshirt with a white ghost on the front.

"Hello," Charlene said as they gathered in the foyer. "Did you have fun?"

"We certainly did," Katherine grinned. "Thanks for your suggestions—we enjoyed the tours very much."

Hailey lifted a decorated cardboard ghost, all glitter and sequins, while Peter showed her his plastic pumpkin filled with candy.

Charlene shared a smile with Katherine, who said, "Kids had a great time but ate way too many sweets. I, however, am ready for a glass of wine."

"Minnie has everything set out in the dining room," Charlene assured her.

Ted sighed and herded the kids up the stairs to drop off the crafts and treats. "Get a drink, Katherine. I'll get these two monsters sorted and be back down to join you."

Katherine waved at her husband and followed the savory smells.

Charlene spent the next thirty minutes conversing with her guests. Minnie passed by with a second platter of mini quiches. Will followed with a silver tray offering wine or champagne. A side table was set up against one wall, across from the large ornate fireplace that burned with cinnamon-scented logs. Above the mantel was an elaborate mirror that she'd found in town at Vintage Treasures.

Everyone mingled and found comfortable niches in which to perch and chat with fellow guests. Three single guys, Phil, Matthew, and Dylan, had rented her top rooms and now clustered together against a wall. Phil and Matthew, both with light brown hair, were in their midtwenties and drank whiskey, while Dylan, just twenty-one, had a local beer.

Dylan had called her in a panic, hoping for a room so that he could meet up with a girl he'd met online. He'd taken the bus into Salem without realizing that all of the hotel rooms would be booked because of Halloween. Something about him reminded her of how nervous Jared had been when they'd first dated.

Charlene greeted Detective Sam Holden's younger sister. "Sydney, did you and Jim have a nice afternoon?"

Petite Sydney had chestnut brown hair, and she'd been the first to book a room at Charlene's Bed and Breakfast— on Sam's recommendation. Charlene accepted a glass of champagne from Will as the trio took a seat on the sofa.

"We did a couple of tours. Saw the House of the Seven Gables, then grabbed lunch at a place called Sea Level. Good food." Sydney chose a spinach tart from one of the trays that Minnie offered. "Right, honey?"

Her husband, Jim, with his curly red hair, reminded Charlene of Prince Harry, and always seemed on the verge of a joke. Putting his glass of dark ale aside, he answered Sydney's question. "The oysters were as good as what we get on Fisherman's Wharf."

Charlene recalled that the Taylors lived in San Francisco, where Sydney was a nurse and Jim a firefighter. "Another great place is Cod and Capers at Pickering Wharf. Sharon Turnberry runs it. If you get there, let her know I sent you and she'll probably give you a discount."

"Sounds good. I wish we had more time here," Sydney sighed. "So many places to explore."

"You'll just have to come again." Charlene stood. "For repeat customers, I'll entice you with a free night, if you return within a year."

"We just might do that." Jim put his feet up on the ottoman,

Silva's usual napping spot, and leaned back in the cushiony chair. Where had her cat disappeared to, anyway? The silver Persian tended to go into hiding when people were around.

Sheila and Sal Harris, teachers and history buffs from Oregon, waved her over from where they hovered by the cookies. The pair was in their midfifties, of medium height, with short gray hair. Like many married couples, they had grown to look alike.

Before Charlene could connect with them, Kevin knocked and entered the foyer. "The bus is outside," he said.

The party was just getting started, but they were on a time restraint. Charlene raised her voice to be heard. "Drink up, everyone. Our bus is here. Dress warmly, as we'll be walking. The streets are broken up in places, so I have some flashlights by the door if you'd like."

One by one, the guests disappeared to their rooms to get whatever they might need, and Charlene searched for Jack. He'd kept to himself for the past hour, which was unusual. Was he sulking because he was going to be left alone for the night? He had Silva to keep him company; the cat could see Jack but not touch him, and it made Silva crazy.

She glanced at the fireplace—no Jack—and then the gilded brocade chair he liked to sit in. Her gaze lifted to the mantelpiece, and the enormous mirror. Seven feet wide and five feet tall, with elegant rope beading in a gilt frame, it was her pride and joy.

Kevin followed her gaze. "That was a great find. You've done a tremendous job in such a short time."

"Thank you." Charlene was about to turn away when suddenly Jack appeared in a flash of blue next to the mirror. She gasped in surprise as Jack laughed; then she placed a hand on Kevin's back, encouraging him toward the door. "We should get going. I'll get my coat."

Kevin studied her closely. "Is anything the matter?"

She dared to peek back. As clear as day, she saw Jack's smirking face as he challenged her not to give herself away.

"No, nothing." Charlene reached for her coat on the coat-tree, safe in the knowledge that she was the only *human* that could see her ghost. At the doorway, she glanced back. Jack winked at her and then was gone.

CHAPTER TWO

Charlene's laughing guests streamed down the porch steps to the twenty-five-passenger minibus. The shiny black vehicle was decorated with spiders, witches, and paper ghosts. Kevin held her elbow as she boarded. "Charlene, take a seat here at the front," he said. "This is our driver, Mac." She smiled at the gray-haired older man behind the wheel in a cheap black suit and orange bow tie.

"Nice to meet you, Mac." She put her large handbag down on the front seat and scooted over to the window, so she could see the driver and keep a friendly eye on her guests. She'd picked up a dozen black flashlights for cheap and was glad to see that everybody had one.

"Are we ready?" Kevin asked, stirring up the crowd.

The family from England cheered the loudest, Sydney and Jim right behind. Hailey and Peter bounced in their seats, and the three single men in the back looked ready to bolt.

Charlene stood, careful not to bang into the overhead compartments, and did a quick body check to make sure everyone was accounted for. This first set of guests would always be special. She brought out her cell phone to snap a photo.

"Smile, everybody!" Charlene captured Matthew and Phil giving each other devil horns—they were friends from Boston who had never experienced a Salem Halloween, though they lived so close. Dylan offered a sheepish grin, not wanting to admit to having fun. Sheila and Sal scrunched shoulder to shoulder in the third row. Sydney and Jim sat one behind the other so they could each have a window seat. Same with the two Jensen kids, though Katherine and Ted were side by side. Charlene made it twelve—a lucky dozen.

"I want to see a witch!" Hailey said to her parents. "One with a broomstick and big pointy hat."

Peter snorted. "There are no such things as witches," the older brother declared. "The reenactments we saw today proved it. The ones you see at the fair are nothing but fake. But there might be real ghosts." He put his hands in the air and made a frightful face, trying to spook his sister, who huddled closer to the window.

"No witches, you say?" Kevin had overheard Peter's remark and spoke into the lapel mic at his black shirt collar. Black jeans and leather boots, scruff at his jaw and his hair a tousled sandy-blond mess of short waves. He was cute, Charlene admitted. No doubt about it.

Kevin tapped the mic. "What's your name, young man?"

Peter whipped around on his bench seat. "Peter Jensen. That's all they talked about on the Witch Dungeon tour today. How those girls lied."

Kevin rubbed his hands together, facing the group from a standing position, and leaned his hip back against the seat.

Mac started the engine. "I'm glad you brought this up, Peter. I'm Kevin Hughes, everyone, and I was born and raised here in Salem. You'll hear a lot of stories about my hometown." He paused dramatically. "And I can guarantee you—we have witches."

Dylan hooted and smacked the seat as Phil and Matthew exchanged disbelieving looks. "Right," Matthew said, heavy on the sarcasm.

"Don't laugh just yet," Kevin warned theatrically. "They walk among us. You'll never know if the man on the sidewalk next to you is a witch. Or the woman who sells you a cup of coffee in the morning. Your neighbor, maybe. Witches come in all shapes and sizes, young and old."

Hailey squealed and covered her mouth, her eyes wide. "Are they bad?"

Kevin smiled reassuringly at the frightened girl with the purple fairy wings. "No. There is no need to be afraid. And on our way, I'll tell you why." The sky was dark, and the fall air had a crisp bite, with clouds blocking out the nearly full golden moon.

"A very long time ago, Salem was a small village with bakers, farmers, mercantile shop owners, and churches. Back then, religious leaders were very strict and there were major consequences for not following the rules. Girls, I'm sad to say, were not valued or equal like they are now."

"Why not?" Hailey squeaked. "They thought boys were smarter?"

"Something like that." Kevin spread his arms to encompass the group. "They were wrong, of course. But the leaders of the community made the rules, and no one questioned them. To do so would bring forth punishment, and their lives were difficult enough."

The bus slowed to a stop, then Mac made a right turn down a neighborhood street. Kids with buckets and bags hustled door-to-door, trick-or-treating. Kevin saw Hailey glance out the window, and reached into his pocket for a few mini candy bars that he tossed to the Jensen kids.

Smart, Charlene thought. A small bribe to keep their attention.

"We'll never know exactly what happened in those days of the witch trials, but we've put together a reasonable accounting. The men in charge of the church used the scariest things they could come up with—witches and magic—to keep their parishioners in line."

"What does that mean?" Hailey asked her mom.

"It is like you being grounded for talking back," Katherine answered.

"Exactly, and if a parishioner didn't go to church on a Sunday, he was promised hellfire and brimstone," Kevin said with an exaggerated shiver. "A much worse fate." He waited for the bus to round the corner, then spoke again. "Now *we* know—but our ancestors didn't—that witchcraft and magic have been around just as long as the Christian church, maybe longer. In fact, Wicca is a recognized religion."

Sydney leaned forward, her arm on the seat in front of her. Her hair was tucked under a knit cap, and she wore a down quilted jacket. "One of my coworkers is Wiccan, at the hospital I work at in San Francisco."

"Modern-day witches are just like you and me," Kevin explained. "Not like in the movies. Remember the Disney films, and the witch who brought a poisoned apple to Snow White? And poor Hansel and Gretel." He hunched down to peer out the window, as if to assess where they were. "Our witches are just regular folks."

Hailey sat back with disappointment. "I want to learn magic. And make you disappear," she told Peter in a whisper. Their mother gave them a stern look.

Kevin chuckled. "Salem is infamous for its history, and we are very proud of it. People who practice witchcraft have been made welcome for at least the last hundred years." He gave a deprecating grin. "Us locals never get tired of talking about it, and people flock to listen."

"Tourism saved Salem," Dylan said from the back of the bus. "According to my econ teacher," he said.

"Your teacher's right." Kevin threw Dylan a mini candy bar. "There are spell books in some of the shops that might be interesting to anyone wanting to learn more. Wiccan practitioners have told me that they live by the rule of three—whatever you do comes back to you threefold, which means that if you are kind, kindness comes back to you three times over."

Peter paused in thought. "If I'm bad, then I get three times bad?" He scowled at Kevin. "Not sure that I like that."

His parents turned in their seats and laughed at Peter with affection. "You? Our perfect angel?" Katherine teased. "You'd only get three times the homework."

He folded his arms across his narrow chest. "That would suck. Guess I just wouldn't be bad."

"That's the idea, Peter," Kevin said, tossing a candy, which Peter caught like a pro baseball player. "No matter what spiritual path you follow, that seems like a decent rule of thumb."

Charlene agreed fullheartedly and put her hand out for a treat. Kevin dropped a chocolate kiss into her palm.

"Okay, everyone—to our right is the Hawthorne Hotel. It's haunted by a young boy, so the legend goes, but is more famous for an episode of *Bewitched* which was filmed on the premises. Who here has watched that TV series?"

"I did," Sheila said. "What woman wouldn't like to wrinkle her nose and get the housework done?"

She attempted to wrinkle hers, and her husband, Sal, laughed. "Forget it, honey. It's not working."

"It certainly made the Hawthorne Hotel a popular desti-nation." Kevin lowered his voice. "Many people have heard the sound of a child crying above their beds, and yet no guest has had a child with them in that room when it's been reported."

"That's pretty terrifying," Katherine said.

Kevin kept his tone dramatic. "Some say the kid died from a fever, and his parents could only slide food into his room but were forbidden to enter."

"How awful," Charlene said, her heart aching for that poor child. Like Jack, he might be stuck in this hotel for an eternity, never free, never to know the peace that Heaven offered.

"On a brighter note," Kevin said, "they have a gorgeous bar—not as nice as Brews and Broomsticks's—but it's all dark wood with an elaborate fireplace, perfect for a hot drink on a cold night."

Mac stopped at a red light and then turned the bus onto Charter Street. "We'll park up here and get out at the shops. The streets will be crowded. Mac won't leave the bus, so if there is anything you want to leave behind, it'll be safe." He glanced at his watch. "I can give you twenty minutes to poke around before we start our walking tour. We will meet at Morganna's Witch House. It's directly up the street, not even half a block. That makes it six o'clock. Please be prompt as we have a lot to take in."

"Do we have time for a beer?" Dylan asked.

Kevin zipped his jacket halfway. "The tour will begin with or without you. We'll go to the cemetery where many people have captured orbs in their photos. Orbs are like spectral energy. Sometimes when I'm doing a tour, I see something moving out of the corner of my eye." Charlene wondered if Jack could be caught on film. "We'll pass by a frightening old house from the sixteen hundreds, haunted by a little boy in the attic window," Kevin added.

"It won't be too scary, will it, Mum?" Hailey asked.

"You can hold my hand," Katherine said.

Kevin looked at each of them with sincerity. "I believe in ghosts—but they can't hurt you."

Charlene recalled their brief discussion at his bar one night about spirits and ghosts. Ghosts were remnants of energy, a memory or an echo, while spirits could be dark energy. She didn't believe that Jack was either of those things. Just . . . dead, and visible to her. Mostly kind. But she'd seen him angry and wouldn't want to face his wrath.

Hailey gave a sigh of relief. Charlene was glad Kevin ended the conversation with that positive note.

Mac opened the door at the front, and Kevin gave each of them a sticker to put on their coats as they exited the bus. "This will give you a ten percent discount at the shops on these two blocks, which is also good for tomorrow. Remember you will have time to shop later," he assured each of them. "Just enjoy the magic that is Salem on Halloween. Oh—and if we get separated, the bus pulls out at ten fifteen."

Outside, people of all ages strolled the streets in costumes. It was the busiest day of the year and felt like a carnival. "Do you recommend any of the shops in particular?" she asked Kevin, once everyone was off the bus.

"Next to Morganna's Witch House is Kass Fortune's Tea Shoppe—she reads tea leaves."

"That sounds interesting," Sydney said.

Jim put an arm around her waist. "Why bother? Your fortune is good—you're married to me."

Sydney laughed. "Maybe I want to know how many kids we're going to have."

"Two is a perfect number. Any more and I'd forget their names."

"Twenty minutes, folks," Kevin reminded them.

Everyone headed off in different directions. Hailey led

her mother toward a candy kiosk, and Ted was dragged off by Peter, who wanted to see the T-shirt store. The three guys ducked into the bar for a quick beer. Sheila and Sal meandered down the street together, peering into the shops as they made their way to Morganna's.

Morganna's Witch House was on the corner next to the tea shop and a souvenir store that had bags and baseball caps at the entryway. The brick building was two stories and didn't appear as old as some of the wooden structures around town.

Being the first to arrive, Charlene glanced inside. Beautiful glass spheres shimmered, beckoning her in. "Those sure are pretty—they look like giant Christmas ornaments," Charlene said. Some of the glass balls were the size of a dinner plate, tied with ribbon and hanging in the window.

"Beautiful," Sheila murmured, coming to stand next to Charlene. "What are they used for?" she asked. "A window decoration?"

"Witch balls." Charlene read the description with a laugh. "Okay, what's the story, Kevin?" But Kevin had drifted away, so she entered Morganna's with Sheila and Sal on her heels.

Incense and sage immediately filled her senses, overlying the less distinct scent of something else burning. Five customers browsed the aisles, which were brimming with glass orbs and custom jewelry. There were rows of various dried herbs along the left wall that connected with the tea shop.

A short woman wearing a tight ruby-red dress and a matching red witch's hat traipsed from behind the counter. Long blond curls bounced at her narrow shoulders. She offered her hand in greeting.

"Welcome, I'm Morganna—you must be Charlene, the new bed-and-breakfast owner Kevin has been talking about."

Surprised, Charlene turned around to see if Kevin had slipped in, but Morganna reached forward and tapped the black-and-orange sticker Kevin had given her.

"I'm no mind reader," Morganna said with a laugh. "He mentioned that he would be bringing you by. I saw you admiring the witch balls?"

"Yes! Nice to meet you. This is Sheila, and her husband, Sal. These ornaments are very pretty, but where would you put them? A sunroom, maybe?"

"The witch balls trap evil spirits when they enter your house." Morganna closed her long red fingernails over her fist as if catching a fly. "You should buy two. One for the front door and one for the back." Morganna brought them to the window display. "I do all the glasswork myself. So customers can order personalized items—like gold to attract money, or sage to cleanse."

"Do you have a factory somewhere that we can visit?" Sheila asked.

"No, these are done by hand. I have a furnace in the back." Morganna waved airily. "I use recycled glass. It's always a surprise. I don't know until I'm working with it what colors it will be. But they are very beautiful, aren't they?"

"Yes. I was hoping to find something special for my bed-and-breakfast." Charlene made a quick decision. "I'd like to order two." But not for inside—just in case it trapped her handsome ghostly roommate.

Morganna arched a blond brow at Charlene. "To keep spirits out?"

She would hate to trap Jack, even accidentally. "How about for good fortune? Can we make it durable, for outdoor use?"

"Certainly—I'll create a thicker glass wall." Morganna turned to Sheila, who stared into a blue ball as if transfixed.

Inside the glass orb was a string of tiny bulbs similar to what Charlene had seen done with wine bottles. "Is the one with fairy lights calling to you?"

What should have seemed like a silly question actually made sense in Morganna's Witch House. Sheila gave a dreamy nod. "It is. Can you ship to Oregon?"

"Absolutely." Morganna took Charlene's hand. "And you, Charlene, think about what you'd like in your orbs to attract good fortune." She tilted her head in question. "Are you psychic?"

Charlene pulled her hand back. "Uh, no. What do most people use?"

"It's personal. For you it might be a houseful of guests, or the interest of a special man," Morganna said. "Dried flowers can be quite pretty. Or something nautical perhaps?"

"Nautical sounds nice. A seashell with some coral? I'm thinking outside in a gazebo."

"I have a selection of coral in rosy pink you might like. Our shops are all staying open until ten tonight because of the festival—I will get your witch balls started, and you can pick them up in two days." Morganna efficiently unhooked Sheila's orb and brought it to the back, where Sheila filled out a shipping label. "The fairy lights are solar powered so you don't have to worry about the battery dying."

Sal spoke up. "We have a ten percent discount from Kevin before you ring up the bill," he told Morganna.

"That's correct. The price will be fifty dollars with the discount, and free standard shipping."

Kevin poked his head in. "You ladies ready?"

"Just about." Charlene checked her watch.

Morganna laughed softly. "Kevin is a Virgo. Always on time."

"Same as me," Sheila said. She pocketed the receipt. "Thank you—and nice to meet you."

"Enjoy the tour!"

Morganna trailed them to the front of the store, sending Kevin a flirtatious finger wave through the front window.

"Did you find something, Charlene?" Kevin asked.

"I did," she said, bringing the collar of her black wool coat up and stuffing her hands in her pockets. "She's going to make two for me—to bring in good luck."

A group of teens in Gothic garb bypassed the shop, and Kevin moved forward. Charlene did a head count—where was Dylan? She was about to ask Matthew and Phil when he came out of the bar, his cheeks rosy under his unkempt dark blond hair. He positioned himself on the sidewalk in front of the big picture window and peeked inside. He hugged his arms—guy was probably freezing in that light-weight leather jacket.

Morganna blew a kiss at Dylan through the glass and motioned him in. Dylan grinned and shook his head no, then stepped over to Matthew and Phil with a bored air. Charlene figured this was pretty lame stuff for a guy his age who would rather be hanging at the bars, chatting up girls.

Because Charlene wanted to make this first Halloween special, she'd gifted this tour at no charge to her guests, which had to be why he was sticking it out.

The Jensen kids were with their parents, Hailey holding on to her mom's hand and eating a caramel apple on a stick. Peter sported a Salem baseball cap that didn't match his pilgrim costume but still looked cool, and his dad had on a new wool hat that covered his ears.

Kevin gathered them together at a corner alley. "Okay, folks! Everyone's here. Stay close and watch your foot-ing—as Charlene mentioned, these streets are uneven. Do

you have your flashlights? We're heading to the Old Bury-
ing Point Cemetery, where on lucky nights we see ghosts."

Charlene brought up the rear to make sure everyone was
accounted for. Dylan used his cell phone to illuminate the
uneven cobblestone paths. Too cool for the flashlight?

Kevin shared his knowledge of local folklore at every
building. He told the story of a boy locked in the attic to
starve away a demon. And how in the seventeenth century
it was thought that affection for your offspring was an offense to God. If you cared too much for your child, you had
to trade with another family—before God got jealous and
took him from you too soon.

They were herded to several homes thought to be
haunted, and though she saw no ghosts, Kevin's stories
kept them entertained. Forty minutes later they reached the
cemetery. Kevin hopped onto a three-foot-high cement wall,
and they gathered at his boots. "This is where I personally
have taken pictures that picked up a woman in a shimmering
sheer gown. I call her my Lady in White." The three guys
all whipped out their phones, snapping away. Sal wandered
toward a broken headstone.

Kevin raised his voice to bring the attention to him
again. "Back in the old days people weren't always dead
when they were buried—which would certainly be a reason
to come back and haunt the place. This is the oldest cemetery in Salem, and is where the hanging judge—" He
glanced at Peter. "Did you learn about this on your earlier
tour?"

Peter nodded. "Judge John Hathorne."

"Very good! You listen well," Kevin told Peter.

"My son also wrote a paper at school," Katherine said
with a proud laugh. "His interest is why we are here on holiday."

"Well"—Kevin pointed toward a headstone—"he's
buried over there. His great grandson Nathaniel Hawthorne

penned *The Scarlet Letter* and added a 'w' to his name to distance himself from the wrongs his ancestors had done."

"How interesting!" Sheila said. "I'll have to share that with my students."

"Anybody have orbs in their pictures?" Kevin stepped down from his perch. "We can look on the bus home too. This is the end of my tour, but be sure to check out some of the other places around Salem."

"Do we still have time to shop?" Sydney asked.

"Yes, you have an hour to visit the open-air Witch Festival and Psychic Fair, or hit the bars—whatever you want. Let's all meet up at ten, at Morganna's where we started the tour," Kevin said.

The three young men took off, but the two couples, including Kevin and Charlene, headed to the shops and festival. The Jensen family walked slowly behind, talking about Salem's history. Costumed people roamed the sidewalks, and most of the touristy stores remained open.

The market was alive with music and vendors selling their wares. The streets had extra lighting, but Chicago-bred Charlene kept her purse tight to her body to thwart pickpockets. They passed a man with a crystal ball, and a woman with long fingernails offering to read their tarot cards.

"What do you think, Kevin?" Sheila asked.

"It's all in good fun." Kevin tucked his hands in his jeans pockets. "But Carmen has the best reputation for actual psychic talent."

Sheila hooked her arm around Sal's. "That's good enough for me. I'm hoping for a raise next year."

"In that case," Sal said with a smile, "I'll ask for the winning lottery numbers."

"I'll be interested in hearing how it goes!" Charlene walked with the enthusiastic couple, Kevin at her side.

A blue-and-white-striped curtain created a "private"

area at the booth if a person wanted their fortune told. A young woman with dyed-blond-and-purple hair smiled at them, the diamond in her nose catching the light. She was so thin Charlene could see her collarbones above the purple witch's corset she wore.

A twentyish man with dyed black hair shaved on one side and long on the other hurried from behind a curtain. "Would you like your cards read, or a peek in the crystal ball?" the young man asked. His Goth clothes were black on black, with lots of pentagram pendants hanging from braided leather chains. "Carmen can fit you in," he said. "The last reading of the night is at nine thirty."

Charlene checked the time. Twenty past nine. Sal and Sheila decided to do one together. Carmen agreed to do a couples reading with the cards—blue and white striped, like the curtain on the tent.

"Are you sure you don't want a reading?" The young man gestured to the cards as if he were a magician's assistant. "I'll see if Carmen can make an exception for one more."

"No, thanks." Charlene and Kevin wandered through other booths that sold everything from talismans to soy candles, but nothing else captivated like the witch balls. It would be easy to lose track of time in the fun atmosphere.

Sydney, Jim in tow, rushed up to them. "I'm so glad we found you guys. We got lost and it's almost ten."

Jim carried several shopping bags, Sydney another two. Charlene laughed. "I see you were successful?"

"I love this stuff," Sydney said. "I bought kitchen towels with the funniest witch sayings to bring back to my friends!"

"Thank you," Kevin said. "On behalf of Salem. The city thrives on the tourist industry." A few minutes later they were standing in front of Morganna's Witch House. Matthew and Phil waited, but Charlene didn't see Dylan.

Sydney hefted her shopping bags. "I'll go put these on the bus."

"The Jensen family is already there with Mac," Kevin said. "I don't see Sal and Sheila?"

Sydney decided to wait, caught by the glass orbs lit in the display window. "I want to buy one of these too."

Charlene peered inside the empty shop. Five minutes till ten. Why was the place obviously closed when Morganna had said she'd be open later tonight?

She cupped her hand against the double-paned glass of the front door, the toes of her boots bumping the wooden bottom half.

Kevin joined her. "What's wrong?"

Charlene tugged on the handle, but it was locked. "I'm not sure . . . I thought that Morganna was going to be working late on the witch balls—she said she'd be open until ten and this place is dark, except for the back room." Costumed folks laughed in the street as they came out of the shops to the left of the block. Why would Morganna close early?

"She works on a special machine," Kevin said, brow drawn with worry. "It gets pretty hot to melt the glass." He, too, cupped his eyes to stare into the store.

Sydney put her bags down. "What's going on?"

All of a sudden Kevin stepped back and yanked on the handle, jerking it. The glass and wood rattled, but it didn't budge.

"What do you see?" Charlene asked.

"A leg." Kevin knocked loudly. "Something's wrong."

Jim used his elbow to break the glass above the lock. "Call nine-one-one," Jim told Kevin. "Keep everyone outside and wait for the police."

The fireman lunged forward, Charlene at his side. "This way." She led him through the shop, past the counter with the cash register. She smelled something hot.

The door was slightly open to the work space, and Charlene slowed as the knee and hem of Morganna's costume came into view. Had there been an accident with the glassblowing machine? Her heart thundered in fear. Was Morganna all right?

Protecting herself from the strange smell, she covered her nose and mouth with her jacket sleeve.

Jim flipped on a light switch, and Charlene came to a halt, her mouth bone-dry.

Morganna's blond curls splayed across the floor, the red witch hat to the side. No blood anywhere that Charlene could see. But Morganna wasn't moving. Her eyes were open, her crimson mouth gaping wide. Charlene's stomach knotted.

The witch was dead.

CHAPTER THREE

"**M**organna," Charlene said softly. Then louder and more urgently. "Morganna!"

The woman's eyes were fixed, her left hand outstretched to the side, fingers curled, as if reaching for the long tube of her blowpipe, askew on the ground next to her. *Dead.* Charlene scanned the room quickly. The twelve-by-twelve door of the barrel-shaped furnace was open, and the smell of almond hit her senses. Whatever Morganna had been making was broken on the concrete-paver floor. Thin blue pieces of glass. A tarot card, and some dried flowers the size of her pinkie.

A witch ball? The overhead light showed a stainless steel bench, a work table, and tools that Charlene didn't recognize. Beautiful glass orbs in various stages of production were lined neatly on a shelf along the wall. There were no personal pictures or knickknacks, as if this space was borrowed. Whatever had happened must have been too quick for the poor woman to escape the windowless room. "Do you smell that?"

Jim, standing at her right in the doorway, had coolly surveyed the scene, and she got a glimpse of the professional firefighter as he kept her from entering. "What smell?"

"Almond?" Charlene sniffed again. "Yeah—like burned cookies."

Jim brought his arm up over his nose, then used his free hand to yank Charlene out of the workroom to the back door, which he quickly opened, and shoved her into the brightly lit alley before him. He propped the door open so that cool autumn-night air filtered into the shop. Merriment from partiers at the bar across the street seemed inappropriate.

"What?"

"Cyanide," Jim said.

"How can that be?" Charlene pressed her fingers to her mouth.

"Not sure, but only sixty percent of people can smell cyanide. We learned about it in our antiterrorism training." Jim peered at her with concern. "Guess I'm not one of them. How do you feel?"

A slight pang stabbed between her eyes—but that could be the shock of finding a dead body. Her belly rolled. She'd just met the woman, but it still made Charlene sad at the unexpected demise. "I'm all right," she said after a hard swallow.

Jim took a deep breath of fresh air. "Breathe . . . the good thing for us is that AC—hydrogen cyanide—dissipates quickly in the air, but a concentrated dose can be fatal." He glanced inside the store. They couldn't see to the front of the shop.

She inhaled all the way to her toes, envisioning clean air in her lungs. "Is that what happened to Morganna?"

"I don't know what happened. I imagine those chemicals she worked with combined with such high heat could be volatile. I wonder if her landlord knew she was working with combustibles? We're lucky the whole building didn't explode."

With a sinking feeling, she agreed—her tummy did another flip.

Jim patted her upper arm. "Come on—let's join the others. I think I hear sirens."

Charlene held her breath as they hustled by the open workroom door. She looked over her shoulder as she followed Jim through the novelty shop. Tea towels and ornaments, magnets and T-shirts. Jim had left the back door wide open. Morganna's blond hair swirled across the cement squares—so tragic.

"Kevin, you called nine-one-one?" Charlene pulled her phone from her purse and texted Sam that there was an accident and possibly cyanide.

Jim propped open the front door, and he and Charlene were careful not to step on the broken glass where he'd gotten them inside.

"Yeah." Kevin looked at Charlene. She gave him a minute headshake, and he recoiled before closing his eyes as if saying a prayer. She silently added hers to his.

The three young men ducked by Sydney, who huddled on the sidewalk with Sal and Sheila. Charlene wasn't going to complain about the cold air. In this case frigid meant safe.

"What's going on?" Matthew stared at the mess. "Why is the door broken?"

"Is somebody hurt?" Phil asked.

"There's been an accident," Jim confirmed, stretching out his arms as if to bar the way. "Stay back, please."

Not heeding Jim's directive, Dylan pushed forward and looked past the counter with the cash register on the right, to Morganna's workshop on the left. Dylan scrunched his nose at Charlene. "I hope it's not that sexy witch. I was gonna see if she wanted to get a drink or something."

Charlene widened her eyes at his callous reaction.

At Charlene's expression, Dylan stopped joking around. "You're serious right now?"

"This isn't a game. Morganna's dead." Jim's stern tone left no room for argument, and he put a hand on Dylan's chest. "Clear the building, and you can help us out by having everyone wait outside on the opposite sidewalk."

Charlene took up a position next to Jim, reacting to the confusion on Dylan's youthful face. "Dylan, if you don't want to wait on the street, then why don't you go to the bus with Matthew and Phil?"

He suddenly looked twelve rather than twenty-one. Had this been his first brush with death? She was getting way too familiar with it. She smoothed the sleeve of his thin leather jacket. "I'm sorry. Maybe you could let Sal and Sheila know to wait on the bus too?"

She figured she'd give him a job to do . . . Instead, he whirled and stumbled between Matthew and Phil out the door to the sidewalk, where he smacked into Kevin. Dylan didn't stop but disappeared into the crowd of Halloween revelers partying on the closed-off street.

The sound of sirens came closer, but the police car had to go slow because of all the foot traffic. Charlene tapped Sydney to get her attention, and Sam's sister immediately turned around.

"Would you mind waiting on the bus and keeping everyone calm?" Sydney's job as a nurse in San Francisco had taught her how to deal with people in an emergency, which Charlene knew she'd need to add to her own skill set. "It will be warmer with Mac."

"Sure, I can do that," Sydney said, tucking her hands into her jacket pockets. She looked at her husband and then Charlene. "You coming, or staying here?"

"I should stay," Jim said. "I think it's cyanide poisoning."

"What?" Sydney gasped. "Did either of you breathe it in?"

"We'll be okay. Maybe a headache. I couldn't smell it,"

Jim said, "but Charlene can, which is what tipped me off. The cops should know."

"Sure." Sydney eyed her husband with a silent communication Charlene remembered from her married days. They'd be talking later. Sydney gathered her packages.

Charlene lifted her cell phone. "I texted Sam about what happened, and he's on his way."

Phil and Matthew, shoulders hunched together, whispered as they ambled toward the bus. Sal and Sheila joined them, Sydney behind.

"What do you know about Morganna?" Charlene put her arm around Kevin's back in sympathy. "I'm sorry that you lost a friend."

Kevin paced before the door, his bootheel splintering broken glass. "We weren't close or anything, but still— poison? How horrible."

"It's terrible." Charlene's voice hitched. "Does she have family around?"

Kevin jerked a thumb overhead. "Not that I know of. She rented one of these apartments—not sure which one."

Charlene turned on the sidewalk to peer up at the row of apartments over the building. Brick on brick. The lights were on in the left two apartments, but the right two were dark above Morganna's Witch House. The big picture window overlooking the street was a testament to the creativity of the woman's work, her beautiful glass orbs and witch balls remained intact. They shimmered prettily in the moonlight, especially the ones with the fairy lights inside. The broken glass by the front door was the only sign of a disturbance.

Charlene's stomach clenched, and she hunkered down in her wool jacket.

It was just she, Jim, and Kevin when the first patrol car arrived, sirens blaring and blue lights flashing. The shop next door to Morganna's Witch House dimmed its interior lights, and the employee inside, a young man with an orange Mohawk, flipped the OPEN sign to CLOSED.

Charlene hiked her collar up against the chill of the October night. She didn't recognize the police officer who got out of the car. The woman turned off the siren, but the lights continued to flash blue and red.

"Who called this in?" Officer J. Jimenez joined the trio on the sidewalk. The woman had a hard jaw, pulled-back hair, and stony gray eyes.

"I did," Kevin said. "I phoned nine-one-one."

Officer Jimenez looked to her partner, a tall dark-skinned man with Y. BERNARD on his name tag, and said, "Detective Holden called in Hazmat, so we need to wait for him—he's on his way."

"All right." Officer Bernard greeted them with a nod.

A large firetruck arrived next, red and yellow lights alternating with the red and blue. The emergency personnel made Charlene anxious.

"I see Detective Holden," Officer Bernard said. His English was barely accented, Haitian, Charlene thought, his frame lean.

Charlene had never felt so relieved to spy the broad shoulders of Sam Holden. Sam's strength, his handsome face, and the warmth of his gaze brought immediate comfort. He'd parked his SUV behind the patrol car, blocking the sidewalk from any curious spectators, though most had steered clear of the police.

Sam's deep, husky voice preceded him. "Charlene—what's going on?"

Charlene had remained calm, almost disbelieving, but now with Sam near, she began to tremble. She hadn't seen him since last week when he'd arrested Jack's murderer at her party.

Seeing Morganna dead, her first instinct had been to call for Sam. "An accident in the back room," she said. "Morganna . . ." Charlene turned to Kevin. She didn't know Morganna's last name.

Kevin pulled his hands from his front jeans pockets. "I only know her by Morganna. She makes . . . *made* hand-crafted blown-glass orbs." Kevin choked up.

Sam's gaze settled on Charlene as he brushed his thick brown mustache. "You okay?"

She nodded, feeling anything but. "We sent the guests back to the bus with Sydney."

"Sydney is all right then?"

"Yes." As a nurse, his sister probably saw death all the time. "Sydney didn't go inside."

Now Sam looked at Jim, his brother-in-law. "Hey, Jimbo. What happened?"

"We'd gathered here to meet before returning to the tour bus, and Charlene thought it odd that Morganna wasn't open for business." Jim's red hair shone with auburn streaks under the streetlamp.

"Because of the Psychic Fair the shops are open until ten," Charlene explained. "And we were here at five till—but the place was dark." She pointed to Kevin. "He peered through the window and saw her lying on the floor. We pounded on the door, and finally Jim broke in."

"I just saw her leg," Kevin said in a heavy voice. "The workshop door was partially open."

"Kevin kept everyone outside while Charlene and I went in." Jim shuffled from one foot to the next, rubbing his arms. "It was obvious that Morganna was dead—and Charlene smelled almonds."

"And that alerted you to cyanide?" Sam asked, thick eyebrow quirked.

"Antiterrorist training," Jim explained. "The military thinks hydrogen cyanide could be used in chemical warfare."

"You do things differently in San Fran." Sam returned

his attention to Charlene. "I'm glad you caught it. Should you two go to the hospital and get checked out?"

"I'm fine." Her headache had lessened, and what she wanted now was her warm house.

Jim shook his head. "From what I understand, this is fast dissipating. I don't believe that there is a danger now that the shop has been aired out. I'd call in your Hazmat just to be sure."

"What's that?" Charlene asked.

"Hazardous materials disposal team. Sam's right—we deal with a lot of strange stuff in Northern Cal," Jim said.

"Hazmat is already on the way," Sam assured them before joining the firefighters to let them know what was going on. He returned with Captain Logan Moreno and introduced him around. The captain was in thick padded coveralls and carried a face mask. Jim and Moreno had things to talk over, so Charlene edged back.

Sam gestured at Kevin. "Please give your information to Officer Jimenez on your way back to the bus."

Kevin gave a nod and joined the waiting officer.

"It was just you and Jim when you found the body?" Sam stepped closer to Charlene and started to reach for her hand but then let his arm drop, as if remembering where they were. He gently took her by the elbow to study her face beneath the streetlamp. "Did you inhale anything? How are you feeling, really? Headache? Nausea?"

"I'm fine, Sam. Just so . . . sad. Morganna was so young. And now she's gone."

He rubbed his smooth jaw. His facial hair was reminiscent of Sam Elliott, but her Sam was even sexier. "Charlene, promise me that if you start to feel at all out of sorts that you'll go to urgent care. Jim and Sydney both know the signs of poisoning."

"I'm okay—Jim got us out into the fresh air." Charlene squeezed his hand out of sight of the other officers. "Thank you for coming so quickly."

"I wish you would call me *before* you walk into a dangerous situation."

"It all happened so fast," she answered softly.

"I just want you to be careful."

With effort, she pulled away from him and gestured toward the patrol car and the police officers who had just finished with Kevin. "Do I need to check in before I head to the bus?"

Sam smoothed his mustache with two fingers. "I know how to get ahold of you, Charlene. I'll be by in the morning to get everybody's statements and to talk with my sis. The fire marshal and me go way back, and I'm sure he won't mind if I help out." Sam checked his watch. "You might want to get home before the witching hour."

"What's that?" Charlene rubbed her arms against a chill.

"Midnight on Halloween—you won't believe the crazy things folks dream up. Mostly kids, but still it's best to get your guests home safely." He leaned close to her, so close his breath whispered against her cheek. "Have a nice night, Mrs. Morris."

Her blood heated at the sultry tone, banishing the cold from the inside out. "Good night, Detective."

She returned to the bus in a daze, thanking Mac for keeping everybody warm for the past thirty minutes. Sydney and Sal had entertained the guests, looking for white spectral orbs in their pictures and telling ghost stories.

"What happened?" Sheila asked as soon as Charlene was seated.

"We don't know yet," she said, then raised her voice to address everyone. "Detective Holden will be by tomorrow, and he might have more information for us."

Peter and Hailey huddled next to each other watching cartoons on a tablet. Matthew and Phil sat with Ted, who seemed certain to have caught the Lady in White at the cemetery.

"Send it to me," Kevin said, "and I'll put it on the website."

Charlene spoke to Sydney. "Sam said he'll catch up with you in the morning. He's going to be busy for the night." She searched the bus and counted heads. "Dylan didn't make it back?" She glanced at Phil and Matthew. "Did he say anything to you?"

"No," Matthew said. "Just took off."

Phil sat back. "He seemed freaked out."

"I was too," Charlene admitted. "Well, I'm sure he'll make his way to the B and B. Probably holed up at a bar somewhere." She shared a sad smile with her guests. "I'm also ready for a nice drink. Who's with me?"

That had the adults on the bus cheering.

They returned to "Charlene's" within minutes. She thanked Mac, and then led her guests up the paved drive to her front porch. Bales of hay and scarecrows decorated the white wooden decking.

Inside, her house smelled like cinnamon from the scented logs she used in her fireplace. The fire had been banked when they'd left, and she coaxed it to life, then offered leftover pastries from their earlier cocktail party.

Sheila and Sal declined, as did the Jensens, but Sydney, Jim, Matthew, and Phil all gathered around the fireplace, too hyped-up to turn in.

The conversation was about Salem and Halloween, and a dead witch.

Kevin stayed for a drink, but he seemed exhausted by the events of the evening and was ready to leave quickly, so Charlene walked with him to the front door.

"I appreciate everything that you did for us tonight—and I'm sorry about your friend." She touched his arm. "Is there someone you can call?"

Kevin glanced down dejectedly. "Friends of hers might

know if Morganna had family. I gave that information to Officer Jimenez."

"I came to Salem expecting to forget my husband's death, and yet death is all around me." She rubbed her arms. "Is it me?"

"Of course it's not you." Kevin chucked Charlene's chin. "The history here is steeped in mysterious happenings. Why should things be any different now than they were centuries before?"

She folded her hands at her waist. "Uh, because we are wiser and more civilized than our ancestors?"

"Are we?" He smiled, but the stretch of mouth was grim. "Call me if you need anything, or if you hear something new. I'll do the same."

Charlene returned to her guests and sat with them for a while, but the day's activities and the night's shocking ending had depleted everyone's energy. When they all went to bed, she turned off the lights, doused the fire, and quietly made her way down to the basement.

Prior to her moving in, Doctor Jack Strathmore had built a wonderful wine cellar. Collecting wine had been one of his and his wife's shared interests. Charlene preferred drinking over collecting—but not alone.

"Jack?" she said softly. This was their safe place to talk without being overheard. She needed his wisdom and comfort.

"How was the tour?" Jack shimmered in front of her, and she wanted to grab on tight and not let go. He wore jeans, and a white shirt under a beige cashmere sweater.

"Not so good." She found the Burgundy she'd opened a few nights back and poured her wine into a balloon-shaped glass. After a fortifying sip she was able to look at Jack without her eyes filling with tears. "Morganna, who runs one of the touristy witch shops, is dead."

Jack's arms crossed. "Who?"

The wine sloshed from the tremor of her hand. "You wouldn't know her because Kevin said she's only been in Salem a year, but, Jack, I was just talking with her! I'd ordered a witch ball. For good fortune . . ."

He hovered near her shoulder. "Charlene, are you all right?"

"No, Jack, I'm not." Kevin had tried to soothe her fears that she was somehow attracting death, but he'd failed. "We found her. Jim and me."

"How did she die?" Jack's temperature dropped as he asked the question. "Were you in danger?"

She reached for the sweater she'd learned to keep down here and slid it over her shoulders. Her headache was gone and her exhaustion natural considering everything she'd been through. "I don't know what happened." Charlene closed her eyes, seeing the attractive woman's blond curls in her mind. Her red witch costume and hat.

"Try to explain?" Jack asked in a droll tone.

Charlene shifted on the barstool and forced her eyes open. "Sorry. She had a workshop in the back of her store, where she made one-of-a-kind witch balls—glass orbs that she created from melted glass in a barrel furnace stove. Reminded me of something you'd see at a fair."

"Sounds dangerous to work on indoors," Jack said. "Was it heated by fire?"

She thought back, recalling a tank next to the shelves of orbs. "I think she used propane—but there wasn't a window in the room. Jim thinks that she died of cyanide poisoning."

"Why?" he asked. "That's very specific."

Charlene explained about the almonds and the antiterrorism training.

"It sounds like you were both very lucky." Jack came

closer to her and studied her face. "Hold out your hands and let me see the nails."

"What are you looking for?"

"Blue. Signs of poison."

"I had a small headache, but it's gone, Doctor Strathmore."

"I can see that you're breathing fine—though you probably shouldn't be drinking."

Charlene moved her wineglass as if he might take it from her. "Hey, now."

Jack's deep brown brows formed a V. "Cyanide poisoning can kill quickly in high doses, but God help those that die slowly."

"What happens?" Charlene didn't want to know—but she had to know. Who better to tell her than a doctor?

"Cellular hypoxia—cyanide doesn't allow the body to use oxygen—which means the body suffocates, even though the lungs are okay."

Charlene drained the rest of her wine. "Jack! That sounds horrible. I think she died quickly—I certainly hope so."

He snapped his fingers and brightened the light in the cellar to banish any shadows.

She began to shake from her toes on up—even her knees felt weak. Poor Morganna. "She was working when it happened."

"Melting glass in an unventilated area isn't smart," Jack said.

"That's what I thought, too, but maybe there was a different system that I didn't see? Jim had us outside as soon as I mentioned a smell."

Jack's energy waned in and out, causing the image he created for her benefit to flicker. "Be careful, Charlene. You've been through a lot since your arrival in Salem. It's a police matter."

"If I'd have left the mystery of your death to them, it never would have been solved." She put her hands on the table and got off the stool.

"To that, I owe you." His eyes caressed her, and he lifted a hand in her direction, but before she could reach for it, he was gone.

"Night, Jack," Charlene said to the empty air.

CHAPTER FOUR

The following morning, Charlene opened the old-fashioned butler's pantry and went inside to gather flour, canned pumpkin, and nutmeg. She brought the ingredients to the counter where Minnie had laid the mixer and bowls. Charlene had purchased a long griddle for the bed-and-breakfast, imagining just such a morning. Minus the dead witch the night before.

Her guests had slept in, but now it was after nine, and they were ready to eat. She and Minnie had coffee, tea, and fruit out on a sideboard in the dining room—the specialty would be pumpkin pancakes like her mother used to make.

"You mean to tell me that you found another dead body?" Minnie asked, her tone hitching. "What a dreadful ending to such a lovely night. I'm so sorry."

"What are the odds?" Charlene answered with horror. "But this was clearly an unfortunate accident."

A blast of cold shot from Jack's chair at the kitchen table, which had been pushed to the side near the cellar door. Then his dark hair appeared, followed by shoulders, chest, jeans, and finally black boots.

"Morning," he said with a salute.

"Morn—mmmmm. Coffee's tasting good." Charlene put her back to him—he'd almost tricked her that time!

Would a witch ball be able to trap Jack? Charlene would have to research the lore regarding the pretty orbs. Morganna had said that they would trap an evil spirit, but Jack wasn't evil. He was kind, considerate—most of the time—and a good sounding board. But she would never want to trap him here when it was time for him to go.

Jack propped his elbow on the kitchen table. "I was very worried about you last night. How do you feel this morning? I listened from your living room in case you needed me."

Unable to argue or converse, Charlene took a spatula from the drawer and set it on the counter next to the long griddle. He'd kept watch over her? How sweet.

Giving Jack a quick smile, she watched Minnie assemble the batter into the mixer, whirring ingredients together with the concentration of someone who had raised three children, managed her own household, worked in other kitchens, and knew how to multitask. The aroma of cinnamon blended with the nutmeg before settling into the comforting scent of fall.

The mixer stopped when Minnie pushed the button. "Will you preheat the griddle? I can pour from the bowl. The kiddos might want pumpkin shapes, but the rest of the folks should be content with round."

"They smell amazing and they aren't even cooked yet." Charlene inhaled, and her stomach rumbled. She'd been too emotional to eat before now.

"Were the guests upset about what happened last night?" Minnie spoke in a whisper and glanced over her shoulder at the closed pocket door that shielded the kitchen from the hall and dining room. She'd clipped her short gray curls back with silver barrettes, and had silver posts in her ears. Blush on her plump cheeks and a ribbon of rose across her mouth—for once not wide in a smile but pressed tight with concern.

Charlene turned the griddle to high. "Some of us stayed up for a nightcap of brandy," she admitted. "But the kids took it the hardest. Dylan"—not a kid, exactly—"wondered if it was part of the Halloween festivities, but then quickly realized it wasn't." Even talking about it this morning caused an ache in her heart. Death should be for the old or the wicked, not for bright, vibrant people who still had a whole life ahead of them.

"If only . . ." Minnie turned on the faucet and dipped her fingers in the running water, then splashed it on the black surface to see if it was hot. The droplets sizzled. She turned the heat down a notch and then poured the batter in a circle. With the edge of the spatula, she elongated the batter for a stem and leaf, creating a pumpkin. "For Hailey and Peter first, poor things."

When the first batch of pancakes was complete, Charlene brought the steaming platter to the dining room, where the Jensen family waited on the far end. Sheila and Sal were on the other, with Matthew and Phil in the center, Jim and Sydney across from them. The long table, now set for twelve, could easily sit twenty with extensions.

There was no sign of Dylan, and it worried her. Sam had said midnight on Halloween could be dangerous—"the witching hour" he'd called it. People got up to some crazy things, and with everyone in costumes partying on the street, that craziness could easily get out of hand. The crowd, the noise, the frenzy—add alcohol to the mix and it could be a deadly combination.

She shoved her fears aside, knowing that if she voiced them it would only fuel the flame of tension at the table.

"Peter and Hailey, you first—Minnie made you pumpkins!" She delivered the savory pancakes to the center of their plates.

The kids grinned, but Charlene noticed that Katherine and Ted each had shadows beneath their eyes. She sent a commiserating look their way and hoped that they hadn't been up all night with the kids, having bad dreams.

"Let me dish these out so you each can have one and I'll go get more from the kitchen." Katherine and Ted lifted their plates, murmuring their thanks, and Charlene hurried back to Minnie, who had another stack ready to go.

"Peter and Hailey loved the pumpkin-shaped pancakes," Charlene said. "Thank you for thinking of it."

"I have grandkids their ages," Minnie said. "It was no bother."

Charlene felt a chill in the air behind her as she offered each guest another pancake. Jack walked around the table, her resident ghost invisible to everyone but her.

How strange it still seemed, but also oddly comforting. In a huge old mansion like this, to never be alone—which made her think of Silva. Charlene searched the dining room until she spied the fluffy tail of her feline diva peeping beneath the curtain of the windowsill.

"Anyone want more?" she asked. "Minnie's starting another batch."

Jim stabbed a fork into his pancake while Sydney shook her head, her dark brown bangs a slash across her forehead. "One is plenty for me. I thought I would just pick on the fruit, but these are delicious."

"No more for me either," Sheila said from her and Sal's end of the table.

Sal took two large pancakes from the platter Charlene offered and grinned. "Nothing bothers my appetite. Never had them made with pumpkin before. Real tasty."

Charlene lifted the dish. "Everything Minnie makes is a delight. I'm going to have to learn to say no if I want to fit into my clothes."

Some people could eat through grief, perhaps taking comfort in food, while others like herself could barely swallow a bite. She'd lost at least ten pounds during the year following her dear husband's death—but was putting them back on quickly!

"As a nurse, I see . . . unpleasant things"—Sydney glanced at Peter and Hailey before continuing—"all the time. Last night was unexpected."

Charlene noticed that Peter had stopped eating his pancake, his face blotchy. Ted rubbed his son's thin shoulder. "Don't eat it if you don't want it," he told him gently.

Jack hovered near the pair, his arms crossed, a concerned look in his eye. Charlene was starting to recognize his empathetic "doctor" expression.

Peter pushed his plate away, his pale English skin even paler. "Can I go upstairs and read?"

"Of course, dear." Katherine watched him closely. "Why don't you take some fruit? An apple or a banana?"

"A banana would be best," Jack said. "I bet he had too much candy yesterday. Compounded with news of a scary dead witch? Nerves. A warm bath would be good too," Jack prescribed.

Charlene bit her lip.

Peter picked up the banana. "My stomach hurts."

Ted ruffled his daughter's dark brown hair and pointed to her almost-empty plate. "How about you, Hailey? Are you well enough for some tours after breakfast?"

"Sure." Hailey spied the cat behind the curtain and jumped from her chair. "Can I play with Silva?"

"Gently!" Katherine admonished as the little girl pulled back the drapes. Silva meowed.

"Maybe a warm bath?" Charlene suggested to Katherine under the weight of Jack's glare.

Peter dragged his feet up the steps slowly, his hand to his belly.

Jack followed to the staircase. "And some of that pink stuff. What's it called?"

"Pepto," Charlene answered.

"Oh! Good idea, Charlene," Katherine said. "Peter, do you need help with the bath?"

Jack laughed. Charlene somehow kept a straight face as she said, "Need some? It's in my bathroom."

"We've got the chewables," Ted said. "But thanks."

"I can do it, Mom," Peter shouted down from their room.

"Kids," Katherine said with a shrug.

Carrying the platter with the few remaining pancakes, she went to the kitchen, making sure to pass Jack as she did so. She nodded in the direction of the empty living room, wanting a word with him—he had to stop tricking her into talking in front of the guests!

After leaving the platter on the countertop, she met him near the fireplace. He was seated in the plush armchair.

Instead of her telling him a thing or two, he said, "Dylan didn't come back last night."

Alarmed, she joined him in staring at the unlit logs prepared for a roaring fire later that afternoon. "How do you know?"

He arched his brow. "I checked."

She wasn't sure how she felt about that. As a ghost, Jack could go wherever he wanted in the house undetected, while she wanted to respect their privacy.

"I was hoping he was upstairs asleep. Jack, now I'm very concerned about him. I know he's an adult and a paying guest, but he seemed most upset last night by Morganna's death."

Jack stood to face her, his hands behind his back. "He's at that age where he is legally an adult." He tapped his temple. "Yet capable of making the worst decisions."

"Where could he have spent the night? Is he safe somewhere, perhaps sleeping it off? I feel responsible." She reached into her jeans pocket and pulled out her cell phone. No messages. She put her phone back. "'Charlene's' is not off to an auspicious start." With a hand on the back of his chair, she searched Jack's deep blue eyes. "Maybe my mother was right. Perhaps I made a mistake coming here."

"That's not true." His expression remained solemn. "I would have been lost forever if it wasn't for you. You have made it possible for me to move on . . . when I'm ready."

"For that reason alone, I'm glad I came."

His pensive mood vanished. "Charlene Morris, you are a smart, caring, beautiful woman. Unfortunately, trouble seems to find you."

"Exactly." She crossed her arms.

Minnie popped her head into the living room and glanced around. "Who are you talking to? I thought you were on the phone."

"To myself," Charlene said with a blush. She had to be more careful. "It's a terrible habit I developed after Jared died."

Minnie smiled companionably. "Detective Holden just pulled up out front. I wanted to let you know." She wiped her hands on her apron. "Should I get the door?"

"No. Thanks, Minnie. I'll let him in." She and Jack exchanged a look.

"Of course." Minnie seemed about to say something, then shook her gray curls and swished back into the kitchen.

Charlene walked to the foyer, smoothed her shirt over her hips, and opened the door. Over six feet of handsome detective waited on her porch. "Sam."

"Good morning, Charlene. How are you feeling today? Any side effects?"

She gestured for him to come in and offered to take his jacket, but he declined.

"Not a thing, physically." She nibbled her bottom lip. "Emotionally? It's hard, but keeping busy helps." She glanced in the direction of the kitchen. "Minnie's made a big breakfast for everyone. Pumpkin pancakes. Still lots leftover. Can I get you a plate?"

"No, but thanks just the same. I had a doughnut already this morning. You know cops and their doughnuts. . . ." His attempt at a joke fell flat. "I came to speak with your guests, and make sure you are all right."

Jack sidled up next to her, his arms at his sides. "Oh, isn't that sweet?"

Ignoring her jealous ghost, she gestured toward the dining room. "I'm more concerned with my guests at the moment. Some of the folks are still at the table—a lot of the tours don't get started until ten, so we've been relaxing after such a crazy day."

Following her inside the room, Sam then stopped to study the curious faces. "Good morning," he said, taking the seat next to his sister. "I won't keep you long, but I just had a few questions."

Minnie brought him a fresh cup of coffee, which he accepted, then doctored with cream. He sat at ease, despite the gray checkered jacket he wore over the holster on his hip. This visit was official, but his posture made it appear less so.

"I hope you had some fun during your Salem-style Halloween," he said, easing into conversation. "Today there will be a Day of the Dead festival, in addition to all of the regular tours."

Hailey wiggled between Katherine and Sam with a gap-toothed smile.

"Hi there," Sam said. "Who are you?"

Hailey giggled and then dashed for the cat, but Silva was too quick for her and darted into the hallway, the girl running, arms outstretched, as she attempted to catch the quick-footed feline.

Charlene silently cheered the Persian, eyeing coffee cups for who needed a refill. Everybody was topped off.

"That was Hailey," Ted said. "I'm Ted Jensen and this is my wife, Katherine. It has been an eventful few days. Our son is upstairs now resting after a feast of chocolate. That and the dead woman have caused a bit of upset."

Jack, arms crossed, nodded.

"Detective Sam Holden. Sorry to hear about that."

Charlene introduced Matthew and Phil, and Sal and Sheila. *Where is Dylan?*

Sydney touched the sleeve of her brother's jacket. "What did you find out, Sam?"

Comparing them side by side, Charlene noticed the same oval shape to Sydney's and Sam's faces and the same chestnut hair.

Jim rested his arm on the back of his wife's chair, and his fingers feathered down to her neck and shoulder. His expression gave nothing away, but his eyes were steady on Sam.

"We are still investigating." Sam shifted in his seat, the antique wood creaking.

"We were hoping it was a prank," Sheila said, pointing between her and Sal. "We had just met Morganna a few hours before." Her eyes filled. "To think she died so suddenly . . . It was awful."

Sal tapped his finger on the tablecloth next to his empty plate. "A terrible shock."

"We're waiting for the fire marshal's report—although the initial finding from Hazmat did detect cyanide." Sam lifted his palm as he looked at Charlene. "Trace amounts, but as Jim mentioned already, it dissipates quickly in fresh air." Then he looked at Jim and said, "Your training kept you and Charlene safe."

Sydney closed her eyes and sank back in her seat with relief. "I worry about you when you go to work, Jim. Not while we are on vacation."

Jim pressed a kiss to Sydney's forehead. "It was Charlene's nose. Not everybody would be able to identify it."

The nurse sat up and focused on Charlene. "I would love to know about that scent thing and how it works."

"It's a certain gene," Jack said.

Charlene made a note to look into it later to satisfy her own curiosity.

Sam drank his coffee and set the cup down. "The coroner has Morganna's body now." He looked around the table to make sure there were no kids around. "They will be doing an autopsy."

Charlene went on alert. She happened to know that law enforcement only did an autopsy if they weren't sure about the cause of death. Did that mean that Sam thought it could be murder? She and Jack looked at one another.

Sam let his gaze touch each of them at the table. "Did any of you see anything out of the ordinary last night?"

Sal chuckled. "I saw more devil costumes than I ever imagined. A dinosaur. What else, hon?"

"A dozen Dorothys," Sheila reported. "And hundreds of witches."

"It makes perfect sense in Salem," Sydney said.

"Well, I don't know if this is helpful. Our family had gone back to the bus early, and so we were watching the trick-or-treaters go by and picking our favorite costume. I saw that dinosaur," Katherine said to Sal. "Anyway, Hailey said she saw a witch holding a magic bubble made of glass. I didn't see it, and I didn't think anything of it—I mean, there were so many witches." Katherine frowned. "But we were sitting near the back alley of the store in the parking lot. The magic bubble might have been a witch ball, with lights inside—I looked them up online after finding out about that poor woman dying."

"What time did you get back to the bus?" Sam asked, bringing out a notebook and short pen.

"By nine, Hailey was complaining about being too tired

to take another step, so we went back first, and Ted and Peter joined us about a half hour later." Katherine looked to Ted for confirmation.

Ted agreed.

"And did Hailey comment on this witch before your husband joined you?" Sam gestured to Ted with his pen.

"Yes." Katherine said that one word with distress.

Sam jotted down a few notes.

So, between nine and nine thirty, a woman was seen leaving the alley with a witch ball. Why, Charlene wondered, could that be of any interest to Sam?

Hailey stopped chasing the cat, forcing herself between Sam and Sydney. She lifted her hand over her head as high as she could. "She had a really tall purple hat and tangled red hair." She sniffed. "Like Princess Merida from *Brave*."

Sam glanced at Sydney and then Charlene, and finally Sheila. The schoolteacher laughed heartily. "Disney—a Viking story, and the girl has incredibly wild red curls."

Hailey ducked under Sydney's arm in pursuit of Silva, who had jumped up to the second-floor gallery, flicking her tail like a dare.

Phil peeled a banana from the fruit bowl in the center of the table. "That Psychic Fair was cool," he said. "I got my palm read by a hot chick in a devil costume. We might be back next year, Charlene."

"Good! Can I get you something more?" She stepped toward his plate.

"Nah—don't want to fall asleep on the drive home."

Matthew scoffed. "I'll keep you awake with some Metallica."

"Anything else?" Sam asked. "You all were back here last night by what time?" Charlene swiveled toward Sam, who sipped his coffee.

"Ten forty," Charlene said. She remembered looking at the time in the kitchen as she'd put together some leftovers.

Over the next thirty minutes, Sam had them tell each of their stories. He jotted the occasional note. "Is that everyone?" he asked.

"Dylan hasn't come down," Matthew said with an elbow to Phil. "Couldn't keep up with us in the whiskey department."

"He's probably still sleeping it off." Phil brushed his knuckles on his chest as if outdrinking the other man was a victory worth savoring.

"Dylan isn't here," Charlene said. "He didn't come back with the rest of us last night. He seemed pretty upset. Might be a girl thing."

What if he'd done more than drinking to drown his feelings—what if he'd passed out somewhere? Recreational drugs were rampant in a time when people snorted bath salts for kicks. Sam stood up with a nod. "I'm sure he'll turn up—Salem can be a wild town, and last night was . . ." His eyes met hers briefly.

"Crazy." Charlene supplied the word.

"Thanks for putting up with my questions," he told the others. "You all have a real good day." He nudged his sister in the arm. "How about dinner later, Syd. Jim?"

"Sounds good, big brother," Sydney said.

Charlene looked around for Jack, but he was gone. Was he watching over Peter to make sure the boy was okay?

She walked with Sam toward the front door. "So, if you see a guy with shaggy blond hair, a lightweight leather jacket, and scruff—possibly with a hangover—can you call me? Far as I know, Dylan didn't have any friends in town, so I'm worried about him."

Sam's gaze reached her heart. "You leave the worrying to me. I was thinking about you when Hazmat came back with that cyanide report. Get some rest this afternoon, and if you don't feel well, get to a doctor. I mean it. This is nothing to play around with."

"I appreciate your concern." She held his gaze for a little too long, and blushed.

"If I see your missing guest, I'll let you know."

"Thanks, Sam." Charlene cracked open the door, and the scent of fall entered her cozy house. "What would I do without you?"

CHAPTER FIVE

Charlene stood at the door as Sam was leaving. She wished she could ask the detective about Morganna's death and why there was an autopsy scheduled, but she knew that he couldn't discuss open cases.

The handle jerked beneath her fingers, and the door suddenly opened with a cold rush of late-morning air. Dylan stumbled in, looking as if he'd been pushed by an invisible hand.

Jack stood there, arms at his sides as he glared at Dylan with relieved disapproval. "Guy walked here," her ghost said with a huff. "Smells like he spent the night in the alley."

Charlene snapped her mouth shut as Jack disappeared; then she closed the door behind Dylan. She took a cautious sniff and discreetly stepped backward a few steps. Was that sand on Dylan's sneakers? A tiny seashell in the cuff of his jeans?

"Dylan, I'm glad to see you home and safe." Charlene wondered if he'd spent the night on the beach, but didn't press. She wasn't his mother.

Sam eyed the youth, taking his measure. If Sam questioned him, Charlene wanted to hear the answers.

"Hey," Dylan said, peering from her to the detective with bloodshot eyes.

"Good morning," Sam said. "I'm Detective Holden."

"Dylan Preston." He shifted nervously, keeping his hands in his jeans' pockets. Charlene noticed that he'd lost his leather jacket somewhere along the way and he was probably cold in his short sleeves. "What's up?"

Sam's demeanor went from casual to cop at the youth's lack of respect. "I came by this morning to talk about the incident last night at Morganna's Witch House. Were you there?"

"Not just me," Dylan said, tilting his head at Charlene. "It was a bunch of us. We did the ghost tour—no offense, but I only went because it was part of the package."

Well, that was honest. He probably would have preferred barhopping. Charlene had been twenty-one once upon a time.

Sam brought his shoulders back, crossing his hands at his chest. "A woman *died* last night," he intoned, not messing around. "I want to know what you saw, if you heard anything?"

Dylan flinched and shifted his feet. "No, sir."

"You left abruptly and had people worried."

"I didn't do anything wrong," Dylan said quickly. "It just creeped me out, that's all."

"Where did you go?" Sam asked.

"I met a girl at a bar. Why—is that a crime?" Dylan glanced toward the dining room area, where the others were listening to the conversation while pretending not to. He rolled his eyes at Matthew and Phil, who were smirking at him from their seats at the table. "We closed down a few bars and then went back to her apartment. Everybody was talking about what happened last night, you know?"

Charlene imagined how rampant gossip about a dead witch on Halloween would be. Probably many of them knew Morganna, by sight if nothing else.

Sam's eyes narrowed slightly. "People at the bar? What did you hear?" he asked.

Dylan scoffed. "Nobody admitted it, if that's what you're asking."

"That would make my job easier." Sam's teeth were gritted, and Charlene admired his patience with Dylan. She thought the kid was kind of likeable, but he wasn't winning any points with the detective.

It seemed to her that Sam was asking more than innocent questions—what was he getting at?

Dylan breathed in and looked at Charlene. "I sure could use some breakfast."

Charlene hated to interrupt Sam, but she was also the owner of this bed-and-breakfast, and it was her job to make sure her guests were taken care of. She decided on a compromise.

"I'll warm some pancakes up for you." She glanced at Sam. "Once the detective finishes with the questions. Okay?"

"Yeah, sure." Dylan bounced the heel of his sneaker against the wood floor. "What else do you want to know?"

"Where were you last night between nine and ten?" Sam didn't bring out his notebook, but Charlene remembered that he'd been specifically interested in that time frame. They must have pinpointed Morganna's time of death.

"With the group," Dylan said. Charlene thought back. He hadn't been with her—but maybe Phil and Matthew? "I met some crazy girls." Dylan slumped as if too cool to be interested. "It's one of the reasons I came here, you know. To meet this girl I'd been chatting with on Tinder, but she was lame—had a boyfriend. Coulda told me, saved me a trip."

So it hadn't worked out, Charlene thought. But being twenty-one, he'd bounced right back.

"Our tour ended at nine. We had an hour free before the bus trip home," Charlene supplied. She looked at Dylan.

"We didn't see you at the Psychic Fair. Were you at the bar during that time?"

"Yeah. I'm legal now, so what's the big deal? I'd had enough running all over the place, seeing old buildings and haunted cemeteries."

Sam gave a curt nod. "Where are you from?"

"Hartford. I took the bus."

"When do you plan on heading back?" Sam asked.

Charlene knew he'd paid for only two nights, unless he extended his stay.

Dylan shrugged. "Today, maybe. I might hook up with that chick Tara later and see what happens. I'm in no hurry."

"Are you in college?"

"Graduated last year. I work as a head waiter at a steak house. It's good money." He eyed the dining room table and took a hopeful step toward it.

"After Jim broke into the store," Sam continued. "What did you do?"

"I ran inside with Matthew and Phil, but we didn't get far before Jim and Charlene told us to stay outside. I thought it was a joke at first, you know, a murder-mystery kinda thing." He ruffled his shaggy hair with a self-deprecating smile. Her heart tugged.

"And then?"

"I left, man." Dylan laughed, and rubbed his stomach, which growled. "I'd asked Matthew and Phil earlier if they wanted to go barhopping, but I think they're more into each other." He said this with a sneer toward his friends, who made derogative gestures in return. "So I grabbed a beer across the street. That's when I met Tara." She and Jared had met in college, around the same age.

"Okay." Sam finally pulled out his notebook. "What number can I reach you at?"

Dylan rattled off his phone number.

"Here's my card," Sam said, choosing one from his jacket.

"If you remember anything else, or hear anything, give me a call."

"Yeah. Sure." Dylan dipped his head at Sam and then wandered into the dining room as if he hadn't a care in the world.

Charlene and Sam exchanged glances.

"You worried for nothing," he said.

"I can't help it. What happened to his jacket, I wonder?"

Sam's head snapped up. "He had a jacket last night?"

"Yes, a leather one—black. It didn't look very warm."

"It probably got lost during the barhop," Sam said. "I have to say, he doesn't seem like the usual bed-and-breakfast client. . . ."

She looked into the dining room as the guys teased Dylan. "What's Tinder?"

Sam grinned, his teeth white beneath his mustache. "A dating site, sort of. Things can get steamy, if that's what you're interested in."

She blushed and gently shoved his forearm. "I feel old."

"You are not old, Charlene. You let me know when you want to go out on the town—no app necessary."

Flustered, she opened the door and ushered him to the porch, reveling in the cool air against her hot cheeks. "Bye, Sam. I'll see you later."

His chuckle echoed through the thick wood of the front door even after she'd closed it.

With a headshake, she entered the dining room. Dylan had devoured the last of the pancakes cold. "Those were great." He reached for an apple from the fruit bowl.

"I could have warmed them for you!"

"No trouble—cold pizza, cold pancakes. All the same to me," Dylan said. "I don't want to put you out any."

Sweet. And what a jerk thing that girl had done to him. "Where did everybody go?" Charlene asked Matthew—the room had emptied.

"Upstairs. The Jensens wanted to check on Peter, and

Sal and Sheila have a tour planned." Matthew finished his coffee.

Phil pushed his chair back and stretched his legs out to pat his belly.

Dylan gestured to the door. "I sure hope they find who killed that cute witch."

Why did *he* think that Morganna had been killed? Why not an accident? "Why do you say that?" Charlene asked.

"He wanted to take her out for a drink, right?" Phil teased. "She was too hot to be into you, little boy."

Matthew laughed but asked Dylan, "Where did you go? I thought you'd come back and we could have a few shots here."

"I was hanging out with some of the Goth kids." Dylan shined the apple with a napkin. "I guess Morganna thought she was a real witch, like, with powers and stuff. She hob-nobbed with a different crowd and treated them like they were wannabes—they resented her for it, and spent their dinero elsewhere."

"Why didn't you tell that to the detective?" Charlene asked.

"*They* didn't kill Morganna, but they weren't sad that she's dead." He pointed his apple at Matthew and Phil. "You guys should have hung out with me—there was some real spooky witching-hour craziness. Partied with the White Witch and a bunch of half-naked chicks chanting by the lighthouse at midnight."

"I'm starting to think we missed a party," Matthew said.

Phil lifted his coffee mug. "I partied plenty, and I'm now paying the price."

"When did you get so old?" Matthew scrutinized his friend.

"Witches?" Charlene sat down, elbows on the table, and gave Dylan a long look. "Were any of them friends of Morganna?"

Dylan shrugged. "Dunno." He chomped away on his apple,

and she could see that he'd clammed up so tight he'd need a steamer pot before she got any more information from him. She exhaled and asked Phil, "Do you need something for a headache?"

"I'm fine," Phil said, "but thanks. Your place is terrific."

Matthew hurriedly agreed. "When do we need to check out, Charlene?"

"One is the official time, but if you need extra, that's fine." There weren't any new reservations for today. She felt a little emotional tug about the three guys leaving. Maybe because they were her first group of guests. She'd have to get her emotions under control or she'd be a wreck within a year.

Phil checked his watch. "We have an hour or so to kill. Can we drop you somewhere, Dylan?"

Dylan read his phone and grinned. "Nope. Just got a text from Tara—inviting me over for a private tour." He tossed the apple stem at Phil. "Loooooosers."

As Charlene watched the stem bounce off Phil to the floor, she realized that maybe she wouldn't miss them quite so much after all.

The Jensens, Peter feeling better after his bath and his Pepto tablets, came downstairs with plans for a trip to Marblehead—Sal and Sheila left next, taking a cab into Boston. Sydney and Jim were off to tour a nautical history museum that the fire captain had recommended last night, and Plymouth.

Charlene was on the front porch saying goodbye to Matthew, Phil, and Dylan when Sam arrived, followed by Officer Jimenez in a patrol car—blocking Matthew's ten-year-old BMW.

Sam got out of his SUV, something black in his hand.

The three young men exchanged cautious looks. Dylan turned white as the first snowfall in Chicago. Charlene reached for him before he—what? What did she expect him to do? Dash off? Confess to a murder?

Dylan bolted two paces to the left before Matthew grabbed him. "Chill out, dude," Matthew said.

Sam lifted Dylan's leather jacket. "Found this at Morganna's. Dylan, I'd like you to come down to the station with me and answer a few questions."

Charlene's stomach clenched. Why had his jacket shown up there? He couldn't have known Morganna. Unless she was the girl he'd been talking to online . . .

Dylan, wide-eyed, said, "I lost it. Thought I'd left it back at the bar. Figured I'd check later when they opened."

"Right," Sam agreed. "We need to discuss where you were at the time it went missing."

Dylan, scared now, said, "I was at the bar, where I met Tara."

Matthew tightened his grip on Dylan. "Man, you just told us you were hanging out at the pier last night for witching hour."

Dylan shrugged off Matthew's hand and straightened his shoulders. "You suck, Matthew—that was midnight. The girl was already dead. Before that I was touring with all of you, dude."

Charlene wondered why Dylan hadn't told that to Sam earlier. Was he protecting his new girlfriend? Or did he have something to hide? She so wanted to believe him, but what did she really know about his life?

Phil lifted both palms and stepped back in a clear removal from the situation. "If you don't need us, you mind if we leave?"

The detective ignored his question, his attention focused on Dylan.

"What do you want?" Dylan demanded, not budging from Charlene's porch. She could tell it was false bravado in the tremble of his voice.

"You can have more privacy for this interview at the station," Sam said—he didn't look at Charlene.

Surely Sam couldn't believe that Dylan was guilty of anything more than youth?

"Tell me right here," Dylan said, chin out. He'd shaved, nicking a tiny piece of skin on his taut jaw. He wore a clean short-sleeved T-shirt but must have packed only one pair of jeans.

"I'd like to know what you were doing at Morganna's?"

"I told you, I wasn't at Morganna's. Not until ten when everyone on the tour was meeting back there." His voice shook. "Am I under arrest?"

"No." Sam displayed Dylan's jacket in an open palm. "I would just like to ask you some questions."

Officer Jimenez took a step toward the porch, her eyes just as hard in the daylight as they'd been last night.

Dylan sent a panicked look to Charlene. She felt his anxiety. Sam couldn't go around accusing her guests! He had an alibi, his girlfriend, and people at the bar should be able to identify him.

"Dylan," Sam said, "you can get into the patrol car and we will drive to the station—nothing on your record—but we need to talk about this jacket."

"I've never even been to juvie," Dylan answered with a scowl.

"Just go with him," Matthew said. "Get it cleared up."

Dylan flipped Phil and Matthew the double bird before going down the porch stairs. "Don't call me, bros." He implored Charlene. "I didn't kill that witch. I was near that shop—the bar was just across the street. But I didn't talk to her. I got kinda wasted. You have to help me, Charlene."

Sam stiffened and finally looked at her with an inscrutable expression.

"You have my number, Dylan." Charlene drew herself up on the porch and spoke with a calm she didn't feel. "Call me when you've answered their questions. I'll come get you. Can I contact your parents?"

"No official charge will be made," Sam said—as if to assure her. "At least not yet."

"It's just me and my dad." Dylan's thin, pale arms had goose bumps in the fall air. "He doesn't need to know."

Officer Jimenez opened the back door of the patrol car. There were no cuffs. Dylan ducked in the back seat, and the officer closed the door with a deafening click.

Sam started to walk toward her but then changed his mind as she was flanked by Matthew and Phil. His mouth became a thin line beneath his mustache as he returned to his SUV and started the engine.

The officers left. Charlene felt powerless against the circumstances. How could Sam possibly think that Dylan was responsible for whatever had happened to Morganna? Or did he hope to frighten the boy enough to get information on the kids he was hanging with last night? She wanted to believe that.

Two things crystalized: She would help Dylan clear his name, even if it meant "getting involved." Secondly? Sam didn't believe that Morganna's death was an accident. She'd been murdered.

CHAPTER SIX

Later that day, she and Minnie cleaned the three vacant rooms. Two long hours went by without word from Dylan.

With each sweep of the broom, she thought back to what she knew about witches—which, before now, wasn't much. But she happened to know a witch—Brandy Flint, who owned Flint Wineries.

Would Brandy have known Morganna? And who might want the woman dead? The Flints had some of the oldest family ties in the community.

Charlene had used Flint Wineries to create a label for "Charlene's" bed-and-breakfast, and they had started off friendly toward one another. Unfortunately, Charlene had questioned Brandy in the previous investigation of Jack Strathmore's murder, and she hadn't liked Charlene poking her nose where it wasn't wanted. Now, Charlene wasn't sure of the reception she'd get. For Dylan's sake, she had to risk it.

Dressed for a chilly afternoon in jeans, knee-length boots, a long-sleeved black tee, and a white parka, she jumped into her Honda Pilot and drove the twenty minutes outside of town.

She slowed when she came to the large billboard that said, WELCOME TO FLINT'S VINEYARD. It had a picture of a beautiful woman with auburn hair holding a wineglass. Brandy Flint. A strong, courageous woman who'd had three husbands, owned and operated a two-thousand-acre vineyard, and didn't take crap from anyone.

Charlene couldn't help but admire her.

She turned right at the sign and drove down a dirt road that curved to the left. After a few minutes, she passed a two-story stone house with a gabled roof, heading to the shop behind the home. Into the horizon, hill upon hill of netted grapevines formed uniform rows. She pulled up in front of the white clapboard winery.

She jumped out of the car and marched to the emerald-green door with the Flint's Vineyard logo on it. Red and green grape clusters combined to make a heart. Simple yet refined, like the wine—for that matter, like Brandy herself.

The door flew open and Brandy stood there. She was tall, possibly five ten—and slender. Her auburn hair fell to her waist in thick waves. Her skin was porcelain; her mouth, a perfect red bow. Not only were her looks intimidating but her emerald eyes flashed anger. "You have some nerve coming here."

"And hello to you, too, Brandy." Charlene waltzed into the store as if there to admire all the fine merchandise on display. "I assume you've had a busy week since you didn't bother to call."

"Why would I call *you*? I'm not sure I've forgiven your insinuation that me, or Theo, could be a murderer." Theo was Brandy's current lover.

Charlene acknowledged that Brandy had a point. "I'm sorry about that—but how was I to know differently? You have to admit that your affair with Theo seemed suspicious."

"I don't have to admit anything—our affair was none of your business." Brandy tossed her head haughtily. "So why are you here? If you need to refill an order, all you have to do is pick up the phone."

"I'll order more because your wine is delicious, but that's not why I came." Charlene tucked her hands into her pockets, wondering how to question her without making their relationship worse.

Brandy hitched her butt on a stool in front of the bar counter and tilted her head. "Well?"

"A woman was killed last night during the Halloween Witch Festival. Morganna, from the Witch House?"

Brandy waited without a blink.

Charlene continued, "My guests and I were on a ghost tour. Jim and I discovered her body."

"Here we go again. Are you trying to find a way to connect me with Morganna?" Brandy's gaze was scalding. "Because we are both witches—is that it?"

"Sam, Detective Holden, has taken one of my guests in for questioning. This young man says he didn't kill her— heck, he didn't even know her—so I'm hoping to clear his name. Did you know Morganna, Brandy? Was she fighting with anyone in the witch community?"

"You are so gullible." Brandy glanced down at her Cartier watch and got up from the stool. "I have work to do, Charlene."

"How do you know this young man didn't do it?" A strikingly beautiful woman with silver shoulder-length hair and the same emerald eyes as her daughter stood at the back-office door.

"Hello, Evelyn," Charlene said. Evelyn had come with Brandy to Charlene's open house last week.

"Was he with you last night, *all* night?" Brandy's mother offered a cool smile.

"No!" Charlene shuddered at the unwelcome thought. "He's young enough to be my son. Just—no." She frowned. "He only came into town for a couple of nights. To meet a girl. He was here to have fun, not to get into trouble."

"Who knows what lies in the heart of a young man? Question is, was he with you when she died?" Brandy asked, zeroing in on the weak point of Charlene's defense.

Charlene exhaled loudly. "No. I don't know where he was, for a fact—we were together, all of us, on a tour right up to about an hour before. After we found her, he took off, said he was at the bar for a while, then later at the pier—for the witching hour at midnight—with other witches. Which is why I am here asking questions. Did you know Morganna?"

"Yes," Evelyn said. "I did."

"And that she was dead?" Charlene persisted, looking from mother to daughter.

"We heard from friends this morning," Brandy said.

Charlene couldn't get a read on how they felt about Morganna. "I imagine the witch community is upset? It was so shocking, and on Halloween of all nights."

"What is it exactly that you want to know?" Evelyn left the doorway, the hem of her long gray skirt brushing the wood floor of the shop. Painted wood bracelets were stacked up her arm to the three-quarter sleeve of her cashmere sweater.

"You better tell her something, Mom, or Goddess knows what she'll come up with on her own." Brandy returned to her position behind the counter and stacked brochures.

Evelyn lifted her hand, and her bracelets clacked together softly. "How can I help?"

"I know nothing about modern-day witches. Would you mind educating me?" Charlene gestured to a round bistro table with two chairs before the window between the shelves of merchandise. "Can I buy a bottle of wine? I'd love to sit down for a *friendly* chat." She made a point of looking at Brandy.

"May I choose the wine?" Evelyn asked. "It's a blend we hope to unveil for Christmas."

"That sounds great, thank you." Charlene removed her coat and took a seat.

"Do you mind getting a chilled bottle, Brandy? And join us, dear," Evelyn said. When Brandy opened the refrigerator, Evelyn spoke in a lower voice to Charlene, "Brandy tends to hold a grudge when she feels she's been wronged, but she will come around."

Brandy returned with two bottles and three glasses. She opened a bottle and put the other in a gift bag on the bar.

Was that an olive branch? Charlene would do her best to keep the friendship door open. "Thank you."

"Let me tell you about this new blend." Evelyn poured three ounces into three long-stemmed glasses and handed them out. She swirled the liquid around in the glass and sniffed it.

Charlene did the same, copying Evelyn's actions.

"This is a wonderfully robust wine with a broad palate. What can you identify, Charlene?"

She breathed in. "It has a floral scent, but I smell apricots, perhaps peach, and honeysuckle."

"Pear and vanilla too." Evelyn took a sip and raised her emerald eyes. "Oh, that's good. Should be ready for the holidays, don't you think?"

"It has a clean, crisp taste," Charlene said. "It's delicious."

Brandy sipped, rolling the liquid over her tongue. "It has a creamy texture. The aroma is mouthwatering." She swallowed. "Mom, we should export this one."

"Hmm. Of course," Evelyn said, "but after we get it out to all our local restaurants and shops, will there be any left?"

"It's all about supply and demand—we want to have just

a little bit less than what they demand, so that next year they want more." Brandy set her glass down.

"I learned that in one of my marketing classes," Charlene agreed. "Did you study, too, or simply learn by doing?"

Brandy's attitude thawed a bit more. "I have my business degree. Mom was all about us getting an education, since she's a professor of medieval history. Didn't want us to rely on magick or good fortune to make our way in the world."

"Magic?" Charlene took another drink of the wine, knowing she'd want at least a case. "Like spells?" Is that what Dylan and the others were doing on the pier?

"Magick with a 'k,'" Brandy said, "is different than ordinary magic. We use spells for the grapes, but we also use the right amount of fertilizer and good soil." She flipped an auburn lock over her shoulder. "Spells are prayers of intent, and no different from people using a vision board to manifest their dreams."

Charlene had created a vision board in college, cutting out pictures of places she wanted to travel. The idea, her best friend Brynne had said, was to imagine your goals and dreams in a visual way in order to work toward them.

Evelyn rose from the table and kept her glass in her hand as she walked around the room, the hem of her long skirt swishing. "What can I tell you about modern-day witches in Salem? We're like everyone else. Some good. Some bad. We don't go around putting warts on people's noses." Evelyn laughed. "Although tempting, it is against the rules."

Charlene didn't want to be rude, but she hoped for better clarity so that she didn't offend anyone in her new town. "So what makes you a witch? How are you different than me?"

Evelyn put down her wine, her back to the bar counter. "I am not fond of the word 'witch,' but I am Wiccan. Wicca is a recognized religion, like Christianity, or Greek Orthodox, Muslim, or any other faith-based practice. There are hundreds of thousands of Americans practicing this religion today, maybe even closer to half a million. Witchcraft dates back to prebiblical times, but Wicca was not an organized practice until Gerald Gardner created the religion in the mid-twentieth century."

Less than a hundred years. "That's not long at all! What faith did your family follow before then?"

Evelyn picked up her glass of wine, swirling it around again before taking another sip. "Our ancestor, Armand Sheffield, was a druid in England before moving here to Salem in 1694. His bloodline runs in the Flint family today." She glanced proudly at Brandy.

"Druid? Is that pagan?" Charlene grasped for understanding. "Could that have something to do with why Dylan and the other witches were on the pier at midnight?" By that time, Morganna had been dead at least three hours.

"The witching hour, when the veil is thinnest," Brandy drawled from her seat by the counter. "How cute that the kiddies still go down to play—I did that myself when I was much younger. Like, high school." She rolled her eyes.

Was it a game, then? Like a challenge or a dare, or hazing?

"The name doesn't matter so much as the understanding that the practitioners were seeking God, which isn't that different than the purpose of religion today," Evelyn said. Her tone was perfectly pitched to capture Charlene's attention. "In this twenty-first century, things are less structured and there is more acceptance in finding a personal path to God," she told her. "What is your faith, my dear?"

"I was brought up Catholic but don't practice it."

"In the past, there were sacrifices, but that was the time they lived in," Brandy said. "Today we gather in circles for prayer and fellowship, but the offerings are flowers and fruits rather than blood."

"Thank Goodness for that!" Charlene said, envisioning young women being led to slaughter. Bad enough a goat.

Evelyn lifted a necklace that had a silver goddess figure as a pendant. "We believe in God and Goddess, and the male-female energies around us."

Brandy laughed. "Her eyes are crossing, Mom. Simply put, nature is divine."

Evelyn paced before the bar counter, her voice growing stronger as her passion increased. "We believe in karma and an afterlife, and the Law of Threefold Return. Whatever you do in this world comes back to you three times over. Good or evil. It is personal choice, and you are responsible for your actions."

She remembered Kevin saying that on the bus tour. "Was Morganna a practicing Wiccan?"

Brandy's full mouth thinned as if she didn't want to talk about it. "She was a member of the local coven."

"I wish we could find another name for coven," Evelyn lamented. "It has a dark connotation."

"You are an elder, Mom. You can suggest something."

"I'm no longer on the council. That will be Martine and Lucas's job to usher in the next generation." Evelyn noticed Charlene's confusion. "The Evergreens are the leaders now."

The women didn't say anything more, but Charlene, rude or not, had to know something that might help Dylan. She had to have information to give Sam in exchange for her young guest. "Did she have a boyfriend? Husband?" Someone had to be grieving for her.

Brandy gave her watch another pointed look before saying, "Morganna had a boyfriend—off-again, on-again kind of thing. Rich Swane."

Charlene committed the name to memory because writing it down might stop the Flints from talking to her. Why should they care about some kid from Hartford?

"Do you know where he lives?" Charlene asked. "I'd like to offer my condolences."

"You are as persistent as grape mold," Brandy declared,

leaning across the counter. "Last answer. He was her land-lord and roommate, but I don't know his exact address. Be careful—he is not Wiccan, and Morganna had a restraining order against him. I guess their fights could be heard from the street."

"Anger and jealousy mistaken for passion," Evelyn in-toned. Yet despite this, Charlene got the impression that the older woman didn't like Morganna.

Realizing that she'd overstayed her welcome, Charlene stood. "Thank you for sharing about your religion. It's been enlightening." She swallowed her last sip of wine, not want-ing to waste a drop. "Let me pay for a case—and could I please have it delivered?"

"We aren't releasing it until after Thanksgiving," Eve-lyn said. "Right, Brandy? Supply and demand," the older woman laughed. "I pay attention."

Brandy stepped behind the cash register. "Take the sec-ond bottle home with you, Charlene. As a gift."

Peace offering, she hoped.

She looked out the office window at the darkening skies. Fall would be winter before she knew it. Next stop, the police station to pick up Dylan—hopefully before it rained. "Thanks again, ladies."

As she started her car she found herself agreeing with Evelyn about the terminology. *Witch* sounded evil, but nei-ther Evelyn nor Brandy were like that. And the world could use a lot more people being accountable for their actions.

CHAPTER SEVEN

Charlene left the vineyard and drove directly to the station. Maybe Sam wasn't aware of the relationship between the witch and Rich Swane—who would need to be notified of Morganna's passing.

She had little empathy for the man she'd never met, since Morganna'd had a restraining order on him. But she liked him for a suspect rather than Dylan.

After finding a parking spot right in front of the brick building, she turned off the engine. It bothered her to be at odds with the handsome detective, but how could he possibly detain one of her guests who had a plausible alibi? Dylan was no more capable of murder than she was.

Charlene palmed her keys and walked into the station.

A young lady in a police uniform, her short brown hair styled in a bob at her chin, greeted her when Charlene entered.

"Hi! Is Detective Holden in? I'm Charlene Morris."

The woman pressed a button and said, "Detective Holden? Ms. Morris here to see you."

"I'll be right out," his deep voice returned.

The officer gestured to a row of plastic chairs in the

waiting area, but Sam arrived before Charlene could take a seat. Two men sat at opposite ends, looking like they'd slept in a dingy alley.

"Ms. Morris! What a nice surprise." Sam glanced at the men seated with their heads down, hunched over. The one on the left began to snore. "Hank? You need a bed to sleep it off?"

Sam's eyes met hers with a flicker of amusement as the lady officer went over to the gent and shook him awake. "I'll get him some coffee."

"Thanks, Patty." Sam's attention landed on Charlene. "Care to come back to my office?"

She knew from previous visits that his office was down the tiled hall to the right. A dark gray carpet runner centered perfectly between the walls muffled the click of her bootheels.

"Thank you for seeing me." She wondered where Dylan was. Surely he wouldn't have been falsely incarcerated? Maybe he was back at the B and B, waiting for Charlene. Or out with his new girlfriend. This part of the building contained offices rather than holding cells.

Sam opened the door, semicasual in black denim, leather boots, and a black button-up shirt rolled at the wrists. Since he held the door, she had to slide past him, and got a subtle whiff of his cologne. It was woodsy, masculine, an outdoorsy scent—appealing, like the man himself.

She took a seat before his desk and unzipped her white coat to cool herself down. "I came to check in on Dylan."

"He's been released already." Sam strolled around his desk and sat, leaning back in the leather office chair with a creak, his elbows on the armrests. "He didn't call you?"

"No." Disappointment warred with relief. She was glad he hadn't been arrested but worried over what had happened.

"A young lady named Tara came to pick him up," Sam explained.

Charlene had been ready to slay dragons and now had to shift tactics. "Oh well . . . I'm glad his story about Tara was true, and that he's not in jail."

"I'm sorry if we disrupted your other guests," Sam said.

That was thoughtful, Charlene noted, but not necessary. "Did he explain the jacket?"

Sam tensed. "I can't discuss this with you."

"Fine." Charlene sat forward, holding eye contact. "I realize you think Morganna was murdered, but Dylan is innocent."

"What are you saying?" Sam asked in level tones. The friendly light in his deep brown eyes dimmed.

"I've learned that autopsies aren't requested unless a death is suspicious. Then you found Dylan's jacket, and *that* for some reason brought questions?" She interlaced her fingers on her lap, searching his face for answers. "I'm not asking, just explaining."

He rubbed his jaw but confirmed nothing.

"I was just at Flint Wineries, ordering a case of wine, and we—Brandy Flint and her mother, Evelyn—got to talking about Morganna and witches in general."

"I hope you weren't discussing the investigation."

She shifted on her chair uncomfortably. "I just wanted to find out if Morganna had any enemies among the witches."

Sam gave a slight shake of his head and straightened his posture. "What did you learn?"

"Brandy and Evelyn are both members of the local Wiccan community, as you already know. Did you know that Morganna has—*had*—a boyfriend?"

He nodded. "Yes. Rich Swane."

Charlene hated the no-nonsense tone delivered from that sexy voice. "Oh. I guess you've already questioned him then?"

His brows lifted. "I wish you wouldn't involve yourself in these things."

They looked at one another across the expanse of desk, which was neat and orderly, without so much as a paper clip out of place. Her own desk was littered with crumpled notes from her endless lists.

"Did you know that Rich was also her landlord?" She twisted her hands in her lap, knowing he hated her butting in. Well, she definitely didn't like Sam arresting her guests.

His right eye twitched.

"And they had loud arguments that could be heard from the street." She hunched her shoulders, thinking that last bit did sound like gossip, but just in case, Sam should know all of the details. "Brandy said that Morganna had filed a restraining order against him—but they still lived together. I don't understand that, but . . ."

"Not everybody has the perfect marriage or relationship," Sam said curtly. "Most of us have to work a little harder to find our life partner."

"I didn't mean to sound judgmental!" Charlene's cheeks heated. Had she been? Dang it. It was hard not to compare others to what she'd known. Jared would never have lifted a hand to her, and their arguments were rarely loud.

Sam pushed himself up from his chair. "Thank you for stopping by . . . I didn't know that he was her landlord for the business, or that they were still living together. I assumed from the report that they had separate domiciles. I will be sure to inform Mr. Swane of Morganna's demise."

Charlene had no choice but to stand as Sam was making it clear the conversation was over. "Sam, I . . ." What could she say? "I want to help. It isn't just Dylan, but being the one to find her body makes me personally involved. You see that, don't you?"

"I understand that and more." His posture looked less stiff; his face hinted at sadness. "It is obvious to me that you still have feelings for your husband. He was a lucky man to garner such devotion."

Charlene looked down and blinked to clear the film of

moisture from her eyes before meeting Sam's searching gaze. "*Time* has helped heal the wound—which is why I came to Salem, remember?"

He nodded, a cautious smile gracing his full mouth. "Let me handle this, Charlene."

"It was a conversation," she said with a toss of her hair. She took her keys from her pocket for something to do with her hands. "And I learned something you didn't know. You wouldn't want me to keep it to myself, would you?"

"No, of course not. But you have a lot of gossipy chats with people you don't really know."

"I didn't object to you chatting with my guests this morning at breakfast. That 'conversation' was helpful, wasn't it?" She remembered he'd taken quite a few notes.

"I was interviewing your guests, not chatting," he corrected, crossing his arms at his chest.

"Speaking of which, your sister is adorable. Her husband is nice too. Jim sure got along well with the captain last night. I don't suppose you've heard anything that you can share about the Hazmat report?"

"I don't have anything on my desk yet." He changed the subject. "You are doing a great job, Charlene. You make everyone feel welcome and seem perfectly at ease playing hostess."

"Thank you. It's so different from my previous career, and not at all like anything I ever expected to do—and yet I enjoy it. Especially with the kids around."

"How is Silva handling all of that attention?"

She laughed, relieved they were back on good terms. The last thing she ever wanted was to hurt Sam, or to lead him on. She liked him too much for that. "Begrudgingly, but she allows it. She would hide if she didn't."

Sam reached out to brush a strand of hair from her cheek, his touch warm and light. "Thank you for coming by. You are always welcome."

She knew that he meant without talking about a crime.

Maybe to say hello, just because. Her heart hummed a little, but she stepped into the hall. "Bye, Sam."

"See you. Oh, will you remind Sydney that I'll be there at four to do an early dinner, before the drive to the airport? Are you free to join us?"

"I can't. I'd love to, but I still have the other guests to think about." Charlene gave him a warm smile and left the station.

She drove home with a lot on her mind, and her eye out for Dylan. She would call him, she decided, later to see how he was doing.

By the time she arrived back at the bed-and-breakfast, it was close to three. It was a quiet Monday afternoon with her guests not yet returned from their outings. Minnie had already gone home and wouldn't be in again until Friday to clean.

The Jensens were to return to England Friday morning. Sheila and Sal would go back to Oregon on Thursday, with Sydney and Jim leaving today. They were already packed. "The house feels empty," she said aloud. Not even Silva was on her sill.

"I'm here," Jack said, materializing slowly before the fireplace, his shirt the same turquoise blue as his eyes. Black slacks, black loafers. *Ah, Jack . . .*

"I'm glad!" She set her purse down on the oval table by the front door and then hung her white parka on the coat-tree in the foyer. She had so much to tell him.

"Let me make tea, and I'll join you. I love that view of the lawn." She glanced past him to the window. "I wonder if we'll get snow soon? It seems cold enough."

"Next month for sure, but we've had snow in early November before. Makes driving around unpleasant, especially on this street of ours."

The "ours" touched her heart. It would always be his home as much as hers. "I think I'll like it. Beats the blizzards. In Chicago we lived in the city, and the snow turned to gray slush. All of the oak trees will make this a winter wonderland."

He concentrated on the drapes, and they opened while she hurried to the kitchen to plug in the electric kettle for tea—something lemony, she thought, as she went through her selection. An herbal lemon zest sounded wonderful, and she opened the bag, dunking it into the mug of hot water.

She grabbed some shortbread cookies from the pantry and returned to the living room, where she settled next to Jack on the love seat.

Through the open curtains, some of the trees had brown and orange leaves, and she could just barely make out the trunk of the oak tree behind the house. "I was thinking about building a gazebo next spring. I'd hire Parker Murdock if you think he'd be the best choice?" The carpenter/handyman had created the wooden wine cellar in the basement, as well as the bed-and-breakfast sign for Charlene's front entrance. He was a master craftsman in her eyes.

Resting his arm along the back of the love seat, Jack agreed. "He's got the talent, and I'm sure he could use the work." He eyed the faded green lawn as if imagining the gazebo. "I can see it. It would be a very nice addition. Afternoon teas . . . cocktail parties?"

"You won't be upset?" Charlene noticed the black curl over Jack's ear and fought the urge to smooth it. If she did, the illusion would disappear. "I mean, it is your home."

"It is our home, and I'm happy to share it with you."

"Me too." She sipped, inhaling the lemon fragrance.

"So any news about the dead witch?" Jack asked. "How are you feeling?"

"I'm fine, Doctor. Not even a hint of a headache." She put her cup down, break over. "Sam brought Dylan in for questioning. It seems that Dylan's jacket was found at Morganna's—Sam didn't say where." She twisted, putting her back to the far side of the love seat.

"Dylan?" Jack repeated. "Well, he had obviously been drinking last night. What happened?" He faced her. "Wait— Sam thinks that Dylan might have been involved?"

She touched her earring, the diamonds from Jared back in place. "He's a person of interest—he hasn't contacted me, although he was released."

Jack folded one leg over the other, black on black, the colors melding without definition of the fabric. "Sam must have something else if they're seriously considering Dylan as a suspect."

"I can't imagine what! Hang on and I'll get his number." Charlene went through the kitchen to her living area and opened her laptop to get Dylan's number from his guest application. She jotted it down on a scrap of paper and dialed, before returning to Jack. It went straight to voice mail.

"Nothing," she said.

"Could be he needs a phone charger." Jack patted the seat beside him.

"I suppose. Remind me to keep trying. I know it is ridiculous. . . ." Charlene sat down again next to Jack. She knew that she wasn't *actually* responsible for him, but feelings were feelings. "I went to Flint Wineries to find out from Brandy about Morganna, and other Salem witches."

"And what did you learn from your witchy friends?" She smiled at his sardonic tone.

"I found out that Morganna had a not very nice boyfriend who was also her landlord and roommate. She had a restraining order against him once but must have forgiven him, because they were still living together."

"The plot thickens," he said, waggling his brows. "Has your detective discovered if cyanide is the cause of death?"

Charlene shrugged. "I stopped by the station to tell him about Rich Swane, to try to clear Dylan. Sam wasn't at all pleased that I was asking questions about Morganna." She sighed. "Of course, he refuses to tell me anything."

"He can't." Jack's eyes were laser beams on her.

"I know." Charlene sipped her tea. "I think an abusive boyfriend is certainly more suspect than an innocent waiter." She put her cup on the saucer, her fingers trembling. "I don't think I'll ever forget that frozen look on Morganna's face . . . eyes wide open . . . her outstretched hand . . . Why would anybody do that on purpose?"

"I don't know. I wish I could help you."

They gazed at each other, she wanting comfort, Jack so clearly wishing to give it.

Just then footsteps pounded up the porch steps, and the sound of Sydney and Jim laughing preceded their entry into the foyer.

Jack disappeared and Charlene stood to greet them. Sydney's hair was tucked beneath a knit cap, her cheeks rosy from the fall air. Jim pulled his gloves off and stuffed them into the pockets of his jacket.

"Hi!" Charlene said, coming around the love seat to the hall. "Oh—you both smell like outdoors. Makes me want to get outside, too, instead of lazing on the couch. How was Plymouth? Did you see the *Mayflower* and the rock?"

"We sure did! It was amazing. And the crowds weren't too bad either," Sydney said. "And the nautical museum was just as great as Logan said it would be."

The captain of the fire department. Charlene looked at Jim. "Oh—was he in touch today?"

"Yeah, he had some things he wanted clarified about last night," Jim said.

"Anything to do with Dylan's leather jacket?" Charlene asked. "Sam brought Dylan in for questioning."

"No kidding?" Sydney shook her head. "I don't believe it."

Jim rubbed his hands together. "Logan wanted to know how open the door was to the workshop, and how much time it took us to break in. Same things Sam was asking this morning, but I think he hoped I'd remember something new." Jim shrugged. "He mentioned that something had been stuffed in the ventilation on the roof. I wonder if that was Dylan's jacket?"

That would certainly give Sam a reason to question Dylan. But how had it gotten up there? Rich, maybe, who had an apartment above the shop? "I've been trying to call Dylan, but his phone is going to voice mail," Charlene said.

"You're going to have to tell us how this all works out," Sydney said as she scanned the room. "You look so cozy. I wish I could join you, but we need to finish the last of our packing." Sydney took her hands. "This has been such a treat, Charlene, despite the . . . drama."

"How about I boil some water for tea—or hot chocolate?" She shifted toward the kitchen, the pocket door open.

"Hot cocoa laced with brandy?" Jim questioned hopefully.

"Sure," Charlene said. "I might even join you."

"That sounds great—can I help?" Jim asked.

"No, I can manage to boil water—so far," Charlene said with a grin. "But you can get the brandy from the liquor cabinet, if you will. I'll rummage up some of Minnie's leftovers. Some cheese and crackers? Or cookies?"

"Both," Jim said, heading for the brandy.

"We won't want to leave," Sydney warned.

"You are welcome to stay!" Charlene watched Sydney hang up both their coats on the rack, and knew she was going to miss them. "Your brother asked me to remind you that he will be here at four to take you to dinner on the way to the airport."

Sydney poked Jim in the shoulder and pulled off her knit cap. "See? I told you. Let's cancel the cab."

"I didn't want to be a bother," Jim said with a shrug. "Especially if he is in the middle of a . . . an investigation."

"He's my brother. It's not a bother!" Sydney pointed out.

Emergency personnel must have a handbook somewhere of what can be said to civilians because Jim was careful not to say "murder." "Sam is very closemouthed about these things, so you might find out what is going on before I do."

Sydney nodded with understanding. "We will share what we can, right Jim?"

"Sure—so long as it doesn't interfere." Jim held up a finger.

"The Jensen family will be here soon. Let me just make the cocoa quickly, and I'll meet you in the living room!" Charlene thought with pleasure about Sam's observation that she made a good hostess. "Give me five minutes."

When she returned with the cups of cocoa, generously laced with brandy, she put the tray in the center of the coffee table. She'd found a selection of cheese and crackers, pâté, and oatmeal cookies fanned out on the side. The Taylors were seated next to one another on the love seat like she and Jack had been—only they could actually touch each other. Jim kissed Sydney's cheek before he helped himself to a drink and cookie, and Charlene's heart pinged with sorrow.

"It's a fact," Sydney said, "that we will be back. I know of two other couples who would also love this place. How else can we help?" She sipped on the hot cocoa and murmured her appreciation. "This is excellent." She put a slice of pâté on a paper plate and added two crackers. "I'll save room for dinner, but we barely had lunch. Just a hot dog around noon."

"Eat and enjoy. I'm sure it'll be a quick meal somewhere." She found a stack of her cards next to the small table at her side. "Pass these around to your friends. Reviews and word of mouth is the best help anyone can ask for," Charlene said.

"Yelp?" Jim spoke around a bite of cookie. "Do you have a Facebook page?"

"Yes," Charlene said. "I was a marketing major before deciding to open a bed-and-breakfast." For once, she didn't add the part about her late husband.

"That explains the gorgeous black-and-ivory cards. A touch of elegance you've chosen instead of witches everywhere. You stand out above the rest." Sydney blew on the hot liquid before taking a hesitant sip.

"It was my intent, yes. I am glad you noticed." She looked around the living area, each piece chosen by her. "I want this to be a home away from home."

She'd love to get to know these two more. Would having a bed-and-breakfast allow her to make real friendships? Or would it be simply a steady stream of strangers passing through her life? After Jared died, she'd realized how sheltered she'd become, just the two of them.

"Are you seeing anyone?" Sydney asked.

Charlene coughed in surprise. "Uh . . . no."

"I think you'd be perfect for my brother."

Jim burst out laughing. "Subtle, Syd, subtle."

Sydney joined in his laughter, her cheeks red from embarrassment rather than the cold. "I'm sorry, Charlene. I just want him to be happy, and I can tell that he likes you. We like you too."

Charlene quickly took a drink of her cocoa, burning her tongue in the process. Her eyes welled.

Jim stood and patted Charlene on the shoulder. "Are you okay?"

"Too hot," she said to explain the sudden tears. But it wasn't the cocoa. It was the idea that life had moved on, and her sweet Jared was in the past.

Was Sam her future? In some ways she hoped so, but as Jack reappeared next to the fireplace mantel with a scowl, she realized that idea didn't settle well either.

She changed the subject. "Right now my attention needs to be on my business."

CHAPTER EIGHT

Sam arrived at four to pick up Sydney and Jim and take them to the airport. Charlene opened the door and asked him in. They stood shoulder to shoulder in the foyer, and for some inexplicable reason she felt almost shy. She was attracted to Sam. What woman wouldn't be? He was ruggedly handsome, big and wholesome, and seemed genuinely kind. But as long as she had a charming ghost living under her roof, she couldn't very well explore her feelings for another man.

Charlene faced the enormous staircase that led to the second and third floor and darted a quick peek at Sam's face. He looked distracted, pensive—probably had a million questions of his own clouding his brain. "Sydney's just finishing up her last-minute packing. She'll be down in a minute."

"I know. I got a text from her as I pulled in your driveway." He checked his watch. "Traffic's going to be bad. Grabbing a bite to eat might not happen."

"I gave them a light snack when they returned, so they won't starve if you can't stop," she told him. "I'm going to miss them. Your sister is someone that I'd enjoy as a friend."

"She thinks the same of you." His dark eyes warmed as he looked at her. "We have similar tastes."

Charlene chuckled. "Well, I thank you very much not only for the compliment but for bringing in business." Jim clomped down the stairs with the larger of the bags, and Sydney was right behind him.

Sydney kissed Sam on the cheek. "Okay, I'm ready, and yet I hate to leave. When are you going to visit us, Sam? Thanksgiving?"

"No saying. It's not like I can just take off in the middle of a case. Gathering verifiable information is a slow process."

Jim said, "Captain Moreno called and asked me about ventilation in the room, and something stuffed in the chimney. Is this an official murder investigation?"

Charlene didn't give anything away as she waited at the door. Would Sam tell his brother-in-law not to get involved? Or would they talk in the car, away from her ears? What did it hurt for her to know if it was official or not?

Sam gritted his teeth before he said, "It is." He shrugged his big shoulders. "I'll try to sneak away for a few days at Christmastime, depending on what's on the books." He looked at Charlene as he hefted the larger of the bags. "You might not believe this, but Salem has a relatively low crime rate." He gave her a half smile. "Or had—it's doubled since a Mrs. Morris came to the neighborhood." He dropped a kiss on her forehead. "Catch you later."

"Bye!" She closed the door behind them. Doubled because of her, huh? And what was the kiss? An apology, or pretending they had something going on to get his sister off his back? She hadn't minded the quick kiss, though.

The low crime rate had contributed to her decision to move to Salem and wanting a safe place to live and run a business. She had every confidence that Sam would find the person responsible for Morganna's murder—so long as he didn't waste time trying to pin it on Dylan.

Before long the Jensen family returned, as did Sheila and Sal. They each conversed with her before leaving for their rooms and a chance to clean up before going out to dinner. She'd recommended Turner's Seafood to the Harrises for fine dining, and suggested Bambolina's on Derby Street for wood-fired pizza to the Jensens, who wanted something more casual.

When they were gone, Charlene made herself a grilled ham and cheese and an iced tea. "Jack?"

He didn't answer. She had no idea where he went when he wasn't here, and he had no explanation for it. It was a new dimension, she supposed, and she felt sorry that he was not of the real world, or the one above. She assumed his disappearances had something to do with his output of energy. When he was angry or upset, or around too long, his energy seemed to drain, his image would shimmer and fade, then *poof*, he'd be gone.

After her light meal, she decided to watch a little television in bed. She loved the Hallmark Channel and romantic comedies, as she was a romantic at heart.

Silva's deep purr kept her company as she immersed herself in a sweet Christmas show that made her laugh while she cried. Petting her silver Persian, Charlene sniffed away happy tears at the conclusion, where the couple got their holiday wish of a new home and a baby on the way.

What would her first Christmas in this house be like? She imagined being surrounded by people, families getting together for the holidays, or groups of singles with no family at all. She'd make it special, she thought as she fell asleep.

In the morning during that twilight time of half sleep, she envisioned a humongous tree filled with Victorian Christmas decorations. The image stayed with her when she woke fully, and she decided to check in with Archie Higgins at Vintage Treasures. He'd been so helpful with her furnishings and the telescope on her widow's walk.

It was the second day after Morganna's death, and she hoped today the matter would be resolved. She knew the police were working hard on it, but for her remaining guests she'd like to give them a conclusion to this terrible drama before they left.

After she showered and dressed, she went into the kitchen to make breakfast. She decided to surprise her guests and made a platter of bacon and sausages, scrambled eggs, and toast—and brought out a package of store-bought blueberry muffins.

The scent of freshly brewed coffee and fried bacon must have aroused her guests as she had just finished preparing the morning feast when Peter showed up at her side with a hopeful expression.

"What are you cooking?" he asked in his prep-boy English accent.

"A huge breakfast." She grinned at him, finding his rumpled light brown hair adorable. "Go tell your mom, dad, and sister that I'm cooking this morning. Everything's ready and waiting." She brushed her hands on the apron she'd put on over her jeans and hot-pink Henley.

"I'll tell them—they're already awake," he said flying up the staircase to the second floor. "Mummy, Daddy, breakfast is ready," she heard him shout.

She smiled. That should wake Sal and Sheila up too. Why not? She snagged a bite of crisp bacon and brought all the platters into the dining room, covering them with silver cloches to keep the food warm. She took dishes from the sideboard and quickly set the dining room table. Silverware rolled in cloth napkins, salt and pepper in the center, near the fruit bowl.

She returned to the kitchen for a pitcher of orange juice, and spotted Jack sitting in his customary seat at the kitchen table. He had linen slacks on and a burgundy sweater. His hair was slightly damp as if he'd come from outside, and slicked back off his handsome face.

"Good morning," she whispered. "I've invited everyone down to join me."

"I heard. It smells wonderful. I miss the taste of food—when it smells this enticing." He gazed at her. "You look very pretty today. Cheerful. I don't see you often enough this way."

"Yes, well, since I've been here I've had a lot of things to worry about."

"That's true enough." He glanced around. "Where's Silva?"

"I left her in my rooms. She was sitting on the chair under the window. You could join her if you like."

"You told me your rooms were off-limits, remember?" His tone was half-teasing.

"My bedroom," she corrected quickly, with an eye toward the dining room. Charlene got out the pitcher, grateful to see Jack but sorry that she couldn't include him in the morning breakfast. It had been a lonely three years for her dear ghost before her arrival. "Do you ever wish you'd left when you had the chance?" She set the juice before him, suddenly sad.

"I have no regrets." His cobalt-blue eyes swept over her, heating her insides. "Stay cheerful, Charlene."

She forced a smile. "Okay."

Peter and Hailey started laughing behind her. "Who are you talking to?" Peter asked.

"Just myself," she answered, shaking her head. Jack joined in the teasing laughter—he loved to trick her into giving him away. "That's what happens when you're alone too much."

"Can I pet Silva?" Hailey asked. She dashed into the dining room, checking under the table and behind the curtain. "I can't find her." She pouted.

"Later, hon. She's sleeping right now in my room." Jack disappeared, and Charlene handed the dish of butter to Hailey. "Do you want to bring that to the table?"

Hailey nodded, and Peter offered to take the juice pitcher, walking very carefully as it was heavy. Charlene spooned some strawberry jam into a serving dish and followed the kids.

Katherine and Ted were sitting at the table, and she'd just poured them a cup of coffee when Sheila and Sal came down the stairs.

"Is that bacon?" Sal asked in as hopeful a tone as Peter's had been.

Charlene waved them to two empty chairs. "Come join us! I made enough for everybody."

"This is awfully kind of you," Sheila said. "Your brochure said that you'd only be doing a big breakfast on the weekends, so this is a treat." She sat near Hailey and smiled at the rest of the Jensen family.

"I woke up this morning inspired," Charlene said with a laugh. "I had a light dinner last night, and my stomach demanded something more than toast and coffee. I have to say that you've all been wonderful guests."

"Morning, Ted and Katherine. Hailey—Peter, we appreciated the wake-up call." Sal used his teacher voice, and Peter blushed.

"We were already up," Sheila hastened to say with an elbow to her hubby, who'd taken the chair next to hers.

Charlene poured them coffee.

"I teach crafting with iron as an elective in Oregon," Sal said. "We're going to check out the ironworks in Saugus."

"What's that?" Ted asked.

"A national park with a mill and forges—if you have time, you might want to see it yourselves," Sheila said. "There are interactive things for the children," she told Ted and Katherine. "We have twins in college. Your kids are at such a fun age."

Katherine spread strawberry jam over a slice of toast. "Peter is the reason why we came—he was so interested in Salem after doing a school project."

"Nice to see parents so involved." Sal served himself two bacon strips and two sausage links, then put the same on Sheila's plate.

"Ironworks?" She thought of the small furnace in the back of Morganna's workroom—it had looked like an oil drum. "Do you ever work with glass?"

"God, no," Sal said, lifting his thick fingers. "I prefer a medium I can't break. Plus glass can be dangerous because of the chemicals that arise when the glass is heated." He said in a lower voice, away from the kids, "We think that's what happened to . . . you know. Have you heard anything?"

They'd been gone when Dylan went with Sam for questioning to the station, but she was mindful of upsetting the children. She shook her head, which was more of an evasion than a lie.

Charlene scooped eggs onto her plate and added a dash of pepper. The couples each thanked her for the recommendations, and she ate as they talked about the highlights of their trip so far. Salem had so much to offer year-round, especially with Boston thirty minutes away.

Charlene turned to Katherine. "What are your plans?"

"We are going to High Rock Tower Reservation today," Katherine said. "There is an eighty-five-foot stone tower wall built in 1905, with a telescope at the top. I wonder if it will be like yours, Charlene?"

"Take pictures," she said. "I want to see."

"You are welcome to come with us," Katherine offered.

"Thank you, but I have plans to visit Vintage Treasures today—the owner is always getting in new antiques." And while she was out on legitimate Charlene's Bed and Breakfast business, she would stop to chat with Kevin as he served drinks.

He knew almost everyone in town, and might have some insights that would help her locate Dylan—she wanted to know Dylan's side of the story. Or Kevin might know who didn't like Morganna.

Dylan remained out of touch, and she feared he was avoiding her on purpose. Kids his age tended to be one-track-minded, and she would blame his lack of manners on hormones. She believed in his innocence.

Ted lifted his coffee cup toward Sal. "But the forge sounds interesting. Maybe tomorrow?"

"We'll let you know if it is worth the trip," Sal said.

Once they'd finished a lingering breakfast, the Harrises went to Saugus while the Jensens bundled up for a day outdoors. Charlene had offered to serve dessert around eight before the big fireplace—in lieu of happy hour, so nobody felt rushed to come back early.

Charlene arrived at Brews and Broomsticks at noon and took a seat at the counter. It was an old building, like many others in Salem, with a lot of character in its shadowed nooks and crannies. Dark wood and brick walls, a long wooden counter that served as the bar. Bottles of liquor were perched in the built-in shelving on the far wall, and due to the early hour, Kevin handled the customers himself.

"Hey, Charlene." Kevin dazzled her with a charming smile. His blond hair shone like dark gold in the dim light of the bar. "Good to see you. Have you still got your houseful of guests?"

"No—I've lost half my group. And how silly is it that I miss them? Even Dylan. Which is actually why I stopped by. Dylan mentioned barhopping Halloween night . . . I guess he made friends with the Goth crowd."

"I haven't seen him."

She leaned forward and lowered her voice. "Kevin, his jacket was found near the scene the night we found Morganna . . . He was questioned at the police station." She saw the shock of surprise in his eyes. "They didn't charge him with anything, but he's not cleared either. I'm hoping you might have heard something, anything?" She gave a helpless shrug. "I feel like I'm the only one in his corner."

Kevin dropped the dry towel he'd been using to polish the counter. "Damn. That's not good. So it's a homicide . . . not an accident, then?"

"Sam reluctantly admitted it was, but he won't tell me anything else. I haven't heard from Dylan since Sam questioned him—and I don't blame Sam for wanting an accounting of his actions that night. Dylan didn't come back to the B and B until the next morning. Said he'd stayed with a girl named Tara after partying on the pier at midnight with some Goth kids. I was hoping you might know something?"

"Geez, Charlene, I wish I could help. But that group usually parties downtown by the Peabody. Cool bar, actually, called Ruin. All dark and gloomy." He wiped the counter with a swoosh. "I'd say go check it out, but it can get wild. If you wait until I'm off work, I'll take you."

She removed her coat and set it on the empty stool beside her. "Tonight is busy, but maybe tomorrow." Would the Goth kids even talk to her?

"You want some lunch, or can I pour you an ale?"

"Too early for me—and I just made a feast for breakfast. What tea do you have?"

He handed her a tray of commercial bags but then took it back. "Wait. I have a friend who owns a tea shop. Want to try a hibiscus-rosehip blend? It's got great flavor without the caffeine."

"Yeah!" Charlene was discovering a love of tea that equaled her love of wine, and easily drank two cups a day. He brought back a steaming ceramic pot with a broomstick painted on the side. She breathed in the hibiscus and smelled the rosehip as well. "Thanks, Kev." She glanced around at the near-empty bar and the half-dozen customers seated at tables. "Quiet today. Does that mean you can keep me company?"

"Sure. Let me grab a cup." He ducked into the back and brought back some thin lemon cookies too.

She let the tea simmer for a minute, then took a refreshing sip. It was hot, but the aroma made her mouth water. "This is so good."

"So, other than Dylan, what else is on your mind?" He poured the dark pink tea from the pot into a shallow cup.

"Morganna." She didn't hesitate. "I know it's not my job to solve her murder and the police are doing all they can, but I can't stop myself from thinking about it. This is the second time since I've been here that I've stumbled upon a dead body. Is this my new purpose in life?" Her laugh had a bitter edge as she didn't find the idea funny.

"Bad luck, that's all."

Charlene tucked a loose strand of hair behind her ear. "I really hope so, Kevin." Kevin believed in ghosts, and she wondered if someday she could tell him about Jack. Would he honor her secret or put her on his ghost tour? "Can you tell me anything about Morganna? Who her friends were? Did she have any enemies?"

"I hate digging into the negative, especially since she can't defend herself." Kevin's eyes dulled and he lowered his gaze.

Which meant he'd heard something—she recalled the flirty wave Morganna had given Kevin through her front window. "I'm sorry if my questions make you uncomfortable. Were you special friends?"

"What?" He tilted his head and unwrapped the cellophane around the cookies. "It's not like we'd ever dated, Charlene," he laughed softly. "I just knew her from the tours and being downtown. Mutual friends."

"Did you ever meet her boyfriend, Rich Swane?"

"Nah, I didn't know she had one. Morganna was a big flirt, so that takes me by surprise, actually."

"Brandy told me that Rich wasn't very nice to her."
Kevin offered her a paper-thin cookie that smelled just like
a lemon. She accepted but didn't bite into it. "Maybe he
was the jealous type?"

"No excuse for violence," Kevin said immediately. "Break
up if you can't make it work."

"I agree." She broke a piece off the cookie. "Kevin, I
had a good conversation yesterday with Evelyn Flint,
Brandy's mom."

"I took one of her classes at the college on medieval history. She's amazing," Kevin said right away. "Brilliant.
What did you talk about?"

"Modern witchcraft."

Kevin sat back and exhaled loudly. "Charlene! I know
you want to help Dylan and find answers for yourself, but
getting involved could be dangerous. Evelyn was a leader
in the Wiccan community—I think she still is."

"I'm trying to understand the people Morganna would
have associated with. Wiccans or witches, whatever you
want to call them. Maybe the reason why someone wanted
her dead has to do with their religion."

Kevin scrubbed at a nonexistent spot on the counter
with his bar towel. "Did Evelyn Flint have any clarification
for you?"

"She explained what Wicca is—although I never did
find out if she performed actual spells." Charlene might
have been distracted by the wine. Had the Flint ladies de-
flected her on purpose? Did her questions or curiosity trig-
ger something they wanted to hide?

"Coming from Chicago, our belief in the supernatural
must seem strange to you, but to us locals, it is just a part of
who we are." He finished a cookie in two bites.

"Dylan told me that the Goth kids didn't like Morganna
because she thought she was better than them. Was that
something you'd seen for yourself?"

"I've heard that she was exclusionary too," he admitted. "A friend of mine invited me to Morganna's initiation ceremony, oh, maybe six months ago?" He raised a palm. "I'm not a member, but I was curious. There is an interview process before you can be accepted in the coven."

"But anybody can be a Wiccan, right?"

"Sure, there are some solo practitioners, but there is greater power when a group comes together." Kevin topped off her cup with tea and then refilled his own. "I can ask my friend and see if the elders would let you witness a ceremony, if you are interested—I was made very welcome."

Charlene considered that. "Evelyn told me their names . . . uh, Lucas and Martine?"

"Evergreen, that's right." Kevin confirmed. "Their daughter, Carmen, runs the Clairvoyant store across from Morganna's, and my pal Kass has the tea shop next door. What did Sal and Sheila think of the reading?"

Carmen had told the Harris couple that they would receive extra money this year and be blessed with a grandchild. "Sal said she seemed like a nice girl, but a little strange," Charlene laughed.

Kevin laughed, too, and glanced around the bar to see if he was needed. He sipped from his tea. "Carmen can be . . . intense. But she was an only child."

"Hey! I was an only child." She nibbled on the cookie. "What do her parents do when they aren't leading the coven?"

"Don't laugh," Kevin said, daring her with an arched brow. "Martine works at the local bank and Lucas owns a bookstore. They are very respectable, extremely normal."

"A bank? Well, why not? The bookstore seems like a good fit, though." She added more lemon to her tea and took a sip. "And Evelyn is a college professor." Her mind was expanding—and to think her mother had worried

Salem would be too boring after living in Chicago most of her life. Nothing like a murder or two to keep boredom at bay.

"One elder in the council sells insurance. . . ." Kevin held up his hand. "I'm not kidding. Stephanos Landis, if you need life insurance."

"I'm good, thanks. I wonder if they use their magick, with a 'k,' to help in their jobs?"

"Maybe, but none of them are rich. Well-off, but not driving Lamborghinis." He finished his tea, not concerned that someone might be taking advantage of the system by using witchcraft for nefarious purposes.

"How many witches are there in Salem?"

"Probably a thousand, if you include the solo practitioners."

Charlene almost fell off her stool. "Are you kidding?"

"No, ma'am."

"That is incredible." Bank tellers, soccer moms, teachers. "Who else do you know that might be able to answer my questions?" She put her palms together and leaned forward invitingly.

"Kass Fortune." He smiled at the mention of her name. "With the tea shop? She's a fellow tour guide and fills in when I need someone—she's one of the best in town. Midtwenties, very smart, and a lot of fun. She's a practicing Wiccan who is also a member of the local coven."

"Can I meet her?" Charlene was more than intrigued. Like Alice in Wonderland, she'd really stumbled into a strange new world.

"I'm sure she wouldn't mind, especially when I tell her how much you love her tea. I'll give her a call right now."

He checked on his customers, then made the call, returning with a card and Kass Fortune's number written on it.

"Thanks, Kevin." More customers entered the bar, laughing and already having fun. "I should run—I want to see if Archie has anything new in his antique shop."

"He's a character," Kevin said, chuckling.

Charlene silently agreed. "How much for the tea?"

"Don't be ridiculous. The tea's on me."

"Thank you." She slid off the barstool, grabbed her coat, and waved to him on the way out. Charlene wondered if anything she'd learned would bring her closer to the truth about Morganna's death.

CHAPTER NINE

Charlene drove to Vintage Treasures, and when she arrived, Archie Higgins was assisting a customer. The place smelled dusty and mysterious, filled with old relics in every available space.

Archie lifted his head at her approach and beamed. He was balding, and his belly protruded over his gray slacks, the houndstooth vest left undone. His half-framed glasses slid down his nose.

"Hi, Archie. I'm just browsing today."

"Take your time, Charlene my dear. I have a few special items I can show you later." He turned his attention back to the middle-aged lady he was assisting, and Charlene wandered the vast store filled with other people's junk and a few priceless treasures.

The main area was dim and musty. Rugs hung from the walls, competing for space with ornate pictures and mirrors, while piles of linen were stacked lopsidedly in trunks or baskets. Tea sets, wine sets, china, and jewelry. Being a nautical town, there were ships in glass bottles, rustic brass wheels, and even a rowboat filled with framed maps and charts, compasses, and a telescope or two.

The assortment of "treasures" made her smile with delight. She spotted old Singer sewing machines, tiny RCA black-and-white TVs, bicycles from a bygone era, trunks that appeared so old they could have arrived on the *Mayflower*.

She had bought her beautiful mirror for her mantelpiece here, and a wonderful Old English Rose tea set in perfect condition. She'd also purchased a marvelous new telescope that made for excellent viewing on her widow's walk. The pleasure she and her guests had from watching the full moon over the harbor and being able to spot the Peabody Essex Museum and Hamilton Hall made every cent she'd paid for it a bargain.

Not having any special item in mind made browsing all the more fun. Every room in her bed-and-breakfast had little knickknacks or specialty items like an antique bed or beautifully engraved headboard, side tables, pretty lamps, and such. She intended to put her stamp on each guest room and have them all charming but different.

A red-faced man in his late sixties entered the shop, looking harassed. "Mary, are you done yet? I'm double-parked, and I've been around the block a few times already."

"Just one minute, dear. This nice man is packaging it up for me so we can take it on the airplane." The woman smiled at Archie. "He's not the most patient man in the world," she called over her shoulder, "are you, Tom?"

The man stormed out and slammed the door behind him, and Archie glanced at Charlene with raised eyebrows. He finished wrapping the set of three framed pictures in bubble wrap and brown paper and assisted his customer to the door. "Have a good flight back to Atlanta, and I hope you find the perfect place to hang your pictures."

"Thank you, Archie." Mary tittered, smiling at him as if he were an Adonis. "I'll be sure to send my friends your way when they come to visit, and I might decide to join them. Serve Tom right, the old crank." A car's horn blew, and making an agonized face, she swished out of the shop.

Archie chuckled and joined Charlene. "Lovely to see you." He took her hands. "I swear you get younger every day."

"I bet you say that to all the ladies, and that's why they keep coming back."

"Now, now, you know that's not true. I prefer a woman of distinction, like you." He dropped her hands and gestured to the overflowing shop. Whatever anyone wanted to sell, they brought to him, and his discerning eye decided its worth.

"Have you discovered a treasure or two?" He rubbed his hands together and his bright eyes gleamed.

"Uh, not yet, but you know me—when I see it, I won't be able to resist."

"Over here, next to the antique French needlepoint footstool? Which is also quite a bargain, if you like that piece."

Her gaze followed where he pointed, and from ten feet away she gasped.

"Oh, Archie. The vase?" Her heart beat quickly. "It's gorgeous."

"It's actually a planter, but it would be beautiful anywhere." He took it down from the small shelf and handed it to her. She read the description on the price tag. VINTAGE NAUTILUS SOLID BRASS SHELL. The price was ninety-five dollars, but she'd have paid twice that for it.

"It's amazing," she whispered.

He grinned with satisfaction. "It's midcentury, a planter in the style of Arthur's court. I knew you'd like it. I purchased it for you."

"You know me too well. I adore it." She held it up to her chest. "I know exactly where I want it placed—on the walnut pedestal in the front entrance."

"Excellent idea. Can I wrap them both up for you?"

"Both?"

"Yes, that and the footstool. It will give you hours of pleasure at night when you're reading a book or watching the moon set."

"Oh, you are too good. Yes, fine, I'll take it as well. With a ten percent discount, of course."

"Of course." He carried the footstool while she kept a firm grip on her vintage planter, placing her treasure on the front desk.

With efficient motions he wrapped them, and she reached for her wallet to get her charge card. "I was dreaming of Victorian Christmas ornaments."

"I'll bring those out next weekend," he assured her. "I was going to call you about the vase if you didn't drop by. I didn't want anyone to buy this but you, so I had it on the shelf, as inconspicuous as possible, until you got here."

"You are sweet, Archie. No wonder it's a pleasure doing business with you." And if Sam questioned her outings today, she now had proof that she wasn't just having conversations.

When Charlene returned home, she took off her coat and boots, then unwrapped her new items. She set her gorgeous brass shell on the pretty pedestal she'd found after moving here.

"Charlene's" was developing character day by day, and it would always be a work in progress, but it was a challenge she enjoyed. Feeling pleased with herself, she went into the kitchen and poured herself a glass of the excellent holiday blend Brandy had given her. She put some brie on a plate, with berries and crackers, for a light lunch.

Remembering the phone number Kevin had given her, Charlene reached for her handbag and pulled the card from the side pocket. After taking a sip of wine, she settled into a chair to make the call. She let it ring several times, then left a message. "Hello, Kass, this is Charlene Morris. Kevin Hughes gave me your number. When you have a minute, would you please call me back?" She rattled off her number.

It wasn't until she'd finished and was rinsing her plate that Kass sent her a text—suggesting dinner at five at the Olde Main Street Pub, since they didn't open for lunch during the weekday. Texting a yes back, Charlene scrolled through her phone. Her mother had left her several calls yesterday, and she hadn't replied. She wished that she could get away with texts to her mother rather than painful phone calls. But, being the dutiful daughter and an only child, she knew she had to do the right thing.

Phone in hand, Charlene entered her private sitting room, took a seat in her favorite chair, and put her feet up on her new ottoman, just as comfy as Archie had promised. Then she hit redial, looking out at the oak tree with the swing underneath while she listened to her mom prattle on. And on.

"Mom, if you don't like your bridge group and think they're cheating, why don't you quit?"

"Well, they can't have the group without me. And I need to prove they're cheating."

Charlene stretched her legs from her sitting position. "It would not be a good idea to accuse them without proof, especially when you've known them for so long. Perhaps they are just on a lucky streak."

"Yes, well, we do play for money, you know. We all put a dollar into the pool for every hand. That amounts to five dollars each time."

"Once a week?" Charlene guessed.

"Yes, that's my point. I used to win at least once a month. Now it's been three months since I came home with any money."

"Maybe you should ask them if you all could play for fun, or put two dollars into the pool each week, and winner take all."

"That's a very good idea. Maybe I'll suggest that." Her mom's exaggerated sigh had Charlene rolling her eyes. "Why didn't you call me yesterday?" she asked. "I've been worried sick."

"I have a houseful of guests. It's the week following Halloween and not everyone has left yet." She didn't want to mention the witch's death. Both words would send her mother off the deep end. "It's been great catching up, but I've got some cleaning to do before meeting someone for an early dinner."

"A male friend, I hope?" Her mother's voice dropped conspiratorially. "How is that detective you mentioned? He sounds like a very promising possibility, and at your age, you might want to jump on the bandwagon while you still can."

"I'm not jumping on anything, Mother. I have more than I can handle right now. I'm sure looking forward to your visit in a few weeks' time. Love you, Mom, and give my love to Dad." Before her mother could say another word, she hit the end button and got off her chair. She really did have cleaning to do.

She vacuumed the carpets, mopped the floors, and dusted, then remade the beds with fresh sheets. It was after three when she picked up her laptop to play around with ad copy for her bed-and-breakfast. Knowing her parents would be here for Thanksgiving, she needed a houseful of guests to take the edge off the visit.

And a full bar.

The business phone rang, and she answered, "Charlene's."

"Hi! I was wondering if you had any rooms available for

this weekend? I'm looking on your website now and I want the room with the view of the oak tree. It would be me and my daughter—she's twelve—for Friday and Saturday night."

The Jensens were leaving Friday morning, which was the room with the best view. "Yes, of course. We have a family in there right now, flying home to England that afternoon. I told them they could keep the room until noon, and then it would have to be cleaned. If you don't mind a late check-in, say four o'clock, I can offer you a late checkout on Sunday. Will that work for you?"

"I suppose so, if that's the best you can do." The woman's irritation was palpable. Would this be Charlene's first rotten guest? Well, she'd make the woman and her daughter feel so welcome she'd change that bad attitude. The important thing was to get them in the door, kill them with kindness, and hope for repeat business.

She took down the reservation and credit card information, then ended the call, checking the time. Almost five! Good thing she lived close to town.

It looked like it might rain, so she opted to drive, plugging in the address for Olde Main Street Pub. It was dark already, wintery, but traffic was light, so she made good time and was just parking in the lot across from the Hawthorne Hotel at five.

She entered the pub and searched the dimly lit restaurant and realized that she had no idea what Kass Fortune looked like. Kevin's description as young didn't really help.

A woman with straight, long black hair and a pale face pushed off from the wall by the long mahogany counter. A gaggle of people chatted and ordered beers, still wearing hats and coats as if they'd just arrived.

"Hi! I'm Kass," she said, holding out a slender hand.

Charlene gave it a shake, finding it warm. She'd been

expecting cold for some reason—maybe because of Kass's vampire look? She was curious to know why this woman had opened a tea shop in Salem, instead of Boston, a far more exciting city, but was more curious about how well she knew Morganna, and whether that poor woman had any good friends? Or known enemies.

"I'm Charlene—thank you for agreeing to meet with me. Kevin speaks very highly of you."

"As he does you." Kass guided Charlene toward a quiet, out-of-the-way table in the corner. "I snagged us this one, okay?" She slid into the corner booth. "I live upstairs and know the owners, and the locals that frequent this place."

The young woman's body was long and very thin, her movements graceful, like an actress on the stage with exact movements.

"I'm over six feet," she said, as if used to people wondering. "But a klutz, so no basketball career for me."

Charlene laughed and sat down opposite Kass, charmed already. "How did you come to Salem?"

Seated against the wall, her elbow on her knee, Kass wore black tailored slacks, a white button-up shirt, and a fitted black coat in a man's style from the 1700s. The androgynous look suited Kass Fortune.

"I came here from Barre, Vermont, to study acting in Boston but fell head over heels for Salem. I see you thinking if you know about Barre, and there is a reason you don't. Nothing ever happens there." She straightened and leaned forward. "My creativity was stifled—here, I can flourish."

"Kevin said that you are Wiccan? Were you practicing in Vermont?"

She held up a thin white finger. "That was also part of my problem—I had no kindred spirits, besides family." Kass exhaled and waved to the hostess, who was walking toward them, menus in hand.

The two women conversed while Charlene perused the menu.

"Wow—Gouda fritters? Deep-fried lollipop kale?" She realized her cheese-and-cracker lunch had been burned off by housework, and she wanted to try everything. "What do you recommend?"

The hostess and Kass exchanged a look; then Kass asked Charlene, "Trust me?"

Charlene decided to go for it. "Sure!"

"No allergies?"

"Nope." She welcomed the ability to try something new.

The hostess returned with two amber beers in frosted mugs and a basket of sweet potato shoestring fries with sea salt and an aioli sauce for dipping, and the lollipop kale.

"I love the fish and chips, but I also love the burger—it is phenomenal, especially with the grilled Guinness mushrooms. So I ordered both, and they are splitting it so we can share. Tony is in the kitchen and will take good care of us."

They made small talk about the delicious food throughout the meal, and when it was over, Charlene decided she'd diet for the next week. "Excellent choices—and the beer paired perfectly rather than wine. I think I could eat that kale for breakfast, lunch, and dinner." Parmesan and something in the oil that she couldn't quite put her finger on.

"Don't bother trying to get the recipe from Tony," Kass said, zipping her lips. "He won't share it, no matter how many whiskey shots you buy him. I tried."

"Got it. Is he your boyfriend?"

"Goddess help me," Kass laughed. "We don't suit. The one thing my mother taught me that actually made sense was to never date a chef. They're so dramatic."

"Says the actress," Charlene chuckled.

"Exactly. I get to be the main event in my life—all of my energy goes to my tea shop and doing the occasional haunted ghost tour, if my friends are in a bind. Everyone around here helps one another out, which is completely different than my hometown."

"The Wiccan community?" Her ears pricked up. Now they were getting down to the reason for her visit.

"Not just the witches—everybody in the *tourist* industry. We have to work together in order to keep people coming back and Salem on the map."

Charlene was in support of that idea too.

"I have three helpers working the tea shop. One is a third generation Wiccan from Salem—but he is very devout and doesn't talk about it. Another is a pagan from Detroit. My assistant manager is a Christian—in the sense that she believes in 'doing unto others' kind of thing. One of the coolest *chiquitas* I've ever met." She smoothed a strand of long hair down her collarbone. "My mother styled herself as a kitchen witch and read tarot—she taught me to read the tea leaves when she realized I'd been born with the gift."

"What gift?"

Kass crinkled her nose and assessed Charlene. "You really want to know? You aren't looking to make fun, or mock my beliefs?"

"Of course not!" Charlene laced her fingers around her water glass. "Since moving to Salem from Chicago, where I worked in marketing and advertising, my mind has opened to new possibilities."

"That's a good thing," Kass said. "Why? The history from Salem got to you?"

Jack had gotten to her, but Charlene wasn't going to share that. "It is compelling. So what are your gifts?"

"I know things. Not always, but sometimes, before they happen." Kass patted her chest, and Charlene noticed three silver rings on her pointer finger and a thick band on her thumb. "It's not always easy. Sometimes 'knowing' is very upsetting, both for me and the person I'm speaking with."

"It must be difficult." She looked into Kass's eyes. "Do you believe in ghosts?"

"I *know* they exist," Kass said in a very serious tone. She glanced out the window at the mansions on the corner across from the pub. "I've seen the one called the captain from my room at night. Supposedly he was a very bad dude, and someone murdered him in his sleep. I catch his energy sometimes, but he can't hurt me. He's stuck behind the veil. Sometimes I see a woman, as well, but I haven't been able to find any history on who she might be. My room is just above here." Kass looked toward the ceiling and then met Charlene's gaze. "What about you?"

Charlene gave a careful shrug. "I don't not believe," she said, hedging. "How do you know that ghosts can't leave?"

"I've always been able to see forms or orbs, sometimes light, but being in Salem with other witches and psychic people strengthens my own abilities. That said, I don't know all of the rules as to why some entities seem to roam while others can't." She tossed her long hair over her shoulder, her dark brown eyes soulful. "Is it anger that keeps a spirit trapped, or love?"

"You think strong emotion?" Charlene and Jack had discussed the trauma that had kept him from passing to the light—discovering who had murdered him was pretty strong emotion, all right. She also didn't know why she was able to see Jack—unlike Kass, who had always seen ghosts, Jack was her one and only spectral experience.

"Maybe." Kass took a drink of water—the ice had melted and the glass sat in a pool of condensation. "The Hawthorne Hotel is haunted—supposedly by Bridget Bishop, who was hanged around here. She was the first purported witch—and being as she wasn't a witch at all, she has a reason to be mad."

Charlene agreed. "I'd say. Nasty people back in those days. Has anybody ever tried to bring the ghosts peace?"

Kass looked at Charlene with approval. "You are a kind soul. Let's go back to my tea shop. I would love to read your tea leaves."

"Oh, I don't know," Charlene said, shaking her head. "Not sure if I'd like that."

"Why not?"

"I just . . ." Well—why not? Trying new things wasn't awful—she'd just discovered deep-fried kale.

Kass rose from her seat. "I can tell you ghost stories for just about every building that we pass."

"Seriously? You see ghosts in every building?"

"Not really." Kass laughed. "But Salem's history is blood-soaked and loaded with religious guilt, which means that there are all kinds of spirits hanging around."

Charlene snagged the check and added a big tip, including a round of whiskey for Tony and the cooks in the back.

Kass put her hand on Charlene's back. "That was very cool! Thank you for dinner. Well, lunch for me. I'm a night owl. Hiring good people allows me to work the midday shift and close up."

"Your place is next to Morganna's?" Charlene wasn't sure how to ask politely and decided to just go for it. "Is her ghost haunting her shop?"

"Not that I've felt or witnessed." Kass's shoulders slumped as they left the pub and headed down the sidewalk toward the pedestrian mall.

"Have you heard anything about her death?"

Kass's head shot up. "Like what? That she was killed? I certainly don't know anyone who'd want to harm her."

Charlene wondered if Kass was speaking the truth—but the woman was an actress, so how could she be sure?

"Our businesses shared a wall," Kass said, stepping over a crack in the sidewalk. "I did a prayer for her passing that I hope eased her toward the light. She died when the veil between the worlds was at its thinnest."

"What does that mean?"

"All Hallows' Eve—when the dead can walk the earth. It is a potent time for spells because magick is more tangible than any other time of the year."

"Seriously? Like zombies?"

"Not that scary, I hope," Kass teased. "We're not talking *The Walking Dead*, but it is a powerful time for magick."

Charlene had a thought. "Are witches able to read their own fortunes? Would Morganna have known what was going to happen to her?"

"Not sure about Morganna, but in general I'd say . . . not always. There are times when the future is clouded to us on purpose because we are too close to a situation. For example, I can ask for the name of my soulmate and not get an answer—doesn't mean my true love isn't out there, but that I need to live my life without searching for a certain person."

Interesting. A brisk wind had Charlene hunching her shoulders as if that would help her get warm. Tea sounded terrific. "Could you go to a different witch and ask?"

"Of course!" Kass shortened her long strides so she didn't get too far ahead. Tourists bundled for the colder weather strolled the shops. "I do readings for my friend Carmen all the time. And I did one for Morganna." Her expression darkened, but she hurried on. "Carmen thinks my angel guide, Raphael, is in love with me and that's why I'm single. He chases the good guys away."

Charlene started to laugh but then realized that for all she knew, it could be true. She would enter the tea shop with an open mind. "So you don't know who your true love will be?"

"Nope, and I'm okay with that. This way I can experience whatever comes my way in the moment, right?"

They slowed as they crossed Charter Street. "Hey—

isn't that the parking lot Kevin used?" Charlene turned to get her bearings. "Yes—there is Morganna's Witch House. It's so dark and sad looking." Like an empty shell.

Kass nudged Charlene with her elbow. "You are very empathic."

"Why do you say that?"

"I just know. You feel what others feel."

"Doesn't everybody?"

"No—in fact, you would be surprised by how many people put up blocks against their own emotions as well as others'." Kass's long strides had her at Fortune's Tea Shoppe before Charlene. "Do you like tea? I dry herbs and create my own blends." She opened the door wide, and Charlene stepped into another world.

Lavender, sage, rose, and vanilla bean collided with the scent of candles. Soft harp sounds melodically led her farther inside toward a gurgling fountain—a ceramic goddess with a teapot continuously poured water into a waiting cup. "Do you have a favorite kind of tea?"

"Orange spice. From Pike Place Market in Seattle."

"I've had that," she said with a nod. "A hint of sweet behind the cinnamon." Kass rubbed her hands together as if excited to get started. "Why don't you peruse the bins of herbs and spices while I get the water boiling. Are you a lemon person?"

"Yes." She could imagine spending days here and still not seeing everything.

"I'll slice some." Kass swiveled on a black bootheel to the lanky man with an orange Mohawk, who looked maybe twenty. "Darren! How was it?"

"Steady business, Boss. We sold out of the lemongrass and chai cookies."

"Good to know. I'll get baking later on."

Kass disappeared into a back room and shut the door behind her. Was that a kitchen, or an office?

Did all the buildings come equipped with workshops?

Charlene turned away from the bins of aromatic spices and crossed to the wall that Kass had shared with Morganna.

Thinking back over their conversation, she realized that Kass hadn't been very forthcoming about the dead witch next door and had in fact steered Charlene away from the subject of Morganna.

What had Kass discovered when she'd done the reading for her friend? Had she seen her imminent death?

CHAPTER TEN

Charlene sat at a small table for two at Kass's tea house, listening to the peaceful gurgle of the indoor goddess fountain. Darren's orange Mohawk bobbed like a rooster as he offered suggestions, giving her a rundown on the health benefits of each. She chose an orange peel, cinnamon, and turmeric blend that smelled as good as what she'd had in Seattle, but with a kick of heat from the turmeric.

He was so good at his job that she had no chance to ask about Dylan.

Kass returned from the back room with a heavy tray of sliced lemon and orange, as well as rock sugar crystals, and set up their pots of water and their steeping cups.

"Thanks, Darren," Kass said. "You want a cup?"

"Nah, if you are here by the counter, then I can finish stocking the bins up front. The new muslin sachets came in." He gestured to the cardboard boxes and a pair of scissors.

"Cool." Kass rubbed her hands together as Darren dragged the box of supplies toward the front of the shop, making his job to restock easier. "Folks are going to love the option of filling their own reusable tea bags." Kass tapped the tea tray between them. "I will get you some of the sachets to try. Do you use a tea strainer when you brew?"

"Oh, I don't brew," Charlene said, breathing in the cinnamon. "I buy tea by the box, prebagged. You know, Lipton."

Kass brought her hand to her head in a dramatic pose. "Charlene! Don't worry—I will fix you up properly."

The door opened, and a striking young woman entered the shop. Charlene recognized the diamond twinkling from the side of her nose, and the blond-and-purple hair over the black leather coat. Carmen, from the Witch Festival, Halloween night. Kass waved. "Hey, Carmen, this is Charlene. She's new in town and just opened a bed-and-breakfast on Crown Point."

Up close, Carmen retained a fragile appearance, as if a hard wind from Pickering Wharf might blow her over. "Used to be the Strathmore place," Carmen said. "My mom thought the doctor was cute." She stepped over to Charlene, her gaze sizing her up.

Charlene offered her hand and got more of a glide-by with Carmen's fingers than a proper shake. "Nice to meet you."

"You too." Carmen shook her purple hair over her shoulder. "Where did you move from?" She circled her palm before Charlene. "I see a strong aura about you."

"Not sure if my aura is strong," she said with a self-conscious laugh, "but I'm from Chicago." What did an aura look like? She imagined a body halo.

Carmen shared a smile with Kass. "Some people can see auras, which is something I turn on when I meet someone for the first time, and shield when I'm in a room of strangers. You are in good health but recovering from something?" She squinted, and Charlene braced herself. "Grief. I'm sorry for your loss."

"Oh!" How could she know that? "My husband died in a car accident."

"Why did you come to Salem?" Carmen raised a pointy black brow.

"Jared and I visited here once for a friend's wedding and loved it. We intended to come back—unfortunately *we* didn't make it."

Kass put her hand on Charlene's forearm. "Carmen has great insight. She's genuine, unlike the fakers in town." She turned to Carmen. "Want some tea?"

"Yes, please." Carmen waggled her fingers at Darren, who grinned and blushed. "The ginger-and-white blend?"

Rain pattered against the window, and Charlene lifted her thin cup. Kass had made this a comforting sanctuary from the weather, but neither the tea nor the ambience soothed her mind. The two women were obviously close friends, and in the same line of work. What secrets did these young witches share?

Kass got up to get tea, and Carmen stole Kass's chair. She leaned forward. "I've got a hunch that you have an interesting story to tell. I read tarot as well as auras."

"I know—I saw you at the Psychic Fair. You did a reading for my guests." And then there was Morganna's death.

Carmen winced as if she'd picked up Charlene's thought.

Kass carried a pot of steeping tea on a trivet. "Oh, here we go. Carmen met you five minutes ago, and now she wants to tell your fortune."

Charlene shrugged. "I'm not sure I want to know. I'd like to think I have many surprises in store."

"And you don't want them ruined by this know-it-all?" Kass eyed her friend affectionately.

"Why not?" Carmen said. "If it's bad, at least you can prepare for the worst."

A shadow passed over Kass's face, and the teasing atmosphere faded. "That's not how it works, and you know it."

Carmen reached into her tasseled hobo bag and handed her a few cards. "Send your guests to me, and I'll give them a discount on a reading. I'm not a quack like some people around here."

Charlene seized the opening. "Like who? Morganna?"

All three pairs of eyes shifted to her as even Darren turned her way. She squirmed in her chair. "What?"

"Morganna was a gifted glassblower," Carmen said softly. "She should have kept to what she did best. Kass is excellent. And Julia Raven is good—she's got a place by the pier."

Kass spoke in a harsh, low tone. "Morganna was not the real deal."

Darren returned to pricing the sachet bags.

"Did that make people mad? Was Morganna pretending to be gifted, when she was actually a fake?" The girls stayed quiet. "Kass, your shop is next to hers. You must have known her well?" Charlene knew she was pushing, but what if she never had another opportunity like this?

Carmen and Kass exchanged glances, and Charlene noticed the warning shake Kass gave Carmen. She wondered what they were hiding. Were they protecting Morganna's reputation or each other's?

"We were more business acquaintances," Kass said in an even tone. "Wouldn't call us friends."

"My mother is a gifted aura reader, too, but she won't do it for money," Carmen said, turning the conversation around. She squeezed lemon in her tea and licked her fingers, then took a sip. "My parents are both leaders of the Wiccan community, and they took over from Evelyn Flint. She is very well known around here."

Again, a look passed between Kass and Carmen, and Charlene wished that the other girl wouldn't have joined them so quickly. Maybe Kass would have been more forthcoming. Or perhaps it was the other way around, and Carmen would be the one to talk?

"I've met Evelyn." At their surprise she explained, "I buy wine for my B and B from Flint Wineries. She's a charming woman, but a force of nature, I imagine."

"That's very true," Kass agreed, twirling a lock of long black hair around her finger. "You pretty much nailed it. She's well respected in the community—disliked by only a few."

"Like Morganna?" she asked. Evelyn and Brandy had shied away from her questions about the younger witch. Kass and Carmen were being closemouthed too. "Nobody seems to want to talk about her," she said, looking from face to face. "I find that strange considering how she died. Usually that would make her the talk of the town." Okay, she'd said it. What were they going to do—put a spell on her? Turn her into a toad?

The door opened, but Darren took care of the customers. Kass frowned and Carmen looked surprised at Charlene's persistence. "Why the interest?"

"I can't believe there is no speculation on how or why she died." Would that rattle the cage?

Carmen stood up, her teacup in hand. "Why are you so curious about Morganna's death? What is she to you?"

Charlene felt guilty at the speculative gleam in Carmen's eye. She swallowed hard. "I found her that night—dead." Charlene looked from Kass to Carmen. "Kevin and I had a tour for my guests. We were to meet up at Morganna's, in front of her shop after the Psychic Fair. At ten," she added. She wiped her damp palms on a paper napkin next to her tea.

"You found her?" Carmen asked, her pointed brow hiking. "How awful!"

"It was." Charlene eyed the wall that the tea shop shared with Morganna's. "Did you hear anything?"

Kass opened a drawer and pulled out a bottle of brandy, adding a healthy slug to Charlene's cup—Carmen held hers out too. "I didn't realize that you had found her," Kass said.

"Darren closed that night. I was helping with a tour, and afterward had drinks with Tony and the guys. Darren told me later that the cops had come but he didn't know why."

Charlene remembered seeing the shadow of a Mohawk as the lights had turned off. "We were surprised that her shop was dark already when she'd made a point of saying she'd be open until ten. Kevin peered through the window and saw her legs sprawled out on the floor—one of my guests is a firefighter. We broke in and . . ." Charlene stopped herself from saying more.

"Well," Carmen said, draining her brandy, "Morganna wasn't a nice person, so if you feel like you need to mourn her, you don't."

"Carmen," Kass warned. "Don't speak ill of the dead."

Carmen sighed and set her cup down on the counter. "It's the truth. At first, our community embraced Morganna . . . until *Evelyn* accused Morganna of stealing her book of shadows."

What was that? Why hadn't Evelyn mentioned it? "But Morganna was in the coven?" Charlene asked. "She was one of you."

"Yes." Carmen gave her an appraising look.

"Kevin told me a little," Charlene said, hoping that the bartender's name would loosen the girls up.

"I liked her at first. It was nice to have another young witch around. But after Evelyn accused Morganna of theft? Uh-uh—she lost favor with me."

"Our community turned against her," Kass admitted in a soft voice, careful of the others around. "There is a rumor that she was going to be excommunicated from the coven at the next ceremony."

Charlene took a drink of her brandied tea. That sounded serious. "What's a book of shadows?"

"It's kind of like a diary," Kass explained. "But you don't write about crushes. It's a journal of your life that is very personal. You might leave it to your kin, or, depending on the witch, burn it at your death."

"So what makes it valuable enough for someone to steal it?" Charlene hadn't had a diary since she was a teenager—once she found her mother snooping, that was the end of that.

"For the spells within, of course. Morganna had no power of her own, and Evelyn Flint is extremely powerful. By stealing the book, Morganna hoped to capture her skills and strengths." Carmen studied Charlene over the rim of her cup. "It's the only reason that makes sense. Has it been found?"

"I don't know," Charlene answered truthfully.

Kass said, "A witch's book of shadows is their personal path as they study the craft. Because of Evelyn's history in Salem—well, you can see why a newcomer like Morganna would want to get her hands on it."

Charlene briefly closed her eyes. The stolen book widened her net far beyond Dylan . . . unfortunately to include Evelyn.

"The Flints are gifted true believers and have been using magick on their grapevines for hundreds of years—and to great success," Carmen told her, then rolled her eyes. "I am the product of a fertility spell. Kass here used magick to find this location for her tea shop. Magick is all around." She paced as if the brandy and tea had given her a burst of energy—it had certainly added color to her pale cheeks.

A customer entered and Darren took care of him, but the moment of sharing was gone, and Charlene could see she wouldn't get anything more out of them tonight.

Carmen teased Kass about a date she'd gone on last week.

"It won't go anywhere," Kass said. "You can't date a tourist."

Which reminded her of her AWOL guest. "Hey, do either of you know a guy named Dylan? Or Tara?"

"Nope," Kass said.

"Thanks for the tea," Carmen said to Kass, "and it was a pleasure meeting you, Charlene. My shop is just across the street from here. I'm heading there now to prep for a guided séance tonight. I'd love to give you a reading, and I'd even do the first one for free. Bye!"

Carmen left. Outside the window, tourists headed to dinner or shops in a parade of umbrellas on the busy sidewalks.

"Thanks for talking to me about Morganna. Do you mind if I ask Darren about Dylan? He was my guest, and now he's missing."

Kass's dark eyes clouded. "Sure, by all means." She stepped closer. "Listen, Carmen is a good friend, but she might be biased when it comes to that stolen book. Her parents took over for Evelyn as leaders in the Wiccan community, and Carmen thinks that Evelyn made it up, perhaps as a cry for attention. She didn't believe Morganna stole it."

"That's odd." Evelyn hadn't mentioned that either. Was there a divide between the generations? "And now?"

"Carmen doesn't talk about it. I was surprised that she opened up to you. But with Morganna dead, why not?"

"Kass, did you know that Morganna had a boyfriend? Rich Swane?" Was it possible he had the book of shadows? He might not even know the significance of it.

Kass's nose wrinkled. "Our landlord? He owns this building. I didn't realize they'd been seeing each other. Honestly, she was such a flirt that I thought she was single."

"I guess she lived in one of the apartments above these shops with him." Charlene shrugged into her jacket. "Do you think he'd answer my questions?"

"He's a jerk, straight up." Kass stacked their empty cups carefully on the tray. "The only time I see him is if I'm late for the rent."

Charlene pulled out her wallet to pay for the tea. "Do you mind giving me his number?"

Kass's nose scrunched, but she went to the directory beneath her counter and copied the phone number down, then handed it to Charlene. Charlene wondered if she had time to catch Rich before stopping at the grocery store. "Don't forget that I warned you. He's a slimeball."

"Noted," Charlene said. Her phone rang, but she didn't recognize the number so she let it go to voice mail.

Charlene picked up her handbag and joined Darren stocking shelves near the entrance. "Hey, Darren. I wondered if you'd met a guy named Dylan?" Salem wasn't that big, and if her missing guest was partying with the Goth kids, it wasn't out of the question they'd know him.

"Nope. Never met him."

Darn it. "Thanks!" She passed Kass and touched her arm. "I'll be sending my guests your way." She waved as she headed out the door.

The rain had slowed to a drizzle and there was a chilly wind. She wrapped a scarf around her neck and hunkered down as she eyed the street. Her car was only a few blocks away. She crossed the road near Carmen's store, anxious to get in the warmth of her Pilot, where she would call Rich.

Carmen's shop door opened, and a pale hand snagged Charlene's arm. She squeaked as she was brought inside. "Carmen! You scared me."

"Sorry! I just wanted to show you my place, so you could recommend it, you know?" Carmen grinned. "Always competing for new business around here, right, Travis?"

"That's the truth," a tall young man said. Charlene recognized him by the multitude of pentagram necklaces around his neck. She'd seen him with Carmen at the festival. He stacked blue-and-white tarot cards along the back wall, next to boxes of wands, à la Harry Potter—and glass bottles labeled with a skull and crossbones. He lifted a heavily ringed hand in welcome.

"Hi." Charlene relaxed and scanned the warm room decorated in blacks, blues, and purples. A round table with a crystal ball in the center surrounded by fairy lights—hers were purple. "That looks like one of Morganna's witch balls," Charlene said, wanting to be on her way before it started pouring again.

"You have a good eye. I asked her to make one for me." Carmen put a hand on her forearm. "Would you like to borrow my umbrella?"

"That's sweet of you, but it's too late. I'm already wet," she chuckled ruefully. At Carmen's studying expression, she asked, "Was there something else?"

Charlene knew she wouldn't be back despite the coziness of the store. If Carmen had been able to see her grief in her aura, who knew what she'd see in her palm, or her tarot cards? Charlene wanted to keep that pain private.

Carmen looked into Charlene's eyes. "There is something I need to tell you about Morganna, and Kass." She looked down and fidgeted before lifting her head, her green eyes bright. "She's my friend, and I feel uncomfortable sharing this, but you were there when Morganna died, and so I feel that you have a right to know."

"Know what?" Things were curiouser and curiouser. Charlene waited next to the door, ready to leave as soon as Carmen finished.

"Kass gave Morganna a dark reading. She used to pop in for tea several times a day. I think she hoped Kass would befriend her and help her regain her favorable position in the Wiccan community. She didn't."

If that was so, why hadn't Kass told her? For the same reason Evelyn hadn't mentioned the stolen book of shadows?

Carmen leaned close. "People aren't always what they seem."

Wasn't that the truth? Charlene said her goodbyes and left—the rain had stopped. When she reached the car, she climbed in and called Rich, but it went to voice mail. She didn't leave her number.

If Kass had given Morganna a dark reading, Kass might have seen her imminent death in her tea leaves. Would she have informed Morganna or kept that a secret? Was it possible Morganna knew her own fate before that night?

Charlene shivered despite the warmth from the car's heater. She was glad she hadn't stayed and had her leaves read. She was determined to embrace life and find happiness again. She certainly didn't want to know what her future might bring.

CHAPTER ELEVEN

Charlene walked into the welcoming warmth of her home. It was half past seven, and she had all the makings for dessert to share with her guests before the fire. She could hear their voices as she entered and was thankful that she'd had timers installed on the kitchen and living room lights in case she wasn't home when they returned.

She peeked into the living room and tugged off her parka. Ted and Katherine Jensen played chess while their son, Peter, read a book on dragons, and Hailey practiced her flute. "Hi there. Sorry, I ran a bit late." She gazed at them fondly. The family she never had, but one of many that her future might bring. "You are very good, Hailey. Have you been taking lessons long?"

"One year. My teacher wants me to play at the school's concert. A solo! Says I'm talented, but Peter says she's just being nice." Hailey grinned and pointed to a gap where a front tooth was missing. "Look! Fell out at dinner." She made a face. "Lots of *blood*."

Charlene shot a look at the unconcerned parents. "That sounds traumatic!"

"We'd already finished eating," Katherine said with a wave of the pawn in her hand. "So we came home straightaway to take care of the tooth. Peter wrapped it in a tissue and put it under Hailey's pillow for the tooth fairy." Katherine made her move on the chessboard. "Hope you don't mind, but we washed her clothes before the stain set in."

"Not at all. Sorry I wasn't here to help." Charlene lifted the cloth grocery bag. "But I brought dessert."

"We've been stuffing our faces since we got here." Ted pushed away from the small table where the chessboard was laid out and rubbed his still-flat tummy. "I'm going to hate going home after this."

"Are you complaining about my cooking?" Katherine asked in a warning tone.

"I know better than that." Ted rose and dropped a kiss to her cheek. "When we get home, I'll be begging for your steak and kidney pie, and delicious mince tarts."

"You smooth talker." Katherine gave him a loving smile. "You just don't want to do the cooking."

"I'm a smart man." Ted winked at Charlene. "Even let my wife beat me at chess. Looks like she's on her way to doing it again."

"Let me beat you? I don't think so. My gramps taught me how to play when I was about Hailey's age," Katherine told Charlene, "and I won the chess championship at our school when I was thirteen."

"That's pretty impressive." Charlene remembered playing with her dad many years back, and he'd made sure she won as often as she lost too. He was also a smart man. "It's a challenging game. I was better at backgammon, or gin rummy."

Peter stretched and put the book in his lap. "I'm bored. Can we all do something? A game of cards? Watch a scary movie?"

"We have board games on the bottom bookshelves. There's

Monopoly, Charades, Scrabble, Connect Four. There's a col-
lection of Wii games down there as well, if you want to do
something more active."

"Go have a look, Peter," Katherine encouraged, with a
grateful nod at Charlene that meant the world.

"If you don't mind, I'll leave you to it—I have some
prep to do with the dessert. Hope you all left room for
that."

"Dessert? What is it?" Hailey asked. "Is it soft?"

"It is," Charlene answered.

"Is it ice cream?" Hailey asked, balancing on one foot,
flute in her hand.

"No," Charlene said. "But one part of the dessert is white
and fluffy."

"Whipped cream?" Peter guessed, rubbing his tummy.
"Over pumpkin pie."

"Close. One more guess . . ."

"Over warm apple pie," Ted said.

"Pecan!" Katherine shouted.

"Bingo!" Charlene laughed. "I'll get the dessert going,
while you all decide on your entertainment for the night."

She dropped her coat and removed her boots in her
room, then headed toward the kitchen just as Sal and Sheila
entered. "You're just in time for pecan pie," she said in way
of greeting. "Did you enjoy the restaurant tonight?"

"It was wonderful. A great suggestion." Sheila waved at
Ted and Katherine as Sal hung up their coats.

"I'll give you guys a few minutes to get comfy, then I'll
serve it at the dining table." She heard the Jensens conversing happily as they switched to a game of blackjack.

Charlene made a pot of coffee, and set the table with
dessert plates, forks, napkins, two cans of whipped cream,
coffee cups for the adults, and iced water for the kids.

Sheila and Sal came downstairs in matching Oregon
State University sweat pants and T-shirts before joining the

others. Charlene poked her head into the living room and invited them to the dining table.

The kids put their games down and raced into the hallway. "I'm getting the biggest piece," Peter said, grabbing a seat at the table next to the large pecan pie.

"No, you're not—is he, Daddy?" Hailey asked. "They should all be the same size." She crossed her arms over her tiny chest and pouted.

Ted took the cutting knife off the platter and waved it in the air. "I'll cut them in equal size," he said with a wicked grin, "except an extra-large one for me."

Katherine shook her head. "After all you ate tonight? I don't think so."

While Ted sliced the pieces and slid them on plates, Sal helped by passing them around. The two women poured the coffee, and Charlene stood back and watched. It was like having one big, happy family, everyone comfortable with each other, sharing the duties. She acknowledged the fact that she was getting well paid to entertain her new "friends."

Charlene made her excuses and left to change into more comfortable clothes. Afterward, rather than rejoining them, she went down to the cellar and was thrilled to see Jack waiting.

"Jack! I'm so glad you're here."

He smiled softly. "I don't have many places to go."

She stepped closer. "I wanted to talk to you about Morganna—but I've *missed* you today."

They exchanged a comforting look. Kindred spirits, but with an intangible wall between them, living together yet separated by a veil linking heaven and earth.

He moved toward the long, rectangular table, breaking the emotional connection. Sometimes he had more sense than her. There could be no romance between them, no true companionship, no mend for her broken heart. A niggle of guilt tickled her conscience—she *was* healing, at last.

"Tell me about your day." Jack watched as she poured a glass of red wine.

She felt his eyes on her. It warmed her inside, knowing that he found her attractive. A woman that he'd desire if he were still alive.

"Well, my day was busy, that's for sure." She took a long sip from her wineglass and sighed with pleasure at the tart berry flavor. "This is good, especially after drinking herbal tea with witches for the past few hours."

"Witches?" Jack's dark hair framed his face as his brow lifted. "Now this sounds interesting." He folded his arms. "How did you meet up with them, and who are they? Anyone I might know?"

"You might. Kevin gave me Kass's name—she's a part-time tour guide, like him, and reads tea leaves at her shop in town. She's Wiccan, and I wanted to ask her about Morganna."

"Did she have any useful information?" He ran a slender finger along the smooth wooden table, and she wondered if he could feel the texture of the wood. No, of course he couldn't. He had lost his ability to touch, to taste, but not to feel.

"I had an early dinner with Kass. I hoped we might become friends, but now I'm not so sure." Charlene shrugged and leaned forward on the high-top table.

"Why is that?" Jack asked, his elbow crooked and hovering over the table as if to rest his arm.

"After dinner we went to her tea shop—it connects with Morganna's." She shot him a look. "Another young woman came in, Carmen. I saw her at the Psychic Fair the night Morganna was killed."

"Go on." He wore a scowl on his face.

What was he thinking? Like Sam, that she should stay at home and mind her own business? For Dylan's sake and to satisfy her own curiosity, she needed to find out who had taken this young woman's life. If Sam would just tell her, she wouldn't have to go running all over town asking questions. How could she help him if he didn't share information?

She took a deep breath. "Carmen is a clairvoyant, Jack, and she read Sheila and Sal's tarot cards at the Witch Festival Halloween night. She claimed to see my aura." Charlene shivered. "Can you see it, Jack?"

"You are getting off track, Charlene." Jack chuckled. "Morganna. Carmen. Kass. What did you learn?"

Charlene sipped her wine. Talking with Jack allowed her to formulate her thoughts like a mental list. "I learned that Carmen's mom thought you were awfully cute." She laughed at the shocked look on his face. "And that Evelyn accused Morganna of stealing her book of shadows, which has all her secrets and spells. The girls said that Morganna didn't have magical powers of her own. She thought if she could use the spells, she'd gain respect in the community, but nobody liked her."

"Did both women admit to not liking her?" He stared directly into her eyes. "Charlene, this is serious. Do you think either one of them wanted her dead?"

"I don't know." She bit her bottom lip. "Not liking someone doesn't mean you'd go out and kill them. I don't see either one of them being a killer."

"You need to be careful, Charlene. I agree with the detective in that. Asking questions from the wrong people could put you in danger. Perhaps they might be innocent, but in their wider circle of friends someone might hear that you're asking questions and decide to silence you."

"Don't say that." She could feel the color leave her cheeks in a rush.

"What else was said? What made you rethink your decision about being friends with Kass?"

Charlene cupped her wineglass tightly between her fingers. "After Carmen left, Kass said that Carmen thought Evelyn was setting Morganna up—lying about the stolen book."

Jack's brow furrowed. "Evelyn lying? No way. I don't believe that."

She sighed. "The Wiccan council was going to have Morganna excommunicated."

"Evelyn certainly could do that if she had a solid reason for not liking a person. She's a respected elder."

"They all knew Morganna was a fraud, but tonight was the first I'd heard of it, and I had to push to get answers."

"I am sure that you handled yourself with decorum," Jack said. "Though does that matter when trying to find a murderer?"

"Jack, things got weirder as I was leaving. I'd just crossed the street when Carmen literally pulled me into her shop. She told me Kass had never liked Morganna, which Kass hadn't said outright—she'd alluded to being acquaintances, friendly but not friends. The whole thing with them both throwing each other under the bus left me with a bad taste in my mouth."

"Witches and bitches—"

"I know, I know, and yet they seemed likeable at the start of the evening." She tilted her head.

His deep blue eyes held concern. "Promise me you'll be careful. Witches are not to be trifled with."

"I never thought witches were real . . . here I am, talking to a ghost." She put a hand to her mouth. "They claim to have real psychic 'gifts'—do you think they could turn me into a toad?"

Jack shimmered as he laughed. "I hope not. Having these conversations with a toad would not nearly be as pleasant."

She laughed, and he teased her some more. "What about Silva? She might decide to have you for breakfast."

"Stop. Enough!" Charlene raised her hands in surrender.

But the laughter had done her some good. "They won't make a toad of me, I promise."

"I love your laughter, Charlene." Jack put his forearms on the table, leaning in her direction. "I'm happier now than I've been, well, since my death."

"I'm so glad for that." She eyed him over the crystal rim. "I don't want you lonely and miserable. Silva must be good company for you."

"The cat is a nuisance. I'd rather have you."

"Jack . . ." Charlene warned.

"I know, you need a real man, not merely a ghost."

"I don't need anything except a good night's sleep, and to find out who disliked Morganna enough to cause her death."

"Here we go." Jack soundlessly rubbed his hands together. "We get to solve another murder."

"I promised Sam I'd stay out of trouble," she said, alarmed at the doubtful tone in her voice. "But I can't, can I?"

Jack scoffed. "Sam doesn't know you as well as I do, if he believes that you will do nothing. Especially if he suspects Dylan."

Charlene had yet to talk to the young man, and her concern grew by the hour. "The stolen book of shadows could be motive."

"Yes." Jack shifted on the barstool. "But not Evelyn. Not her style."

"I told Sam about Rich Swane, who was her landlord. He already knew about him, but not that they were still living together."

He put his fingers to his chin and looked thoughtful. "Not sure about Sam. He isn't a very good detective, if you ask me."

"Hey! I didn't." Charlene peered into the last swallow of red wine at the bottom of her glass. "He's probably ready to make an arrest any day now. Can't arrest someone on circumstantial evidence, so he's making sure he has sufficient proof."

"That's what a good detective would do. But Inspector Clouseau"—Jack lifted a shoulder—"probably not."

She laughed. "Don't you dare compare Sam to that idiot in the Pink Panther movies."

"So you know it? Thought you might be too young."

"No. Jared and I used to laugh ourselves silly over those old movies."

"Well, I meant no offense to your good friend Sam. But, if the shoe fits . . ."

Before he could complete the sentence, his form began to fade.

"Jack. One more word, and I'm out of here."

But Jack beat her to it.

"Sam's here," he said—in voice only, before that too was gone.

Sam? Charlene went upstairs just in time to hear the knock at her front door. The clock on the kitchen stove read nine. That was kind of late, but she heard the Jensens and the Harrises laughing as they played games in the living room.

She opened the front door. "Sam!"

"Sorry about the time," he said, shoulder slouched against the frame. "Can I come in?"

"Of course!" Charlene looked into the living room, and her guests all waved to Sam. He wore an open dark blue wool coat but no hat—as if he were on his way home from the station and decided to stop in.

"Hi, everyone." He lifted his hand but didn't make a move to join them. "Can we talk in private?"

"Sure—my sitting room?"

"Fine."

She led the way from the foyer through her narrow kitchen. "Can I get you anything to drink? Or a slice of pecan pie?"

"No. This is an official visit, sort of—you have a way of blurring the lines, Charlene."

"I don't know what that means." She gestured to her yellow love seat and the armchair beneath the window. Sam shrugged off his jacket and took the armchair. She recognized the Ralph Lauren plaid shirt from one similar to Jared's, and he wore dark blue jeans and boots. His thick hair curled enticingly around his ears. "What is it?" she asked.

He gave her an admiring look as she sat opposite him. "Damn, but you're pretty, Charlene."

She brought her hand to her throat and touched her beating pulse. "That doesn't sound like business, Detective, but thank you. You're awfully pretty yourself."

"I'm flattered, ma'am, but I prefer the word 'handsome.'"

She lowered her head and laughed.

"So"—he cleared his throat—"Captain Logan Moreno said that he'd tried to call you but didn't get an answer?"

Charlene remembered her phone ringing while she'd been talking with Kass and Carmen. "Oh? There was no message, and I didn't recognize the number. Was there something he wanted?"

Sam smoothed his mustache and stared at her as if making a decision. "Have you heard from Dylan?"

"No. I've tried calling, and it doesn't even go to voice mail anymore." She scooted to the edge of her sofa. "I'm worried about him."

"I have enough evidence now to hold him."

"What?" Her breath whooshed from her lungs. Sam had to be mistaken. "Why? What did he do?"

"I can't explain, but I can't locate him either—but if he comes to you, please tell him to find me at the station. Can you do that?"

"I'll tell him. If I see him." Shoot! "Does he need a lawyer?"

Sam nodded. "Might be best."

"What did the captain want?"

"Wants to know if you remember the furnace? And if the glass inside was liquid, or if it was in chunks? He's trying to pinpoint the time of Morganna's death."

Charlene hummed before answering right away. "What can you tell me about that? Off the record, even?"

Sam blew out a breath. "The official cause of death is cyanide poisoning."

She lifted a single shoulder. "I knew that already."

"Once Logan can zero in on the time of death, he will have a better idea on how the poison was applied, which is where you come in."

She looked down at her fingers folded across her knee. Sam wanted answers, but so did she. . . ." Have you talked to Rich Swane?"

"He was in jail that night on a DUI, so that lets him off the hook."

Charlene raised her gaze, thinking of Kass, right next door. Had a man gotten in the way of their friendship? Wouldn't be the first time it came down to murder. "Have you checked into her past? Maybe she had enemies that followed her here."

"Matter of fact, Swane told me that Morganna learned her glassblowing techniques from some guy in Ohio, at one of those traveling festivals. Her real name was Linda Crane, and she took off with this guy's truck and supplies."

"Linda Crane?" Charlene repeated what Sam had told her. "I figured that Morganna had to be a stage name. Did she have family?"

"None listed," Sam said, then blew out a heavy breath. "She was thirty-three. Born in Cleveland, Ohio, with intermittent shoplifting charges between five and ten years ago. No felonies. Married twice, divorced twice. Not squeaky clean," Sam said, "but not a hardened criminal either."

"Why are you telling me this?" Charlene asked.

"Everything I've told you is a matter of public record—if you knew where to look."

"How sad that she died alone. What will happen to her . . . ?" Charlene just couldn't add the words "dead body."

"Once her body is released from investigation, she'll be buried. Nothing fancy, but in Massachusetts unclaimed decedents are buried at the cost of the state rather than cremated, in the event of religious beliefs."

"Religion is a powerful thing, isn't it? It forged Salem into what it is now." Raised Catholic, she still carried residual guilt, but she and Jared had not been religious. She didn't believe sacrificing chocolate or ice cream would make her a better person. She practiced a "do unto others" dogma and did her best to be kind and honest.

Jared had never harmed anyone, yet he'd been taken away by someone who had no right to be behind a wheel. She was working on forgiveness.

"Religion has toppled countries," Sam said.

"True, but who would commit such a brazen act, right on Halloween? Thousands of revelers had been on the street that night."

"Hard to say why anyone would take a life, but they do." He rubbed his jaw. "I know the means in which she died, but not why," Sam said. "Rich Swane continued to pay her bills despite her filing a domestic violence charge. Those glass orbs were nice and showed talent. Some guy taught her everything he knew, and she stole from him. Then we have your kid Dylan. He seemed taken with her—reason unknown."

"Dylan is young enough to be attracted to any pretty female. But, yes, I've heard she had lots of boyfriends. Some women just have an allure," Charlene said, "that draws men like bees to honey."

"Are you suggesting that Morganna cast a spell?" Sam's right brow hiked upward in disbelief.

Charlene hesitated before answering, and Sam immediately leaned forward, his upper lip in a mocking smile. "If a guy goes to bed with a lady, it's not magic, honey, or any Wiccan spell. It's sex, pure and simple."

"I get that you don't believe in the supernatural." She held his gaze, her chin lifted slightly. "I used to feel the same way as you. Now I don't know. There are things that I've seen since moving to Salem that make me wonder what else can't be explained with just five senses." *Like ghosts.*

Sam groaned and sat back, arms across his midriff. "Charlene. If Salem's history teaches you anything, it should be that witchcraft was not real."

"In that instance, yes, you are right. But Kass Fortune claims to have psychic gifts. She can read tea leaves, and Carmen could see that I had been grieving. I don't think Kass told her anything. Some people really have a gift."

"Maybe yes, and maybe no. Kass Fortune?" Sam said. "Another stage name?"

"I don't know," Charlene said, her cheeks heating. "That isn't the point. She says that she was born with these supernatural abilities."

"Show me proof." He braced his palms on his knees. "Psychics have come into the station a few times, promising this and that—but never once helped us solve a crime."

His phone dinged with a text, and he rose, their visit over. "Do you remember about the glass?"

"Just that the orb on the end of the pipe was broken, and the glass was thin, as if she was still working on it. The little door to the furnace was open and the glass inside not completely melted—I hope that helps."

Charlene got up to walk him out. At the door, he leaned in close to look her in the eye. "For the record, I can talk to whoever I want to, but my concern for your involvement has always been a personal one. I don't want *you* getting hurt."

Her toes curled in her boots and her mouth dried as she absorbed the warmth in his gaze. "Oh."

"I'd prefer to keep our friendship separate from my police work. All right?"

Charlene made no promises. "Night, Sam."

CHAPTER TWELVE

Thursday morning the Jensen family left early for a whale-watching expedition that would keep them out all day. By nine, Charlene waited on the front porch with Sal and Sheila Harris for their cab to the airport, and then Oregon.

"I hope you enjoyed your stay?" Charlene wrapped her light jacket around her middle. The sun peeked between gray clouds, but at least there was no rain.

"We did!" Sheila patted her tight gray curls. "We will tell everyone we know about how wonderful you are, and how you took such care of us."

"Tell your guests about the ironworks," Sal said with enthusiasm only a teacher could muster. "It's fascinating to see how weapons were made, and tools."

Charlene privately didn't share his excitement about tools, but she thanked him for the brochure and would add it to her list of things to do. They left, and she quickly ducked into her warm house once the taillights were gone.

She took a mug of hot tea and a muffin to her sitting area and fired up her laptop to post pictures of their Halloween event on her website. She grinned when she saw that Sydney had sent a friend request on Facebook, which she quickly accepted, then perused old photos of Sydney, and, of course, Sam.

He'd always been gorgeous, she noted, scanning the pictures of his rugged face.

Sam had told her that Linda had learned her craft at a Renaissance festival—which made sense, considering the furnace had been portable with wheels. She wondered what had made her leave Ohio and come to Salem, only to find more difficulties here. It made her sad to think of that poor woman's body not claimed by any family.

Sam might not be able to tell her everything, but that didn't mean she couldn't find out for herself. She typed in "Linda Crane," which came up with too many hits to search, so she then typed in "Linda Crane, Ohio, glassblowing."

Charlene gasped aloud, and Silva, who had been purring on the other side of the love seat, lifted her head and cocked an inquisitive ear.

Morganna was platinum blond with curves. Linda Crane had black hair but her smile was the same, with a slightly crooked eyetooth.

Charlene clicked on the pictures and discovered that in most of them Linda was with a man named Hammond Cobb. Tall and sturdy, he was also dressed in medieval garb, with a thick belt around his hips that held a beer stein like a holster. Shaggy, long brown hair and a beard.

Hammond the Glassblower? Surely all of that facial hair was a job hazard.

Charlene kept clicking her way through the pictures. Hammond seemed genuinely enthralled with Linda/Morganna. In love. And Linda with him. Was Linda's affection all an act?

She clicked on his profile and saw that he'd taken his old profile picture down, of him and Linda cuddling, and changed it to one of him drinking from a large leather mug. She scanned the images and old posts—he'd cared for Linda—but then there were no more Linda posts or pictures . . . as of a year ago? When she'd come to Salem, trading her medieval persona to an enticing witch. Had they broken up? Did Sam know any of this stuff? If she could find it this easily, then he surely had too. Had he already questioned Hammond?

Linda's ex-lover had to be more of a person of interest than Dylan, surely.

Was Hammond aware of Morganna's death?

Her fingers paused on the keyboard. If someone she'd loved had died alone, wouldn't she want to know? That special someone about to be put in a lonely grave with nobody to mourn? The answer was yes. Having been in that man's half boots, she knew without a doubt that it was better to know.

Charlene knew this crossed Sam's line of interfering in police business, and it made her squirm in her seat. But her soft heart wouldn't allow her not to act. She sent off a friend request to Hammond, unable to share a private message any other way.

He must have been online because he accepted right away.

Now what? She'd lost someone she loved and knew the pain, so she was very careful with her message informing him of Linda's passing in Salem.

She couldn't help but hope that Hammond still loved Linda—enough to come and claim her body and bring it home to Ohio for a proper funeral. It would be the happiest of endings, considering the tragic circumstances.

I am sorry to inform you that Linda Crane has passed. I see that she was someone special in your life and thought you might want to know. She has no family. If you have any information, contact Detective Sam Holden at the Salem Police Department.

She waited, seeing that he'd read the message.

Rather than answer, Hammond got offline.

Sitting back, she hoped that her message mattered, and that he might have family contacts to give to Sam.

Jack appeared before her with a blast of cool air, and she brought her hand to her chest. "Oh!"

"What are you doing?" Jack asked, taking a seat in the armchair to her right. "You look guilty."

He knew her too well. "Maybe just a little. I know Sam will think I'm interfering, but I hate the idea that Morganna, who is really Linda Crane, died all alone." She smoothed a line in her brow as she frowned. "That could be me one day."

"It won't be you."

She waved his words off. "Unless you are suddenly able to read the future, you can't know that."

"You have family."

"My parents only had one kid—me. And they are now in their seventies. I guess I could stay in contact with my cousins, but I never really liked them. Seems hypocritical to try and be friendly now. Bobby made me eat an ant when I was five." She shuddered. "I never forgave him."

Jack chuckled. "You have friends, Charlene."

"I had Jared—we loved each other to the point of exclusion. Jared and I came here for my best friend's wedding, and yet Brynne and I haven't talked in a year."

"That happens sometimes—but you can change it."

She shifted on the love seat. "I am making new friends. Even more important, I am creating a *home* here. And the point is that I can't help feeling bad that Linda had nobody. I hope that Hammond calls Sam with information about her family, or that he loves her enough to come and get her himself."

"Tell me about her." Jack crossed his legs at the ankles as he stretched them before her. "Linda? That's Morganna's real name?"

"Yes. Last name Crane. From Ohio." She updated him on the new information. "What if he'd broken her heart?"

Her email *ding*ed with a notification from Facebook.

"It's a message! From Hammond." Charlene scanned the reply he'd sent and then looked up at Jack with a rapidly beating pulse. "And it says, 'Linda can rot in an un-marked grave for eternity. She stole my kiln, my money, and my livelihood. Seems karma is a witch, and she's found Morganna. You know I gave her that name? Don't message me again!'" She brought her hand to her throat in shock. "He just unfriended me!"

"I'm sorry," Jack said with a grin. "But you have to admit that the 'karma is a witch' line is funny."

Charlene gave her handsome ghost a look that sent him scrambling, his laughter an echo in the air.

After finishing her muffin, Charlene went upstairs and stripped the sheets off the bed in Sal and Sheila's room. She'd have to look them up on Facebook to see if they posted pictures—which reminded her that she'd just been unfriended by a man she'd attempted to do the right thing by. Charlene dropped the soft sheets in the hall, and Silva dove into the pile like it was a new game, tail flicking back and forth.

Hammond's rudeness stung her pride. She'd thought she was doing something nice for a stranger. As Charlene vac-uumed, she considered Linda Crane, aka Morganna. Ham-mond hadn't said anything positive about his ex-lover.

It seemed the woman had a history of theft. Petty theft, according to Sam. Maybe Carmen didn't believe Evelyn's book of shadows had been stolen, but it was possible that Morganna had done just that.

Charlene brought the linen to the laundry room, dodging Silva's antics as she took the stairs with her arms laden. "If I fall, Silva, who will feed you?"

The cat loved the warmth of the dryer and was perched on

top by the time Charlene started the washer, blinking gorgeous golden eyes at her—completely innocent, of course.

After laundry she tackled her household accounts—it was nice to see money in the plus column. Was money why Linda had left Hammond to seek a new future in Salem? Had she grown tired of blowing glass at the Renaissance festivals and figured she could make a pretty penny here? What kind of woman was she? What drove her?

Charlene wrote down *Linda*, then a few dollar signs with question marks. When Charlene had moved it was because she wanted to start over. Her husband had died and she needed a fresh start, a place where she didn't see his face everywhere she'd go. Linda had Hammond—so what had spurred her toward Salem to start over as a witch? And why a witch, since she supposedly didn't possess psychic qualities?

Charlene doodled a witch ball next to Linda's name as something to talk over with Jack when he came around.

By two in the afternoon, Charlene was caught up with her daily chores and had just put a pork roast in the Crock-Pot for pulled pork sliders—in case the Jensens returned hungry—when a knock sounded. She dried her hands on a soft cotton towel and dropped it on the kitchen counter before going to the front door.

She peered out the side window since she wasn't expecting anyone and felt a jolt of surprise. Styled silver hair, a belted crimson coat appropriate for the fifty-degree weather, and low-heeled black boots.

Opening the door, she said, "Evelyn! Come in." She stepped back to welcome the beautiful older woman inside. Evelyn made silver hair look *good*.

"I hope I'm not intruding?" Evelyn entered up the stairs and looked around the foyer, the stairs, toward the living area and dining room.

"Of course not." Was she searching for Silva, or to see if there were any guests?

Evelyn untied the belt at her waist as if prepared to stay awhile.

"Can I get you some coffee, or tea?"

"Oh, coffee for me, dear. You know we Salem natives prefer coffee ever since that whole tea party fiasco in Boston." Evelyn turned around to shrug out of her jacket and hung it up on the coat-tree.

Charlene bit back a laugh. "The one in 1773?"

Evelyn lifted a straight finger and gave her a wag, along with a hint of a smile. "Seventeen seventy-six. You may have noticed that we are very proud of our history. Even the naughty bits."

Was that how the older generation referred to the hanging of innocent people? Charlene led the way into the kitchen. "Do you mind sitting here, or I can put a tray together for the living room before the fireplace?"

"Oh, no, please don't go to any extra effort. I love the informality of the kitchen." Evelyn eased herself into Jack's usual chair—since Jack wasn't around, Charlene hoped he wouldn't mind. Silva sauntered out from Charlene's living room and eyed Evelyn in a feline way.

"I wonder what she's thinking?" Charlene said.

"She's happy to be here," Evelyn answered after studying the cat.

Charlene didn't reply but turned to her Keurig. Could Evelyn read the cat's thoughts, or was the older woman being polite? "Dark roast, decaf, or I have a vanilla bean?"

"Dark roast, if you don't mind." Evelyn settled at the kitchen chair while Charlene had her back to the unexpected guest.

What was Evelyn doing here? Charlene handed her a full mug and chose the vanilla bean and waited for her own cup to brew. Facing Evelyn, she asked, "Cream or sugar?"

The older woman's face belied age, giving her timeless beauty. Straight posture, slender fingers. Her emerald-green eyes were bright with intellect. "Black is perfect." Her crimson tunic top and oxblood jewelry set in chunky silver, paired with black jeans, suggested a woman of fashion without pronouncing her beliefs—she didn't have to dress the part; she just *was*. Charlene noticed the black leather tote at her feet.

"Can I hang up your purse?" Charlene asked, gesturing to the coatrack.

"No, thank you. Not necessary."

Charlene brought her mug to the table and sat down.

"You are probably wondering what I'm doing here." Evelyn's silver brow arched.

Charlene started to deny it but then shrugged and smiled. "Yes, I am curious—though you are very welcome."

"Thank you." Evelyn sipped her coffee, then said, "You were asking about witches when you came to visit the winery?"

She'd been asking specifically about Morganna and had gotten nowhere. This time she'd go more slowly and not lose sight of her goal to find out how Evelyn really felt about the woman.

Charlene went into the pantry for a box of chocolate chip cookies and brought them back to the table with napkins. "I'm just learning about this modern-day witchcraft, finding it surprising since Salem is renowned for the witch trials when all those innocent girls were hanged. It doesn't seem right somehow."

Evelyn nodded once. "Even in the sixteen hundreds, news of the atrocity traveled the world and attracted Armand Sheffield, from London. I told you that he is our ancestor? The Flints are the only branch still true." Evelyn sipped her coffee and hummed with delight. "Is this Sumatra?"

"Yes," Charlene said. "It's one of my favorite blends." Kass and Carmen had mentioned Evelyn's pride in her ancestry. Were the younger girls jealous? Or just annoyed millennials?

"Anyway, Armand was a powerful druid in England, but when he arrived in Salem, he discovered that there were no actual witches here. So he formed the original coven with others who had come in search of the pagan faith." Evelyn smoothed a silver strand back from her slightly lined cheek.

"Why are you sharing this with me now?" Charlene shifted on the kitchen chair.

"I dreamed that you needed to know." Evelyn's gaze remained unwavering.

Charlene wasn't sure what to say to that. "A dream?"

"Don't you dream, Charlene? Some believe that our dream state is when our spirit guides can contact us with portents. Information to benefit us or warn us from danger."

"Sure, I dream," she said. "I don't usually remember them. And when I do, they don't make sense."

"Oh . . ." Evelyn tilted her head to study Charlene again. "Your soul might be one that wanders during the night."

"What?" Charlene straightened, her hand to her heart to make sure all her parts were intact. "That sounds scary."

Evelyn chuckled. "It's only scary if your soul gets lost."

She thought of Jack. "Is that possible?"

"Anything is possible, my dear. With the right spell, at the right time, in the right circumstances." Evelyn's voice hardened. "Magick is powerful and not to be played with."

The conversation unnerved Charlene. Spells and witches were in fairy-tale books, not in the real world. Yet here in Salem and in her kitchen it was being stated as fact.

If the young witches were correct, Morganna was a fraud who'd chosen the wrong people to play with, and probably had paid the ultimate price. "Have you found your . . . journal?"

Evelyn positioned the mug before her. "Journal?"

"Your book of shadows," Charlene clarified, hoping she

wasn't saying the wrong thing by bringing up the incident. "Spell book? I heard that it was stolen, and that you thought it was taken by Morganna."

A wave of distaste traveled across Evelyn's features.

Charlene realized that Kass and Carmen were correct about one thing. Evelyn didn't care for Morganna.

"I hate to pry," Charlene said, taking a cookie, "but I can see that you are upset."

"Morganna took us all in with her charm. Her eagerness to be a protégé. I brought her close, and the little viper bit me."

Evelyn's bright green eyes turned icy cold, and Charlene shivered.

"I am a powerful witch—I say this not because I am bragging but because it's true. I have handed that power to my daughter and granddaughters. I made the mistake of allowing her into my circle. I lowered my guard."

"Because she asked you to teach her?"

"She appealed to my pride, yes," Evelyn admitted, "but I am usually more cautious than that." She took a cookie and placed it next to her mug. "I welcomed her into my inner circle—until I caught her in an indecent act. Once I did, her glamour immediately dropped away and I could see her and her black heart."

"What did you do?" *What had Morganna done?*

"I accused her of adultery and theft, and proposed that she be cast out at the next full-moon ceremony—a banishment spell that would need to be performed with the entire coven to show her for the fraud that she was, to reveal her weakness."

Charlene sat forward, listening intently as Evelyn opened up to her. She felt Evelyn's shame, her need to make things right. "Did you ever find it?"

Evelyn eyes glittered before she gathered her thoughts. "No."

"You could ask Detective Holden if Morganna had it."

Kass had wondered if it had been in Morganna's office.
What if Rich had it, unknowingly, in Morganna's personal
things?

"Morganna stole it, I know she did. I know *when* she
did—during an ancient ritual that required more psychic
strength than I had on my own or I wouldn't have invited
her. That is how I found out that she was no more a witch
than Bridget Bishop."

The first innocent woman hanged in the 1600s.

"How did she gain the coven's trust?"

"I don't know why we were so gullible." Evelyn broke a
corner off the cookie. "When I discovered her fraud, she
got back at me by stealing my book of shadows, which has
spells so powerful even an untrained acolyte could make
them work."

Charlene drank her coffee and shook her head. "How
could she take anything from you, if you had the power? It
doesn't make sense."

Evelyn jammed her palm flat against the kitchen table.
"Somebody helped her."

"Who?" Charlene nudged her mug aside. "Since I'm not
familiar with this, I don't know how this power thing works.
Did someone else physically overpower you and steal your
book? Is that what you're saying?"

"I can't explain the ritual to someone who doesn't understand magick. Just know that someone very powerful assisted Morganna. I was the fool to let my guard down."
Evelyn glanced out the kitchen window, her mouth a stern
red line, the cords in her neck tight.

Charlene didn't understand, but the betrayal on Evelyn's
face was clear to read. She may very well have wanted
Morganna dead.

"I called for a meeting of the council, and we decreed
that Morganna would be excommunicated and run out of
Salem." Evelyn met Charlene's gaze. "She had to go before
she poisoned anybody else."

Poison. Like cyanide? Or a more figurative poison? Revenge was a powerful motive. "But she died before that happened."

Fear tickled Charlene's spine. Was Evelyn here to confess?

"I need to find my spell book. It's too dangerous to be out among the neophytes in Salem. With power comes responsibility." Evelyn reached across the table for Charlene's hand. "If anything would happen, the fault would be mine."

"You believe that your book in the wrong hands could do unspeakable harm."

"I do," Evelyn said. "Goddess help me."

Charlene thought of the Goth kids and how Morganna had treated them like they were fakes when she was the fraud all along, with her created name and stolen furnace. "What do you know about Morganna's death?"

Evelyn scoffed. "She got what she deserved."

Charlene wondered if she might be having coffee with a murderer.

"I didn't do it, Charlene," Evelyn said with a brisk laugh. "You should see the look on your face right now."

Charlene bowed her head and cleared her expression. "Sorry. This is all so new for me."

"Witchcraft? Murder?"

"Both." She took a deep breath. "Have you asked if your book has been turned in at the police station?"

"It hasn't. Morganna might not have been a witch, but she knew someone who was . . . someone who knew how to use a cloaking spell. Otherwise, I'd be able to track it. My guides would know and tell me. But it is blocked."

Charlene didn't know about her spiritual guide, but it didn't hurt to ask questions. "Have you asked the other people in your coven?"

Evelyn's sigh ruffled a napkin on the table. "The Wiccan community has been a place of flux in the last month since I discovered Morganna's treachery. Well," she considered, "maybe even longer than that. When Stephanos and I were the leaders, before Lucas and Martine, our coven thrived."

"Who is Stephanos?" She memorized the names to look up later, pretty sure that Evelyn wouldn't like it if Charlene got up to take notes.

"Stephanos Landis." Evelyn smiled softly. "We did our best to guide the community for almost twenty years."

"Wow! And how long have Martine and Lucas been in charge?" It would be very difficult to step into a position like that, especially if the previous leaders had been admired.

"Six months." Evelyn twisted the silver bangle at her wrist. "The Evergreens should have been a good choice—Martine's family has been here in Salem for generations. They've always been a part of the community, and when I wanted to step down, Stephanos did too. It made sense to bring in another couple as deeply involved in the faith."

"I've met their daughter."

Evelyn clapped her hands together and sat forward. "How Lucas and Martine wanted a child! And they were finally blessed after a fertility ritual."

"What is that?" Charlene had visions of debauchery in her head, and she gave it a shake.

"Rose quartz, essential oils, gifts for the Goddess and God. It is a beautiful thing, Charlene, and they were blessed with a child at long last, despite many miscarriages and previous disappointments. For that reason, they are true believers in the Wiccan faith, perfect to bring the next generation of young witches into the light of love."

She and Jared had wanted children, and she'd looked at all the options when it came to in vitro and fertility specialists. The procedures were very costly, and there was no guarantee.

"It sounds like they are a wonderful family, just the three of them." Charlene went to take a drink but realized her mug was empty. "What happened?"

Evelyn's voice dropped to a chilly zero degrees. "Morganna happened." She bowed her head and murmured something that sounded like a prayer.

Or was that a curse?

CHAPTER THIRTEEN

How had a fake like Morganna managed to cause such angst in Evelyn, a woman with such great power?

Despite the coziness of her kitchen, Charlene's stomach was in knots. Should she offer comfort, or leave Evelyn alone? All of this witchcraft stuff sounded like something out of an old Disney film, like *Snow White*. Or maybe *Fantasia*. Those cartoons had given her nightmares as a kid.

Evelyn's face had gone white, aging her ten years, and Charlene couldn't stop herself from reaching out. "Are you all right?" She held out her hand, palm up.

"Of course I'm all right." Evelyn's eyes snapped with fierce determination. "And as much as my faith demands forgiveness, I can't say that I regret her death. She left a mess in her wake that has rocked our community—though Stephanos and I have done our best to keep it quiet. What else have you heard?"

Charlene wet her lips. If she turned the clock back to two, three months ago, she would never think it possible that she'd be having this conversation with a self-professed witch—or that she might consider the things Evelyn told her to possibly be true.

"I didn't know about the adultery charge—who was it?"

Evelyn shot out of her chair, her black bag tipping to the side by her feet. "I can't say." Charlene knew she'd crossed a fine line, and for a second she was afraid that she might be in danger too. She closed her eyes and held her breath, then felt cool air drift in.

Jack?

When she looked up, there he was, next to Evelyn's shoulder. Dressed in jeans and a burgundy sweater that complemented his masculine features.

Her heart pounded as their eyes met.

Had he come to protect her? Did she need protecting from this strong-willed witch? "I'm sorry," Charlene said, realizing that Evelyn was truly rattled. "I'm just trying to understand who might have wanted Morganna dead."

"You don't believe it was an accident?"

Before thinking better of it, Charlene countered, "Do you?"

As if feeling a chill, Evelyn rubbed her shoulders, and glanced around the kitchen. Did Evelyn sense Jack's presence?

That might not be a good thing, for Jack or Charlene. Time for Evelyn to go, she thought.

Evelyn took another long, hard look around the kitchen, her gaze passing over Jack's ethereal figure as he stood by Charlene. "Do be careful, my dear. You can't go around accusing people of murder, you know. It makes them angry."

Was Evelyn referring to Brandy? Was that a warning for Charlene to be careful of whom she talked to now? Or a simple witchy observation . . . ?

Charlene got up on the pretense of checking the pork roast in the Crock-Pot and lifted the lid. Garlic and rosemary escaped and gave her the time to gather her thoughts before turning back to Evelyn, who was righting her spilled tote.

"I wasn't accusing anyone, certainly not you. The more

I hear, the more I realize that nobody grieves Morganna's passing."

"No," Evelyn agreed. "They don't, but that doesn't mean they killed her, does it?" She crossed her arms, as if challenging Charlene.

Why had Evelyn suddenly turned defensive? Had she told Charlene what she wanted Charlene to know—and if so, why? Was she protecting someone?

Before she could reply, she heard Jack's voice in her ear. "Take care, Charlene. I grew up with talk of witches and ghosts, didn't believe a word of it, and yet here I am."

Jack had a point. "Evelyn, I'm afraid that I've offended you with my Midwest sensibilities. Salem has broadened my mind, and I'm learning new things all of the time. Like spells, for example."

"Spells are prayers with guided intent." Evelyn trembled, skirting around Jack, who had moved to the counter next to the kitchen sink. "Witches are regular people who believe in different dimensions, not just one."

Evelyn paced in front of the wine cellar door, rubbing her arms. "We are not afraid to delve into the unexplainable. Science is now backing up what was once 'magic,' and I imagine that as time goes on, more mysteries will be revealed." Evelyn laughed at herself and blushed. "There I go sounding like a professor again."

"Would you like another cup of coffee?" She avoided looking at Jack, who stared intently at Evelyn.

"She can sense me," Jack said.

"No thank you, dear," Evelyn said. "I've said more than enough." Evelyn picked up her black tote and brought it to the tabletop, rifling inside for her car keys. "Brandy says that I tend to lecture, so forgive me if I went on too long."

"I am sure that you had students lined up at the door for your classes. Thank you for coming. I enjoyed our conversation." She'd be willing to bet Silva's red collar that Evelyn had wanted to give Charlene certain information—it would take some time to decipher just what.

Evelyn brought her coffee mug to the counter by the sink. She inhaled the garlic coming from the Crock-Pot, and the savory pork. "Life is full of twists and turns. I know that you are widowed, but I sense love and bounty all around you."

Charlene stepped back in surprise, her hip bumping the chair. "We had a wonderful marriage."

"You are fortunate in that, Charlene. But I don't think love is done with you yet." Evelyn's eyes narrowed, and she straightened. "Well, thank you for the coffee and letting me ramble on."

The woman hadn't rambled at all, Charlene thought as she walked with Evelyn to the door. She helped her into her wool crimson coat and waved at her from the porch as Evelyn got into a classic silver Porsche.

Once inside, Charlene said, "You're right, Jack—she knew you were there. What did she want, exactly? And did I give it to her?"

Jack studied Charlene with care. "I'm not sure how much power the witches actually have, but if I can exist in this dimension, who knows what someone like Evelyn might be capable of?"

"She says that Armand Sheffield is her spirit guide. Do you believe that?" She looked at him thoughtfully. "Is that what you are, Jack? Can you see any other entities like yourself?"

"I don't know what I am, Charlene. I can't see or feel anything in the place that I exist when I'm not with you." His shrug broke her heart and she reached for him, but her hand met only the cold of his essence and not the arm of the man she saw before her.

Charlene tugged at her diamond earring, her back to the closed front door. "Jack, witchcraft and magick are so hard for me to take in. And yet I have to accept that there is more to life than meets the eye. Like you."

He shimmered, fading before coming back in vibrant outline. "You are strong, Charlene. Just don't forget to be careful. You can't protect yourself against something you can't see or hear." Jack strode from the foyer to the stairs to the dining room, dark now, and empty until the Jensens would return. "Could the witches have used a spell to kill Morganna?" He paused and rubbed his jaw. "Evelyn talked about poison."

"As far as I know, Morganna died from cyanide poisoning—not magick. But there is more going on. Why would Dylan's jacket be in the chimney?"

"I've been thinking about that. Perhaps whoever did it had another motive."

"Like what?"

"To block ventilation in the workroom?" Jack offered. "You said there was no window. Maybe there was a vent in the ceiling leading up to the roof?"

"I don't know. I'll check Kass's place next time I pop in," she said. "But why Dylan's jacket? Why not a newspaper or a wool blanket." Charlene wished she could see that work space again. "I wonder if I could get inside to see?" She headed to the living room and took a seat on the sofa. Jack joined her. "Evelyn very clearly said that the leaders of the coven wanted Morganna gone. That would be Martine, Lucas, Stephanos, and Evelyn."

"Gone is not the same as dead," Jack said. "I remember Martine from school—a shy brown-haired girl who always had the sniffles, she was very thin and hung out with drama kids writing poetry."

Charlene compared that image to the one she had of Carmen—also thin and artsy. Kass was too—maybe that was part of the theatrical side of the tourist industry. Darren, with his Mohawk, Carmen's assistant in black and pentagrams that night at the fair. Dylan was too "normal" for the Goth crowd and was the one that didn't fit.

Was he trying too hard? What would he do to prove himself? "We need to find Dylan—or we need to find the real killer." Charlene stopped herself from reaching for Jack as he got up from their seat and walked to the unlit fireplace. "Dylan wouldn't make it in jail. He'd be eaten alive."

"I agree with you, so our job is to keep him out. Have you heard from Rich yet?"

Charlene's stomach flipped with nerves. "No. I've called twice, but he doesn't answer—and what would I say in a message? 'Hey, do you know who killed Morganna?'" She shifted. "I think I better just go over there."

Jack crossed his arms, the fireplace behind him showing through in shadow. He wasn't strong right now, but she knew he wanted to help her and was pushing himself to stay. "I don't like that idea, Charlene. That could be dangerous. If I could go with you . . ."

"It's daytime—he won't be expecting me." Charlene sat forward on the couch. "If Morganna is the one that stole Evelyn's book, what if Rich has it, unknowingly?"

"How will that help Dylan?" Jack's brow furrowed.

"It will prove that Evelyn is telling the truth." She brought her thumbnail to her lower lip. Which helped *Evelyn*.

"Maybe Rich will know who else Morganna was sleeping with? That could be a motive for murder . . . I have to try." She couldn't sit by and do nothing while an innocent kid was possibly in way over his head. "I just know in my heart that Dylan wasn't involved."

She rose quickly, which must have startled the cat.

Silva raced around the couch as if her furry tail were on fire, and she tried to twist her body around Jack's legs from where he stood. The cat fell through Jack's essence to the stones on the fireplace with a frustrated tail flick.

"There she is," Jack said as he looked down. "Little fuzz ball."

Silva cocked her head and let out a meow in protest.

Charlene saw something dangling from the cat's mouth and wondered if it was a dryer sheet. "That can't taste good, you strange cat." She leaned down and tugged. "Silva, let me see." Charlene sat down, and the cat jumped into her lap.

"Netting?" The white ball was the size of her thumb and smelled like flowers—or herbs—and was tied with a lavender string. Looked almost like a muslin sachet from Kass's tea shop. Had Kass given it to her? Charlene didn't recall seeing anything else like that in the store. "Where did you get this?" She looked from Silva to Jack.

Her spine tingled as she recalled Evelyn's tote spilling over.

Jack joined her for a closer look. "Could Evelyn have dropped it?" he asked quietly.

"Maybe—and Silva found it. I hope our cat didn't steal it." That didn't seem likely. She sniffed the ball. Rose and lavender.

"Be careful," Jack warned.

"You think it might . . . contain a spell?" Charlene dropped the sachet. Silva swiped it like it was her latest cat toy and ran off with it down the hall.

"I'll try to find it later," Jack said. "I know where Silva hides her favorite things."

They looked at each other for a long moment, and she thought of the witch balls meant to trap spirits. "Jack, I don't want you bothering with it. Who knows what's inside?" She checked the time. "I have just over an hour until the Jensens get back. I'm going to Rich's."

Jack's anguish was palpable in the dimming of his blue eyes. "I don't like this. Maybe you should call Sam. Or take Kevin with you?"

"I'm a grown woman going to a public space in the middle of the afternoon. I will be just fine. I think I still have pepper spray from when I lived in the city that I can stick in my purse. Evelyn might carry a sachet with spells, but I've got something better."

Before she could talk herself out of it, Charlene found the unused bottle of pepper spray in a box in her closet and dropped it in her bag, zipped up her jacket, and headed out the door to her Pilot. The gray skies seemed ominous as she drove downtown and parked in the lot closest to Morganna's Witch House.

The corner storefront was dark, though Kass's next to it had a cheerful glowing light from within as customers streamed in and out.

Would Rich be home? How did one get to the upstairs apartments? There was a black metal fire escape on the side. Charlene got out of the car and walked toward the building.

A man in a Boston Bruins jacket and cap came out of a door that had been hidden by the metal stairs.

Going on impulse, Charlene called, "Rich? Mr. Swane?"

He stopped with a chuckle, holding the black metal door open with his foot. "Mr. Swane is my granddad. What can I do ya for?"

His face was round, his hair light brown and dull, his cheeks ruddy—Rich appeared to be in his late thirties but it was hard to tell beneath the cap.

"Hi! I'm Charlene Morris." She held out her hand.

He shook it with curiosity.

"I'm a friend of Morganna's," she said.

As if repulsed, he dropped her hand and moved back a step. His face was guarded.

"Linda Crane?" Charlene added, as if to prove they were indeed friends.

"Yeah, I know. I lived with her, didn't I?" He shuffled his sneakers—gray with use—and looked over her shoulder as if to see who else might be around. Nobody on this side of the building. He shoved out his chest, and she swallowed hard.

"I was wondering if I could get her things? I know she doesn't have family. . . ."

Rich's chuckle wasn't friendly but had a "piss off" tone. "Too late, lady. I already gave her suitcase, which she'd already packed, by the way, to the cops. Not that she had much. Not even a cell phone. I think whoever done her in stole it, but the cops don't believe me. They think I sold it or something. Jerks."

He started to leave and let the door close, but Charlene moved around him to keep it open. Could she go inside? Did this lead up to the next floor? And if it did, how would she get in?

"What are you doing?" Rich asked. His tone was not amused as he looked from her hand to her body. Her purse was at her side, and she wished that she'd put her pepper spray in her pocket. Although right now she was the one out of line. What did she expect for Rich to do? Invite her in for a drink?

"What about her diary?" Charlene said, grasping specifically for the book of shadows. Would Morganna have told him she'd stolen it? She had no idea so she said, "I'd love to connect with her poetry."

"Nope," Rich said. "No diary. No spell book, like the cops asked about. No money. No will. She didn't bring nothing but her glassblowing supplies that she stole from some idiot in Ohio."

Charlene bit the inside of her cheek.

Rich was on a roll now, red-faced. He snorted. "I tell you what, lady. Don't waste no tears over Linda Crane—she was a liar, a cheat, and a fraud. I haven't shed a one." With that, he smacked his hand against the metal of the fire escape, and Charlene jumped.

The door closed with a click of a lock.

Rich's gaze narrowed with suspicion. "Unless you're such good pals that you plan on paying me what she owes for her lease, why don't you get outta here?"

Charlene was only too happy to comply. Her pulse raced as she hurried back to her car and got in. She searched the street and sidewalk for Rich, but he was gone. She had to wait for a few minutes for her hands to stop shaking before she was able to start the Pilot and drive home.

Rich was not a nice man—but if he wasn't lying, that meant that he didn't have the book of shadows. Morganna's bag had been packed? Whom had she been going to meet? And why was her cell phone missing?

The outer door to the apartments on the second floor required a key. How had Dylan's jacket gotten up to the roof? Had Rich somehow got his hands on it? Maybe he'd shown up that night at her shop, found her with Dylan in the back room, and . . . what? If he'd killed her in a fit of rage, he'd never have used cyanide. He'd have used his hands.

She tried to call Dylan again—nothing.

Charlene parked in the driveway, went inside, and had just taken her coat off when the Jensens burst through the front door. Hailey wrapped Charlene's legs in a hug. There was no sign of Jack. "We saw a whale! It was as big as Mum's car!"

Charlene greeted her guests and made them at home even as her mind whirred with what she'd learned.

Nothing to clear Dylan. Or Evelyn. And Rich had violence simmering beneath the surface. He had the most reason to want Morganna/Linda dead. The woman had cheated on him and was planning on leaving, stiffing him on the money for her lease.

What reason would Evelyn have to commit murder? A stolen spell book? Covering up an affair that Morganna had with someone of importance? Maybe that pride of hers was at stake by accepting her into their clan only to discover that Morganna was a liar and a fake.

She shook the questions from her mind to focus on her guests. After a feast of pulled pork sliders and coleslaw, and a game of trivia that Charlene lost to Peter, she said goodnight to the Jensens and went to the kitchen to fill Silva's bowl with tuna fish.

"There you go. Enjoy. I really hope that you didn't steal that sachet from Evelyn's purse. She might come back and turn you into a dog."

She poured herself a glass of the special winter blend from Brandy and Flint Wineries but paused before she took a drink.

What if Evelyn had left that sachet on purpose?

CHAPTER FOURTEEN

Charlene drank the last of her Earl Grey tea the following morning as she worked on her website. The Jensens were due to return to England later that day and had already left for breakfast by the wharf. Needing another caffeine kick to keep her energy going, she searched the butler's pantry for a box of tea—any kind would do—but the shelves were bare. She eyed her Keurig, not wanting another cup of coffee.

Rather than the grocery store, she thought of Kass Fortune's Tea Shoppe. If Dylan's jacket had been used to block ventilation in Morganna's workshop and Kass's back room was the same as Morganna's, she wanted to see if there was a vent. There weren't any windows.

It would also give her an opportunity to ask about Carmen's parents. Evelyn had mentioned that they'd taken over for her and Stephanos as coven leaders, and those were pretty big shoes to fill. Maybe the Evergreens felt that Morganna's theft and fraud reflected on them as leaders.

It seemed extreme, but Charlene was determined to uncover answers so that Dylan stayed out of jail.

Charlene stepped outside into the fall air—gray clouds

and a bite that reminded her of a snowy Chicago day. She flipped on the heater once she got behind the wheel of her Pilot. In less than ten minutes, she'd parked her car in the familiar lot a half block from the strip of brick shops.

Blue police cars flashed red and blue lights, and she was immediately reminded of the night Morganna had died. Tension rose and her fingers shook.

Afraid for Kass, Charlene ran the remaining distance and burst into the tea shop. With overwhelming relief, she saw Kass talking teary-eyed by the register counter with the police. Officer Bernard, taller even than Kass, took notes. The shiny black rim on his blue hat reflected the overheard fluorescent light.

Pale, her hair in a twisted braid over her shoulder, her brown fisherman's sweater loose on her slender body, Kass used her hands animatedly as she gestured to the back area.

Charlene hesitated awkwardly at the entrance, until Kass waved her forward. The racks of merchandise were in order, although the indoor water fountain hadn't been turned on, which made the goddess figure seem forlorn.

Kass reached for Charlene's elbow and said, "This is Charlene Morris, a friend of mine."

"Hello. We met the other night," Charlene said to Officer Bernard.

"Ma'am," he responded politely.

She looked around the shop for Officer Jimenez but didn't recognize the other officer with him. Short and sturdy, Officer P. Tanner had light red hair and freckles. "What happened?" Charlene put her hand on Kass's back.

"Someone broke in," she cried, distraught. "Destroyed my back room."

The uniformed officers nodded—Charlene noticed that Salem police even included their witches in a patch on their dark blue uniform. They appeared to be finishing up, because Officer Bernard put his notebook in his pocket. "We will be in touch," he said.

"If you can think of anything else"—Officer Tanner handed Kass a business card—"call me directly."

Kass slid it in her jeans pocket and walked them out of the store.

Charlene was so grateful that Kass hadn't been hurt that it took her a moment to realize that the front of the shop seemed undisturbed. Whereas Morganna had witch balls in her display window, Kass had filled hers with interesting-shaped teapots, wooden crates, and tea towels.

"Just the back?" Charlene squeezed Kass's elbow when the young woman returned. "Was anything taken?"

"No . . . I don't think so. Everything was dumped out of my file cabinets, and someone overturned my desk. Thank the Goddess that my teas are all stored in a nearby ware-house. I keep very little money in the till." Her voice hitched.

"Do you mind if I take a look?"

"No, go ahead." Kass sniffed.

Charlene stepped around the counter toward the back door—it was the same layout as Morganna's. A big work-station to the right, with a stove and sink in addition to her desk. She looked up at the ceiling. Sure enough, a rectan-gular white vent that had to lead up to the roof. Would plugging the stack on the roof have created fumes in Mor-ganna's workshop?

She couldn't imagine Rich thinking up such a devious plan. Dylan might have been interested in Morganna and hoped to get lucky, but he certainly wouldn't climb up on the roof and stuff his jacket in the vent and hope to kill her.

Kass lifted a recipe book from the floor and put it on the counter, bringing Charlene back to the present. "When I re-alized this place had been tossed, I figured I might be next." Her lower lip quivered, but the tears slowed, and an undecipherable expression crossed her wan face. "I . . . I don't know what's going on around here. Who would kill Morganna? Is this supposed to be a threat, to me? I don't know anything."

Charlene searched the breakroom-office space. Kass had fun photos on a corkboard with her and Darren, and two other employees Charlene hadn't met yet. There were shelves for magazines and books. It had been gone through, but not *vandalized*.

Whoever had broken in had been looking for something, but what? The only thing that she knew of that had been stolen was Evelyn's book. "What did the police say? Do they think this break-in is related to what happened next door?"

"They didn't offer any information." Kass tugged on the sleeves of her big sweater, clearly distraught. "I'm glad it was me that opened today," Kass said in a small voice. "Darren called in sick with the flu."

Charlene felt goose bumps run up her back. Darren had said he didn't know Dylan—but was that the truth? If someone was setting Dylan up, that pitiful kid might be in serious trouble. "You didn't see anybody around?"

Kass wrapped her long, thin arm around her slender waist as if to give herself a hug. "No! I didn't stop to think when I saw the back door ajar. I ran right in. What an idiot thing to do."

"Poor girl," Charlene said. "Of course you didn't stop to think of the consequences—you were worried about your shop." She scanned the back room once more. "Can I help you put this together? It won't take long." Had the book of shadows been here? Or some other evidence that needed to be destroyed?

"No, that's okay." Kass filled a kettle with water and put it on the stove. The floor was linoleum tiles rather than cement pavers, like Morganna's had been. Rich must have known about the furnace if he'd helped her set up flooring.

"So I met your landlord yesterday—you were right. He's a jerk."

Kass looked over from the stove with surprise, tears trickling down her cheeks. "What happened?"

"I wanted to ask about Morganna, that's all. Rich seems to be the closest thing she had to a family or a friend."

"That almost makes me feel sorry for her," Kass said wryly.

"Do you have access to the roof from here?"

"Yeah—I guess so. From the outside fire escape? I've never been on the roof or to the upstairs apartments. They're probably pretty similar to mine." Kass's long hair flowed down her back. Tiny braids with tiny beads were interspersed that reminded Charlene of a pirate.

Charlene righted the oval plastic table and a chair. "I hope the police will offer extra protection in the evenings. After what happened next door, perhaps you should close early, at five every night, until the person is caught."

"The police don't seem very concerned. I mean, they questioned me about Morganna right after it happened, but not since. This morning I asked them if they'd discovered anything, but Officer Tanner wasn't exactly talkative."

Charlene understood her frustration. "I'm sorry, and I'm worried about you."

Kass gave another sniff and her eyes welled. "The first time I spoke with the police, I said Morganna and I were friends, and the other officer—I didn't get her name, something with a 'J'—said that she was aware we'd had a falling out." She got out two mugs from a shelf. "How'd they know about that?"

Charlene could guess who might have shared the incident—Carmen had wasted no time in telling Charlene and would likely have spilled the beans to the police. "It might have been best hearing it from you."

"Morganna and I still talked—we weren't enemies." Even though the shop was empty, she whispered, "I'd given her a tea reading, and it was dark. I didn't know that she was going to die! All I read in the leaves was trouble coming. It could have been anything."

Charlene's heart went out to the young woman. "She was upset?"

"I was careful how I worded it, but, yes, I gave her a gentle warning. She got angry and told me I was jealous of her friendship with Carmen, which isn't at all true."

"Is there another reason you didn't get along?" Charlene asked. She knew that Morganna had wanted Kass to support her against the elders, because Carmen had told her. Would Kass admit it? Or hide it? Kass settled back against the counter, her body loose. "I am not into the local politics, you know? But Morganna believed that the younger witches needed to be more involved in the community, and she made disparaging remarks about the elders' ages all the time. It was embarrassing, actually."

"How so?" Charlene set another book from the floor on the table.

"We could be at a meeting and everyone would get along fine—then Morganna would spark the drama with a snide comment on Evelyn's crone status, or Stephanos no longer being virile enough to lead. She wouldn't say it to the whole congregation, only to the person next to her, but the word got around."

"Ouch!" Knowing Evelyn, she imagined that hadn't gone over well.

"Evelyn and Stephanos have always been respectful to me. Same with Martine and Lucas."

Charlene thought back to Hammond's opinion on the woman and commiserated with Kass. "She doesn't sound like she was a happy person. In fact, I'd say troubled. She obviously made a lot of waves in this community."

"Maybe it's wrong, but I was glad that she was going to be excommunicated. Morganna was that drop of negative energy that spoils the whole pond." Kass took the kettle off the stove and gestured for Charlene to follow her out of the back area to bins of dried tea.

Kass chose a calming chamomile and lifted the selection to Charlene.

"Sure—whatever you want."

Tears pooled in Kass's brown eyes. "I wish that the message in the leaves had been clearer, because then maybe I could have helped. I would never have wished her harm."

"Of course not," Charlene said. "You are not responsible for another person's choices." She glanced around the room. "Kass, you know that Evelyn's book of shadows is still missing? Do you think someone might have been looking for it here?"

Kass's brows arched. "*I* don't have it."

"What if someone thinks that you do?" Evelyn said it was very powerful and could be harmful in the wrong hands. If Morganna had stolen the book of shadows, what had become of it? She had a hard time imagining Evelyn in a ninja suit breaking into buildings after dark.

Confusion brought more tears—Charlene traded the dish of dried chamomile for a box of tissues near the cash register and dotted Kass's mascara running down her cheeks. "You're a mess, honey. Go wash up, and then we can have tea, and clean your back room."

"I'll need to do a cleansing ritual to clear the negative energy," Kass replied, taking the tissue. "I'll have to smudge the whole room with sage before I can open for customers again—that just means burning a bundle of dried sage—and say a cleansing prayer."

"How long will that take?" Charlene asked.

Kass crumpled the tissue in her palm. "I'll do it myself, tonight at the moon's zenith. I have sea salt and bundles of sage at the warehouse."

The front door opened, and Carmen rushed in, her brow drawn with concern. The diamond stud in her nose twinkled, and her strands of purple hair perfectly matched her velvet coat. "Nettie called from the T-shirt shop and said she saw a police car here! Are you okay?"

Kass walked into the young witch's hug. "Yes, just shaken up. Someone went through my back room."

Carmen petted Kass's long black hair. "I think somebody tried to break into my shop too." She stepped away from Kass, her green eyes wide with fright. "Luckily, I had the lock bolted from the inside, but I heard it rattle. After what happened to Morganna? I never leave it open."

Charlene looked at the two frightened girls. "What *is* going on?"

Kass sighed. "You better inform the police," she told Carmen. "What if we're both in danger?"

"What if somebody is targeting witches?" Carmen asked, her pointed black brows high.

Charlene straightened with shock. She hadn't considered that possibility—but why not? Who knew what prodded a killer? Killing witches had happened back in 1692—what if someone wanted to re-create the mania? "Please, call Detective Sam Holden and let him know what happened."

"I called my mom and dad," Carmen said. "They're going to meet me at my store—Kass, you should come. I know they'll want to make sure that you're okay too."

Kass shuffled from one foot to the next. "Okay. I'll put the 'Closed' sign on the door. We should call Stephanos, if this is a witch hunt."

"Why Stephanos?" Charlene asked. "I thought he was no longer a leader?"

"He's still on the council," Carmen said. "Evelyn too." Her eyes glittered with excitement, and Charlene was reminded of their youth. "Dad says he doesn't know what he'd do without Stephanos." Carmen shrugged. "I don't think Dad gives himself enough credit, but I could be biased. I think he's pretty great."

Kass laughed softly. "The Evergreens are this perfect little family. They actually like being together." Kass scrunched her nose. "I never met my dad, and my mom is not the motherly type. I have a bunch of half siblings, which makes things very noisy around the holidays. Do you have brothers and sisters, Charlene?"

"No, I'm an only child. Most of the time I like my parents." She liked them better now that she'd moved to Salem and her mom wasn't dropping over all the time with an agenda for Charlene's life.

"Me too!" Carmen said. "They went through a lot before they had me—Dad never lets me forget that I'm their blessing from the Goddess."

Carmen and Kass cracked up, and then Carmen looked around the shop. "Come with me—I have something a little stronger than tea. Better than brandy too."

"Thank you for offering to help me clean up the back office, Charlene, but I'll do it later—after the cleansing."

"No problem," Charlene said, suddenly feeling like a third wheel. The younger witches hadn't done it on purpose, but Charlene didn't have their shared history. "I have guests leaving this afternoon and new arrivals to greet. If you both are okay, I should be running along."

"You've been a great help, just by being here," Kass told her. "I'll be open for business again tomorrow."

The young ladies headed across the street, and Charlene hurried to her car. She got in and quickly clicked the lock button, feeling ill at ease now with the two break-ins in this neighborhood, and Morganna's murder unsolved. Something very wicked was going on in the Wiccan community. Could somebody be targeting witches?

But then why would Dylan be under suspicion?

Kevin sent a text that he'd have to reschedule their trip to Ruin until after the weekend, since he was filling in for a tour.

When she arrived home, the Jensen family was in the

kitchen with Minnie. It being Friday, she had worked all day, cleaning the vacated guest rooms and ensuring they would be ready for the mother and her daughter later.

She removed her coat and boots, feeling ridiculously pleased to be in the warmth of her home with boringly sane people instead of witches and covens. "Hi, everyone! What are you all having for lunch?"

Minnie greeted her with a sweep of her wooden spoon. "I made a big pot of chili, and we have all the toppings." Charlene saw bowls of grated cheese, onions, and sour cream. "Picked up some delicious sourdough from the baker's on the way in today."

Peter dropped his spoon on his side plate, making a clatter. "Do we have to leave?" he whined. "I love it here."

Katherine laughed, and Ted pretended to smack the back of Peter's head. "He wrote four pages today, a school report, all about the history of Salem, and the executed witch." Ted wiped his mouth. "I'm sure he'll be a big hit when he gets back to school. Keep us informed, Charlene, and let us know when they find out who was responsible."

She swallowed her concerns that there might be another witch-killing spree and put it down to drama—both women were theatrical, and she'd gotten pulled right in.

"I'll do that." Charlene washed her hands at the kitchen sink and wiped them dry on the towel. After filling a bowl of chili for herself, she took the vacant seat next to the family. She kept the break-ins to herself, not wanting them to worry. "It's going to be lonely here without you all. I've loved having you this week."

"We've enjoyed it too." Katherine gave her a warm smile. "You've done an amazing job with this place, Charlene. Minnie was telling us you haven't even been open two months."

Charlene said, "You should come back next year once the gazebo is finished."

Katherine looked at her husband. "We probably won't get back this way for many years, but I'm sure some of our family and friends would love a visit. We'll send business your way, don't you worry."

"That's kind of you. Please take some brochures with you. Where's Hailey?" she asked, glancing past the kitchen door in search of the girl.

"She's in the living room, saying her goodbyes to Silva," Katherine answered. "She wanted us to pack the cat away in our suitcase, but I told her you'd miss her too much."

Before Silva, Charlene had been anticat, but her sweet Persian had entwined her silver tail around Charlene's heart. "I would." She loaded her chili with cheese, sprinkled on the onion and a dollop of sour cream, then took her first taste. "Excellent, Minnie. As always."

Ted pushed back from the table. "Yes, you have a wonderful cook. I want to pack *Minnie* in my bag and take her home with us." He winked at Minnie. "What would your husband, Will, say about that?"

"He'd probably supply the bubble wrap." Her plump cheeks grew rosy, and she put her hands on her ample hips. "But he'd miss me aplenty."

"I would hog-tie you here, Minnie," said Charlene. "Don't want to lose you, that's for sure."

She pushed her bowl away and stood, knowing she had to stop enjoying Minnie's home cooking quite so much or she'd be twice the size. "Is there anything I can help you with? Order a cab? Pack some snacks for the long flight home?"

"No, thank you." Katherine got up from her chair. "It's sweet of you to offer, but we found a great candy store and picked up some peanut brittle for us, and some gift boxes for family."

"Ye Olde Pepper Companie," Charlene said. "The oldest candy company in America. I try to stay away, but every so often I just have to buy a little something."

Hailey had snuck up behind her and pulled at her sleeve. "Charlene, I made something for you."

"What is it, hon?" Charlene faced the sweet little girl. Her brown curls had been tamed back with a head band.

Hailey pulled a piece of paper from behind her back and grinned. Her missing tooth didn't seem to bother her a bit. "It's a picture. Of the witch."

Charlene accepted the lined notebook paper and admired the drawing as if she were standing in front of the *Mona Lisa* at the Louvre. A very tall witch with a very tall purple hat, and lots of red spiral curls, seemed to be holding a fish bowl filled with sparklers. "Why, it's beautiful. I'll have it framed." She showed it proudly to Minnie, then Ted and Katherine. "Thank you, Hailey."

Peter stuck his tongue out at his sister, and Charlene asked, "Do you have time to show me your school report? I'd love to read it."

"Sorry, son," Ted said. "It's already packed. We need to brush our teeth and get washed up before the cab arrives. Should be here in half an hour."

The Jensens climbed the staircase to complete last-minute packing, and Charlene helped Minnie put away the dishes. "I'll change the sheets as soon as they leave."

"You don't need to do that," Minnie answered. "I'm the employee, and you're the lady of the house. You go get yourself fancied up to meet your new guests. They called from the airport—she sounded like a nasty one, she did."

Charlene rolled her eyes. "I got that feeling as well. But nothing we can't handle, right?"

"I hope so." Minnie snickered. "Otherwise, I'll add another ingredient to their bowl of chili—like a spoonful of Silva's favorite tuna."

"You wouldn't!" Charlene looked down as Silva nudged her head against her leg. "She'd never forgive you."

An hour later, the Jensens were on their way to the airport, and Charlene lit a fire to make the room cozy for her arriving guests. She would do whatever she could to make their two-day visit enjoyable.

She heard the cab pull up in front of the house and opened the door to greet them. Standing in the frame of the door, she noticed the driver get out, go to the rear of his yellow cab, and pull out two carry-on bags.

The woman was about her own age, early forties; her daughter, tall for twelve, slender, with brown hair and a swinging ponytail. They carried their luggage up the white porch stairs and looked surprised when they saw her standing there.

"Hi, I'm Charlene." She widened the door for the two of them to enter. "Mrs. Robinson, and you are Natalie. Welcome to my home, and yours, for the weekend."

Mrs. Robinson brushed past her and dropped her designer purse next to the staircase. She glanced around. Sniffed the air. "What is that?" Silva, head in the air, looking very regal in her red bling collar, had come to greet them as well.

"Our family pet. Silva."

"I'm allergic to cats."

Charlene looked at the haughty woman with the too-thin lips, her hair pulled back in a severe bun, and her plain daughter. "The cat stays. If you'd like different lodging, I'd be happy to help you find something."

Mrs. Robinson made a distasteful grimace, picked up her bag, and said, "Just keep it away from us, and we should be fine. Will you show us the way to our rooms, please?"

Charlene wanted to show her the way to the road; instead she climbed the staircase and walked them to their room. The beds were big, with luxurious duvet covers; fresh flowers arranged in a floral vase sat on their side table; and the curtains were open so they could enjoy the view.

"I suppose this will have to do."

With that, Charlene turned around and walked out, wondering how many minutes were in forty-eight hours.

CHAPTER FIFTEEN

Charlene needed an excuse to leave her home before she lost her patience with the uptight Mrs. Robinson, who had demanded that room—and then dared to complain. Hmph. She'd have to hold the memory of her first week of guests close to the heart and stay out of the nasty woman's way.

She said goodbye to Minnie, then decided to swing by the cop shop and see if Sam was in. She was worried about the two young witches after their break-ins and hoped the police were taking it seriously and adding protection. She couldn't get rid of the feeling that something bad was brewing in their neighborhood and more lives were in danger.

Unfortunately, she *really* wanted to dump on Sam all the things she'd done behind his back, because she believed they were important to the investigation. Since he was unable to confide in her, he might not know that Hammond Cobb was not wallowing in grief but anger. If she dared to tell him about her Facebook chat with Cobb, Sam would not be pleased, but she just had to brace herself for the storm. He needed to know that Morganna had at least one enemy from her past.

She marched up the stairs, past the waving American flag, and into the station around noon. The front desk was unoccupied so she texted Sam that she was in the lobby, half hoping he was out on the job and she could leave a message instead of facing his wrath. As deserved as it was, she still would prefer to avoid it. Her palms grew damp, and she might have turned and fled if she hadn't heard the steady click of his boots against the carpet runner. Too late to slip away.

"Charlene!" Sam's outstretched hand preceded his smile. "What a wonderful surprise."

He was so happy to see her, and she was about to disappoint him again. Her mouth dried. "Hi, Sam." She accepted his hand, and he pulled her into a quick hug. "It's nice to see you too."

"Come on back. I just finished up some paperwork, so I have a few minutes to talk." He gestured to his office. "It's been mayhem around here lately, and you're a breath of sunshine."

"I hope you still feel that way after I tell you what I did. . . ."

He grimaced and ushered her inside his office. She took "her" chair, and he sank down into his. Bringing his elbows onto his desk, he looked at her across the tidy expanse of wood. "All right. Let me have it."

"Sam . . ." She unzipped her jacket but kept it on, knowing she had to make this short. If she kept looking at him, she might not have the nerve to tell him what she'd come to say.

He brought his thumb and forefinger to his smooth-shaven chin. "Let me guess—this is not a social visit. You're here about Morganna."

"Linda Crane, yes." She cleared her throat. "I got to thinking that she must have friends back home, perhaps even family. Someone who loved her. Maybe someone to claim her body." She forged ahead. "I looked through Linda's social media pages on Facebook and located a man named Hammond Cobb. They were obviously close from the photos I saw, but something happened, and they broke up—she started over here in Salem."

She didn't mention tracking Rich down or their brief conversation. She didn't want to drive Sam over the top. He'd been in such a nice mood when he first saw her; now his face had darkened, and his jaw was set with anger.

Sam sat back slowly. "What did you hope to achieve by making this Facebook connection? A new friend?"

She attempted a laugh, which sounded wrong. "Of course not. I'd hoped that Hammond cared enough for her to claim her body. Or maybe he'd be able to tell you how to contact her family. I'm sharing this with you, Sam, in case you didn't know. Hammond Cobb is *happy* that she's dead."

His expression turned incredulous, and he snapped his jaw closed. "I don't even know what to say to that."

"Did you know about Hammond Cobb already?" Before waiting for his answer, she asked, "Is he coming here for her?"

Sam pulled a paper tablet from the middle drawer of his desk and read from the line of notes. "Yes to knowing him. No to his claiming her body." He glanced up at her, and she tried not to wince. "We've got a call in, but he hasn't returned it yet. Maybe we should have gone through you first."

Charlene heard the sarcasm in his voice and straightened her back. She was only trying to help solve this murder—which she wouldn't feel obliged to do if he hadn't accused one of her guests. Questioning Dylan, when Sam should have been looking at Morganna's enemies—she had a long list of them, starting with the local coven. "Well, he's very angry. Not sure if he was angry enough to drive from Ohio and kill her, but you might want to add him to your list of suspects."

Sam put his hand up. "Did you actually talk to this man?"

"No, no—over messaging."

He swallowed and looked at the ceiling as if praying for patience before he returned his hard gaze on her. "Charlene. This man could be dangerous, do you understand that?"

"Yes, but he lives in Ohio."

"Rich Swane is the one who told me about Hammond— you want to know why?" He smiled, not his heartwarming smile, but more like a shark's. She felt like the bait.

She put one leg over the other, feeling antsy. She knew she wasn't going to like the answer.

"Because Hammond did drive to Salem to beg Linda to return to Ohio with him, all sins forgiven."

Charlene's stomach fluttered, and she could feel her face grow warm. "When was he in town?"

"Halloween." The night Morganna had been killed.

"Oh." Had she reached out to console the man who'd murdered Linda? "Oh . . ." She put a hand over her mouth.

"Exactly," Sam said. His eyes had narrowed into mere slits. His voice was deceivingly calm. The shark was closing in.

"Hammond found out that Linda was living with Rich— it seems Linda and Hammond were still in contact via text messages, behind Rich's back—and the two men got into a fistfight outside Pirate's Bar." Sam's jaw was clenched. "Rich told Hammond to get lost, and Hammond said Linda had asked him to rescue her. We picked Rich up later that night for a DUI—he spent the evening in jail, as you know."

"Okay, I get it. So why don't you go to Ohio and bring Hammond in as a suspect?"

"He might not be in Ohio."

"Sure he is. He just messaged me," she said. "Yesterday."

"That doesn't mean Hammond Cobb is there." He leaned closer, and she could hardly breathe. "He can do that from anywhere." Sam rose slowly from his chair. "Charlene, I know I'm frightening you, and I intend to. You must be more careful. The man is a danger, and he could still be around. When did you last correspond with him?"

"Yesterday afternoon." She raised her eyes, hoping he'd see that she was sincerely sorry. "I know you're angry. I'm only trying to help. I'm worried about Kass and Carmen too. Maybe someone is attacking the witches in the city."

"Thank you for your concern. Is there anything else we can do to make you feel safer?"

Was that more sarcasm?

"No, no. It seems as if you're handling the case just fine. I guess I'll tend to my guests while you catch the killer. I just want to see this case close quickly, and not have any more deaths around here."

"We appreciate you being a concerned citizen, and, trust me, we are working to meet that end." He walked her to the front door of the station. "Right now, I'd like to go back to your house with you and see your computer and the message."

"Okay, but he unfriended me, so I don't know if it is still there." She wasn't sure that she wanted an angry Sam Holden in her house. Jack was protective of her and might react unfavorably if Sam got upset. And what would Mrs. Robinson have to say with a police detective coming to the house on official business? "Why don't I just call you if I can find the message?"

He pressed two fingers between his brows. "Doesn't matter—we have a computer wiz that can find anything. We already know about Hammond's and Linda's communication with each other."

"You have Linda's phone?" she asked.

"No. It's still missing." His brow arched, but he didn't ask how she knew. "But I have the phone records. Now, we might need your computer."

"But . . ." Charlene bit her tongue when she saw the line of tension across his brow. "All right. Sam, when I mentioned the witches, I was serious. Did you know that Kass Fortune's Tea Shoppe was broken into? The shop next to Morganna's? Carmen's Clairvoyant shop too."

His frame blocked the door as he stared at her. "You can't help it, can you?"

"I went to buy tea, Sam. How is that my fault?"

"It's like you are a magnet for trouble, Charlene."

"I didn't used to be . . . I used to have a very nice life. Steady, with breakfast in bed on Sunday mornings. Not a single dead body in all my forty-two years."

Surprised, Sam looked at her, blinked, and then started to laugh. "Charlene . . . all right. I'm listening. Come back into the office and tell me what happened at the tea shop."

As he passed the front desk, he spoke to the sergeant on duty. "Patty? Find out what officers responded to a break-in at Fortune's Tea Shoppe this morning. See if there were any other break-ins reported over the last seventy-two hours. Also, keep calling Hammond Cobb. If we are not in contact with him in an hour, call the Ohio police department and dispatch them to his last-known address. Oh, and have the rookie call all of the local hotels to see if Hammond Cobb checked in."

Back in his office, Sam faced her, and she had to swallow back a sigh. Was there anything more attractive than a confident man?

"Have you discovered anything else about Morganna's death? Kass is afraid because nobody has been apprehended . . . It has to be related somehow."

Sam folded his hands in front of him on the desk. "You know we can't discuss this, but let's say we're getting close."

"Do you still suspect Dylan?" She put her hand to her heart. "He has no possible motive. I think he was just hanging out with those Goth kids."

"I asked him to voluntarily give me his prints, and he did. We are still trying to find an answer as to how his jacket ended up at the crime scene. He hasn't recanted losing it earlier that night."

"Hartford is probably safer for him than Salem." She bit her bottom lip.

"I can see that you are worried about your friends. Tell you what—I will put an extra patrol around the neighborhood of the shops. We don't want any more trouble, that's for sure. But with October over, things should quiet down some."

"That's good." Charlene would feel better knowing that Kass and Carmen had more protection. "Have you found Evelyn Flint's book of shadows?" she asked.

"No. Why do you ask?"

"She came to visit me yesterday."

His left eye twitched. "Again, why didn't you tell me sooner?"

"She came for coffee!" *And to tell me about witches.* "You already knew that her book was stolen."

"Tell me again the significance of it—it's a diary?"

"No, a personal spell book. Evelyn's family traces its origins back to Armand Sheffield. He set up the original coven in 1694."

Sam's scowl didn't detract from his rugged good looks. "Are you saying witches existed back then?"

"Since before biblical times, she says. Evelyn is a professor of medieval history, so she would know. Anyway, she's concerned that the wrong person might try to use the book and get hurt."

"I questioned some of the Wiccan community," Sam said. "Evelyn Flint has a very good reputation, and some were sorry when she stepped down as leader. They feel that whoever stole her book will have bad luck." He shrugged. "Morganna certainly did."

Charlene said, "The law of three—whatever you do comes back to you threefold."

"Death is a severe punishment if someone was looking to make a statement."

"Carmen Evergreen said Morganna thought that Evelyn was lying about it being stolen, and just wanted to get rid of her, so accused her."

"Drama and politics." Sam shook his head. "Never mind—any other tidbits I should know?"

Charlene thought back, trying to decide what to tell him. She decided on the simple truth. "Evelyn questioned Morganna's abilities as a witch. Thought she was a fraud. And a thief. She wanted her to be excommunicated from the coven."

"I guess I'm going to have to call Evelyn Flint and Carmen Evergreen back in for more questions."

"You've already questioned them?"

"Evelyn and Morganna's disagreement was common knowledge, so, yes, we've had a few conversations."

He didn't say anything more.

A knock sounded at the door. Officer Tanner and a female officer, an OFFICER PASQUALE from the name tag, waited. "You wanted to see us, sir?"

Sam invited them in, and Charlene took that as her cue to leave. She rose and asked, "Did you want me to bring my computer in?"

"No—I'll stop by later." He checked his watch. "After four okay?"

"Sure." Charlene slipped past the other two officers and out the door to the hall.

They went inside Sam's office and shut the door.

As she reached the lobby, her cell phone rang. It was Flint Wineries.

Would it be Evelyn, with more news from her dream guides? She didn't dare laugh at the woman or hang up on her, either, but she did want a little reality in her life.

"Hello," she answered.

"It's Brandy," the woman on the other line said.

"Oh! Hi."

"Can you meet me for a late lunch, or early happy hour? I'm at Cod and Capers."

Charlene checked the time—just a little after two. It was good she'd had only a small bowl of chili for lunch. "Sure. When?"

"I'm already here, actually, but I can have a glass of wine while I wait."

"I'm just finishing up an errand," Charlene said, thinking that sharing she was at the police station might not be a good idea. "I can be there in fifteen minutes."

"Wonderful!" She sounded genuinely happy to be seeing her.

The last time they'd talked, Brandy had been cool, so Charlene was naturally suspicious at this sudden change of heart. Had Evelyn shared her visit to "Charlene's"?

Charlene wished she had the ball of herbs to return on Evelyn's behalf.

All she said was, "See you there."

CHAPTER SIXTEEN

Charlene arrived at Cod and Capers and scanned the restaurant from the entryway. The full bar was to her right, where Sharon served drinks. Brandy was seated at a window table and looked as beautiful as ever. Her flaming red hair fell over her shoulders in galloping waves, and her emerald eyes were highlighted with dark brown liner. She wore a wool calf-length shirt, brown boots, and a long-sleeved tee, with a knotted scarf at her neck. Yet she seemed pensive holding her glass of wine.

Not sure what to expect, Charlene joined her. "Hey, your call was a nice surprise." She slid into the chair opposite and glanced at the wine. "Is that the new blend?"

"Of course. I can't be seen in town drinking anything else. I've got to endorse my product. Want one?"

"I've actually been craving a Corona, no offense. With fish and chips." Charlene shrugged off her jacket and draped it on an empty chair. "So how's Theo?"

"Don't worry about him," Brandy said with a satisfied smile. "I'm keeping him company in that huge king-size bed. I might be ready for husband number four, or is it five?

I'm starting to lose count." Her eyes flashed with humor. "He's growing on me."

"Oh, that would be awesome," Charlene said in all sincerity. She wished Brandy well, and had no reason to dislike Theo. Although he'd married Jack's wife—within months of his untimely death.

"Yes, well. Don't get too excited. That's this week." Brandy signaled to a young brunette waitress with dimples.

"Hi! I'm Tammy. Would you ladies like a lunch menu, or are you just having drinks? We have a nice mussel appetizer. And the best calamari!"

"Hi, Tammy. I know what I'd like. A Corona Light, slice of lime, and your delicious fish and chips." Charlene glanced at Brandy. "Do you need a menu?"

"No." Brandy swayed her near-empty glass. "I'll have the blackened grouper with fries, and another wine, please."

Tammy dazzled them with a superbright smile, gathered the menus, and bounced away to hand in their order. *Exhausting.* She shifted toward Brandy.

"So do you still have a houseful of guests, or is it quiet now with Halloween over?" Brandy ran her finger down the stem of the glass, then picked it up and swirled it before putting it to her full red lips.

"A wonderful family left yesterday, to be replaced by a dragon lady and her child, who seemed too overwhelmed by her mother to step out of line." She made a little face and chuckled. "Hopefully, they will be busy with the tours. I'm not complaining about the business, but I think I was spoiled with my first guests." They'd felt like friends when they'd left, especially the Jensens. Hailey's picture was on the refrigerator door.

"And what do you do all day in that big house of yours?" Brandy unfolded her paper napkin to free her silverware, giving her an intense look that Charlene couldn't decipher.

"I'm not all the way settled in yet, and I've got plans to

decorate for the holidays, so I don't get to be a lady of leisure, if that's what you think. . . ."

"And here I pictured you stretched before the fireplace with a romance novel and bonbons." Brandy smoothed her wool sweater down her forearm. "Seriously, though—what does the average day look like for you, Charlene Morris, bed-and-breakfast owner?"

"I don't have a full-time housekeeper, so there is plenty to do. Minnie comes every second day, or when I need her. She's very flexible, depending on the guest schedule."

"You do housework?" Brandy scrunched her nose. "With all those bedrooms and baths?"

"It isn't that bad." Charlene wondered what Brandy's point was in this line of questioning. Tammy dropped off their round of drinks, and Charlene raised her bottle. "Cheers." She took a sip of the beer with the tart lime and resolved to not let Brandy intimidate her. "I like what I do, and it's my business, like you have yours."

"Yes, but mine includes a lot of wine tasting, not cleaning toilets." Her grin took the sting away from the words. "I'm sorry—that sounded awful. Being in business for yourself means doing the hard jobs, and it's admirable that you shoulder the load."

"What is the worst thing you've ever had to do?" Charlene kept her voice teasing. "Drink a bitter merlot?"

"Ha!" Brandy settled her elbow on the table. "The worst thing that ever happened was getting stung a hundred times. I must have disturbed a nest because the swarm came at me so unexpectedly. Mom wondered if someone had cast a spell on me."

Charlene felt her jaw drop and closed her mouth.

Brandy waved her hand, the glitter of her diamond ring flashing in the afternoon sun. "Mom and Stephanos gathered the coven and did a cleansing ritual of all negative energy over the vineyard. It never happened again—although

I retain a small anxiety around bees. The buzzing noise gives me the shivers."

"I don't blame you," Charlene said, bringing her jacket around herself. "For the record, I'm happy doing the work. Why not? It is *my* reputation on the line."

"To each his own." Brandy took a swallow of wine. "So is anybody keeping you company on those nights you're alone?"

"Uh . . . no! I don't have a man friend if that's what you're asking." Charlene settled back in her chair, wondering why Brandy had really asked her here. She knew it wasn't for chitchat.

Brandy leaned across the table. "My mother is very intuitive. The night of your party she sensed something in your house. Something not of this world."

"I have no idea what she *sensed*, but my home is fine. However, I think Evelyn must have dropped something from her purse when she was there for coffee." Charlene watched Brandy closely and pinched her fingers together. "A small, round sachet-type thing tied with lavender ribbon. I don't think it was valuable, but . . ."

"Ah yes." Brandy gestured dismissively. "It is nothing to worry about."

"So it wasn't important?" She reached for her Corona again. "That's good. Silva was playing with it, and I may have thrown it out."

"If it's what I think it was, it was only chamomile and lavender, with a pinch of dried dill?" Her lips twitched. "It's used to ward off ghosts."

"Ghosts!" Charlene reached for her napkin and dabbed her chin. She had a feeling that Brandy enjoyed shocking her, but she wouldn't be tricked into revealing her secret. "Why in the world would she carry that?" She remembered Evelyn rubbing her arms and walking around glancing in corners—she'd been aware of Jack, but unable to see him.

"Well, knowing Mom, she probably thinks your place is haunted." Brandy toyed with the scarf at her collar. "Come on, tell me. Is it?"

Charlene laughed and crossed her legs under the table. "What nonsense. Would I be living there if it was?" She caught Sharon Turnberry's eye and waggled her fingers, wondering where their food was. *Come on, Tammy. I need it sooner rather than later!*

"Well, it depends. If it was a male ghost, and a friendly spirit, it might be kind of fun." Brandy's green eyes glittered.

"Seriously? You have a very active imagination. Are you sure you're not a writer or something? Penning mysteries late in the evenings—harvesting wine as a hobby?"

"Some hobby!" Brandy scoffed. "Trust me, running the winery is a full-time job. Why do you think I was curious about the bed-and-breakfast business?"

"You are curious by nature," Charlene said. *Like me.* "Oh, here's the food." Charlene made room on the table for the two plates, eyeing her golden fish and chips with anticipation. "This looks wonderful. I'm sure I'll be taking a box home with me." Leftovers were a single woman's best friend.

"No problem," Tammy trilled. "I know it's a really big order."

"Mine looks perfect," Brandy declared.

Charlene agreed that the blackened fish on Brandy's platter even smelled delicious, but there was something about deep-fried cod with lemon and malt vinegar that satisfied her taste buds.

She took her time squeezing lemon all over her fish, nipping at a fry before they got cold. Why had Brandy invited her for drinks? Was it to find out if her place *was* haunted? Why would that matter to her?

"I'll let Mom know she *lost* it at your place." Brandy sliced a piece of her grouper and took a dainty bite.

They ate in silence for a few moments, but Charlene could feel Brandy watching her, so she set her fork down. "It was a nice surprise when you called, and I'm happy to have lunch with you. I would like us to be friends even though we got off on the wrong foot."

"I would also like that," Brandy admitted.

"So why did you invite me to lunch?" Charlene bit down on a fry.

"Detective Holden has been questioning my mother, and I wondered if you knew why?" Brandy sat back in her chair, all pretense gone.

"Afraid not. He doesn't confide his police business to me." Charlene kept her tone polite but raised her guard against an interrogation. "Why don't you ask your mother?"

"I did, but she won't give me a straight answer." Brandy scooted her seat closer to the table. "You and Sam Holden seem rather close. You're telling me that he doesn't talk about the case with you?"

Charlene swallowed her lemon-soaked bite of whitefish. "He doesn't." No matter how many times she'd tried. She glanced around the room at the other diners. A group of women surrounded one table, talking kids and school soccer leagues. Across from them were two couples looking at tourist maps. Businessmen reading their tablets or phones. Everyday people smiling, chatting, exchanging pleasantries. Why couldn't she and Brandy just have lunch? "I'm sorry I can't help you."

"You and the detective are friends. . . ."

"It's complicated." Charlene ran a finger down the condensation on the Corona bottle. "And a nice break from cleaning toilets."

Brandy choked on a laugh. "Okay, I guess I deserve that." She covered Charlene's hand. "I'm sorry, but I'm really worried. Does he think my mother is a suspect in Morganna's murder?"

"How do *you* know it's a murder?"

"Because he wouldn't be interrogating people like my mother if it was deemed an accident."

True. "They're calling it a possible murder investigation." Charlene picked up another fry to nibble on, getting uncomfortable with this line of questioning.

"He's been out to see my mother twice." Brandy gave her a long look. "Does he know that Morganna stole her spell book?"

She'd told Sam herself, in order to keep the heat off Dylan. Charlene thought of the divide between young and older witches in the Wiccan community. "Could someone besides Morganna have taken it?"

"Look, Charlene. No playing games. I want to know what you know and whether you think my mother is a suspect. If you think that for one moment"—her voice hardened—"then we will never be friends."

Friendship with Brandy was not going to be easy. She closed her eyes for a sec, then let out a sigh as she opened them again. "Honestly? I don't think your mother would kill someone. Do you?"

"Of course not!" Brandy sounded affronted. "If anybody wanted that fraud dead, and with ample reason, it was Martine Evergreen."

Charlene's fork slipped from her fingers and clattered on her plate. "Why?" From what Kass had said, Charlene thought of the Evergreens as tight as the Three Bears.

Brandy studied her as if on the fence about something.

"I understand that Martine and her husband accepted Morganna"—Charlene stumbled over the young woman's name—"into their community only to discover that she was a phony. But that is no reason for murder." She'd almost slipped up and called her Linda, a giveaway that she knew more than she was saying. Her mouth went dry. Picking up the bottle, she then took an extra big sip of her beer.

"There's more to it than that." Brandy tapped her knife on the table, her pretty face lined with anxiety.

"Tell me? What could be so bad?"

Brandy's emerald eyes widened. "You met Morganna. She was young and beautiful, a very confident, appealing woman."

The meeting had been less than fifteen minutes, but Morganna had exuded all of those things. "Okay." Charlene leaned back in her chair. "What does that have to do with it?"

"She was sleeping with Lucas."

"Lucas? Martine's husband?" Her mind whirled at the revelation. "But I thought they were one happy family."

She laughed bitterly. "You thought wrong."

Charlene recalled how Evelyn hadn't said who the people involved in the adultery charge were—was she protecting the coven leader, whom she had backed to take her place? She'd assumed incorrectly that Evelyn had been protecting Stephanos.

Charlene stared at Brandy. Could Martine have killed Morganna out of jealousy? Passion, love, and greed were the most likely reasons to kill someone. Had she acted alone, in order to keep their positions as high priest and high priestess?

She preferred thinking that Martine was guilty compared to Evelyn, but that wasn't exactly fair. Should she tell Sam to look at Martine as a suspect, or would her "meddling" only irritate him more?

"Tell me again about Martine and Lucas," Charlene said. "What do they do?"

"Martine is an account manager at Salem Federal Bank, and Lucas has a bookshop on the other side to the wharf."

"A witchcraft bookstore?"

Brandy sighed. "I think he collects antique books and manuscripts. The usual New Age stuff but not completely touristy. It's been years since I've been in. He and Mom would go on about medieval authors and actually understand one another." She sipped from her water glass. "This has been very hard on Mom."

"Morganna's death?"

"Yes, that—but, also, she's lost respect for Lucas, someone she'd believed had integrity. Human failings can be hard to watch."

Could Lucas have killed Morganna, somehow thinking her death would save his marriage?

"I always wondered if he harbored a tiny bit of resentment"—Brandy pinched her fingers together—"over the fact that his wife and daughter had more magick in their pinkie than he had at all. Maybe the affair placated his pride."

Charlene put her knife and fork together on the side of her plate. "I've lost my appetite. It was so good too," she said sadly.

"I don't think I can eat anymore either." Brandy pushed her platter of grouper away, and Charlene signaled Tammy over.

"We weren't as hungry as we thought. Could you please box them both up? I'll take the check."

"No, you don't." Brandy stopped her from taking out her wallet. "We'll split it since we are both working girls."

"Fine." She had to share this information with Sam and hoped it wouldn't mean the end of her and Brandy's fragile friendship. Or hers with Sam.

"Will you do me a favor and convince your detective to interview someone other than my mom?"

"I can't make Sam Holden do a thing," Charlene said. "But if the conversation comes around to Evelyn, I'll let him know that I don't think she is responsible. It's the best I can do, Brandy."

The ladies left the restaurant together, Brandy driving home to the winery. Charlene sat in her Pilot for several minutes, thinking things over.

It was only three in the afternoon on Friday, and Sam wasn't due at the B and B until after four. Martine Evergreen had a lot at stake with her husband, the leader of their Wiccan community, having an affair with the sexy wannabe witch in town.

Did she have enough time to pay Martine a visit and open a new account at Salem Federal Bank?

CHAPTER SEVENTEEN

Charlene looked up the address for Salem Federal Bank and plugged it into the GPS, then drove the short distance, skirting pedestrians who dashed across main streets with no regard for safety.

From everything Charlene heard, she believed Martine to be a loving mother and wife, but even good women did bad things when they discovered their husbands had been unfaithful. Mrs. Lorena Bobbitt was living proof.

She found a parking spot on Washington Street, only half a block from the bank.

The bank was a midsize historic brick building similar to others in Salem, peppering the landscape with deep reds. The Georgian Colonial architecture with its boxed edges and multiple windows on both front and sides was even more striking against the fall trees. She pushed open the door to the bright and cheery lobby. Brandy had said that Martine was the accounts manager, so Charlene's plan was to transfer her savings account from Chicago to Salem and meet a key player in this drama.

A row of tellers faced the door, with three people in line. On the right-hand side were individual glassed-in offices:

one for the manager, one for loans and mortgages, another for business accounts. To the left of the entrance were two desks, each with a woman seated behind a computer. One had a customer; the other did not.

Charlene made her way to the dark-haired fortysomething woman who had her head down, fingers flying over the keyboard as she transferred information from a folder to the computer. "Hi." Charlene spoke quietly, sorry to disturb the woman's work.

Preoccupied, the lady looked directly at Charlene, her thin lips pinched. "May I help you?"

The other employee's customer had just left, and Charlene was tempted to ask *her* about how to find Martine when she noticed the woman's name on her desk. MARTINE EVERGREEN. The pale woman rose to offer her hand and introduced herself as the new accounts manager.

Charlene kept a neutral expression as she tried to put this woman, so fragile as if suffering an illness, with her daughter. Carmen oozed confidence and turned heads by walking into the room. The girl had to take after her father.

Martine seemed more frightened brown mouse than murderess, and Charlene almost changed her mind.

How many times had she been told in the past week that people were not as they appeared?

That thought prodded her to step forward. "I'm so pleased to meet you." Charlene shook her hand. "I'm Charlene Morris—I own the bed-and-breakfast on Crown Point Road."

"Ah yes. Ernie Harvey was in before Halloween, and he mentioned that you'd bought the place." Martine brought her hands together at her ultraslender waist. "So how do you like it here? Are you settling in well?"

Good ol' Ernie. My no-good, swindling realtor. Charlene kept her smile in place. "Yes, I like it very much, and business has gotten off to a nice start."

"Wonderful. Would you like to open a business account

with us, or personal? I only do checking and savings, but Mr. Garwood handles the business, and he doesn't have anyone there with him." Martine glanced to one of the glassed-in rooms where Mr. Garwood was polishing his lenses.

"Most everything is online, so I haven't been in a hurry to transfer my accounts, but I'd like to open a personal one here. Do you have time for me now, or should I make an appointment?" Charlene was conscious of the ticking clock and Sam.

"Now is fine. Please have a seat." Martine gestured toward the wooden folding chair with beige upholstery over a thin cushion. "I'll need your current address and phone number. Do you have your license updated?"

"Yes." Charlene perched on the edge of the seat and opened her large bag, reaching for her checkbook and wallet. Her fingers brushed the hard plastic case of the pepper spray she'd decided to keep near until the murderer was caught.

She handed over her driver's license, noting the framed picture of the three Evergreens, before Carmen dyed her hair. The trio faced the camera with smiles, Lucas and Martine on either side of Carmen, beneath an oak tree. "I've met your daughter, Carmen, and her friend Kass."

"Oh?" Martine gathered the items before her, avoiding the photo. Charlene noticed that Martine wasn't wearing a wedding band. Was that a Wiccan thing? But, no, there was a pale strip of skin that suggested a band used to be there, probably for a long time.

"She's beautiful."

Martine gave a slightly proud maternal smile. "We value things besides looks, Mrs. Morris."

"Charlene, please." She inched closer, her shoulder to the other employee seated at the next desk. "Like the rule of three?"

Martine dropped Charlene's license and glanced at the employee at the next desk as if worried the other woman, typing information into her computer, might have heard. Her mouth worked as she stared at Charlene. "What an odd thing to say," she managed in a small, hurt voice.

"I've learned so much since I've been here. About witches and the Wiccan faith."

Martine's body jerked, and her wan face grew splotchy. "I don't discuss religion in my workplace. Are you here to open an account or pry into my business?"

"I'm sorry," Charlene said. "I just assumed that in Salem . . ."

"One still needs to blend in." Her eyes sparked with annoyance. "Our faith is accepted because the town thinks of it as a joke, or as a way to bring in tourists. I am not about to parade my beliefs before you to satisfy your curiosity." She peered into Charlene's eyes as if reading her mind. "If you want to know more about our way of life, then my daughter or my husba—Lucas can help you."

Charlene sat back at the rebuke. This woman's faith was sincere, but not everybody believed it. Had she somehow picked up on Charlene's reasons for being here? A fishing expedition?

Martine rose, and Charlene saw true strength behind the woman's fragile appearance as she gathered Charlene's paperwork. "I have a headache. I'm sorry." Her tight brow gave proof to her pain. "Barb, will you please help Charlene set up her account?"

Without taking anything, not a purse or a phone, not even a jacket, Martine simply walked out the door and onto the street.

Where could she go in this weather? It was windy and chilly, in the low fifties.

Charlene stood, and the young woman behind the desk a few feet away gave her a sympathetic smile, as robust in her demeanor as Martine had been delicate. "I'm happy to help you. Martine is prone to migraines. Never had one, but everyone swears they are painful. Sit!" Barb pointed to the vacant chair before her desk. "We can have you set up in a jiffy."

Charlene went through the motions, wondering if Martine had truly just read her mind. She was the high priestess of the Salem coven, a woman of power in her community. Her own daughter said that her mother had a true gift. What had spooked Martine into leaving like that?

Going to her car, she called Sam and left a message asking to postpone his coming to the house until five. Martine had told her to check with Lucas—maybe not in a sincere way, but Charlene had to meet him. Where did he fit in this situation?

Something was up with Martine. The woman was clearly frightened, but of what or whom? Was she hiding information to help someone, or did she have a secret too heavy to bear?

Martine had motive to kill Morganna. But then so did Lucas. He had a very good reason to want Morganna gone— to save his rocky marriage. It was obvious that Martine was suffering.

She searched online for the bookstore, finding one by the name of Evergreen's a mile away. Within moments she pulled alongside the store with a green awning in front. After lucking out with a parking spot, Charlene went inside with uncertainty.

A bookstore has a certain smell that book lovers absorb, and as soon as she entered, she was hit with paper, old leather bindings, and the promise of escape.

Unlike his wife, Lucas Evergreen was the picture of health: a big, strong man who exuded charm and energy. Stylishly messy dark blond hair, brown eyes that warmed in greeting.

"Hello!" He circled the counter, dressed in dark jeans, black boots, and a nubby black sweater. "Welcome to Evergreen's!"

Charlene was drawn farther inside. "Thank you. You must be Lucas?"

"Have we met?" He clasped her hand for a firm shake.

"No, but I've met your daughter." It was on the tip of her tongue to compliment her, but Charlene stopped, remembering Martine's reaction.

"Ah, Carmen." His eyes crinkled at the corners with his smile. "Our clairvoyant? Down by the Peabody? She is something else, isn't she?" he said with fatherly pride.

"Yes—her shop was very . . . theatrical." Charlene gave herself points for being diplomatic.

"Did you have a tarot reading?" He tucked one hand into his pocket and leaned the other against a bookshelf filled with ink pots and feather pens for sale.

"No." She glanced around the walls of books, wishing she had more time. She'd love to have a bookshelf at the B and B, so her guests could learn more about the history of Salem and the neighboring towns during their stay. "I prefer to keep my future a surprise."

His laugh boomed. He was a larger-than-life kind of guy. She could see his appeal to women—especially to someone like Morganna, who enjoyed the company of men and had few scruples.

"What's your name?" he asked. Unlike Martine, he wore his wedding band and had pictures of his family behind the cash register and on the wall.

"Charlene Morris. I moved here from Chicago at the end of September."

"You have the old Strathmore place, don't you? Carmen was telling us about it."

"I do!" she agreed.

"I've always loved that house, and I bet it makes a perfectly charming bed-and-breakfast. I'd be curious to see what you've done with it."

"Just call before you stop by—I'll give you a tour of the

place. Come for happy hour on Friday or the weekend, if that suits you better. Bring your wife!"

"Oh—have you met Martine?"

"Briefly, at the bank. I'm afraid I offended her, and that was not my intent. I brought up your family's belief in Wicca."

He sucked in a breath and widened his eyes. "Never at work, that's the cardinal rule. Though Carmen, like all children, forged her own path." He leaned forward confidentially. "I don't mind as much. Then again, I don't work at a bank."

It seemed like a confining career when one could work at a bookshop such as this. But to each his own. "I'm sorry if I embarrassed or made trouble for her."

"I'm sure it's fine. Martine's been at the bank for fifteen years. Me, I would be stifled, but Martine likes the order of numbers. Most days it suits her perfectly." He shifted back a step and crossed his arms in front of his chest.

"Would you convey my apologies when you see her? She had a migraine. . . ."

His eyes clouded. "Ah. She will be home in a dark room for a while then, poor dear. I've learned that when the ladies of the house don't feel well, it is best for me to work late." This was said with a conspiratorial wink.

"I hear they are terrible. I hope Carmen didn't inherit her migraines?"

"She's had some health issues. You know about her . . . gifts?"

Charlene hesitated before saying, "Psychic gifts? Yes."

"She is a true visionary." His face glowed. "Carmen and Martine are both powerful witches. I think this takes a toll on them physically. It is my job to care for them and protect them."

Would he be jealous that his power was not as great? Might that be a reason to dally with Morganna, to boost his ego, as Brandy had suggested?

"Evelyn Flint is a friend of mine, and her daughter,

Brandy." Charlene watched Lucas's face for his reaction—his jaw clenched before he smiled.

"Ah, Evelyn. We used to talk about books and a great many other things. A most intelligent woman."

She recalled Brandy saying that Evelyn felt as if she'd lost a friend in this man who had shown human fallibility by cheating on his wife. He seemed very fond of Evelyn, and it must have been hard for him to lose her respect.

His affair had come at a great cost to them all. Did he regret it? Had he resented Morganna for it? Enough to have plotted her death? With all the books in this place, it wouldn't be hard to gain knowledge about certain chemicals that could induce death. He was strong, intelligent, and confident. He also had motive. She steered the conversation a safer direction. "So you support Carmen's store?"

"Oh yes—and Martine does in her own way, don't get me wrong. We love our daughter very much. In fact, I carry these tarot cards that she designed. She's infused them with magickal properties."

Charlene followed Lucas to the box of tarot cards, which were a deep aqua, like the Caribbean. She recognized them from the night of the murder when Carmen had a booth at the festival and had done a reading for Sal and Sheila. "How many of these sets are there?"

"A limited edition," Lucas said, pride evident. "Only five decks. Carmen insisted that she didn't want the power in them weakened by making too many." He made a flourishing gesture with his hands. "So what can I interest you in today? Historical books, something for the coffee table?"

Her phone dinged, signaling a text. Sam, asking if everything was okay.

"Oh, I'm very sorry, but I have to go," Charlene said reluctantly. "But I will be back to browse—and buy." If he wasn't a murderer. "You have a terrific store."

"Thank you, thank you. And don't worry about Martine.

She is having a rough time right now, but I am doing everything in my power to make things right."

He walked with her toward the door.

"If you see Evelyn, let her know I send greetings?"

"I will."

Charlene thought about his words the whole ride home.

How would he "make things right"?

Murder?

CHAPTER EIGHTEEN

Her mind spinning like a rabid lab rat, Charlene drove straight home to get there before Sam, who was on his way to pick up her computer. What in the world would she tell him? That she'd casually run into Martine and Lucas today—at the bank, and then the bookstore?

Dang it, why did he have to be so difficult? A murderer was on the loose, and she hated to think it might be Lucas, but if it was, then he needed to pay for his crime. No good deed goes unpunished. Well, that went for bad deeds too.

She parked her car in the driveway and marched to her door, carrying her tote and leftovers from Cods and Capers. She hoped the fish wasn't tainted, but the cold weather was probably as good as the fridge.

Above, the sky had darkened and thunder roared. A crack of lightning split the clouds in half. The wind had picked up, and the oak trees ominously waved their heavy branches. She went inside and quickly locked the front door behind her.

With her back to the door, she took a couple of deep breaths. It had been a nerve-racking hour with Martine and Lucas, digging for information. She'd discovered that

Martine was not happily married and had known about her husband's affair. Lucas wanted to make things right. Could he?

She understood that stirring the pot might make people angry. But what choice did she have? Dylan's freedom was at risk, and she feared for her young Wiccan friends.

Silva darted from beneath the stairs to greet her. "Hey, kitty, did you smell something good?"

The beautiful silver Persian responded by wrapping herself around Charlene's ankles, rubbing her head against Charlene's calf. The final touch was the throaty purr.

"Okay." Charlene caved as she brought her things to the kitchen table. "But it's my dinner, not yours. You can have one little piece, all right?"

Silva raced her to the cat dish, tail high. Charlene broke off a piece of fish and tossed it into the bowl. With a mere twenty minutes to spare, Charlene logged on to her computer in her private living room and took off her coat.

As a professional woman, she'd learned to be organized with folders and used the cloud to back up all her files, and a second external drive for extra protection. Gnawing on her bottom lip, she leaned on the backrest of her love seat and looked out the window to the oak tree.

It wouldn't hurt if she opened the conversation with Sam by saying she'd gone to the bank and met Martine Evergreen when opening a new account. It was the truth—and harmless.

Then she might share her observation that Martine was in poor health. Dare she say that Brandy had suggested Martine might have been seeking revenge on Morganna for sleeping with her husband?

Charlene hadn't asked for that information—Brandy had dumped it on her so that she'd tell Sam and get him to back off Evelyn.

Martine certainly had reason to want Morganna dead,

but Charlene couldn't see that mousy woman doing something so vile. She couldn't imagine fragile Martine climbing the rickety black metal fire escape up to the roof to stuff Dylan's jacket in the vent. At night.

Not that she was dismissing anyone as a suspect. Not even Lucas—who she'd liked on the spot.

Silva came from the kitchen to her love seat and jumped next to her with a deep rumble. Petting the cat, she realized that no matter how she told Sam what she'd learned, he wouldn't be pleased.

A blast of cold preceded the presence of her roommate. "Jack?"

A wavy shadow strengthened before her until forming the full image of a man. Jack, in black denims and a crimson Henley, reclined in the armchair beneath the window. "Yes?"

"You're here!" She closed her laptop. "It's been a long day, and I'm so glad to see you."

"What's wrong?" He straightened, leaning forward, his forearms on his knees, focusing his attention on her.

She sighed. "I had lunch with Brandy. Evelyn can sense you. That net thing that Silva was playing with? It's supposed to banish ghosts."

Jack's laughter reverberated around her in warmth. "Didn't work, obviously. Is that what has you worried? I'm not going anywhere, Charlene."

Charlene nervously rubbed her hands together. She saw herself as a regular person. She wasn't one of those people that walked around seeing dead people, yet she could see Jack while others couldn't. What did that make her then? Did she have special abilities that she didn't know about? The idea made her stomach flip.

"That's good news, Jack. I don't want you to get accidentally sent away. Not by magic in a sachet, or by a witch ball, no matter how pretty they are."

"It's not going to happen. I'll decide when it's time to leave, no one else. Happened once, won't happen again," he assured her.

She headed for the kitchen. "I am out of tea, which is a long story. Want some cocoa?" she asked her friendly ghost in jest.

"Wish I could join you. So tell me about your day. Was it good or bad?"

"It was interesting, I'll say that." She microwaved a cup of hot chocolate, added a marshmallow, and carried it over to the table, waiting for Jack to sit in his favorite chair. She propped her elbows on the tabletop. "Brandy also told me that Sam has questioned Evelyn about Morganna's murder twice. She mentioned Morganna slept with *Lucas*, the new high priest."

"This is like a daytime drama. No wonder you look a little shaken up."

"Do I?" Charlene pushed her long, disheveled hair off her face and tucked it behind her ears. "It has been that sort of day."

Jack chuckled. "What else happened?"

"I went to see Sam to give him some information that he already knew. He's furious with me for asking questions and getting involved in the murder investigation. But I didn't mean to—I went to buy tea from Kass at her shop. Because we're out!" She glanced down at her cocoa.

Jack's brow lifted as if he didn't quite believe her motive to be true.

"When I got there, the police were out front because she'd been broken into. Then Carmen showed up saying someone had tried to get into her place as well."

"Uh-huh." He crossed his knee over the other and drummed his fingers on the table. "Charlene, that doesn't sound like anything that might make the detective mad."

"Well . . ." She cupped her hands around the hot chocolate. "I told him that I'd messaged Hammond Cobb on Facebook."

"Now, that might do it." She heard the humor in his voice and peeked at him through her hair to see that he was trying not to smile. "And what did our detective friend say to that?"

She swallowed a lump in her throat. "He said that Hammond was not grief-stricken in Ohio but that he'd been here, in Salem, on Halloween, the night his girlfriend was murdered."

Jack straightened and braced both feet on the floor in a whoosh of cold air. "What?"

"Yeah. Rich Swane, Morganna's boyfriend, found out that Hammond had come to town to see Morganna, wanting her back. They got into a fight. Sam doesn't know if Hammond is still in town or back in Ohio. Obviously, Hammond isn't answering Sam's calls."

"Obviously."

A hard knock sounded on the front door. Before she could get up to answer it, there were two more sharp raps. "Sam's here. For my computer. You might want to leave."

"No," Jack said, his blue eyes full of concern. "On the contrary, I would very much like to stay."

"Suit yourself." Charlene answered the door. The scent of rain rushed inside.

Sam stood on the porch, shaking out his umbrella over the railing to the shrubs below. His dark hair was damp, and his broad shoulders hadn't been adequately protected under the small fold-up umbrella. He grinned when he saw her. "I almost had to take the boat," he joked.

"Come in." She laughed. "It's nasty out there."

"You can say that again." He remained in the doorway, and a few drops fell onto the foyer carpet. "The road up here was a muddy mess, and rain is predicted all night. Best if you stay in tonight."

"That was my plan." It had been a long, stressful day. "I'm having cocoa. Would you like a cup? Or a coffee?"

"Better not. I don't want to mess up your floors." He brushed drops from his shoulder and forehead.

"You won't. Stay there for one second and take off your boots. I'll get a towel."

He did as he was told, and she returned with a hand towel for him to mop up with. "Cocoa or coffee?"

"You got a strong coffee in there?"

"Dark roast or bold?"

"Either works, thank you."

"Want to sit next to the fire? It'll be more pleasant than the kitchen."

She had to scoot Silva off one of the chairs to make way for Sam. She couldn't see Jack, but she doubted that he'd gone far away. His curiosity would get the better of him.

"Cream or sugar?"

"Cream, please."

When she came back with the two cups balanced on a small serving tray and a plate with four cookies, Sam was already sitting down, his feet on an ottoman. Jack stood facing the fire, his back to Sam.

She took the seat next to Sam and offered him a cookie. Jack turned around, his face glowing from the warmth of the fire. His cheekbones stood out, his dark hair was swept back, his blue eyes almost black. Like the devil himself.

Well, if he was jealous, it was his own fault! She'd told him to leave.

Sam couldn't see Jack, so when Silva jumped up and snarled at the fire, scratching her paws in the air, he just laughed. "That is one crazy cat."

"You got that right. I never thought I'd be a cat person." She nibbled on the edge of a shortbread cookie. "Sam . . ."

"What?" He sipped his coffee with pleasure, then shot her a look of disappointment. "Don't tell me you've been meddling again."

"Who, me?" She gave a short laugh. "I don't have to meddle—people just seem to want to tell me things." She shrugged and widened her eyes.

"Like what?"

"Brandy called before I'd even left the station today and invited me for a late lunch. She wanted to know why you've been questioning her mother." Her instincts were telling her to shut up now and drink her cocoa, but her tongue kept flapping away. "Brandy said you should be looking at Martine, that she has more reason for wanting Morganna—Linda Crane—dead. You want to know why?"

Sam balanced his cup and saucer on his knee, the short-bread halfway to his mouth.

Charlene spoke with triumph. "Morganna was sleeping with Lucas, Martine's husband."

His cookie fell into his plate. "No shit."

"Don't swear."

"Sorry." He put his mug down on the coffee table, his fingers to his lips in thought. His damp hair curled around his ears and weathered forehead. He wasn't a pretty boy, but a *manly* man.

"So?" He didn't seem mad. Not yet, anyway. She picked up the rest of her cookie and dunked it in the cocoa for a proper bite.

"So that's interesting. What else did she tell you?" His gaze roamed over her, heating her from within.

"Not much. Brandy was more interested in what I had to say, but I didn't say anything. Not about Morganna's real name, or that Hammond was here—nothing like that. You'd have been proud of me." She practically batted her eyelashes for Sam's approval.

Jack stood behind her and whispered in her ear. "What are you doing, Charlene? Flirting?"

Sam's eyes narrowed in on hers.

She perched on the edge of her chair, refusing to let a ghost have the last word. "Sam, what are you going to do about Hammond? If he's guilty, he won't contact you. If he's not, I'd think he'd call. Don't you?"

"Agreed. The longer he hides from me, the more he becomes a person of interest." Sam finished his cookie in two bites. "Course, he could be dead."

"Dead? Holy crap! Please, no more death. I've had enough." *Like any sane woman.* Trying to keep the tone light she asked, "Do you really think it's possible that I might be a magnet for trouble?"

Sam wasn't in the mood for jokes. "No. I was merely trying to get you to be sensible and stay out of trouble."

"You're a magnet, all right," Jack said, moving around the chair to watch her face. "He's attracted to you. Can't you see that?"

She turned her head so she wouldn't have to look at her angry houseguest. She almost purred when she spoke to Sam. "Sam, can I get you some more coffee? Or something stronger? A shot of brandy perhaps?"

"No. I have to get back to the office, unfortunately. I've asked the tech department to come in even though it's Saturday. They're none too happy."

"I hate to give up my computer, but I suppose for a few days I can use my iPad. Will you call me when it's ready?" She gave him a long look, wondering why she was acting this way. She felt Jack's anger, but it was all so unfair. She was living with a ghost, but there were times in the past two years when she'd missed a flesh-and-blood man— being held as if cherished.

The events of the day, between Kass's break-in, the Jensens leaving, the dragon lady arriving, Brandy's assurance that Evelyn knew this house was haunted, the fear that Jack might leave, and Martine's fragile demeanor caused by Lucas, who exuded good health and good will, all combined to make her feel rather vulnerable. Sam's strength beckoned. What would it be like to lay her head against his chest and just have him hold her?

The tray of cookies tipped over and landed on the carpet. Silva pounced.

Charlene jumped up, knowing Jack had tipped it and not Silva. "Let me fix this. Then I'll get you the computer." Before Jack went for something bigger than the cookie tray.

"You go," Sam said, dropping to a knee. "I'll clean these up."

She hustled off to her living area and gathered her laptop, putting it in a spare case. Jack was not around. Probably just as well, or she'd let him have a piece of her mind.

Charlene returned to a tidy pile of mugs and saucers set carefully on the coffee table, and Sam standing before the fireplace.

"I've backed up my files, in case anything goes wrong." She handed the case over by the shoulder strap.

"Smart, but my team is pretty good."

She shrugged. "Oh—I suppose that now isn't a good time to ask if you'd heard anything else from the fire marshal?"

Sam's sigh would have shaken the rafters, if she had any. "Nothing I can share with you." He strode toward the front entrance. "I'll get this back to you within a few days." He didn't bother putting his coat on, instead draping it over her case.

It had stopped raining, and Charlene waited at the threshold until Sam reached his car. He turned and waved, and she slowly shut the door.

"Jack! How could you?"

But he was no longer there.

As Sam's SUV rolled out of sight, a cab entered the driveway to drop off Mrs. Robinson and her daughter.

The last thing Charlene wanted to do was entertain this woman, but she'd chosen this career, and dealing with all sorts of people was part of it.

"Hello!" she said, widening the door for them as they clattered up the porch.

Natalie smiled in response while her mother said nothing.

"Did you have a good time? What did you see?"

The little girl practically shook with excitement as they entered the foyer and took off their coats. Mrs. Robinson reached for Natalie's and held them both out to Charlene.

"We saw real witches and ghosts and old-fashioned buildings, and we had pizza, and I'm so glad we came." Natalie lifted her head to look at her mother. "Thank you, Mama." She turned to Charlene. "It's my birthday present. Mom got to have me for the weekend."

Charlene thawed toward the little girl and realized that the uptight Mrs. Robinson might have a reason for being so tense and angry. If Charlene had children and had to share custody, she wouldn't like it at all.

"That sounds perfect. Happy birthday, Natalie." Charlene gestured to the couches and chairs and merrily crackling fire. "You are welcome to use the living room. There are games and a television. Would you like some cocoa?"

"That won't be necessary." Mrs. Robinson hefted her pointy chin. "We are cleaning up and then taking a cab to dinner and a play in Boston. We will be late returning home. Is that a problem?"

"No! You have your key—that sounds like a wonderful night." Charlene was very curious as to how these two guests had discovered her bed-and-breakfast, but no matter what, she would make sure they were welcome.

CHAPTER NINETEEN

Saturday morning, Charlene made a large pot of coffee for herself and her guests, pulling out sausages and eggs from the refrigerator to serve a nice weekend breakfast. Whether she had two guests or twelve, her brochure promised a full breakfast on weekends, and continental during the week—included in the nightly fee.

She hadn't heard any movement upstairs, so she enjoyed her first cup of java while listening to some eighties music on the radio. Her business number rang with two women needing a place to stay that night. Sharon Turnberry had recommended her bed-and-breakfast, and Charlene gave a silent thanks to the owner of Cod and Capers. She took their credit card information over the phone, gave directions, and said their rooms would be available by noon.

Before she could be too pleased with herself, Mrs. Robinson appeared in the doorway of the kitchen, hair loose, wearing a gray floor-length robe. "Good morning." She spoke in a commanding kind of way rather than friendly. "I hope I didn't startle you, but you were rambling to someone on the phone. I tried to get your attention."

"I'm sorry." Charlene inwardly bristled. "It was a new reservation."

"Well, if it's not too much trouble, my daughter and I would enjoy coffee, juice, and muffins for our room." She stood there, as if the order would magically appear.

Not a hint of warmth showed on her face. Charlene was ultrapleasant as she asked if they'd liked the play in Boston. "What did you see? I haven't been to the theater in years, but my husband and I loved to go. We lived in Chicago, you know."

The woman froze her with a glare. Not a morning person, then, she thought.

Charlene, determined to be polite even if it killed her, said, "I normally do full breakfast on the weekend."

"No need for that," Mrs. Robinson responded. "Muffins are fine. Maybe a piece of fruit if you have something easy."

"Very well." Charlene put together a tray as the woman watched over her shoulder. She added a banana and an orange, following the women's request.

"Thank you," Mrs. Robinson said, lifting the tray with shaky hands.

"I'd be happy to bring it upstairs," Charlene offered.

"I can manage." The woman looked so rigid, her back iron straight, chin determined as if she were going out to battle instead of relaxing for a weekend.

Charlene felt sorry for Natalie, having this tense woman for a mother. She was wired so tight that at any moment she could break.

Then it happened.

The woman collapsed into tears at the kitchen table, the tray sliding across the top. Jack appeared at her side, studying the woman with interest.

"Mrs. Robinson, are you all right?" Charlene glanced

over at Jack, but he shook his head, as confused as she was. "Do you have medication that you need? Can I get anything for you?" She gently placed her hand on the woman's shoulder.

The woman didn't reply but shook her hand off. Charlene tried again. "What is wrong? How can I help?"

Mrs. Robinson sniffed into her gray flannel sleeve. "I'm a terrible mother," she whispered in a broken voice.

Jack said in a soft tone, "Ask her why she thinks that? She seems on the verge of a breakdown." He scanned the woman and breathed in the air around her. "I don't see any sign of alcohol or drug abuse. I think she has a malaise of the heart." He lifted his eyes to hers. "Emotional issues. Go ahead, ask her."

Clearing her throat, Charlene then asked, "Why do you say that? It's obvious to me that your daughter adores you."

"Her father is a very wealthy man and can buy her whatever she wants. How can I compete with that?" Sobs shook her body, but Mrs. Robinson didn't wait for an answer. "I lost full custody because he had better lawyers."

"You have joint custody then?" she asked, knowing that most working couples in a divorce situation had to accept this new reality. The child flip-flopped between two homes.

"Yes. He has her every second weekend. This year I lucked out to get her over her birthday. He tells her things and is trying to turn Natalie against me. He's an evil man, but nobody sees it. I have a good job. I'm responsible. She's got a great home with me. I have money—just not as much as him."

Jack hovered with concern behind the woman. Charlene took her trembling hands and squeezed. "Your daughter knows you love her—and she loves you. I saw the two of you together yesterday. And you are doing what she wants for her birthday. What a nice present! But probably time with you is the best gift."

"Raj texted me this morning—he wants me home Sunday afternoon, so he can celebrate a part of her birthday with her. But this is our weekend, not his. He takes and takes, and is so demanding that I usually give in. But not this time."

Charlene braced her shoulders as she listened.

The woman's lip quivered. "He's a very forceful man, and I try to keep the peace, but Nat and I only have these two days and I don't want to give them up. Would he do that for me? Never." Her voice rose.

Charlene handed her a paper napkin, and the woman wiped her eyes as the tears slowed but didn't stop.

"It just makes me so angry, and there is nothing I can do about it. The more I fight back, the worse he behaves. Late with the checks, poisons Natalie's mind by saying bad things about me." She sobbed. "He's told her I'm mentally ill." She looked into Charlene's face. "He drives me crazy, but I'm not!"

"Tell her not to give in, to be strong," Jack suggested. "And if things get worse, she should call her lawyer after documenting *everything*. I helped a patient against an abusive husband that way once."

Charlene nodded and then realized Mrs. Robinson couldn't hear Jack. "You have to be strong, for Natalie's sake. She sees that you love her—you are her *mother*." She patted the woman's back. "If I were you, I'd just enjoy the day and ignore his threats and bullying. Are you documenting everything that he does? Even the small things. You could present it to your lawyer."

Mrs. Robinson sniffed and wiped the last of her tears from her face. She drew in a deep breath and tightened the belt around her robe. "I haven't been, but I will start. I'll create a file, so that I have documentation in the event things get worse." Her eyes grew fierce again. "That's a great suggestion, actually." Her red-rimmed eyes misted. "It was Nat who found this bed-and-breakfast online—she wants to swing beneath the oak tree. She's fascinated by the history of Salem." Mrs. Robinson flipped her loose blond hair back. "I grew up in Boston. I didn't realize how much I've missed it until seeing it again."

"Is that why Natalie chose this area? Because of the things you've told her about growing up, and maybe she could see how happy you were then?"

The woman's brow furrowed. "She's such a sweetheart that I shouldn't be surprised." She rose. "Thank you very much for your kind words—and advice. Please, call me Diane."

Footsteps raced down the central stairs, and Natalie, wide-eyed with worry, entered the hall. Diane's smile was soothing and filled with deep maternal love. Charlene brought her hand to her heart and exchanged a look with Jack.

Charlene quickly organized the tray once more. "Here you are. Your mom was bringing you breakfast in bed."

Natalie wrapped her arms around her mother's waist, and Diane squeezed her daughter close.

"Hungry, peanut?" Diane asked, petting Natalie's hair.

"Yum! Let's sit by the window and look out at the tree. It's so pretty here. Peaceful. Not like Daddy's house. He never lets me watch cartoons in bed."

"Well, we can do anything you please, young lady. Spend all day in our pajamas if we want."

Charlene watched the two of them walk away, and, smiling, she turned to Jack.

"Thank you, Jack." Charlene shook her head at him. "I was so wrong about her."

"The one thing that I learned from being a doctor that took me by surprise was that people are complicated creatures. You think that A plus B equals C, but everybody is different."

"We certainly are." She laughed wryly at the realization that though she'd been warned that people were not what they appeared, she'd still misjudged—and made a promise to herself to be better.

"Which brings me to my next subject. Evelyn Flint. I need to talk to her about Lucas and Martine, so after I clean up I'm going to drive out to the winery and surprise her. Be nice to Minnie. She's coming in today. No tricks, okay?"

"I wouldn't dream of it," Jack huffed, and disappeared.

Charlene arrived at the winery at noon to find Brandy working in the shop by herself. Her green fringed sweater hung to her knees, over black leggings and knee-high boots. Her long red hair fell over her shoulders, in artful waves.

Some people had all the luck. Charlene had to use electric rollers to get her hair to do that. A ponytail was simpler.

"Hello there," Charlene said.

"Hey," Brandy answered. "What's up?"

"I was wondering if I could speak to your mother? Is she around?"

Brandy ran a feather duster over the wine bottles. "Take a number. You might have to wait in line."

"What does that mean?" Was Brandy being cryptic? Was Evelyn all right?

"I'll tell you what I told Detective Holden, and Stephanos, and Martine. Mom is volunteering at Old Town Hall," Brandy said. "The woman turns seventy-five and all of a sudden she's the most popular woman in town." She batted her long lashes over her catlike eyes.

Charlene bit her lip to keep from laughing at Brandy's exaggeration. "She is very well thought of. You're not jealous, are you?"

Brandy adjusted a wine bottle on a display. "Of course not!" she snapped. "It's all to do with the 'investigation,' so very mysterious, with Mom's book of shadows at the center of the chaos. Jealous? No. I'm just not sure what to think."

The investigation kept gaining suspects, to Charlene's mind, but Evelyn could answer some questions and perhaps provide clarity. Then again, Brandy also knew everyone in town, and all their secrets. "Is there another explanation of where the book could be?"

"Mom's a lot of things but she's not a liar." Brandy held up a palm. "Morganna was an awful person, and I'm convinced she stole it. Mother is so respected within the community that only someone new would think they could get away with stealing something of this importance from a very powerful witch. Only 'Morganna'"—she made a mockery of the name—"fits the bill."

If the younger witches hadn't brought up doubt regarding Evelyn's claim, then Charlene wouldn't have questioned the accusation. "Still, somebody murdered her, Brandy. That isn't right, no matter her crimes—moral or otherwise." Had one of the Wiccan community taken justice into their own hands?

"I happen to agree with you, but I don't like what this investigation is doing to my mother. She's a sweet old lady," Brandy said.

Charlene's brow lifted.

Brandy started laughing and leaned forward to touch Charlene's arm. "Goddess help me, but she'd kill me if she heard me call her that. And she's not exactly sweet."

Charlene and Brandy headed toward the long counter at the back of the office. "Your secret is safe with me."

"In that case, I will tell only you . . . She likes to walk through the old cemetery to unwind after her shift. If you hurry, you can catch her—and she'd probably love a mug of coffee."

"Not tea—she told me. The Boston Tea Party."

There was pride in Brandy's smile. "I should be so lucky to have her spunk. My youngest daughter is the most like her, though. Serenity is at college in Boston."

"What a pretty name. And if she looks anything like you, well, I'd probably want to lock her up for the next dozen years or so."

"No." Brandy tossed her head back and laughed. "The girl is a butterfly, and smart as a wiz. I worry more for the men she's with than my daughter." She rounded her lips. "I was hopeful that the name would guide her personality, but that never happened. She's a hellion and a cute one."

"Sounds just like you," Charlene said.

"My mother was *stunning*—still is really. It has been hard for her to accept the silver of her hair, to move into the season of the crone."

"What is that exactly?" It sounded awful.

"Our goddess has three phases. The maiden, young and nubile. The mother, nurturing and warm. And then the last is the hunched old woman, wise but dried as a prune." Brandy snickered and put a hand over her mouth. "It doesn't sound appealing, does it?"

Kass and Carmen had mentioned the divide between the young and the old in the community, saying that Morganna had publicly ridiculed the elders. Morganna had instigated a rebellion, but it had backfired, and the elders had planned to get rid of Morganna.

"Did your mother share her suspicion with you that Morganna only posed as a witch but hadn't the skills? Maybe that's why she wanted the spell book—to learn?"

"My! Mom was quite the chatty Cathy with you." Brandy's gaze narrowed as she studied Charlene.

"No, she left me with more questions than answers. I don't understand something," Charlene said, then laughed.

"There is a lot I don't understand—but how can a person without psychic skills learn to be a witch?"

Brandy brought out a bottle of water for each of them from the mini fridge. "Why do you want to know that? Are you asking to be an apprentice?"

"No! Absolutely not." She quickly uncapped the water for a drink.

Brandy went to the front door of the office and looked out at the empty parking lot before she continued. "That is a good question, and I can understand your disbelief. But it *is* possible that someone with more power than Mom could have assisted Morganna. Perhaps this someone wanted that book of shadows and used her to get it."

"Who?" It was too much to hope that Brandy would give her a name.

"I can't say because I don't have proof, only suspicions. I know it wasn't Lucas Evergreen. But go, walk with Mom, and maybe she will tell you. She's protecting someone, misguidedly, perhaps. Perhaps not."

Other than her family, whom else did Evelyn care about? She had no husband. Charlene thought of Stephanos—her handsome partner and council leader. Lucas's best friend. Who would Stephanos side with if there were a division in power? His best friend, who'd had an affair, or Evelyn?

"Thank you for the help." Charlene stepped toward the door and pulled her keys from her jacket pocket.

"I want you to realize that Mom didn't hurt that little twit, and then you can tell your detective so that the police can find out who really did kill her."

"I will, Brandy. I want the same thing you do." But for Dylan's sake.

"Morganna had something of an Eve nature, where men came to her aid. That is a certain kind of witchcraft," Brandy said. "I wouldn't be surprised if the killer is a woman."

"A jealous woman?" Charlene thought of Martine Evergreen but couldn't see her doing the dirty work. "Or a man who wanted to possess her but couldn't?" Someone like Dylan . . . Was that possible? She hoped not.

"Go talk to my mom." Brandy shooed her out the door and into the fall afternoon.

Chapter Twenty

After the long conversation with Brandy, Charlene got into her Pilot and checked her phone messages. Nothing from Sam via voice mail or text, and nothing from Hammond on Facebook.

She drove downtown, then parked on the street in the old historic district. After finding a coffee shop, she bought two large coffees. She recalled Evelyn drinking her coffee black, but stuffed packets of creamer into her pocket just in case.

The cemetery was old, early 1600s, if not older. Large trees, most of them without their summer foliage, surrounded the acreage. Brownish lawn with a few strands of green interspersed added to a gloomy feeling and ambience of those forgotten. Headstones, crooked or cracked by time, didn't seem to be in any order.

She remembered Kevin's tour on Halloween night. The bright moon, the guys snapping pictures and hoping to catch an orb. Hunching her shoulders against a cold wind, she remembered the witch balls and the handblown glass orbs and Morganna. How long ago it seemed, and yet it was less than a week.

Charlene sat on the stone half wall. Dylan had been with them for the picture taking but had he remained throughout the tour? He'd been smitten by Morganna, and shocked when she'd been killed.

"Which means he is either a very good actor or probably didn't do it," she said aloud, preferring to think the latter.

She spied Evelyn walking down the broken sidewalk toward the cemetery. Her gorgeous silver hair was stylishly tucked beneath a black knit hat, and her wool coat was also black. A thick cable-knit scarf in gray hung loosely around her neck.

Evelyn saw her and sauntered over.

Charlene lifted a coffee, and Evelyn's mouth twitched in a smile.

"Brandy texted me that you might be here," Evelyn said. "I hope you brought dark roast?"

"Yes. I have creamer, but I don't think you use it."

Evelyn peeled back the plastic lid to eye the dark brew inside. "I'll have one, please. This is not the quality of your coffee."

They sat on the wall with their beverages in silence before Evelyn got up and gestured toward the tallest tree in the center of the cemetery. "Shall we? It gets so stuffy sometimes in those old walls that I need the open air. Such secrets they whisper to me."

Overhead, dark stormy clouds blotted out the sun, and a north wind blew. Charlene shivered but followed her through the random headstones and then around the lonely, bare tree. "This feels so desolate, like we're the only ones here but people are watching," she said.

Evelyn eyed her before sipping her coffee. "Not a single whisper from souls who know no peace. Today, it's quiet, exactly what my mind needs. So what is it that you want to know?"

"I found that sachet, tied with lavender." She glanced at

Evelyn's face to read her reaction. "I wasn't sure if it was something more . . . important?"

"Did you really come here to discuss a harmless charm bag?" Her voice was serene.

Charlene didn't believe that finding it had been an accident, but she didn't want to insult Evelyn and have her leave. She decided to use caution. "No. I have more important things to discuss."

"I thought so." Evelyn stared at her with intensity before moving her gaze to the gray sky visible between the bare branches of the tree.

"I asked Brandy if a person had to be a psychic to be a witch."

"For true power, the answer to that is yes. Now, even the tiniest seed can be nurtured and grown, but if there is nothing to guide or groom, heartbreak and disappointment await."

What the heck did that mean? Charlene nodded as if she perfectly understood the strange-sounding words. "I see."

Evelyn continued walking through the headstones. After another few minutes she said, "My sister had none, and she hated me for it—and trust me, I would have shared it—I tried! But the gifts are given without explanation. My son was born with a sliver of Brandy's power, and it was too much of a divide between my children. He's turned his back on the craft and sells expensive homes in New York— doing very well for himself, of course."

Charlene laughed. "Well, I'm glad he's doing well. We can't all be into witchcraft, now can we?" She tried to make a joke. "Too many touristy shops as it is."

Evelyn gave her an appraising glance, and Charlene wondered if she'd failed some kind of test. Her shoulders straightened as Evelyn's voice rose like she was in a lecture hall.

"I can see that you don't get it, Charlene, so it's no use

trying. But magick does exist. Oh, maybe not in your world, but certainly in mine."

"I meant no disrespect," Charlene said. "I'm searching for answers, that's all."

"During the ceremony which I had invited Morganna to be a part of, I discovered that, at her core, she had no magick. None. Zilch. Possibly like you." Evelyn gave her a dismissive look. "Now, I can see by your expression that you're skeptical, but believe me." She lowered her voice. "Someone of great power lent her theirs to try and bind me and strip me of mine. To get the book of shadows. How I would love to know who . . ."

Brandy thought that her mother knew. "What is in your book of shadows that is so valuable? I understand it contains spells, but do they have meaning to others besides you?"

"The entire book is valuable! To me—it is my essence, my legacy to my daughter and granddaughters. But Morganna and whoever infused her with power were after Armand Sheffield."

"What?" Charlene thought back to Evelyn telling her about him. "Your ancestor that came to Salem after the witch trials, believing there would be actual witches here? Why were they after him?" She glanced around, hoping no tourists overheard this crazy conversation.

Evelyn sighed and finished her coffee. "Armand created this first coven here, which is where the Flint family can follow their bloodline. That in itself holds great power."

"I don't understand."

Evelyn's eyes dimmed. "I believe the page in my book of shadows that Morganna was after was the summoning spell for Armand."

"Why?" She couldn't wait to tell Sam this. No, better not. Jack might help her understand. "I mean, it's not possible, right?"

"His spirit remains in Salem—he is a guide for me, and for the Flint women."

The coffee tasted acrid in Charlene's mouth and she swallowed, but the bitterness didn't fade. She thought of Jack. By not going to the light when he'd been called, had she doomed him to stay for hundreds of years?

Evelyn continued her story. "Armand's pagan magick is tied in with my family and our magick. If he were caught by another, he could be"—her cheeks seemed to sink into the bones of her face—"dispersed or banished into the ether, and I don't know what that would do to our power."

The two women had completed a full lap around the cemetery. She could escape if she wished, yet Charlene didn't have all the answers she'd come here for.

"I still have a few questions remaining. But first, do you realize that Brandy is concerned for you?"

"Bless her—she should know not to worry."

"Why?"

"I told you—I did not kill the girl." Evelyn sounded offended that Charlene even questioned her motives.

"Help me understand," Charlene said. "You and Stephanos were co-council in your community. Were you, um, more than friends?"

"Lovers? Oh yes, we were lovers. Beneath the summer moon—we created magick." She huffed. "But that was over a decade ago. Now, those love spells are meant for the young."

"Stephanos is Lucas's best friend—would he cover for him? Deny or keep his affair with Morganna a secret, to keep the coven together?"

"Who told you that it was Lucas having the affair?"

"I have my sources," Charlene said, keeping Brandy's secret.

"I can guess—but I won't. We did our best to hush that mistake up and to put an end to it immediately. Martine deserved better, after staying with Lucas through hard financial times. And the difficulty in conceiving took its toll on her."

"I thought the Evergreens were the perfect family?"

Evelyn scowled. "You need to be careful, Charlene, of who you talk to." She kept walking. "Martine wanted a baby so badly, but Lucas was more interested in the *image* of being a mage. He had a trickle of actual ability." Evelyn put her thumb and forefinger together. "Enough that he could do simple tricks. Martine was sweet and ethereal, a Salem native with lots of magick. She fell head over heels for the handsome Lucas. They handfasted on a summer's eve, but despite their enthusiasm, she never quickened."

"Handfasted?" Charlene was looking at Evelyn and stumbled over a stone. The language the professor used would be perfect in a medieval romance.

"Yes. They used rituals and ceremonies, but it wasn't until she convinced him to try a fertility doctor that they were able to conceive. What a celebration we had! We wanted them to be happy, you understand? They were in their midthirties by then, and financially this would be their only chance." A shadow passed Evelyn's face.

"What?"

"Sometimes Mother Goddess has a plan. Carmen was born premature, and we all prayed around the clock that the babe survived. We knew her loss would . . ." Evelyn trailed off.

"I've met Carmen, with Kass Fortune."

Evelyn nodded. "Powerful young witches both—now. It was touch and go for Carmen throughout her childhood. Lucas and Martine were very protective." She clamped her mouth tight.

"What aren't you saying?"

"It was the three of them against the world, victorious. Stephanos and I knew that word of Lucas's affair would devastate Martine." She tapped her temple. "She was never strong."

Lucas had mentioned making things right, but unbeknownst to him was Martine aware of the affair? And unable to forgive and forget?

"Do you think Martine found out, despite you and Stephanos?" Charlene and Jared had been so in tune that she knew when he had a bad drive home from the gym. If he'd loved another, she would have felt it in her heart.

"I don't know how. I trust Stephanos with my life."

"Maybe Lucas confessed?"

"He is aware of his wife's fragile nature." Evelyn shook her head with sorrow. "Always remorse after the incident. Never *before* they drop their pants."

Charlene held back a grin. "You may have a point."

Evelyn and Charlene followed the curve of the path, staying on the outer edges of the cemetery. "It is a shame that we can't see people for who they are right away," Evelyn surmised.

Thinking of her most recent house guest, Charlene agreed. Which reminded her that she had two ladies arriving and should hurry back.

"Did you know that Morganna was from Ohio?" Evelyn glanced at Charlene as they walked. "It's where she learned to blow the glass orbs."

"Yes," Charlene answered. "Her name was Linda Crane. How did you find out about that?"

"After the incident where she robbed me and tried to bind me, I dug into her past. Evil people leave a trail that isn't hard to find—just discover who they hurt last." Evelyn tightened her scarf around her neck against the chill.

"Hammond Cobb?"

"He was furious at her," Evelyn said, her eyes narrowed. "This was a month before Halloween, and your detective has already questioned me about the timeline. I know that he was here that night, but I haven't seen him or talked to him since that first call when I reached out to him. He was at a festival in Ohio, drunk and angry. But he was forthcoming because I was the first person he could talk to about her." Evelyn shuddered. "If he is the one that killed her, I led him to Salem. There might be guilt in that."

"I don't think so—you didn't know."

"He told me that she'd used him for a year, learning everything from him, and then up and disappeared with all his money and his furnace. He is not a wealthy man, so her theft hurt more than just his pride."

Black clouds rolled in overhead. A fat raindrop landed on Charlene's cheek. "I'm parked on the side street—can I give you a ride?"

"No . . . My car is behind Town Hall." Evelyn grabbed Charlene's hand. "Thank you for the coffee. But be careful, will you? I sense danger. Drive home safe."

Evelyn hurried off in the opposite direction.

Is this how Morganna felt when Kass had given a cautious warning from her tea leaf reading?

There was a helplessness in not understanding the nature of the trouble coming. Charlene drove exactly the speed limit and double-checked each stop sign and breathed a sigh of relief as soon as she hurried inside.

CHAPTER TWENTY-ONE

Charlene got home in time to check in her last-minute guests, Gloria Smith and Lori Romero from Kentucky.

Lori was less than five feet tall and a bundle of energy. Moving quickly around the living room, she finally took a seat next to her friend Gloria, who was half a foot taller, with a full head of bleached hair.

"Thank you so much for fitting us in. We didn't realize there would be so much to do in Salem, so we'd booked Boston for four nights. Now we will go there for three and spend tonight here." Lori's knee bobbed in place.

"Charlene, this is a beautiful mansion."

"Thank you, Gloria. We had a full house last weekend over Halloween. I hope Salem wasn't too quiet for you?"

"Not at all," Gloria said.

"We consider ourselves quite lucky." Lori grinned. "We didn't have to wait in line for the tours or the restaurants. It was perfect."

"I'm glad to hear that." Charlene waved at Minnie, who had been making last-minute preparations for their new guests.

Gloria pocketed some of Charlene's business cards.

"We both work in administration for the University of Kentucky and will tell all the professors about this place."

"Wonderful! A personal recommendation is always the best." Charlene gave them a heartfelt smile. "Oh, tomorrow is Sunday, so we'll have a big breakfast set up in the dining room, along with fruit and pastries."

"Sounds good," Lori said.

"You will find a bottle of our signature rosé in your room this afternoon, along with a cheese tray. We try to do a happy hour when we have more guests, but I figured this was the simplest solution."

"How thoughtful," Gloria said, glancing at her friend. "Sharon at the restaurant spoke highly of you, and now we see why."

"I always recommend her restaurant as well. The lobster roll is terrific, and the fish and chips—everything I've tried has been great."

"I'm sure Boston will be a disappointment after this," Gloria lamented.

"It's a beautiful city—where are you staying?" Charlene scooted forward on her chair.

"The Copley Square, in the Back Bay area."

"Yes, I know of it. Haven't stayed there myself, but it has a very good reputation. You might have to pay for your bottle of wine, though," she teased.

Lori laughed. "Wine in the room, you say?"

"Yes—do you need a hand with your bags?"

"No, we're good, thanks." Gloria easily rolled hers across the floor to the stairs, with Lori following behind. She'd put the ladies next door to one another in rooms decorated in the Victorian style.

"Top of the stairs, first two rooms on the right," she told them, leading the way.

After getting them settled, Charlene went back downstairs to find Minnie in the kitchen.

"Thank you for getting their baskets ready. The fresh sprig of pine is a nice touch. Lori took hers to Gloria's room, and they couldn't be happier."

Minnie blushed, pleased. "They seem like nice ladies. How's Mrs. Robinson?"

Charlene shared a little of their conversation. "Much kinder, after she'd unburdened herself."

Minnie went home, and Charlene hurried down to the wine cellar, calling for Jack to discuss the investigation, but he wasn't around. *Oh well.* She collected her iPad and sat on the love seat in her private sitting area and checked her e-mails, and then Facebook. Though she and Hammond weren't friends, she could see his activity in the name search. Nothing new.

Frustrated, she put Dylan's name into the search bar—he hadn't been active on the social media site since Halloween. She enlarged a photo of him smiling with a bunch of Goth kids outside somewhere—blue, purple, orange—the many hues of hair these days made it impossible to know what was a costume and what was real. It was too dark to tell exactly, but it looked like they were by the water.

Her mom called, and Charlene had no good excuse not to answer. "Hi, Mom." She opened the fridge and found an opened bottle of chardonnay, then rummaged for some hard, white cheese.

"Hi yourself, young lady! Where have you been? Too busy to talk to your own mother?"

Charlene rolled her eyes. "Mom, if you could record yourself, you might realize why I don't call as often as you'd like." She loved her mother, but after Jared died, her mom became overly protective, wanting her to move home. As if!

"And what is that supposed to mean?" She could hear the tartness in her mom's voice and wondered what had soured her so much. Growing up, her mother, though never warm and fuzzy, had been amusing. Fun. There was no fun left, and it was sad to see.

"Never mind. I'm looking forward to your visit next month. How is Dad doing?"

"As well as expected for a man of his age, who doesn't do much but sit around all day and make a nuisance of himself."

Poor Dad, she thought. He really needed a hobby, just to get out of the house and away from her mother.

"And your bridge group?"

"They'll be over Friday. Good thing. It gets your dad out for a few hours. He's taken to going to the movies by himself. Probably one of those girly shows, sitting in the dark, doing heaven knows what."

"Mom!" Charlene nearly dropped the wine bottle. "What a terrible thing to say! Dad is a sweetheart, and you're so mean to him."

"Mean? I do everything for that man. Cook, clean, even call his daughter who doesn't have time for us anymore."

"I'm running a new business. That takes a little time too. Sorry if you feel neglected, but I'm forty-two and can't be calling you every day. Once a week is sufficient."

Her parents were older than most, in their midthirties when she was born. They'd had a hard time trying to have a child, and she had been an unexpected late-life gift. In their seventies now, her father had long retired, and her mom couldn't stand having him under her feet all day.

"You got a boyfriend yet? That's probably what you're doing all day. Too busy to call your mother. And your poor dad sits looking at your framed pictures. But do you call? Do you care if he cries himself to sleep every night? No! You're out with your new boyfriend, having a good time. Who cares about us?"

"I don't have a boyfriend."

"Well, you should get one. You're not young anymore, and time is a-wasting."

"I've got to go, Mom. Someone's trying to call, and it might be a reservation, or who knows? A new boyfriend?"

"Don't get smart with me." Her mother released a long-suffering sigh intended to make her feel guilty. She wasn't buying into it.

"Goodbye, Mother. I'll call soon." She ended the call.

Her parents planned to visit over Thanksgiving, and hopefully when they saw her place and how well she was doing, it would put their minds to rest. Kevin had called, leaving a message that he was just checking in to see how she was, and if she'd heard anything new. He suggested going to Ruin on Monday and to talk then.

Charlene was thinking about dinner—go out or order a pizza in—when she got a text from Kass asking her to meet her at the tea shop.

She texted back. **OK. 30 mins. Dinner after?**

Not waiting for a response, she got her down-filled jacket from the closet for the cold night. She pulled a wool cap over her ears and grabbed her gloves, then locked up, leaving the usual lights on for her guests.

As she drove the short distance to town, she remembered Evelyn's warning about being in danger. It made her extra cautious as she drove, and she half wished she'd stayed home. Not that she was superstitious or anything. These so-called witches knew more than they were saying, and she hoped Kass might come clean.

It was half past five when she parked her Pilot and headed down the street. Night had fallen, but the streetlights and shops made the short journey safe enough. Still, she huddled in her warm jacket and held the scarf against her face to block the harsh wind.

Taking a short cut behind the buildings, she saw someone dashing across the street after two other guys—one in all-black gothic garb, the other with an orange Mohawk that sliced through the evening. Darren? Had he just gotten off work?

The young man following them wore a hoodie and didn't see the car bearing down on him, going much too fast on a busy street. In the nick of time, the large SUV slammed on the brakes, just missing the pedestrian. He turned around to glare at the driver. The headlights outlined his face, shaggy blond hair poking beneath the black fabric.

Her stomach lurched. What the heck! Dylan. He'd come from the direction she was headed. Why was he still hanging around here? Near Morganna's shop—or Kass's? Why had he never returned any of her texts or calls? She'd hoped he'd gone back to Hartford.

"Dylan!" She called out his name, but he kept walking at a fast clip. She decided to follow him through the back alley. She gave the black metal fire escape a look of interest. Had Dylan come from up there? Or from inside the building?

She was passing the back door of Morganna's when she heard something heavy scraping against metal. A clang. Standing still, she listened again. Should she follow Dylan or investigate the noise?

The place was sealed off due to the active murder investigation. No one should be inside. There were no windows in the back of the building at shop level. *Screech.* There it was again. Like furniture being moved. Was it the heavy furnace? The propane tank? Knowing she shouldn't—she couldn't help herself—she stepped quietly up to the back door.

Charlene glanced down the alley toward the main street to see if anyone else was around. There was no sign of Dylan. Had he been following Darren, or hanging out with them? If she called Sam, she knew what he would say— that old buildings made strange sounds. The place was supposed to be locked up tight.

She'd just turn the handle to make sure it was properly

locked. If it was, she'd be on her way to Kass's and put the incident out of her mind.

The knob turned in her hand. Crap! *Now what?*

Her heart hammered. Kass's shop was next door. Charlene could get her, and they could explore the noise together. But if someone was in there right now, they might get away. What if they were stealing evidence of their crime? Linda's killer would never be caught. Dylan had run away. It couldn't be him! She had to prove his innocence and that meant catching who was involved.

Her pulse raced, and her heart thudded inside her chest. *Danger.*

Should she heed the warning? That would be what any sane, sensible person would do. Call the police and let them know Morganna's Witch House wasn't locked. That would make Sam proud and show that she respected his opinion and concern.

Heck, for all she knew it might be Hammond Cobb in there, and she'd be no match for a man his size.

Be sensible, she told herself. *Walk away.* This was police business, not hers. Still, even telling herself that, she straightened her shoulders and took a deep breath. *Just one peek, that's all.*

Charlene opened the door and glanced inside from the alley. Her vision blurred as her eyes adjusted from the dark outside to the gloomy interior—not pitch-black because of Morganna's front display window, which allowed some light from the streetlamps. The orbs that had hung there were gone.

She smelled the faint odor of propane. She pushed the door a few inches wider and stepped one foot in. Broken glass littered the floor. Her gaze traveled to the front, and the empty window.

Were these colorful shards of orbs from the display, or from the shelves in the back workshop?

Her skin prickled with fear, but she inched forward, careful of her steps. She hadn't realized before that a thin industrial rug had been laid over cement, though Morganna had used cement pavers in her workstation—a safety measure?

Charlene said a little prayer. She smelled a strange odor. What was it? Sage! She could smell sage over the scent of gas. And something else. A familiar scent, like alcohol.

Charlene held her breath as she stepped down the hall, her back against the wall, seeing that the workshop door was closed. She made her way past the counter to the front of the store, searching for who might be here.

A screech of iron against cement—she whipped around, her senses on alert. The sound emanated from the workshop. A footstep. Could that be the killer? Her heart raced, and she swallowed hard. Danger! Evelyn was right. Why hadn't she listened?

Sam! Forgive me, Sam.

She slipped the cell phone out of her pocket and rushed toward the back door, trying to dial 911. Her heart beat so loud that she couldn't hear her own breath. Her feet seemed clumsy. Keeping an eye on the shop door, which she had to pass to get out, she quietly retraced her path toward the exit.

The workshop door burst open. Charlene let out a scream. Moving quickly now, no longer worried about being heard, she stumbled into something and banged her hip into the counter. Reaching out with both hands, she dropped her cell phone. Footsteps, heavy, rushed toward her.

She couldn't escape. Scrambling now, she hunched over in the gloom, looking for the phone. Her lifeline. Reaching beneath the counter, she clawed at the frame and brought it to her, frantic to hit the buttons. 9-1-1.

Her skin crawled, and it felt like someone was hovering over her. She could smell the scent of alcohol again. Phone in hand, she eyed the door. Could she feint to the right and run left to get away? Kick out with her heel? Scream bloody murder?

Before she could act at all, a bright light flashed in her eye and something smacked her head.

Dazed, Charlene collapsed, broken glass crackling under her weight. Then there was nothing. Silence. Darkness.

CHAPTER TWENTY-TWO

Charlene woke to someone shaking her. Shards of glass underneath her crunched when she tried to move, but they didn't penetrate her heavy coat. Her head hurt.

But I'm alive.

She slowly opened her eyes. Then blinked again.

Kass! Her friend had found her. Dressed all in black, rail-thin Kass looked down at her with an inscrutable expression.

Had she heard the noise and come running, or had she been here all along? "Kass?"

"Charlene, what are you doing here?" Kass hunched down and ran her slim hand over Charlene's forehead, brushing back her hair. Blood darkened Kass's fingers in the dim light of the shop.

"I'm bleeding?" Charlene struggled to sit up, but a blinding headache kept her down on the thinly carpeted floor, the cement beneath it cold as ice. "What happened? Did you see who was here?"

"No, I heard a scream and a crash and came running. And there you were. Lying here like you were dead. You scared *me* half to death!"

"Did you see who hit me?" Charlene's vision blurred, and she reached for Kass's arm.

Kass's teeth chattered. Her thin black sweater was no match for this icebox.

"No. I was too late to see anybody, but I called the police right away." Kass shifted on her knees at Charlene's side.

"Thank you. My head hurts." She tried to sit.

Kass gently pushed her back. "A scratch at your temple, but you have a big lump on the back of your head." She glanced around the rear of the shop as if searching for who had done this to Charlene. "I don't want you to move, though, okay?"

Blue lights flashed through the front window, but Sam and the local police came around the back. Charlene recognized Officer Tanner and Officer Bernard.

Sam went directly to Charlene, and Kass stepped away.

He touched her cheek, his gaze running over her quickly to categorize her injuries. "An ambulance is on its way."

"I don't need an ambulance, Sam. I'm all right. Just a little sore."

"You're flat on your back, and the woman who called said you were unconscious. That doesn't sound okay to me." His voice was gruff. "Can you give me an explanation as to what you are doing here? Didn't the crime scene tape, and the Do Not Enter sign, mean anything to you?"

"Uh, I was just passing by. Going to Kass's." Charlene gestured to Kass, who had her arms crossed in front of her, her hands tucked beneath her elbows for warmth.

"I'm the one that called," Kass said.

"Thanks. Charlene, did you faint? I smell propane fumes." Sam stood to look around.

"No," she said in a low voice, not really wanting to see his reaction. "I heard someone moving things in here, and I should have called, but I was afraid that if I went next door and called from there, whoever was *here* would get away."

"Inside this shop? And yet you entered?" Sam rubbed his chin in agitation. His mustache vibrated along his top lip.

"I didn't see anybody, but I heard them, and when I stumbled, I lost my cell phone. I was trying to get away, so I could call you." She pleaded with him to understand.

The two officers were asking Kass questions, but Charlene wished they would intervene so she wouldn't have to answer to Sam.

"Well, that was good thinking, wasn't it?"

She cringed at the heavy sarcasm, which made her head hurt. She balanced on her arms to sit up.

"Did you see this intruder?"

"No, it was too dark." She looked up at him. "You were the first person I thought of."

"How nice." His voice was steely. "Again—what made you enter believing someone was in here? Common sense would dictate that you'd stay on the outside, in the clear, and call nine-one-one."

"Yes. My common sense did tell me that, and yet here I am. I just wanted to catch the person that is responsible, Sam."

"That's my job!"

"I'm sorry." She stared at the black toes of his boot and the black fabric of his pants. "Sam, before coming inside I saw Dylan running across the street."

"From inside this shop?"

"I don't know. I'm not sure." Charlene gingerly touched the back of her head. "It was possible that he was here with someone—maybe looking for that book of shadows?"

"Charlene . . ." Sam dropped down, so they were nose to nose.

"Someone knocked me out, Sam. A person. Not the gas."

He gritted his teeth. "Maybe they were frustrated by the fact that you keep turning up at their crime scene?"

Her eyes narrowed at him. "You're an officer of the law. You can't say things like that."

"You want to make a bet? Criminals come back to the scene . . . They can't help it. Officer Tanner has been watching the shop."

"And obviously missed something!" Charlene kept her hands folded on her lap instead of touching her aching head.

"Is that true?" Kass asked. "About criminals returning to the scene of the crime? I thought that was just in movies." She shivered so hard her teeth knocked together.

Sam rose again, his expression set. "Just be careful, Kass, and keep your door locked. I will double the patrol in this area." He stepped back and gestured for the EMTs to take care of Charlene.

She glanced up at Sam, but he'd left her and was talking to the two officers. She heard the sound of wheels against broken glass and tried to turn, but it hurt.

"You have a stretcher for me?" She squealed. "I don't need that. I'm fine."

"You could have a concussion," a voice admonished, kneeling down at her side where Kass had just been. "You have a head injury. Best if we get you checked out." The female EMT was probably around her age, dark skinned, heavyset.

"Checked out? I guess so. We could do that here?" Charlene closed her eyes, more embarrassed by her actions of breaking in than her actual pain. Yes, her head throbbed, but her dignity had taken a bigger hit. "I don't want to go to the hospital."

The woman snapped a penlight in her eyes with a huff.

Sam and Kass were to her right, and from Charlene's sitting position on the floor she heard him ask, "What did you hear, exactly?"

"A crash," Kass said, "that's all. I was waiting for Charlene to come over."

"Business or social?" She couldn't get a clear view of Sam, though she imagined he'd be tugging on his poor mustache.

Kass hesitated. Charlene tried to move her head, but the EMT kept one arm on Charlene's shoulder to hold her in place while she took her pulse. Kass said, "I'd offered her a tea reading before everything happened and was going to do one for her."

That was news to Charlene, and she wasn't sure Kass was telling the truth.

Sam didn't answer—that Charlene could hear.

"Stay still now," the female EMT said. The latex gloves felt smooth against Charlene's forehead. "You might need a stitch or two. I highly recommend that you go to the hospital."

Pain washed through her. Charlene gave a slow, head-pounding nod. "All right."

"Hang on," the other EMT said in a cheerful voice. Male, youngish sounding, so she was surprised by his gray hair and brows when he came into view. The pair lifted her carefully onto the stretcher. The woman attached the straps over Charlene's body. "Ready?" the man asked.

"Wait," Charlene said.

Kass told Sam, "I was surprised that someone would be in the shop. I figured it might be the same person or persons who ransacked my place. So I called Officer Tanner and came in through the back door, which was open." Kass picked up a bundle of dried herbs that Charlene recognized as sage.

Maybe Kass had been in the shop to try to cleanse it of negative energy, as she'd done her own? But Kass wouldn't have hit her on the head, and then called the police, would she?

The female EMT clucked her tongue against her teeth at Charlene's obvious eavesdropping. "Can we go now, princess?" Charlene didn't answer.

The man pushed the stretcher while the woman walked backward. Wheels crunched over the broken glass by the front entrance. They'd just reached the sidewalk outside when Carmen ran toward her, with Lucas and Martine behind.

"What happened, Charlene?" Carmen's green eyes exuded concern.

Martine bowed her head as if to say a prayer. Lucas placed a comforting hand on his wife's shoulder.

"'Scuse us." The female EMT was not a ray of sunshine as she motioned for the trio to get out of the way. The Evergreens seemed surprised by the EMT's rudeness. Charlene smiled apologetically, but even that movement hurt.

She lifted her fingers in a half wave. Nausea burned up her throat, and she wondered if she hadn't been affected by something else after all.

The doors closed on the ambulance, leaving Charlene in dim interior lighting, surrounded by screens and an IV machine. Charlene, certain that she was just fine, didn't wake up again until she was at the hospital.

CHAPTER TWENTY-THREE

Charlene had never spent the night in the hospital before Salem, and she didn't care for it. The rooms were kept as cold as the refrigeration section at Albertsons grocery store, and the nurses woke you up every two hours to ask you how you were feeling. She would have felt a lot better if they'd left her alone and allowed her to sleep.

By seven a.m., she'd had a light breakfast and a cup of tasteless coffee, and was waiting for the doctor to discharge her after his morning rounds. By ten he still hadn't made an appearance, and her inquiry to the Boston Irish day nurse, Kelly Fisher, was met with a noncommittal answer delivered in the same tone. *Soon.*

"Was my cell phone brought in?" she asked when the nurse came to check her vitals. Pulse, temperature, and who knew what else.

"Just your purse," Nurse Fisher answered. "I put it in the drawer of the side table." She wrote the results on a small chart on the foot of the hospital bed.

"Can I get dressed?" Charlene hated to complain, but she was cold in the paper gown despite the blue fuzzy socks the hospital had supplied.

"Let's wait for the doctor," she said. The desk phone rang, and the nurse rushed out to answer it.

Charlene found her jeans and sweater in a plastic bag in the same drawer as her purse and warred with temptation to defy the nurse's directions and get dressed anyway. In the end, she settled back against the thin pillow and dumped the contents of her bulky bag onto the white sheet. The black cylinder of pepper spray mocked her. Why hadn't she used it last night? She'd wanted to find the person responsible, and all common sense fled before that want.

Half a roll of mints, a stick of gum, wadded up receipts. No cell phone. She put it all back but the garbage, which she tossed. Still no doctor.

Charlene called Minnie at the bed-and-breakfast, and the housekeeper answered on the first ring.

"Charlene's," she said.

"Minnie, it's Charlene."

"Where are you?"

The concern in Minnie's voice made Charlene quick to explain, "I'm fine—there was an incident that I will explain later." Minnie and Will spent Sunday afternoons with their grandkids. "I know you like to be gone early on Sundays, but do you mind checking out the guests for me?"

"Are you all right?"

"Yes, I promise. I'll be home later!"

Sipping cold water through a straw from a plastic cup on her adjustable bed table, she considered a mad dash for the hall just outside her partially closed door.

A knock sounded, and then Sam peeked in. Her shoulders bowed with relief. "Yeah! You've come to save me." She sat up straighter and ran her fingers through her tangled hair. "I must look awful. I feel like a pin cushion— they've pricked me so many times."

"You earned a private room?" He strode toward her, carrying two large coffees. His presence did her spirits a world of good.

She extended her lip in an exaggerated pout. "Have you come to spring me out?" She accepted the insulated to-go cup and sighed at the warmth to her fingers. "Thank you."

"I don't know that you are going anywhere anytime soon."

"Why not?" She winced at her whining tone.

"They ran some blood tests on you, pretty standard procedure, but I asked them to check for cyanide poisoning." Sam sat on the edge of the bed and removed the plastic cover on her coffee, and then his own. He looked at her in a way that made her insides tingle with pleasure. He had a bad habit of doing that.

"But it's been a week!" She breathed in the aroma of dark roast, her eyes fastened on him. Charlene used one hand to pull the sheet higher, feeling underdressed and vulnerable. "And I didn't smell almonds, Sam. It was propane, I think. Sage. Something else too." She scrunched her nose in memory. "I felt sick in the ambulance. But I don't remember much after that."

"They gave you something for the nausea." Sam stood up, choosing the chair next to the bed, crossing his legs at the ankles. "Which could have been caused by chemicals locked in that back room in addition to being smacked on the back of the head. You hit your temple when you fell."

"Chemicals other than cyanide?"

"Yeah. I found Hammond Cobb. Among other things, I asked him about the possibility of cyanide in melted glass. He said that glass is often made of recycled material, and you don't know what might be inside. Once it heats, it could emit something poisonous. We are having the glass in Linda's furnace tested now."

She thought back to that night. "I remember that she had her blowpipe next to her. There was a pan in the furnace, like a bowl—the liquid semihard, as I told you already. Did Hammond say if this is a common thing?"

"Hammond is sitting in jail, thinking about his story, which keeps changing—but he says it is very odd for Linda to have been killed by cyanide unless the room had no ventilation, but the door to her workstation had been ajar. It would have taken a very condensed amount to happen so quickly." Sam lifted his coffee toward her. "I came by last night to tell you, but you were out cold."

She sipped cautiously from her hot cup. "You were here last night?"

Sam's slow grin warmed her better than a fleece robe. "Where else would I be?"

Charlene leaned back on the bed, wishing she could walk out with him right now. Hammond in jail. Then she sat up, spilling a drop of coffee on the white sheet. "Wait—so someone *added* more cyanide to her glassware that she was going to melt, hoping to make it look like an accident?"

"That is one theory." Sam blew on the coffee and took a deeper drink of his joe. "We will know more once the tests on the glass come back from the lab."

"Where did you find Hammond?"

"My officers tracked him down to a Motel 12 outside of town. He was brought in—about an hour before we got the call from Kass last night."

She frowned. "Guess that means he couldn't have been the one to hit me over the head."

"Yeah." Sam shifted in the chair, holding her gaze. "I'd sure like to find Dylan."

It was on the tip of her tongue to defend him, but even she was beginning to wonder how Dylan was involved.

"Hammond would know how to add cyanide—that's his

business, right?" Charlene said. "And he was going to run off with Linda."

"Hammond admitted to being in a fistfight with Rich Swane on Halloween night." Sam gave her a straight look, as if wondering how much she knew. "According to him, he didn't go near Linda or her shop after realizing that she'd set him up. They'd been texting romantically back and forth for a week . . . after she found out that she was going to be excommunicated from the coven. He was her fallback plan, and Rich let him know it." Sam balanced his coffee cup on his bent knee.

"You think he did it?" Charlene just wanted whoever it was to be caught. And if it was a lover's quarrel, that meant there wasn't a witch killer loose in Salem. It also meant that Dylan would stay out of jail.

"Hammond was angry, no doubt about it. Fooled once, shame on her. Fooled twice, shame on him. He says he didn't do it. But he can't give me an alibi." Sam patted his jacket pocket, pulled out her cell phone, and returned it to her. "You left this in your rush last night."

"Ha ha." She set the phone on the bedside stand. "Did you ever find Linda's cell?"

"No. But it'll turn up. Hammond sent her an unanswered text at nine, demanding to know what she was up to—he'd just gotten into that fight with Rich, who was so upset by it all *he* ended up with a DUI—lucky he ran his car into a ditch and didn't hurt anybody."

"What a job you've got. Dealing with the criminal element all the time. Being patient, and methodical. Leaving no stone unturned." She thought with embarrassment of her dash into the dark shop to supposedly catch a killer. "I would never make a good police officer."

"We can agree on that." Sam held up a finger as if she'd argue, but she knew it was true. "Because you don't listen to the warning of danger, Charlene. You'd be the rookie killed in her first year, rushing in to save the hurt kitten from a drug house." He stood up and brushed his knuckles just under the bandage at her temple. "You think with your heart."

Her heart was doing some serious thumping at Sam's perusal.

He stepped back and tapped his temple. "A cop has to think with their head."

Her cheeks heated. "Not my strong suit, but I am willing to learn."

Sam's cell phone rang. He set his cup down on the wheeled table and turned away to answer. "Uh-huh? Okay, I'll be right there."

Charlene waited for him to turn around and asked, "What?"

"Officer Jimenez just spotted Dylan down by the wharf. I told her to keep an eye out for me."

"You can't suspect him of anything, Sam—not if you have Hammond in jail."

Sam sighed. "Hammond said that anybody who has taken a science lab could figure out how to make homemade cyanide. Dangerous, yes, but possible."

She didn't like the sound of that.

Sam's bootheels clicked against the linoleum floor. "Guess what Dylan Preston minored in?"

Charlene braced herself for the news. "What?"

"Chemistry." Sam shook his head at her. "I was going to try and get you out early, but I think you're safer here. I know where you are."

"Sam! Come on—I promise to go straight home. I have to feed Silva." And she needed a dose of Jack's wry humor.

"If there is a hint of cyanide or other chemicals in your system, I want you in this hospital for observation."

She slumped back against the pillow.

"But if there is none, then promise me you will go home and rest, okay?" Sam asked.

"Yes!" She thought of her clean sheets, her warm bed, and was suddenly exhausted.

"I'll see what I can do. Stay out of trouble." He walked to the door, but then came back and looked down at her face, as if memorizing it. "Please, stay out of trouble?"

"I will." And she meant it—she really did.

It was noon before she was actually discharged—with a clean bill of health—and she called a taxi to get home. Charlene was so tired that the idea of stopping to get her car first just seemed overwhelming.

Besides, she'd promised Sam. And sharing what had happened with Jack would help her feel better too. She was thankful her two lady guests had stayed only overnight, and that Natalie and her mother would be leaving as well, if not already gone. She felt too awful to be a good hostess. Minnie would take care of everything.

She arrived at her slate-blue home, the black-and-ivory CHARLENE'S BED AND BREAKFAST sign glossy and elegant in her front yard. She went inside, and Silva meowed from the upholstered chair in the foyer—had the cat been waiting for her?

"Hey, sweetie. Mama's home."

Silva headed straight for the kitchen.

"What? I'm just your meal ticket?" Charlene laughed low but made her way down the hall to the kitchen. She could tell that the house was empty, and the note from Minnie on the table confirmed that everyone had enjoyed their stay. "Food for you, then bed for me."

Cool energy centered by the wine cellar door, and then Jack materialized.

"Where have you been, Charlene? I was worried when you didn't come home last night. Is that a bruise on your head—a bandage?" He was next to her in an instant, his chill making her shiver.

"I'm fine, Jack."

He studied her, looking into her eyes as intently as the doctor had done. He lifted his hands to touch her, but he couldn't, of course. Goose bumps broke out along her flesh where he'd tried. "Tilt your head for me," he instructed. "Take off the bandage. Two stitches. Decent work. Concussion?"

"I bet you were an amazing doctor, Jack Strathmore."

"What happened?" He snapped his fingers, and the electric kettle clicked on.

Charlene poured Silva's dry food in the dish and then chose a can of soup from the pantry. "Well, Kass asked me to meet her last night at her tea shop. But then she told Sam she was going to do a reading for me, but we hadn't talked about that—I've decided I don't want to know. Evelyn Flint warned me to be careful, that I was in danger. How does that help, I ask you? It doesn't."

Jack sat on the kitchen counter next to the sink. She got out a big bowl, dumped the can of clam chowder in, and microwaved it.

"Do you know what Kass wanted?"

"No. I suppose I could call her, but I promised Sam I would stay out of trouble and just go to bed and rest." Her lids weighed heavily.

"I agree with the detective for once."

"You do?"

"Yes. Charlene, I was powerless to help you last night—I worried but couldn't do anything, being stuck to this house." He smacked his palm down against the counter, but it made no noise.

"I'm fine." She removed the steaming bowl of soup and placed it on the table to cool. While waiting, she reached for a notepad and pen. "Jack, you had to take chemistry, to be a doctor."

"Yes?"

"Sam has arrested Hammond, who told him that any-body with basic science knowledge could make homemade cyanide."

He scowled. "I guess so—but it would be dangerous. Hammond killed Morganna, er, Linda?"

She couldn't get the image out of her mind. Linda, red dress, blowpipe just out of reach.

"What is the fastest way for cyanide to be lethal?"

Jack considered this. "Inhalation."

She drew a pair of lips. The long pipe.

Jack slid off the counter to stand over her shoulder and look at her doodles. She pointed to the picture of the witch on the fridge. "Not as good as Hailey, but . . ."

"What is it?"

"Linda had to blow into this metal tube—it's about four feet long, and thin. She hadn't planned on leaving right away, though Rich said her suitcase was packed. The furnace takes time to heat, and she must have been firing the ma-chine up for more work to start the glass melting—the glass wasn't completely liquid. Could she have inhaled the poison from there?" She sucked in her breath, imagining the tube like a whistle.

Jack fluttered her notepad as he moved around the table. "Ask Sam to check the mouthpiece of the tube as point of entry. Her mouth would show signs of poison burn. It wouldn't be an easy death."

"How awful! And even if it is true, we still don't know *who* did it. Hang on." Charlene texted Sam about the mouthpiece of the pipe. She saw that he'd read the mes-sage, but he didn't reply. Hopefully, he wasn't busy tossing Dylan in a jail cell next to Hammond. She caught Jack up on Dylan's activities all over town and concluded with "So Dylan took chemistry classes in college."

Jack sat opposite her at the table. "Doesn't every four-year student have to take some form of science? That doesn't mean Dylan killed the witch. That's a reach, even for your detective. Has the book of shadows showed up?"

"It's still missing." She was so tired she didn't know how to untangle all the names of suspects in her head. "The only person who we can say for sure didn't kill her is her abusive boyfriend, because he was in jail. How sad is that?"

Jack shimmered in his seat. "The detective must not completely believe that Hammond is guilty or else he wouldn't be searching for Dylan. This isn't over yet, Charlene. Lucas was sleeping with the witch. Does he have an alibi?"

"I don't know. But I can ask around. What if Lucas wasn't the only person Morganna was having an affair with? She was living with Rich, texting Hammond, and flirting with every man in sight." Charlene blew on her chowder to get it to cool. If she didn't eat it soon, she might fall asleep in it.

His gaze challenged her to think carefully. "Can you think of anybody specifically?"

"Brandy had suggested to me that Evelyn might be protecting someone. I really want to talk to Stephanos Landis—he and Evelyn were very tight."

"Just be careful, Charlene," Jack warned. "Meet in a public place."

Charlene finished her chowder and rinsed the bowl, exhaustion clouding her mind. Had Stephanos been doing more than protecting his best friend by wanting to banish Morganna, or could he be covering up his own affair?

CHAPTER TWENTY-FOUR

B efore Charlene napped in her bed, the soft, plump pillows beckoning, she went upstairs to do a walk-through. She read the note of thanks signed by Diane and Natalie, and pressed it to her heart as she wished the mother and daughter well. Minnie would change the sheets on all of the beds tomorrow.

The house was cozily empty, and Charlene was glad that she didn't have to entertain for the afternoon. She drew the chain lock on the front door and then shuffled to bed, followed by Silva. The cat's low purrs immediately lulled Charlene to sleep.

After two hours of rest, she awoke not quite refreshed, so she spent the afternoon on the sofa in her sitting room, watching old movies, playing sudoku, and reading a few chapters from a romantic suspense novel on her tablet. The heroine was smart and savvy, not the too-stupid-to-live kind, like she'd been the night before.

Poor Sam. She certainly knew how to try his patience. Once she was on the mend, she'd sign up for a self-defense class and learn not to think with her heart so much in an emergency. He hadn't answered her text about the blow-pipe, and she hoped he wasn't giving up on her.

She took two ibuprofen to ease the pain and tried to snooze on her love seat. Unfortunately, her mind wouldn't shut down. Finally, she sat up with a sigh. "Jack? Are you there?"

Maybe talking these things out would help her find resolution. The pieces of the puzzle didn't fit, and her brain strove to make sense of them.

He joined her at once, his presence a refreshing burst of cool air.

"You called?" He bowed formally to make her laugh.

She patted the love seat next to her. "Jack. You realize that the murder happened a week ago today?"

"All Hallows' Eve. Full moon." Jack shifted as if to get more comfortable—how, she wondered, could he be *un*comfortable? "How is your head?"

"Sore, but fine. It's my imagination that is giving me a hard time." She nibbled her lower lip. "Why hasn't Dylan gone back to Hartford, where he could be out from under Sam's radar?" She recalled Dylan's wide eyes as he'd faced the SUV driver in the street. "The more I think about yesterday, the more I wonder if Dylan was *following* Darren and his friend? I mean, Dylan was so intent that he almost got hit by a car."

"I know you want to trust Dylan, but you don't know him well." Jack crooked his knee so that his heel rested on his opposite leg. "Why are you so attached?"

She snugged her afghan around her lap. "The truth? Dylan reminds me of Jared when we first dated—not that they look alike, but Jared had been an awkward college student, and so afraid to ask me out. When he did?" She smoothed the blanket. "I couldn't say yes fast enough." Her heart sighed at the memory.

Jack emanated understanding. "I get it. But you know that Dylan is not Jared?"

"I know," she said. "I saw a picture on Facebook of him with his new Goth friends around the water, dated Halloween night." What if she'd been mistaken in her trust?

"What if I'm wrong?" she whispered. She looked at Jack. "Last night, I'd smelled propane, which makes sense, because Linda had a tank in that back room. Whoever hit me was inside that room."

Kass—thank heaven for Kass—had come to her rescue before the killer had time to finish her off. Or . . . what if Kass had set her up? Had been hiding in that room? She'd smelled sage.

Charlene, uneasy, tossed off her crocheted throw, suddenly too warm. "I hate not knowing who to trust. Kass is the one who called for me to meet her."

Jack tilted his head in thought. "Could this still be about Evelyn's book of shadows? Maybe somebody is determined to find it."

"At this point, why?" Charlene asked. "Morganna is dead."

Jack strummed his fingers along the love seat cushion. "What if whoever killed Linda needs to find the spell book in order to protect Evelyn? I don't think Evelyn would have the strength to hit you over the head."

Charlene thought back. "It was very gloomy inside the shop. I had dropped my cell phone, which is when I was hit."

"It keeps coming back around to Evelyn," Jack said. "Maybe she went to Morganna's Witch House that night to confront Linda about the stolen book?"

Charlene considered this scenario with a pat to where Jack's hand should have been on the cushion between them, and met cool air. "And Evelyn just happened to have some extra cyanide in her pocket, next to her antighost charm?"

Jack sat back with a chuckle. "Good point."

She checked her phone. Nothing from Sam. Stifled by her promise to the detective to stay home and rest for the day meant she'd need to wait to pick up her Pilot in the morning. "I think Sam is giving me the silent treatment," she said.

"Or he's busy," Jack countered.

"I hope he's found Linda's *real* murderer." Sam had said he still wanted to talk to Dylan, and all Charlene could think of was his frightened face yesterday. Her phone dinged.

Hazmat has the blowpipe. Rest.

"Jack—Sam says Hazmat has the metal pipe. Do you think we helped? Oh, he's going to hate that." But it did wonders for her headache.

"That's wonderful, but as you said before—it doesn't name the killer."

"Kass knows everybody," she said. "And I need tea."

"You've lost me. . . ."

"For the business." A whisper of guilt surfaced because she had no guests registered, though she had two couples and a single for next weekend.

Before she could change her mind, Charlene dialed Kass, who she hoped was at her shop and not filling in as a guide for a haunted tour.

Kass picked up right away. Charlene put the call on speaker so that Jack could hear, and set the phone on the coffee table. "Charlene! How are you feeling? You home yet? I've been thinking of calling all day but didn't want to bug you if you were sleeping."

"They released me around noon. Two stitches and a headache."

"That's terrible. Can I bring you anything?"

"No, no. I want to thank you for saving my butt last night. You took a big risk by doing that!"

"I'd called Officer Tanner," Kass said. "I knew help was on the way. I was very worried, Charlene, I don't mind saying. I don't want anything bad to happen to you."

"Neither do I," Charlene laughed. "I acted on impulse, not smarts." She exchanged a look with Jack. "I have to pick up my car in the morning, and I wondered if I could place a tea order to pick up. Every time I try to drop in, something happens, and I'm down to my last packet of instant hot chocolate."

Kass snorted. "Can't have that. What would you like?"

"Make an assortment for me, would you?" A doubt whispered from her mind that if Kass was actually her enemy, she was handing her the perfect weapon via muslin sachet.

"Sure. You like orange, and cinnamon?"

"Yes. Uh, do you know Stephanos well?" Charlene jotted his name down on the back of her sudoku puzzle, putting a fancy circle around it.

"Oh, yeah. He and Evelyn used to be on the welcome committee for new Wiccans in town." Her voice held humor. "A very handsome and charming man—single, if you are interested?"

"No! Sheesh." She glared at the phone and ignored Jack's chuckle. "But I would like to meet him." She wrote Kass's name down, too, making little flowers around the *K*.

"Charlene, I was just kidding about the hookup—he is handsome, but he's got to be thirty years older than you."

Jack laughed so loud that she was surprised Kass couldn't hear her ghost.

"Kass, be serious! You've been so open about your religion, but I still have a few more questions on how things work inside the Wiccan coven. I'd like to meet him—but make it casual, okay?"

There was a long silence, and then: "Charlene, I realized last night when I found you in Morganna's that you are trying to find her killer. Am I right?"

Charlene almost swallowed her tongue. "Uh . . ."

"Stephanos is *not* your man, trust me. I'll see if he can meet, but no promises. The elders are more discreet when it comes to talking about religion—and murder within the community? This has been bad press so he's working double time to keep it quiet. I thought he was going to *pass out* when Carmen and I suggested that a witch killer might be on the loose in Salem."

"Well, that's it. He knows everyone in the coven. Maybe he has insight as to why someone would want Morganna dead. Gone, I can understand, but why not just buy her a bus ticket out of town?" *Morganna*, she wrote, adding an orb beside her name.

"And the break-ins have to be tied in somehow," Kass said. "I want to lift the town vibe. This is very negative energy."

"I see why you don't want her to be guilty." Jack paced before the television. "She sounds very interesting. But don't let your guard down, Charlene."

Kass snickered. "I know just how to get him to show up. 'Hey, Stephanos, this really hot chick from Chicago wants to grill you about a murderer among the coven. Ten okay?'"

"You're *hysterical*," Charlene said in her driest tone. "Casual, remember? Either way, I'll see you in the morning. Ten is great."

"Will do. And get some rest. Hey, Detective Sam was sure ticked last night. You two got a thing going on? He's awfully cute."

Jack's chill was immediate, and she feared frostbite on her nose.

"Uh . . . no. No 'thing.' We're just friends." She jotted down *Sam*, with a heart.

"Sure you are!" Kass observed. "Friends don't look at each other the way he looks at you. And I saw you looking back."

"Bye, Kass." She started to hang up but then remembered her question: Why had she wanted to see Charlene? It hadn't been for a tea reading, like she'd told Sam. "Kass?" The dial tone buzzed in her ears. She called right back but got a busy signal. "I guess it can wait till morning."

Jack returned to the love seat next to her. "What can wait?"

She flipped the puzzle book over so that Jack couldn't read her doodles. "The real reason she asked me to her shop."

"Charlene, I know I can't stop you from meeting her and Stephanos in the morning, but you need to be careful. Have your phone with Sam's number on speed dial. Call him if there is a hint of danger."

"I will." Her eyes drooped sleepily now that she had a plan for the next day.

"If you were my patient, I'd recommend rest and laughter for the remainder of the evening."

Charlene followed the doctor's orders and put her phone on silent so they could watch movies and take her mind off Linda, and Dylan. When she woke up the next morning, curled on her side of the love seat, the television and lights were off, and she'd been covered with her afghan.

Sweet Jack.

Charlene took a long, hot shower and gingerly washed her hair, devising her plan for when she met the handsome, charming Stephanos. He sounded like a lady-killer, but could he kill in cold blood? If Evelyn was protective of him, then maybe he was just as protective of her.

She dressed in black wool slacks, a pink silk shirt, and a

fitted black cloak that she used to wear to work in Chicago. She called for an Uber to take her downtown.

"Bye, Jack! Bye, Silva!" Neither roommate answered.

Charlene's five-minute trip was just long enough for her to decide to keep her Pilot in the parking lot. She had the driver drop her off at Fortune's Tea Shoppe. The morning was cool but bright. She entered and was immersed in peace and harmony via herbal scents and soft sounds. The goddess fountain gurgled merrily.

"Kass!" Her tall friend had added tiny turquoise feathers to some of her braids, which matched the ivory pirate shirt and tight black pants.

"Charlene, I've got you all set up." Charlene spied a box on the counter with her name scrawled on the side. "And I've given you the employee discount."

She thought of Darren and looked around the shop, but the lanky guy with the orange Mohawk wasn't there. She desperately wanted to talk to him about Dylan. Maybe he knew where Dylan was staying. "Thank you!"

"I've got the water boiling. An oolong with orange zest?"

"Yes, please. Is Darren in today?" Charlene took off her cloak and draped it on the stool next to her.

Kass fixed each of them tea, adding thin slices of lemon. "No, he's taking a couple days off. Funny you should ask."

"Why's that?" Her nape tingled.

"Well, he's the reason I wanted to talk to you the other night." Her blue feather dangled precariously close to her teacup. "He's been acting weird since Morganna's death, so I asked him what was going on, you know? Maybe he had a secret crush or something and needed to talk." Kass waved the scent of tea up to her nose.

Charlene had wondered if Morganna might have had other lovers. Surely Darren was too young? "What did he say?"

"It's probably not important. He and his buddies were on the pier, beneath the full moon. . . ."

"Halloween night?" She recalled the picture of Dylan near the water, on his Facebook page. "And?"

"That kid you were asking us about, your guest? Well, I guess he got into an argument with Darren's friend Travis."

"Tall kid, works with Carmen?"

"Yeah." Kass added honey to her tea.

"But, you heard me ask Darren if he knew Dylan the other day and he said no."

Kass flushed pink. "I didn't know he was lying to you, I promise."

"So what happened?" Dylan hadn't mentioned a fight that night, just a party.

"Let me explain about the kids around here. While I think every person has their own spiritual journey, Morganna didn't like the Goth crowd." Kass stirred the honey at the bottom of her cup. "In order to be part of this Wiccan coven in Salem, you have to prove that you have some psychic ability, or else be accepted as an apprentice—an acolyte. Morganna treated them like dirt because she was a part of the coven, as if that made her better than them."

Evelyn had said that Morganna had *zero* psychic power.

She wouldn't have been accepted into the coven without it—unless she'd agreed to be an apprentice.

Charlene lowered her teacup. Evelyn had figured out that Morganna stole her book of shadows to trap the spirit of Armand Sheffield—intending to use his powers to stay within the coven? Who had taken Morganna under their wing, in secret?

"So—the kids were at the pier, partying. What did Dylan and Travis argue about?"

The pitch of Kass's voice was so low that Charlene had to lean in to hear her words. "Someone had Morganna's cell phone. I don't know how, and Darren said he doesn't know, either, but they were doing a spell beneath the full moon."

Charlene bit her tongue.

Kass squeezed lemon into her cup, not looking at Charlene. "Kids like to show off, pretend they have more power than they do. Anyway, Darren said that Travis decided they should try to capture Morganna's spirit. Using something of hers, the phone, to draw her into one of her own witch balls."

"What?" The whole thing sounded outlandish.

Kass put her hand to her chest. "I've never seen it done. It would take a very powerful witch to capture a spirit—not a group of kids."

"Do you think one of them killed her—maybe to prove themselves to the coven?"

"Shh! I *really* don't think so," Kass said, her mouth pinched. "But your guest threatened to go to the police, so Travis reacted and tossed Morganna's cell phone into the water, far off the end of the pier. Darren said that's why he lied."

That's where the phone went! "I have to call Sam. Why haven't you gone to the police with this information?"

"Maybe they were partying hard. . . ."

"Drugs?"

Kass looked very unhappy as she sipped her tea. "They're just kids."

"Playing with magic." At the least. Poor Dylan! If Dylan had threatened to call the cops that night, why had he then stayed in Salem to hang out with them all? Had his girlfriend influenced his decision? Or was he a typical college kid, experimenting with something new?

Sam needed to find Linda's killer. It seemed as if Dylan knew more than he'd told the detective about what had happened that night. "Can I get Darren's phone number? I really have to talk to him about Dylan."

Kass paled. "I don't feel good about that. Darren said he had nothing to do with Morganna's death, but he's been sick over it."

Charlene felt sick too. "Were you at the pier, Kass?"

"No—Darren closed, and I went home after the tour, then drank shots with Tony and the guys at the bar downstairs. We heard later what had happened and didn't believe it."

Charlene looked at the teacup clock behind Kass's register. Ten a.m. had come and gone, and it was now half past ten. "If you can't give me Darren's number, would you please have him call me? I haven't heard from Dylan, and I'm worried about him." Maybe it was a good thing she didn't have kids—she'd be a mess. How did any parent handle not knowing if their child was okay? She made a note to be nicer to her mother.

"I can do that," Kass said. "But he's scared, you know?"

"If he knows anything, Detective Holden is the one to contact." Charlene reached for her cloak. "It doesn't look like Stephanos is coming."

Kass sighed. "I told him that you had some questions about the workings of the coven." She put her hand on Charlene's wrist. "Oh, wait. Here he comes."

Charlene turned on her seat. Stephanos Landis's elegant form showcased wide shoulders, a tall, lean frame, and a commanding presence. His dark blue suit was visible under a camel coat, and his leather gloves even *looked* soft. He had a wool scarf wrapped around his neck; beautiful, thick white hair slicked off his face; a strong, straight nose; a square jaw; blue flashing eyes that lit up when they saw her; and a warm lady-killer smile.

Easy to see why women joined the coven, if this guy was their leader.

She put her coat down and stood, offering her hand. "I'm Charlene Morris. Thanks for agreeing to meet me."

The news about Morganna/Linda's stolen phone could wait a few more minutes, she decided. Especially if this interview with Stephanos went well. Had he been having an affair with Morganna too? She couldn't think of anyone else Evelyn would go to such lengths to protect.

"My pleasure." Stephanos smoothed the lapels of his coat. "Take your seat. Kass, would you like to join us?"

"I have a few things to do first," Kass said. "Can I get you a tea, Stephanos? Or something stronger?"

"A strong brewed coffee with some room," he said, showing a silver flask.

Kass tossed her hair over her shoulder with a chuckle. "Coming right up. How about you, Charlene?"

"Better not," she said. "It would go straight to my head, and I'm dizzy enough after getting smacked the other night."

"Kass told me about that." His voice was rich and deep. "Terrible thing." He removed his coat and folded it neatly over the back of his chair. "How are you now?"

"Fine." She touched the bandage at her temple.

"What happened there?" he asked, eyes narrowed.

"Hit the counter going down," she said.

"Not sure what is going on in this town of ours. It was never like this. Not before . . ."

"Yes, that's what I wanted to speak to you about." She folded her hands. A customer entered the shop, and Kass greeted her cheerily. Charlene whispered, "Do you know of any reason why someone would want Morganna dead? Or any of the witches hurt?"

Stephanos gripped the table so hard his knuckles turned white. "No." He glanced at Kass, who guided the customer toward the loose-leaf tea. "That woman was *no* witch. She was an imposter and a seducer. She used her feminine wiles to get what she wanted because she had no magick."

He raked a hand through his hair. "I know I should not speak ill of the dead, but I saw through her right from the start."

"And Lucas?" Charlene kept her voice low. "Could he see through her too?"

Stephanos gave her a discerning look that made her shift uncomfortably on her seat. If he could see right through Morganna, then why hadn't he stopped her before she'd done her damage?

Kass broke the heavy silence when she arrived with his coffee. He added a slug of golden booze and stirred, the scent like oak. He took a large sip and put the mug back down. "Excellent. Thank you, Kass."

"Welcome." Kass returned to the customer, who smelled each dried blossom or herb bin to create her own blend. Kass spoke animatedly about the variety of flavors, her long arm flung wide.

Stephanos sat back and studied Charlene, his finger to his lip before he lowered his hand. "I talked to Lucas about the affair, warned him plenty of times. But a man does what a man must, and he wanted to believe the best in her, because he was quite enamored. Head over heels in lust." He drank again. "Men are weak when it comes to beautiful women and temptation."

"I don't imagine that you are weak, Stephanos." She stared at him in a frank manner. What would he do to protect his coven? His family, and friends?

"You flatter me, my dear."

"I didn't mean to." She fiddled with the napkin next to her cup of tea, tearing it into shreds. "Do you know if Morganna was seeing anybody else within the coven, sexually? Romantically?"

"No." He stroked his chin.

"Were *you* attracted to her?"

Stephanos snorted. "*No.* It killed me to see the damage

she was doing to the Evergreen family. Not that Martine ever complained."

Charlene recalled the pale strip of skin on the woman's wedding finger. "She didn't seem happy with the status quo."

"Evelyn warned me that if we tried to keep Lucas and Morganna's affair a secret, it would be found out." He sighed. "And as we feared, Martine has taken it very, very hard. She isn't a strong woman. Lucas mentioned that you were at his bookshop, asking questions?"

Charlene heard censure in his tone and regarded him with her head high.

"What were you looking for at Morganna's? I can't imagine it worth your life," he said.

"I heard a noise. The witch balls in the front display were no longer hanging there, and there was broken glass by the back door." She didn't tell him about the real reason for her involvement—a kid she'd met a week ago. "On purpose?" She shrugged.

His eyes were guarded. "I can't imagine why anyone would intentionally break them. It seems like a random act of vandalism."

"Could someone be searching for Evelyn's book of shadows?" She pushed a lock of hair behind her ear, touching her diamond earring for luck. Although Stephanos was pleasant enough, a palpable tension weighted the air.

"I suppose," he said slowly—too casually. "It might be worth looking for." He leaned back, crossing one leg over another.

Charlene wasn't about to lose this opportunity to question Stephanos directly. It didn't matter whether or not she believed in witchcraft—they did. "Who do you think has the psychic power in your community to use Evelyn's spells? Does Kass?" She looked at the tea shop owner.

He shook his head.

"Do you?"

Stephanos didn't falter beneath her steady gaze. "I have psychic gifts, as does Martine . . . Lucas, not so much, but he does have a glimmer. Before you ask if we are responsible, the three of us were hosting the Witch Ball at the Hawthorne Hotel, with hundreds of witnesses, when Morganna was killed."

She filed the information away to be double-checked later.

"Are you trying to solve this murder yourself?" His white brow arched regally, and she felt about ten years old. "You really should leave this to the police. Asking questions could lead to more trouble." What did he know that he wasn't telling her? She noticed that his gaze kept landing at the bandage at her temple. Was that concern, or a warning?

The door to Kass's shop jangled as more customers arrived. Charlene, uneasy, got up and reached for her purse—and the pepper spray she'd moved to the side pocket within easy reach.

"Thank you very much for your time," she said.

"You take care of yourself." A tiny line of moisture dotted his brow and just above his mouth. It was a chilly day, and not warm in the shop. The whiskey? Or covering up for someone, as Evelyn had done? Would he protect Evelyn, and Lucas, as a leader of their community? Would Stephanos have had the strength to pop her on the back of the head night before last?

The tea roiled in her stomach.

Somehow, she managed to put her cloak on. Kass met her at the register, where Charlene paid for her cup of oolong and the assortment of teas, as well as Stephanos's coffee. She needed fresh air and a clear head to figure out what had just happened.

"Thanks for introducing us, Kass." She offered her hand to Stephanos. "It was a pleasure meeting you."

"And you." He didn't sound like he meant it any more than she did. Charlene balanced the container, just larger than a shoe box, in one hand and left Kass's tea shop. She stepped out on the street and breathed deep the crisp fall air. She looked around for Dylan, or Darren or Rich, before she started her brisk walk to her car, her purse in front of her with the pepper spray in easy reach.

What had caused the elegant Stephanos to break into a sweat?

CHAPTER TWENTY-FIVE

Charlene unlocked the doors to her Pilot, placed the box with the tea samples on the floor in the back, then slid behind the wheel. She turned on the heater. Chills ran over her like someone walking on her grave. It was a strange new world she lived in now, where witches and ghosts were the norm and people were not what they seemed.

She reached for her phone to call Sam but realized she was two blocks from the station and might as well just drop by. She could use a dose of down-to-earth Detective Sam Holden after her meeting with Stephanos.

Charlene was not one to believe in magic, just like she didn't believe in Santa or the Easter Bunny. However, she had a ghost for a roommate, so she knew that there was something more—she just didn't know what.

She parked in front of the station and walked inside. Officer Tanner, pale and freckled, sat at the front desk, typing one-fingered on the keyboard of the computer, his ear to a black phone receiver.

Sam said from behind her, "Charlene? What are you doing here?"

She whirled and put her hand to her rapidly beating heart. "Sam!"

He smiled cautiously. "You okay?"

"Can we talk?"

He took her by the elbow and guided her down the front brick stairs of the police station and around the back to a manicured lawn shaded by oak trees. Six faded picnic tables were around the grounds. All were vacant, so Sam brought her to the first one, where she sat on the wooden bench.

He studied the bandage, and unlike Stephanos's perusal, Sam's felt gentle and caring. "I meant to call—how are you? We've been busy. Hazmat just sent back the numbers to Captain Moreno and me—thirty minutes ago. You were right about the mouthpiece. How did you know?"

"I didn't," she said. "I just kept remembering how it seemed Linda was reaching for the blowpipe." She could never tell Sam about Jack in a million years. "Sam, I just went to pick up my car and get some tea from Kass."

Sam sat down opposite her at the picnic table. "And?"

"Her employee said that the Goth kids were partying on the pier Halloween night. One of them had Linda's phone." She took a deep breath. "Did you find Dylan?"

"Kid is one step ahead of me," he said, his jaw tight. "Go on?"

"Well, Dylan was there that night, and when he realized that the phone belonged to Linda, he threatened to call the police."

Sam smoothed his mustache in a cool manner.

"And," she continued in a rush, "the guy, uh, Travis?— threw the phone into the water off the pier. I don't know if that will help you find it?"

"Why were they on the pier *exactly*?"

"Midnight. Full moon." She swallowed uncomfortably, knowing that Sam did not believe in the paranormal at all.

"They were trying to bring back Morganna's spirit with her phone and trap her into a glass orb like she used to make."

Sam gave her an incredulous look, then leaned his elbow on the picnic table. "Do you have Travis's last name?"

"No, but Darren would . . . He . . . works at Kass's. Travis works with Carmen Evergreen."

"Did Kass know about the phone? Was she a part of this party on the pier to trap Linda's spirit?"

"I don't think so. Sam, she just told me about Darren, and I told her I was coming to you. I asked to talk to Darren myself about Dylan, but she said he was taking a few days off."

Sam scowled.

Charlene rushed in. "Sam, remember that I told you that I saw Dylan, before I went into Morganna's? Well, it looked like he was with Darren and another guy—but what if he was following them? What if someone is setting him up?"

Sam knocked his knuckles against the wood of the table. "Charlene, I will say this about you—you are loyal to a fault. I don't know what this kid did to earn your trust. I hope that he doesn't let you down."

His sincerity tugged at her. She breathed in the scent of leaves and earth around them, the breeze from the wharf. "Have you looked into Stephanos Landis?"

Sam's posture snapped up straight. "Why?"

She skipped over the fact that she'd set up the meeting and said, "He stopped by while I was buying my tea. He kept staring at my bandage, and I think he warned me to leave the investigation to the police."

"Was it an actual threat?"

She thought back to how the words were spoken. "Not something I could swear to, no. But he had a shot of whiskey in his coffee when he was there with Kass and me. Why would he need fortification?"

"Maybe he's an alcoholic."

"I had an uncle that was addicted to vodka and his eyes were bloodshot all the time, his skin jaundiced. Stephanos wasn't like that." No, Stephanos was strong and healthy, physically capable of knocking her over the head. "But I must be wrong. He couldn't have killed Linda because he said that he, Martine, and Lucas hosted the Witch Ball and they have alibis for the night of Morganna's death."

Charlene studied her fingernails rather than see Sam's "butt out" look. If Kass was telling the truth, that meant four main possibilities were all accounted for and Charlene's list was shrinking.

At Sam's exhale she finally looked up to brave his censure. Sure enough, his jaw was clenched. "Kenny Chang, one of my boys, has been tailing Stephanos. Like you," he said with no hint of camaraderie, "we also figured him for a key player. A person of interest, as well as his buddy Lucas. Especially since he was in a relationship with Linda."

"So you already knew Stephanos was at the tea shop this morning?"

"I know a lot of things, but I can't tell you what, now can I?"

"You didn't know about the phone. . . ."

"That will be a help."

Charlene thought over what she'd learned this morning, glad to have shared it with Sam. It was a little annoying that he couldn't tell her things, but she didn't take it to heart. His civic duty meant keeping her in the dark.

"I'll interview Darren, and that Travis kid. Dylan was there—do you know who else was on the pier that night?"

"No. But there is a picture of a bunch of kids on his Facebook page." Dylan's trip to Salem had gone so wrong.

"I'll handle it, Charlene." Sam stood, eager to get back to work. "I'll call later—can you go *home*, please?"

Her head pounded, so she managed a yes without a single nod.

The weather had cleared to a gray sky without rain, and her drive home took only a few minutes. She put the selection of tea into the pantry and grabbed a can of tuna for Silva. The cat meowed next to her empty dish as if she hadn't eaten in months. "Hey, baby, you miss me?" Charlene petted the silky softness of Silva's fur as the feline proudly arched her back, purring with contentment.

A draft behind her made her whirl around with relief. Sam couldn't talk to her, but Jack sure could—and that mattered very much.

"You're here!"

He took his usual seat, his gorgeous blue eyes warm and concerned as he looked at her. "You have purple shadows on your cheeks, Charlene. Perhaps you should have stayed in the hospital longer."

"No, I'm fine. I really am." She rested her hip against the kitchen counter. "I have so much to tell you."

"Stephanos showed up?"

"He did." She crossed her arms. "But more importantly, Kass finally told me why she'd asked me over the other night."

Jack leaned back in his chair, and she noted the stretch of light-blue knit across his broad shoulders, navy slacks, loafers on his feet. His hair waved around his ears, and a dark lock had escaped and lingered on his forehead.

"Don't keep me in suspense!" Jack sat forward in a rush of air. "Did she confess?"

"No." Charlene pulled out the kitchen chair to sit down too. "But Dylan is involved somehow—the Goth kids had Linda's phone and were trying to trap her spirit at midnight in one of her witch balls. Kass said that they had to use something that belonged to Morganna, to call to her on the night when the veil is thinnest."

"Ah—so Rich wasn't lying when he said he didn't have her phone." Jack tapped his fingers against the table soundlessly. "Have you talked to the detective?"

"Yes—I told Kass I'd have to. I just don't think she felt comfortable 'ratting' on her employee. I guess there were drugs involved." Charlene scooted back so that Silva could jump in her lap. She gave Jack the condensed version of Dylan, the fight, and Linda's phone in the water, ruined.

"I feel so close." She rubbed the tips of Silva's ears. "Like the answers are just on the edge of my fingertips, and yet out of my grasp. Dang it! I forgot to ask Sam if Hammond was still in jail." Charlene eyed her cell phone on the table but didn't pick it up.

Jack studied her before asking, "Was Stephanos able to help enlighten you on the folks in the coven?"

"There is something off about him, despite his charm. He said that he, Lucas, and Martine were visibly running the Witch Ball. But Sam has an officer tailing him. How well do you know Stephanos?"

"We attended some of the same parties or events. Salem's not that big of a city, and the locals with ancestral roots seem to stick together." He interlaced his fingers— his hands on the table. Hovering just above without touching—but Charlene had to really look to realize the illusion.

"Yes. I've learned that already." Salem Hall had an entire floor dedicated to Salem's ancestors. "What else do you know?"

"He and Evelyn made a dashing couple for several years. Not sure why they didn't end up married. They seemed very close."

"I can imagine them together. Both so elegant, kind of like you," she teased.

"We would have made an elegant couple too," he said in a serious tone.

"Yes," she told him sincerely, but Sam's face, his smile, came to mind. "I treasure our friendship, Jack." She didn't want to think of Sam when she was with Jack, or vice versa. She enjoyed the company of them both, but their friendship or relationship would never equal what she'd had with Jared.

She shared about Stephanos's seeming nervous. "Was he a drinker, do you know?"

"I saw him drink socially but never drunk." Jack rubbed his chin.

"Another thing—when I brought up the book of shadows to Stephanos, his demeanor changed. He acted like it didn't matter, but I think it does to him, and to Evelyn."

She remembered a hovering presence, the smell of sage, gas, and alcohol before she'd lost consciousness. Whiskey? But it was high-end. She knew the scent—oak! Did that mean that Stephanos had clunked her over the head?

Charlene placed the cat on the floor and hurried to her liquor bar, uncapping her expensive Glenlivet. She inhaled the oaky notes. "It was this that I smelled the other night. Scotch."

Jack joined her at the cabinet in the dining room. "Good taste."

"Distinctive smell. I think I interrupted Stephanos in Morganna's workstation."

"No wonder he was sweating during your conversation today." Jack's expression drew tight with anger. "He hit you!"

"To keep me from discovering him." Her stomach rolled with nerves, and she put the bottle back in the cabinet. "What was *he* doing in there?"

Jack pounded his fist down in a swoosh of cool air. "Maybe you should invite him over? We could question him ourselves."

She laughed weakly. "Like you did to Ernie? Frightened the daylights out of him."

"Served him right, the weasel."

"I have to tell Sam that I remember the scotch smell—specifically the brand. That might be enough reason for him to bring Stephanos in for questioning."

"You shouldn't have to help the detective do his job. Running 'Charlene's' is yours." His gaze went to the bandage at her temple, which was nothing compared to the throb at the back of her head.

"All I want is a houseful of guests." And Dylan to be in touch. Maybe she should institute a "Charlene's" policy of nobody under the age of twenty-five. Nobody that would make her care. But when she thought of Diane and Natalie Robinson, where she'd listened and made a difference . . . she accepted that she would have to open her heart.

This emotional risk was part of her new life. She carefully touched her head as she hoped the physical one wouldn't be part of it too.

"So, if you don't crave the excitement or the mystery, prove it, and give it up." He walked behind her, and she turned her head to take him all in. It was a fine day when she'd met Doctor Jack Strathmore, her hauntingly beautiful ghost.

"I can't," she said truthfully. "Dylan is on the run until we find who really did kill Linda. Who had the 'power' to help Morganna?" She strode back to the kitchen and returned to her chair.

Jack materialized before her. "If, as Stephanos said, he, Martine, and Lucas all hosted the Witch Ball, and it turns out that Kass was with Tony—you'll need to find out for sure—then who might Morganna have given the book of shadows to?"

"Kass, Carmen, Rich, Hammond, and I guess Lucas were friends of hers at one point." Charlene gave a rueful laugh. "Nobody is admitting to being her friend now. The Goth kids never liked her. Stephanos never liked her."

"Now she's dead."

They had the same thought at the same time.

Jack voiced it. "What if Stephanos comes back to try and kill you again?"

Charlene lifted the phone. "It's time to call Sam."

CHAPTER TWENTY-SIX

Charlene checked all the locks in the house to make sure her home was secure and paced the foyer, pepper spray in hand, until Sam arrived—her laptop in her leather case over his shoulder. His scowl forbade her from saying a word as he placed the laptop on her kitchen table. She discreetly dropped her pepper spray back in her purse.

He strode from one end of her narrow kitchen to the other, concern on his face, but he was also struggling with something that she couldn't rush.

At last he stopped and straightened. Jack, seated on the counter, exuded tension.

"Your call about the scotch was timely. Stephanos was at the station for questioning regarding his alibi for the night of Halloween. The Witch Ball is a madhouse, but the hotel has video footage, and it seems Stephanos is not always on film."

Charlene gasped.

Sam stared at her, his brown eyes intense. "When you said he was sweating and nervous this morning, that raised a flag. He'd been cool as ice earlier this week during two separate interviews—so what had changed between the night of the murder and today?" He pointed at Charlene. "The break-ins."

Jack clapped behind him. Silva jumped into Charlene's lap.

"As soon as I mentioned that you remembered the smell of Glenlivet that night when you were hurt, he broke down."

Her heart raced with apprehension. "Has he been arrested? I can't believe he killed Morganna. . . ."

"I don't think he's guilty of murder. Despite the lack of video footage, there are a hundred eyewitnesses of him there all night at the ball."

"What did he want, then?"

"As much as it pains me to admit it, you were right about that diary, or spell book, or whatever you call it."

"Book of shadows."

"Yeah. Stephanos believed that Morganna had it, and he was trying to help Evelyn get it back." Sam tugged his mustache.

"So he broke in to Kass's store, looking for the book, and Carmen's shop too?"

"Salem has city cameras, and we have matched footage of a cloaked figure approximately Mr. Landis's size in the alley the night of Kass's break-in. We are still investigating Carmen's burglary, but I don't know that we need it to hold him."

Charlene exhaled with relief.

"He's lawyered up and isn't saying much else, but, Charlene, he said that *you* requested the meeting at the tea shop. Something you neglected to mention earlier. Would you like to explain?"

She winced. "Not really."

"Humor me."

After drawing in a long breath, Charlene released it slowly. "Sunday, I stayed home, just as I'd promised you. I realized that Stephanos was the perfect person to ask if Morganna had other lovers besides the ones we knew about. Evelyn was protecting him. I wanted to know if *he* had also been sleeping with Morganna."

Jack chuckled behind her. "You aren't winning any points. I think I see smoke coming out of his ears."

She ignored her ghost and focused on Sam. "I knew Kass was friends with him, and it was a public place . . . He said no, about an affair with Morganna, but it seemed like he was hiding something." Her mouth twisted downward. "Like the fact he was the one to clobber me."

"Charlene." Sam's voice was deceptively smooth, but she kept her guard up.

"Yes?" She bit her lip, knowing he was furious with her. When he'd release his fury, she was going to feel really bad. She should listen to him. He only wanted to keep her safe. He cared about her. As she did him.

"What don't you understand about not questioning people and leaving the detective work to the detectives?" His soft voice made her eyes water.

"Not as much as you would like." She looked away, telling herself to be strong. Chin up, she said, "I understand your concern, but as you can see, I was perfectly safe."

"Uh-oh," Jack said, scooching farther back on the counter.

"You . . ." Sam's voice could freeze lava. "You met up with the man that knocked you out and put your life in danger. You could have died."

"I didn't know that it was Stephanos—how could I have?" From the corner of her eye she saw Jack shake his head. He'd moved from the counter next to the refrigerator and the picture Hailey had drawn of the witch with the tall purple hat, wild red hair, and necklaces with stars on them. Why couldn't all of her guests be like that sweet girl? Unlike Dylan, who was in real trouble.

Charlene shifted so she couldn't see Jack at all. "Sam, I am sorry that I set up the meeting—I thought I was helping."

"Who, Charlene? Who are you helping?"

"Dylan. He is too young to go to jail. He has his whole life ahead of him—he came to Salem to meet a girl, not to fall in with murderers and witches."

Sam looked up at the ceiling and then at her. "For the record, if Dylan is innocent, then he won't go to jail—I need to question him to find out. I am asking you as a personal favor to let me handle this. I am very, very close. I can't do my job if I am worried about you. Do you understand?"

"Oh, he's good," Jack said.

Charlene folded her hands together. "Yes, I do."

"Now—I am going back to the station to finish the paperwork on Stephanos. You have your laptop. Is there anything else that I can do for you?" His tone dared her to suggest even one thing.

"No, thank you."

Sam clenched his jaw. "Stay home, Charlene. I'll be in touch."

She and Jack walked Sam to the front door, and Jack *tsk-tsk*ed as the detective drove away.

"Well?" Jack said. "What's the plan?"

Charlene peeked at Jack through her bangs. "What do you mean?"

"I saw your body language change from 'willing to listen to the detective' to 'protective' as soon as he said he still wanted to question Dylan."

She closed the front door, her hand on the knob. "He fell in with the wrong crowd!" She snapped her fingers. "Hey! Kevin mentioned a bar called Ruin where the Goths hang out. We were supposed to get together today, actually."

Suddenly the front door opened, and Dylan slipped inside. "Dylan!" She was so relieved to see him that she pushed aside her natural alarm when he was followed by a very tall young man with hair shaved on one side and the other long and black.

Like the night he'd been helping Carmen at the Witch Festival, he'd worn layers of pentagram necklaces, adjusting them as he came from behind a curtain. Carmen's assistant.

Jack, to her right, said, "I told you he'd turn up, like a bad penny."

She stared at the young men and remembered that the very tall man's name was Travis. He and Dylan had fought over Morganna's stolen phone Halloween night at the pier when Travis and Darren had been trying to perform a spell. Why was Dylan with him now?

"Charlene, can you come with me and Travis? Carmen wants to give you a tarot card reading." Dylan's eyes darted around the room as if he couldn't stay focused.

Heart thundering, she backed up a step. "I'm sorry, Dylan." What was wrong with him? "I have plans for the night," she improvised.

"Stay here," Jack said, reaching for her in a cold swoop. He looked from Dylan to Travis.

"You are coming with us," Travis announced. He pulled a blue-and-white tarot card from his back pocket. She remembered seeing that in the room next to Morganna—and in Lucas's bookstore.

"I don't want a reading," Charlene said, her pulse rising in panic.

"Get her keys," Travis told Dylan. He came behind her, but Jack pushed him away with a sudden gust of air.

Dylan shrugged apologetically at her, looking around for the source of wind. "Charlene, where are your keys? Just come with us and you won't get hurt."

She didn't believe that.

Jack slammed the door closed so hard the frame shuddered. Dylan's eyes grew wilder, and Travis curled a fist to punch Charlene. Jack shoved him back, and the young man knocked over the coat-tree. Silva yowled from the staircase.

Dylan saw her purse strap hanging on a kitchen chair and ran for it, dumping her bag out on the kitchen table until he located her car keys. The can of pepper spray rolled across the floor like a tired joke. "Travis, dude—chill out. I've got them." He brushed by her, skinny pale arms bare in just a short-sleeved T-shirt. His jeans hung on him like he'd lost ten pounds in the past week. "You said you wouldn't hurt her."

"What are you doing, Dylan?" She'd been so worried about him, and still was—but it was tempered with growing fear. Travis gripped her wrist hard.

"Helping out a friend," Dylan said. He refused to look at her.

"What friend?" Charlene asked, scratching at Travis's hold. "Travis?"

"Shut up," Travis demanded. He struggled to open the front door, fighting against Jack, who had it closed with all his spectral might.

"What is going on?" Dylan scanned the foyer, eyes wide. Her vintage shell vase crashed to the floor as Jack pushed Travis backward. She jerked her wrist free and took two steps—unsure where to go. Upstairs? Her rooms? They had a lock—the wine cellar?

Jack's rage was a red torrent of energy as he slid Travis across the floor.

Dylan shook off his shock and leaped across the planter to Travis, helping him to his feet. Charlene darted toward the kitchen, but Travis snagged her hair, and she fell back on her butt hard enough to crack her teeth together.

Jack used all of his supernatural strength to pin the door closed.

Travis pulled on the door—Dylan joined him. In the instant that Jack had to regroup his energy, Travis opened the door and shoved her out to the porch. Dylan flew down the steps as if he couldn't leave fast enough.

"Drive," Travis told Dylan, who headed for the driver's side of her Pilot. "And make sure that bitch cop is gone."

Travis held her wrists behind her back. Jack was a whirlwind around the two young men, knocking down branches and blowing up dust.

She was forced into the back seat, a flurry of energy shimmering next to her. She knew it was Jack but couldn't see his form. Travis wrenched her arms behind her, gripping them in place. Dylan peeled out of the driveway. Once they crossed the property line, she heard Jack tell her to fight them, and then he was gone.

Her mind scrambled to put the players in order. Morganna and Carmen had been friends—Carmen had psychic power. Her mother, Martine, was very powerful, and Carmen must have inherited that power along with her mother's migraines.

She thought back to the picture of Dylan that night on the water. She'd thought nothing of the multicolored hair on Halloween—but did one of the women have purple locks? Had Carmen been on the pier that night with the Goth kids?

"Travis, why did you steal Morganna's phone?" He couldn't have killed Linda because he'd been at the festival. With Carmen. This didn't make sense to her at all.

No . . . at Carmen's booth. She recalled the Jensen kids saying they saw a very tall woman with red hair and a purple witch's hat running from the shop to cross the street. Carmen wasn't tall. But her assistant sure was. He'd been stocking powders labeled with a skull and crossbones.

"Did you go to college, Travis?"

"Chemistry major," he said proudly.

"Drop out," Dylan added shrilly from the driver's seat.

"Good enough, ain't it?" Travis reached into the front of the car from the back seat to smack Dylan on the ear.

She hadn't caught her breath yet when Dylan parked in front of Clairvoyant Carmen's. It was dusk, twilight, the eerie moments before dark. "What do you want from me?" She struggled against Travis and tried to make eye contact with Dylan, who acted like he was on something—wide eyes, nervous tic.

"We want to please our mistress," Travis said.

Dylan opened the door to Carmen's, and Travis pushed Charlene inside. She heard the sound of a metal dead bolt behind her.

The dark purple velvet curtains shut out all light but the flicker of candles. Dylan said, "We brought her to you, mistress."

Carmen, seated at the round table in the center of the shop, waved her hands around a crystal ball—shaped like an orb from Morganna's shop. Lights glittered within. But Charlene had seen the illusion at Morganna's workshop with tiny lights inside the balls.

"Well done, acolytes," she intoned. "Bring her here."

That's what Brandy called someone who was learning witchcraft. Had Dylan bought into the fantasy? Charlene pulled against Travis. "Let me go, Carmen."

The young witch's green eyes blazed, and Charlene saw the glint of madness in them. What had happened to her? All three of them seemed frenetic.

"You should have stopped asking questions," Carmen said flatly. "You almost caught me at Morganna's, breaking the orbs." Carmen flicked her fingers toward the candles, and the flames went from orange to blue.

Carmen had been there too? "Why were you there? I thought Stephanos . . ."

"I was searching for the book of shadows, as was Stephanos. I found it first, hidden in plain sight among those delicate orbs on the back shelf of her workstation." Carmen's smile was devoid of humor. "It was a pleasure to smash them to the ground. Chilling sounds of glass destroyed, the breaking of a soul."

Carmen had the spell book? A chill raced up her spine. According to Kass, Carmen had the psychic abilities to use the book, for good or evil. "Where is it?"

"Not your concern, Charlene."

Travis dropped to his knees beside Carmen, his head bowed, the shaved side to Charlene. "She knows about the phone, mistress."

Dylan held her arm now, his grip hurting her.

Carmen laughed shrilly and made circles with her palms around the crystal ball. "Charlene. Is there any chance you will sell your business and move back to Chicago?"

Charlene swallowed hard. "No . . ."

"I didn't think so. Linda lied to me about going back to Ohio with her ex-lover. She should have gone—I gave her the choice, but she too stayed too long." Carmen made clicking noises as her hands swirled faster, around and around the ball.

Drawn to it, Charlene stared down into the depths of the ball. What had been black became clouded, and then she was able to see faint images. Was that her mansion? Her mother? Oh no—Jared?

With a cry of alarm, Charlene pushed back from the table, rocking the crystal ball. "No! I told you I am not interested."

Carmen's head dropped forward, and she swayed from side to side. "You have a very strong will, Charlene. Would you like to be my acolyte?"

"No." It was obvious the young woman was not in her right mind. She yanked her arm from Dylan's grasp as he became entranced by the spinning orb and studied the dark room. How could she get free?

On the back wall next to the small glass bottles with the skull and crossbones was the purple witch hat and the red wig. The hat wasn't abnormally tall, which meant the person Hailey had seen had been. She'd drawn stars. Pentagrams could be drawn as a star shape, by an eight-year-old. "It was Travis that killed Morganna."

Carmen hissed, her fingers circling the orb.

As a chemistry dropout Travis could make cyanide—and drugs. Meth? Who was in control? Anybody? It was a madhouse, and Charlene wanted out. "Did he do it for you?"

Travis rose from his kneeling position at Carmen's side like a monster from a horror movie, face pale, lips pulled back, exposing his yellowed teeth.

Charlene leaped for the front door.

"Stop her, Dylan!" Carmen ordered.

Dylan blocked the door, skinny arms stretched across. He still didn't look at her. Was there a way to save him from this? To get them both out?

Charlene turned back to Carmen, searching the space. There was a phone on the counter next to the cash register—she'd have to taunt the witch in order to get by. "Why? Why did she have to die? Because she slept with your dad?"

Carmen's head whipped up so fast her blond and purple hair lifted behind her. "Shut up. Linda Crane was a fraud." Her green eyes narrowed to slits.

Charlene breathed out. The room dropped in temperature—but unlike Jack, this young woman meant Charlene harm.

A sheet of paper, torn at the edges, with a paragraph in neat script fluttered down by the crystal ball. Charlene wondered if this spell was from Evelyn's book of shadows.

"She was a liar!" Carmen flung her arms out. Travis scuttled backward. "A *whore*!"

Fear rooted Charlene's feet to the floor.

"I will trap her spirit and make her pay." The candles went out before coming back to brightness. "She betrayed the circle of trust with her false smile. We were going to lead the coven."

Carmen chanted something undecipherable. Charlene rushed by for the phone, but Travis pushed her backward and she tripped over a cord, unplugging the lights beneath the round table. Candles flickered.

"You should have left it alone," Carmen said in a growly voice. "Now it is too late for you!" With a convulsive jerk of her arm, she lifted the ball in the air, spinning it higher. "I command the spirit of Morganna to enter the ball!"

Charlene realized this was her chance—Jack had told her to fight, and she would! She knocked the candles over. Flames licked up the purple velvet curtains. Smoke immediately filled the room, and Travis, instead of going for the front door, went to the back wall to scoop the bottles of skull and crossbones into a Clairvoyant Carmen shopping bag.

Charlene shook Dylan, who'd been spellbound by the spinning orb. "Snap out of it!" She smacked his cheek, and his eyes blinked clear.

She unbolted the front door from the inside and shoved it open, dragging Dylan by the elbow with her to the sidewalk. He swayed, in a daze.

"Charlene?" Sam tugged her arm to search her face in the near dark. "Are you okay?"

"Sam!" How had he known that she'd been kidnapped?

Behind them, smoke curled out in gray and black waves. "Carmen and Travis are in there. I knocked over the candles," she said, her pulse erratic with nerves. "We need the fire department."

"On the way," Officer Tanner said before he dove into the shop.

A crash sounded like a thousand glass orbs falling to the ground. The smell of smoke overwhelmed her, and she stumbled to the curb. Kass raced toward her from her shop across the street.

Sam covered his mouth with his jacket and stormed inside—he returned quickly with a soot-faced Carmen crying hysterically that Morganna's spirit had been in her grasp but was gone forever.

Travis, escorted by Officer Tanner, stumbled out next. The police officer dropped the shopping bag of "potions" at Sam's feet. "Found our source," he said. "I stomped the flames out."

The fire truck arrived in a blare of sirens and red and gold lights. Captain Logan Moreno hopped down from the side of the massive truck. "Detective," he said to Sam. "Ms. Morris."

Officer Tanner kicked the bag. "I had a quick peek in the back, Captain. All kinds of chemicals. Could be the makings of White Witch—meth with cyanide. Added danger increases the thrill."

Charlene looked at Sam, who stood close enough his shoulder brushed her arm. "What's that?"

"Street drug we've been tracking." Sam hooked his thumb in his coat pocket. "Logan, want me to call Hazmat?"

"I'll do it. We're getting pretty tight these days." The fire captain walked back to his truck, the fire-retardant beige coveralls heavy and formless. Two firefighters passed him to go inside Carmen's.

"Travis was a chemistry dropout," she told Sam.

Sam pretended not to hear her, but she saw his jaw tighten before he went inside with two officers she didn't recognize.

Officer Tanner read Travis his rights and brought him to the patrol car parked crooked in the street. Officer Bernard got behind the wheel to take them to the station.

Dylan sank down on the curb beside where she was standing. "Charlene? I didn't want you to get hurt. I just couldn't think straight." He bowed his head, his shaggy blond hair a mess.

"What happened? How did your coat get up on the roof?"

"Travis put it there after the fight about Morganna's phone, to set me up."

She'd known it had to have been a frame. "Why didn't you go back to Hartford? Tara?"

"No, Tara was nobody special. Travis hooked me up with White Witch. That's all that I wanted." He sniffed into his arm.

She put her hand on his thin shoulder. "I'm sorry, Dylan."

"I want to go home."

"I hope that Sam lets you. Just cooperate with him, okay? No more running. Call your dad—he's probably worried."

He folded forward and rested his head on his knees, eyes closed.

The paramedics arrived. For Carmen? The young woman trembled and shook as she stood next to Kass.

Kass snapped her fingers before her face. Carmen's head lifted at once. Her eyes focused as she slowly came out of her trance. Seeing Kass, Carmen's lower lip quivered. "It's the wrong time of the month to summon a spirit," she said in a singsong voice. "The moon must be full. The veil between worlds thin. I told Travis today was too late, but he thought that maybe with a blood sacrifice . . ."

Kass looked from Carmen to Charlene in dawning horror. "Carmen! You would hurt Charlene?"

"She was looking for Evelyn's book of shadows. Travis said she had to be stopped before she discovered the truth." Carmen lifted a thin arm.

The truth being his drugs, or the murder of Linda Crane? "You said he was your acolyte," Charlene said, trying to understand who had the power.

"The greatest magick is an exchange of male and female energy. I was his acolyte in love, and he was mine in the craft." Carmen's tone remained a child's.

Charlene shivered from shock as well as the chilly evening. A blood sacrifice. *Hers.*

One of Kass's blue feathers blew free in a gust of wind. "Why did you kill Morganna?"

"I helped her fool everyone by making her my secret acolyte. I tried to give her magick, but she had none. So she stupidly thought to go over my head to my dad, the high priest? He barely had enough magick to get into the coven." Hysterical tears rained down her cheeks. "She slept with Daddy."

Knowledge of the affair had broken the emotionally frail young woman.

After taking her vitals, the paramedic said, "She should be checked out at the hospital."

Sam had heard the confession and motioned for Officer Pasquale, who had just arrived with other officers. "Have one of the rookies ride to the hospital with her. She is a person of interest in the murder of Linda Crane."

Kass wrapped her arms around her middle. "Should I call her parents?"

"No—why don't you go on back to your shop? I'll have Officer Tanner inform them of the situation." Sam nodded at the waiting officer. He had soot marks mixed among his freckles.

"Martine works at Salem Federal," Charlene said.

"Her dad owns the bookstore on the wharf side," Kass added.

Sam breathed deeply. "You know I am capable, ladies, right?"

Charlene didn't see the humor. "How did you know that there was something wrong?"

"Officer Jimenez was doing a drive-by to make sure you weren't in further danger, and noticed the front porch lights flashing. A silver cat waited at the end of the driveway, and she went to check it out and saw the front door wide open, the planter knocked over, as well as the coat-tree—signs of a struggle, but nobody was there. She called me right away. I put out an APB, and Officer Tanner said that your Pilot was parked at Carmen's."

"That was really fast," she said—there would be no more making light of Sam's skills.

"We were already suspicious because she'd never filed a burglary report, so we wondered if it was a cry for attention when the city cams never showed anybody at her back door at that time. We have confirmation via Linda Crane's cell phone plan, that Carmen had been the last number that had texted her."

"And Travis?"

"Carmen wanted Morganna dead, and Travis had just enough chemistry skills to make it happen. We've got him on a drug and murder charge." Sam looked at her. "Not to mention kidnapping."

Charlene exhaled, her vision swimming. Jack had gotten a message to Sam that she needed help? Sam reached out to steady her.

"Thank you." She gazed into his eyes, and her heart stirred.

Now wasn't the time for her to be feeling all warm inside toward a certain detective, so she straightened up, curbing the impulse to hold on to his strength for a little longer. "You won't believe this, Sam, but I really do just want to go home."

"Are you all right to drive yourself?" Sam asked. "I can have Officer Jimenez take you."

Dylan started to slip away, but Sam hooked his arm. "Not so fast."

The young man didn't try to fight. Kass waved goodbye and returned to her shop.

"I'm fine." To prove it, Charlene got into her car for the short drive home.

CHAPTER TWENTY-SEVEN

The sky was dark with turbulent clouds, and thunder rumbled out a warning. It was drizzling rain and would only get worse.

All she could think of on the ride home from Carmen's was Jack. Was he okay after expending all of that energy to signal the police, to save her? Her mind churned with worry.

When she got home, the porch light was on, and the chandelier in the dining room was lit as well. She picked up the coat-tree and hung up her coat. "Jack?"

He had helped her today—somehow he had found a way to bring Sam to her in her hour of need. How he had accomplished it she wasn't sure, but in the past, whenever he'd expended a lot of energy, he would be gone for a while afterward.

She righted the oval table by the door and centered the shell-shaped planter. She shook out the rug and set it over the hardwood floor. Silva was nowhere to be found either. "Here, kitty kitty."

She turned on her electric kettle for a cup of tea, her body shaking as the shock of it all caught up to her.

"Jack, come to me, if you can." Sometimes when he went away she feared he'd never come back.

They'd become so close in the last few months, like two kindred spirits—she of this world, he of another. She didn't want to think of a time when he might leave her to go to the light, or heaven, or whatever it was out there. Yet it was because she cared for him so much that she couldn't ask him to stay.

"I'm here, Charlene." A tornado of cold air wrapped around the kitchen as if Jack were trying to surround her. She saw nothing but felt his energy, before he finally appeared before her. "I've been worried about you. You're all right?"

"You saved me, Jack!" She swung around to look at him clearly. His handsome face, his strong shoulders, the concern in his deep blue eyes. "If it weren't for you, Sam might not have found me in time. Were you flashing my lights? A squad car came by to check on things—you know Sam." Wanting to protect her, and he had.

"I was so angry when you were taken, and I was trapped by this property—I'd hoped the lights might get some attention. It worked?"

"Yes—thank you." She poured hot water into a mug with a rosehip tea sachet and quickly caught him up on it all, including the new drug in town, White Witch. "It has traces of cyanide in it. What are these kids thinking?"

"Oh, Charlene, I wish I could have been there to protect you."

"It was one of the scariest things that ever happened to me, but I broke free and ran out of the shop, with Dylan." A few tears slipped from her eyes, which she quickly wiped away. "Sam was there. You brought him to me."

"I'm glad it's over." His warm gaze held hers. "I will stay with you tonight. But you should get some rest now. I can see you're exhausted."

"Where's Silva?" she whispered. "I called for her, but she didn't come."

"In your room, waiting for you."

"I wish it could be you," she said, wanting to reach out, to touch him just once.

"Not as much as I."

She didn't deny it, what was the point? They could never be together, but what she had with him had to be enough.

Sam showed up the next morning with two coffees and bagels. He kissed her on the cheek after she let him in. She'd brushed her teeth, washed her face, and clipped her long hair back, which had to be good enough, since he hadn't called ahead.

"Good morning, Charlene. I hope I'm not too early? Adorable pajamas—are those black cats?"

Her flannel pjs were warm, and she had pink slippers on her feet. "They are comfy."

"I figured you'd probably stayed up half the night wondering what happened."

"Not half the night. Only a few hours." She accepted a hot coffee while he waved a bag of bagels that smelled like heaven. "Mmm, this is a nice surprise." She removed the lid. "French vanilla?"

"I thought you could use something sweet."

"I can, and I do appreciate it. Thank you." She took a sip and saw Jack "sitting" at the counter. She walked past Jack to get plates from the cupboard and motioned her head toward the door for privacy. He shook his head no.

They sat at the kitchen table, but then Charlene got up to show Sam Hailey's drawing. "I realized yesterday that she'd seen Travis in a wig and witch costume—his necklaces gave him away. The outfit is on the shelves beneath the tarot cards at Carmen's."

"Travis is in jail, but Dylan's dad drove from Hartford to

pick him up. He wasn't part of Linda's murder—I hope this was enough to scare him straight. He said to tell you he's sorry, and thank you."

She put her hand to her heart. "Dylan isn't a bad person deep inside," she said. "He tried to protect me from Travis but just wasn't strong enough. I think he got in way over his head and didn't know how to back out without ending up like Morganna."

"Could be," Sam said. "He made plenty of wrong choices."

"What about Carmen? Her parents had to see how troubled she was. . . ." Her father had mentioned illness.

"They've been trying to get her help in the medical world as well as the homeopathic field for years, they told me. She seemed to be getting better until she discovered her father's affair with her supposed best friend. She and Morganna were going to usher the coven into the next century."

Charlene looked out into the gardens and the early-morning sun. When she'd tripped over the power plug, she'd unplugged the blue and yellow lights that had "flickered" from Carmen's fingers. She wasn't sure how the ball had lifted, but she wouldn't be surprised if there had been a trick.

But Jared's image? She couldn't explain it.

Charlene pushed aside the other half of her bagel. "Carmen was smart, beautiful, and loved. She had everything, and yet it wasn't enough. Did the rest of the coven know about her troubles?"

"Maybe, but Martine and Lucas tried to shield her as much as they could. Travis entering the picture brought her out of their control. Drugs never help a situation like that, and this White Witch was very addictive."

His phone beeped. "I've got to get back to the station. So are you going to tell me how you got your porch lights to flash like that? Officer Jimenez said it was very strange."

Jack chuckled. "Go ahead, tell him."

Charlene cleared her throat. "Must've been a short. They are fine now."

"These old houses have faulty wiring," Sam said.

She didn't tell him that hers had all been updated. "Thanks for coming over so early this morning."

Sam stood and slipped on his blue jacket. "So, now that we have this behind us, how about I take you out for a nice dinner?"

Jack rumbled behind her, "Dinner?" His turquoise eyes flashed as his jaw set.

Silva must have noticed the change of energy, because she jumped off the counter, and Charlene bent to pick her up. "I wouldn't mind going to Finz, or Turner's. I've heard very good things."

"Excellent. I'll make the reservation." After ambling toward the door, he put an arm around her waist, and she didn't pull away. "No matter what the tour guides say, neither one of them are haunted. I think we deserve a nice, quiet, sane place for dinner with just the two of us. No ghosts."

Charlene bit her lip to keep from laughing. "I can't wait."

As Sam drove away, Jack glowered before her.

"Don't be angry, Jack. Sam needs us—and I need you."

Please turn the page for an exciting sneak peek
of Traci Wilton's next
Salem B and B mystery

MRS. MORRIS AND THE
GHOST OF CHRISTMAS PAST,

coming soon wherever print and e-books are sold!

CHAPTER ONE

It was dark at seven thirty, the seventeenth of December, when Charlene Morris entered Bella's Italian Ristorante with her parents, Brenda and Michael Woodbridge. Her frayed nerves required some serious holiday cheer, and tonight's charity auction to support the Felicity House for Children was exactly what she needed. Her mother had been with her for only two days, and it was two days too long.

David Baldwin, the manager and maître d', greeted her with a broad smile. She'd eaten at Bella's many times in the three months since she'd moved to Salem from Chicago and liked it so much that she recommended it to all of her guests at Charlene's Bed and Breakfast.

"Charlene!" David crooned, arms outstretched to give her a hug. "So nice to see you again." He had a natural charm, salt-and-pepper hair, and black glasses, and a slight paunch in his black suit revealed his love for pasta.

Her mother eyed David with interest, until her gaze landed on his thick, gold wedding band.

From the podium, Charlene peered into the restaurant. Each of the round tables had been decorated with a candle-

and-pine centerpiece. Baskets of auction items sparkled with red and green bows on long folding tables set up against the walls. Savory Italian spices wafted from the kitchen. Half the price of every meal purchased tonight was to be donated to Felicity House, and Bella's was packed.

"David—this place looks great. Really festive." The décor, and the cause, kindled her holiday spirit.

"It's all about the kids tonight," David said cheerfully. She'd read the big news in the local paper that he'd won the lottery last week. Would she still be at work if she'd won ten million?

Maybe—she loved her bed-and-breakfast, which had come with a resident ghost. Until three months ago, she'd never believed in such things, but Dr. Jack Strathmore was part of the reason she required some cheer. He wasn't fond of her mother—and though he'd promised to never disturb the guests, he couldn't seem to help himself around Brenda. He moved her boots just out of reach and kept hiding her reading glasses. He even put salt in the water she used for her false teeth.

His antics were mostly innocent and sweetly protective but had to stop—she couldn't call him out in front of her parents, as he was visible only to her, or she'd look like she'd lost her mind, and they'd *never* leave.

"I'm glad we reserved early," she said to David. "You have a good crowd."

A metal rack in the doorway handled the surplus of coats for the evening. They handed theirs to an orange-haired teenager Charlene hadn't seen before—a new hire?

David flung his arm toward the ten-seat bar at the rear of the restaurant. "We have a lot of supporters here for Felicity House. Even my wife has graced us with her presence." He pointed at a petite bleached-blond woman in a gold sparkling sheath, who leaned her elbow on the bar to chat with the bartender. "I'll bring her by later to introduce you, Charlene."

"I'd love to meet her."

David peered over the rims of his black glasses as he studied her mom and dad. "Are these your parents? I think I see a resemblance." He smoothed the lapels of his jacket. "No, no, this young lady must be your sister."

Her mother tittered like a Victorian maiden—all she needed was a fan. "Oh, you sly fox. I'm Brenda, *her mother*."

Her father reached out his hand. "Michael Woodbridge."

"David Baldwin, manager and part owner of this lovely establishment."

Part owner? Charlene hadn't realized he'd been so invested in Bella's. Would he buy the place now that he had millions, or sell his investment and move on?

"You must be so proud of Charlene," David said. "Her bed-and-breakfast is an outstanding piece of property."

Her father nodded, while her mother had to think about it before she said, "It is beautiful, I'll give you that, but we miss having her in Chicago."

David chose three menus and gestured at Jessica, waitressing tonight. Charlene genuinely liked the young woman, who had just become a physical therapist, from very humble beginnings.

She'd lopped her cocoa-brown hair to a new style at her shoulders, and greeted them cheerily as she took the menus from David. "Hi, Charlene. Glad you all could come tonight. Should be a fun evening." Jessica patted her red half apron. "You must be Charlene's parents—she said you would be her dates tonight. It's going to be super busy, so get your bids in early."

"I've put Charlene and her family by this first window," David said, pointing to his right.

"Perfect." Jessica touched David's arm. "Tori wants you."

David's expression dimmed slightly, but he kept his smile. "Enjoy your dinner. Be sure to look over the raffles and auction items—let's give these kids a holiday to remember." He moved on, wending his way through the crowded restaurant, pausing at various tables to say hello on his way to the bar.

"This way." Jessica bypassed an oval table for two at the very front of the restaurant to the next round table, which had a merry view of the Christmas lights outside. She could see the two-lane street, bare of snow, and the strip of businesses across the road—none open. A giant red Santa holding a toothbrush twinkled from the dental office.

Jessica handed them each a menu once they sat down, pointing out the auction items listed on a sheet of green paper bordered with holly. "You'll see that Charlene donated a stay at her bed-and-breakfast."

"She's always had a generous nature." Pride emanated from her dad as he looked at Jessica over his menu. "Charlene was in first grade when she donated her tooth fairy money to a kid in her class with leukemia. We added a check for more, of course."

"Dad, no embarrassing stories—you promised," she said with a laugh. When Jessica had approached her last month for a donation and explained about the kids at Felicity House, she'd welcomed the chance to give a week-long stay, and in the process had gotten to know Jessica and Jessica's success story—all because of Felicity House.

"It's going to raise a lot of money," Jessica assured her. "Can I start you off with some drinks?"

"Merlot for me, please," Charlene said. "The house wine is superb. Mom, Dad?"

"Let's get a carafe for the table," her father suggested.

"I suppose," her mom conceded and then removed her

red-framed glasses to gaze at Jessica. "We'll need some bread too. *Before* the drinks?"

"Absolutely." Jessica hurried to the kitchen.

Charlene had taken the chair closest to the window so her mom couldn't complain about a draft. It also gave her the advantage of seeing everyone in the room dressed up for the event.

Kevin, the scruffy blond bartender from Brews and Broomsticks, wore a navy suit and sat hip to hip at a table with a woman Charlene hadn't met before—girl-next-door pretty, with long light-brown hair. Even from across the room, Kevin looked besotted. She hoped he was on a date. Around Halloween, he'd hinted at an attraction to her, which she'd ignored, though he was cute, kind, and funny.

Her husband, Jared, hadn't even been gone two years. Her heart was not quite as raw, thanks to a certain gorgeous ghost, and a very much alive detective, Sam Holden of the Salem Police Department. Sam had invited her out numerous times, but she'd always declined. Her heart wasn't ready yet.

Charlene spotted Brandy and Evelyn Flint sharing a table with Theo Rowlings and whispered to her parents, "See the auburn-haired woman near the baskets, with the silver-haired lady?"

They both turned to look.

"They own Flint Wineries and can trace their ancestry back hundreds of years in Salem, which is very important to the locals," she said. "They supply the house wine here at Bella's, as well as my label for 'Charlene's.' "

"I'd like to see the winery," her mother said. "Do they offer tours?"

"I can ask." Charlene wouldn't mind a peek behind the scenes.

Jessica dropped off a selection of breadsticks, a sliced baguette, and a dish of savory oil for dipping. "I'll be right back with your wine. One of our servers called in sick, so we have Avery, from Felicity House, stepping in to help out. She's very new, so please be patient."

"Don't worry—we're not in any hurry," Charlene reassured Jessica.

Her mother picked up a thin, crisp sesame breadstick and broke it in half, not interested in any excuses. "This is hard, and it's cold."

"A breadstick *is* hard, Mother." A loud laugh came from the back, and Charlene turned toward the sound.

"Tori." Jessica barely bothered to hide her dislike of David's wife as she smoothed her hair behind her ear. "She keeps the bartender's attention, which slows the drink orders—but I can get your wine myself."

Her mother perked up at the hint of drama and craned her neck to get a look at Tori, who bared a lot of thigh. "Hmm. She's a hot one. Second marriage?"

Jessica shifted the empty tray from one hand to the next. "I think for both of them. David has a son just a few years younger than me."

"No offense," her mother said, which always made Charlene cringe, "but I bet his new wife is about your age too."

Jessica's eyes rounded in surprise at her mother's bluntness. "Uh, maybe . . . Let me get that wine."

After the waitress was out of earshot, Charlene said, "Mom, do you have to be so critical?" She tapped the laminated menu. "Why don't you decide what you want to eat?"

Charlene leaned back in her chair and exchanged a glance with her father. He was unaffected—having decades of practice at ignoring his wife's negativity. There had been a time when her mom hadn't been so hard. What had changed? Charlene had memories of her mother being happy. Now it seemed bitterness seeped from every pore.

Charlene had escaped, but her dad? How did he handle it day and night, years on end?

"Maybe breadsticks are supposed to be hard, but these are enough to break my teeth." Brenda dropped the half-eaten stick to her bread plate.

"Dip it in your water," her dad suggested, going back to the menu.

He couldn't be serious! "Try the baguette." Charlene offered her mom the basket. "And the oil." The girl who had taken their coats rushed by and accidentally bumped the back of Charlene's seat. She was pale, skinny, and utterly out of place in a too-big apron. Avery from Felicity House, Charlene guessed. A spider tattoo was visible on the back of her neck.

Her mother pointed in the direction of the bar and David's wife. "Look at her ring. Can you believe she's flashing that gaudy thing around? I bet she bought herself some new jewelry with David's lottery money. New wealth makes a person trashy. They can't help it. They gotta buy, buy, buy just to show it off."

"And you know this how?" Charlene folded her burgundy cloth napkin across her lap.

"I watch the crime shows," her mom said with a huff that stretched her green plaid sweater across her ample top half, above her stilt-thin legs—her mother's figure reminded Charlene of a long-legged bird. Not a flamingo, but a crane, maybe, that had to make trouble to get anyone to notice her at all. The thought surprised Charlene, and she felt a sudden spurt of tenderness toward her mother, who, at seventy-five, wouldn't be around forever.

Her balding father's black reading glasses were poised on the edge of his long nose. He looked like the art professor he'd been for half a century as he scanned the menu.

Life had cruelly taught her that death could happen at any time.

The candles on the tables flickered when the restaurant door opened again, bringing with it a rush of cold air. Sharon Turnberry, a faux-redhead, and her husband, John, arrived, and Jessica seated them on the opposite side of the room. Charlene waved at the manager of Cod and Capers.

Another creak from the front door, another swoosh of cool air, made Charlene shiver as she turned to the podium, where David greeted a short, squat gentleman with dull gray hair and a silver mustache who wore a black trench coat and black cowboy boots. "Vincent. Glad you could make it. I saved you a table by the bar."

"You were very mysterious telling me to be here tonight," Vincent said, his demeanor hard. "You better not be wasting my time."

Jessica returned with the wine. "Here you are. I made it, unscathed," she said dramatically.

"Who is that?" Charlene asked, subtly pointing at Vincent.

"Oh—Vincent Lozzi. David's business partner and our 'silent' boss." Jessica, a tray in one hand, used her free fingers to make air quotes. "We don't see him around that much, but now that David's won the lottery, you wouldn't believe how many people have come out of the woodwork. Even one of his old college buddies, he told me."

Jessica scurried off to assist Vincent. He tossed his jacket over the chair, sat down, and plunked his elbows on the table for one. The co-owner glared at Tori, who waggled her bejeweled fingers at him. He refused to let Jessica hang up his trench coat.

Charlene pulled her gaze from *that* drama to continue her perusal of the diners—she couldn't have asked for a better seat.

A plump woman in evergreen velvet, her hair a mousy brownish gray, smoothed in a bun with a red silk poinsettia tucked in the knot, rubbed her hands together and beamed with pride as she went up and down the length of baskets for the auction. Charlene recognized the rosy cheeks from the photo for Felicity House on the table. The director, Alice Winters.

Her mother held the green paper and pointed to the picture of Jessica. "It says here that our waitress used to live at Felicity House, before she was adopted."

"That's true, and she's also a physical therapist." Charlene admired the young woman's drive toward success.

"Why is she working here?" The question was asked in a snide tone that made Charlene twist her napkin.

"I imagine because she wants to, Brenda," her dad said. "Don't you dare ask."

Jessica arrived to take their order, and her mother thawed slightly. "I'll have the veal Parmesan, with a salad."

"Wonderful choice," Jessica said, turning to Charlene. "And you?"

"Lobster ravioli. I'll also have the salad, instead of soup. Dad?"

Her father collected their menus. "Chicken scaloppine, and pasta e fagioli. Thank you."

"I'll get these in so you can enjoy your meal by the time the auction starts!" She hustled off, her hair swinging.

Charlene peeked out the window at the barren trees. "Snow sure would be pretty."

"It's in the forecast, according to *The Weather Channel*," her dad offered.

"If you want snow, you should live in Chicago." Her mom's mouth thinned into a red seam.

"I'm happy here, Mom," Charlene said. "Can't you be happy for me too?"

"I am! What kind of mother would I be if I wasn't happy for my own child?"

Jessica arrived with their salads and soup, saving her from having to answer. "Enjoy!" she said, circling her way to Sharon's table next.

At precisely eight o'clock, David tugged the lapels of his black suit jacket. "I'd like to introduce Alice Winters and Pamela Avita."

Pamela, the cochair for the charity event, was the opposite of dowdy Alice, in a sleek green skirt and fitted jacket, styled black hair, and pearls.

"Now there's a woman who knows how to dress," her mom said. "Tori should take notes."

David had moved the podium so that it faced the diners, and Pamela stood behind it. She was a natural auctioneer, listing each item with a starting bid, and creating excitement as she worked the crowd, the patrons generous to the cause of Felicity House. Alice would declare the winner's name, and Tori, whose gold-sequined number showed off her dynamite figure as she paraded before the baskets, delivered the prizes.

They ate during the show, Jessica expertly maneuvering around the action.

Her mom raised her hand to bid on a pair of diamond earrings, which she won, but she lost the mystery box from Vintage Treasures to a woman sitting next to Brandy's table. Charlene had her eye on a cashmere scarf and gloves but was outbid by Kevin's dinner date. Her dad put in a lackluster bid on a whale tour, but was more content with his soup.

Before she knew it, all of the items had been presented and Pamela announced the auction a success. Her eyes shone brightly. "I'd like to thank everyone on behalf of Felicity House."

Alice clapped, and the whole room erupted with applause—except for Vincent, who hadn't bid on a thing as he'd nursed his drink. Whiskey on the rocks?

"Check the website tomorrow for our silent auction winners—the children are so appreciative." Pamela gracefully returned to her seat with a flip of her head, exposing a large pearl in gold at her ear.

Alice rose, her cheeks as bright as the silk poinsettia in her hair. "Thank you for hosting our event, David. I hope to do this again next year at Bella's."

Vincent Lozzi smacked his hand on the table. "We'll see about that," he groused.

Charlene's pulse raced—the show of aggression at odds in the festive atmosphere.

David clenched his hand as he glared at his partner. What was going on?

Alice whispered something to him, and David gathered himself. "I'd like to give my thanks to Jessica," he said, nodding at Jessica, "for bravely sharing her adoption story. And to all of you for your generosity tonight. We're just getting started, my friends, and I plan on doing more."

Charlene applauded, hoping that his windfall would be put to good use. With a promise to herself to help Salem's at-risk youth, she folded the green sheet with Alice's name and contact information and put it in her purse.

David, his back to a pouting Tori, gestured for the bartender. "Bring the Dom Perignon," he said, then faced the rapt audience. "As some of you know, we have much to celebrate."

Low laughter and hoots resounded. Ten million dollars was indeed a lot.

"Lottery winners are never happy," her mother said in a foreboding tone. "They don't know how to spend their newfound money."

"Be happy for them, Mom, will you? I wish them the very best."

The door swung open, and Charlene rubbed her arms at the frigid temperature. A young man with dark brown hair and heavy brows unwrapped his scarf and scuffed his motorcycle boots along the small carpet at the entryway next to David's podium.

Tori saw him and rolled her eyes. "Kyle," she drawled. "Why am I not surprised?"

David whirled toward the young man. "Son! What are you doing here?"

"I left a message for you earlier, Dad." He waited by the oval table between Charlene and the door. "I need to talk to you."

Tori's mouth puckered like she'd downed sour apple schnapps.

David looked to Jessica. "Jess? Will you see if the kitchen can make up something for Kyle?"

"Don't bother." Kyle checked the time on his phone. "Ten on the dot. Kitchen's closed, right, Dad?"

"It will only take a second," Jessica said. "If you aren't picky?"

"I don't want anything but a few minutes of my dad's time." Kyle helped himself to the lone chair at the table near Charlene.

Jessica disappeared into the kitchen, and the scent of garlic escaped.

A clatter sounded to her right, and Charlene turned. Avery, orange hair quivering, knelt to pick up plate shards around a woman's high heel. Sauce coated the lady's shoe, and Avery's apron. "I'm so sorry," Charlene heard the girl say. She dabbed at the woman's foot with a table napkin.

"Just get me some water," the woman snapped. "I'll clean it myself."

"Yes, ma'am." The girl sniffled and kept her head bowed.

Alice took a protective half step in Avery's direction.

David apologized to the woman but glared at Avery. "Finish up in here. Don't come back tomorrow," he said under his breath.

What a terrible way to speak to her—Avery was no more than a child. This was a new side to David, one Charlene didn't like.

Kyle, still in his motorcycle jacket, rose, sympathy on

his face. He grabbed her arm, but Avery shrugged off his hand. "Don't, Kyle."

The teens were friends?

Jessica delivered Perrier and a white linen cloth to the woman with the marinara-doused stiletto, and a plate of pasta with red sauce to Kyle.

David, like a consummate actor, gazed at the jubilant faces before him in the dining room as if his son and Avery didn't exist.

"You should all have a flute of champagne." He held his glimmering glass high. "To all of you, for coming here to help Felicity House. Thank you again for your generosity tonight. Cheers!" He snagged Jessica as the young woman tried to pass him on her way to the kitchen.

"Wait!" He poured Jessica a flute. "Jessica has been with me since I first opened Bella's five years ago. My thanks, my friend."

Tori scoffed and twirled her diamond tennis bracelet. Her pettiness diminished her beauty, and Charlene almost felt sorry for David.

"Not only are we gathered for the auction"—David raised his voice—"but I've invited some of you here to deliver extra holiday cheer." He lifted the bottle of Dom and spoke sincerely. "I have not always been the best friend, or husband, or business partner, or father"—he turned to Kyle, and then back to the group—"but I want you to know how much you all mean to me."

He drained his flute and set the glass on the table of unclaimed baskets.

Jessica, standing close to Charlene, sniffed back tears welling in her eyes.

Kyle slurped a forkful of spaghetti, his suspicious gaze on his father.

Tori's phone dinged, and David eyed her with anger.

"Sorry," she murmured, quickly checking the text. The

light from her diamond ring flashed brightly from the candles on the centerpieces.

"Let me see your phone," he whispered angrily, reaching for it, his "friends" momentarily forgotten.

"No—it's nothing." Tori shifted on her gold heels, pressing buttons as if deleting messages.

"It better not be Zane," David said, his mustache trembling. "I warned you."

"David, please," Tori snapped. "Get on with your show, would you?"

He turned his back to her and pulled a stack of envelopes from the podium.

Who is Zane? Charlene sipped her excellent champagne. This was a madhouse—she couldn't wait to tell Jack all about it.

David handed an envelope to Jessica, who smiled at him affectionately and slid it into her apron pocket without a look.

He gave one to Brandy and Evelyn Flint, one to Vincent Lozzi—whose anger still simmered judging by the scowl on his face—and another to Alice and Pamela. With each passing check, Tori's mood seemed to deflate. Charlene noticed the young woman continually touch her tennis bracelet, as if to assure herself it was still there.

"Is there an envelope for me and Mom, Dad?" Kyle pushed his empty plate aside.

David winced. "Not tonight," he said. "But I haven't forgotten you, son." He went back to the podium and the bottle of champagne, slyly watching from his post.

Vincent opened his envelope and then snorted an ugly laugh. "This is nowhere near what you owe me. I thought you'd be signing it over." He got to his feet, grabbed his coat, and strode between the tables to David at the podium, hand clenched. "My lawyer will be in touch."

David didn't back down. "That amount is fair, and you know why."

Vincent glared at David, and then glanced at Kyle before lowering his fist—racing out the front door on a flurry of cold air.

The others who had received envelopes opened them and peeked inside. Brandy used a butter knife to slit the envelope open. She showed the check to Evelyn with a nod and put it in her purse.

Jessica immediately grabbed a bottle of champagne and started topping off everyone's glasses. Kyle smirked from the sideline, as if he knew something about his father that nobody else did.

Charlene felt terrible for David—everybody had their hand out. But why was he doing this? "It's so ugly," Charlene said under her breath to her parents.

Her mom sipped her water sagely. "Winning the lottery isn't guaranteed good luck."

Alice, seated next to Pamela, opened her envelope, and her plump, rosy complexion turned the color of curdled milk. She showed it to Pamela, who gasped, quickly covering her mouth.

David took off his glasses and scanned the room, resting his forearm on top of the podium. "Winning the lottery has been a miracle, but my funds are not immediately accessible. I will donate more when my bounty comes in."

The majority of diners had not received an envelope, so they applauded David's intent. From Charlene's table she saw Tori, who stood next to David, whisper, "You don't owe anybody. That money is ours."

Ignoring his wife, David announced to the diners before him, "Dessert will be served—and again, I thank you all for coming. Felicity House thanks you."

The crowd cheered, but Charlene was just as eager to leave as she had been to arrive. She checked the time on her phone. Ten thirty. What would Jack think? The whole check-giving thing had been awkward and in poor taste—as if David had wanted to prove a point.

David walked over to Kyle and put his hand on his son's shoulder. "I'll be sending a special Christmas card to you and your mom, okay? This was business."

"I wanted to talk to you about a call I got today, but I can see you're too busy." Kyle stood and looked his dad in the eye, his voice hoarse. "Why can't you follow through, just once?" He zipped his black leather jacket and darted out the front door. Moments later, a motorcycle roared and peeled off.

Poor Kyle!

"We need to talk, David." Tori tugged at David's arm to have a heated discussion by the kitchen door. The waitstaff brushed by them with trays of cannoli.

Charlene waved at Jessica, ready for the check rather than dessert. Her festive joy was squashed by the greed surrounding David's lottery win.

Alice rose and stepped shakily toward the long table with unclaimed prizes, but Pamela urged the older director to enjoy the cannoli while she loaded the SUV.

"Get Avery to help," Alice suggested, tugging the silk poinsettia from her hair.

"Good idea," Pamela said. "Save me a bite, would you?"

Jessica delivered the bill, the envelope from David peeping from her apron pocket. She hoped for Jessica's sake that David had been generous. Charlene's dad insisted on paying for dinner to do his part for the kiddos at the center.

Within moments they were ready to leave, and Charlene got to her feet, looking for David. "Let me just say goodbye. . . ."

David, Tori clinging to his side like a golden leech, left his spot by the kitchen door and stalked toward Charlene, and the window over her shoulder, his bushy brows arched in surprise above the frames of his glasses as he focused on the streetlamp outside. His body quaked with fear, and he shook Tori off. "No!"

"What?" Tori's hand flew to her mouth. "I told Zane to stay away, I promise."

"Freddy?" David asked in confusion. "But no—it can't be." Concerned, Charlene reached for David as he swayed unsteadily, not from drink, but shock. He stared out the window—she turned, seeing nothing, then focused on David.

He wobbled, grabbing the back of her empty chair. Was he having a heart attack? Her lobster ravioli flipped in her stomach as she recalled what she knew of CPR.

"Doug is supposed to be dead!" David's shaking finger touched his bottom lip in sheer terror, and then he lunged away from her and raced out the front door of Bella's restaurant.

She turned to Tori. "Who is Doug?" It all happened so fast—the next thing she knew, Charlene heard a sickening thump. Slowly, slowly, she glanced outside the window, to where David's body sprawled across the centerline of the road, his glasses shining beneath the streetlamp. Nobody else was there.

Connect with

Us

Visit us online at
KensingtonBooks.com
to read more from your favorite authors, see books
by series, view reading group guides, and more.

for sneak peeks, chances to win books and prize packs,
and to share your thoughts with other readers.

facebook.com/kensingtonpublishing
twitter.com/kensingtonbooks

Tell us what you think!

To share your thoughts, submit a review,
or sign up for our eNewsletters, please visit:
KensingtonBooks.com/TellUs.

Grab These Cozy Mysteries
from
Kensington Books